Crime Files Series

General Editor: **Clive Bloom**

Since its invention in the nineteenth century, detective fiction has never been more popular. In novels, short stories, films, radio, television and now in computer games, private detectives and psychopaths, prim poisoners and overworked cops, tommy gun gangsters and cocaine criminals are the very stuff of modern imagination, and their creators one mainstay of popular consciousness. Crime Files is a ground-breaking series offering scholars, students and discerning readers a comprehensive set of guides to the world of crime and detective fiction. Every aspect of crime writing, detective fiction, gangster movie, true-crime exposé, police procedural and post-colonial investigation is explored through clear and informative texts offering comprehensive coverage and theoretical sophistication.

Crime Files Series Standing Order ISBN 978–0–333–71471–3 (hardback)
978–0–333–93064–9 (paperback)
(*outside North America only*)

You can receive future titles in this series as they are published by placing a standing order. Please contact your bookseller or, in case of difficulty, write to us at the address below with your name and address, the title of the series and the ISBN quoted above.

Customer Services Department, Macmillan Distribution Ltd, Houndmills, Basingstoke, Hampshire RG21 6XS, England

---

Late Victorian Crime Fiction in the Shadows of Sherlock

Clare Clarke
Trinity College Dublin

First published 2014 by
PALGRAVE MACMILLAN

Palgrave Macmillan in the UK is an imprint of Macmillan Publishers Limited, registered in England, company number 785998, of Houndmills, Basingstoke, Hampshire RG21 6XS.

Palgrave Macmillan in the US is a division of St Martin's Press LLC, 175 Fifth Avenue, New York, NY 10010.

Palgrave Macmillan is the global academic imprint of the above companies and has companies and representatives throughout the world.

Palgrave® and Macmillan® are registered trademarks in the United States, the United Kingdom, Europe and other countries.

ISBN 978–0–230–39053–9

This book is printed on paper suitable for recycling and made from fully managed and sustained forest sources. Logging, pulping and manufacturing processes are expected to conform to the environmental regulations of the country of origin.

A catalogue record for this book is available from the British Library.

A catalog record for this book is available from the Library of Congress.

Typeset by MPS Limited, Chennai, India.

Contents

List of Illustrations

Acknowledgements

Like all good works of crime fiction, this book started with a handful of confusing clues and stories, leading to a range of red-herrings, wrong suspects and futile investigations. Again, just like the fiction I've been studying, my own detective work has benefited immeasurably from the fantastic help that I've had with my investigations. I first began this work at Queen's University Belfast, where I was privileged to be supervised by a generous and supportive team. Sincere and heartfelt thanks to Andrew Pepper, whose expertise and feedback helped me tremendously as a researcher and a writer. Without his input this book could not have been written. Thanks also to Caroline Sumpter, who helped reawaken my love of Victorian literature and has always been on hand to offer support and advice. Thanks also to the School of English at Queen's University Belfast for the Special Research Scholarship, which funded two years of research on this project and made an academic career possible. Lee Horsley and Sinead Sturgeon were generous examiners, and Lee has been a kind and supportive ally in subsequent years. At Trinity College Dublin, I have benefited from the support and expert assistance of Jarlath Killeen and Darryl Jones. Sincere thanks to Jarlath, who has been an attentive reader of my draft manuscript over the last year. Significant thanks also to the generous financial support of the Irish Research Council, and institutional support of Trinity College, whose fellowship funding facilitated the final push necessary in getting this manuscript ready for publication. Huge thanks also to the patient, helpful, and professional editorial team at Palgrave Macmillan, particularly Clive Bloom, Paula Kennedy, Felicity Plester, Peter Cary and Monica Kendall, who have been a pleasure to work with.

I would like to thank the staff of various libraries for their help in locating and copying many of the numerous primary materials used in this study. Thanks especially to the staff of The British Library and British Newspaper Library, the McClay Library at Queen's University Belfast, and the libraries at Trinity College Dublin. For help with Robert Louis Stevenson's correspondence thanks to the staff of the Beinecke Library, Yale University. For help with materials on Arthur Conan Doyle thanks to Catherine Cooke of the Sherlock Holmes collection at Westminster Library, London, and Jon Lellenberg of the Conan Doyle Estate. For help locating Arthur Morrison's manuscripts and correspondence thanks to the staff of the Manuscripts Department at the University of Cambridge

Library, the University of Reading, and the rare Books and Manuscripts Department at the Ohio State University Library. For help with Guy Boothby's correspondence I would like to thank the Special Collections department at the Brotherton Library, University of Leeds. For help with Israel Zangwill's papers thanks to Rochelle Rubinstein at the Central Zionist Archives, Jerusalem. Many thanks to the Conan Doyle Estate for their permission to reprint Arthur Conan Doyle's sketch, 'The Old Horse'. Thanks also to the State Library of Victoria for their permission to use the image *Collins Street – Looking East*.

I have been fortunate to present some of the material in this book in embryonic form at conferences and in print. I thank Roger Luckhurst, Kate Flint, Maurizio Ascari, Heather Worthington, Kate Macdonald, Janice Allan, Elizabeth Foxwell, Dino Felluga, John Maynard, Adrienne Munich, Clare Horrocks, Patrick Leary and Andrew King for giving me the opportunity to present these ideas, for their encouragement and for their feedback. A small section of Chapter 3 has been published in Kate Macdonald, ed., *The Masculine Middlebrow 1880–1950: What Mr Miniver Read* (Palgrave Macmillan, 2011). Part of Chapter 5 has been published as 'Horace Dorrington, Criminal-Detective: Investigating the Re-emergence of the Rogue in Arthur Morrison's *The Dorrington Deed-Box* (1897)' in *Clues: A Journal of Detection* 28.2 (2010). Part of Chapter 6 has been published as 'Imperial Rogues: Reverse Colonization Fears in Guy Boothby's *A Prince of Swindlers* and Late-Victorian Detective Fiction' in *Victorian Literature and Culture* 41.3 (2013). I am grateful to Palgrave Macmillan, Cambridge University Press, and McFarland and Co. Publishers for their permission to reproduce this material. Every effort has been made to trace all copyright holders, but if any have been inadvertently overlooked, the author and the publisher will be pleased to make the necessary arrangements at the first opportunity.

Queen's University Belfast and Trinity College Dublin introduced me to a number of colleagues who have become great friends. Heartfelt thanks especially to Eadaoin Agnew, Clare Gill, Sonja Lawrenson and Beth Rodgers, for all their professional encouragement, their proof-reading skills, but most of all for their wonderful friendship. Without their support I would have lost faith long ago. To my parents, and my grandparents, especially my mother, Carole Ireland – thank you for your belief that I was capable of this project and for your help providing the means and opportunity to see it through. But most of all I would like to thank my biggest supporter, my husband and best friend, Peter Clarke, without whose unfailing enthusiasm, belief and support (intellectual, financial and emotional) this project could not have been started, never mind finished. I dedicate this book to him.

Introduction

> If the abundance of supply affords any accurate
> test, the demand for the detective novel is great and
> increasing. Novels of this class must surely be counted
> amongst the greatest successes of the day.
>> 'Detective Fiction.' *Saturday Review* 4 Dec. 1886: 749

This book examines crime fiction in the years 1886–1900, a formative and fascinating period in the history of the genre. The 1880s and 1890s have been termed the 'First Golden Age of Detective Fiction' (Smith, *Golden* iii). These were the years in which detective fiction firmly established itself as a genre and sealed its popularity with the reading public.[1] At this time the very first print article to refer to detective fiction as a separate genre was also published. The piece – entitled simply 'Detective Fiction' – informed readers that the 'demand' for detective fiction was 'great and increasing', and that the genre was one of 'the greatest successes of the day' (749). Indeed, thousands of detective stories and novels were produced in these years, eagerly consumed by the new mass literate readership brought about by the passing of Forster's Elementary Education Act in 1870. As a clerk employed at one of London's many W.H. Smith railway book stalls told an interviewer for the *Speaker* magazine in 1893, '*Any* detective story, whatever its merits might be, I could sell from morning till night' ('A Literary Causerie' 383).

This book investigates representations of detectives and criminals in both canonical and forgotten crime/detective/mystery fiction at this key juncture, challenging studies of the development of the genre which have given undue prominence to a handful of figures.[2] My study offers an alternative, and much fuller, account of late Victorian crime fiction, concentrating particularly on the frequently overlooked stories which illustrate the nascent genre's often overlooked capacity for narrative and moral complexity. It examines a selection of stories where detectives are criminals and murderers, where criminals are heroes, or where crimes go unsolved. Arthur Conan Doyle's canonical Sherlock Holmes stories and Robert Louis Stevenson's novels are considered alongside works by neglected authors Fergus Hume, Israel Zangwill, Arthur Morrison and Guy Boothby. Together these fascinating 'Shadows of Sherlock' showcase the often wholly overlooked formal and moral diversity of late Victorian crime writing, forcing us to rethink our preconceptions about what the nineteenth-century detective genre is and does.

The detective genre is generally taken to have been born in the USA of the 1840s, with Edgar Allan Poe's short stories, 'The Murders in the Rue Morgue' (1841), 'The Mystery of Marie Rogêt' (1842) and 'The Purloined Letter' (1844), starring the investigative hero Chevalier Auguste Dupin. British literature featuring detection by police constables, such as Charles Dickens's *Bleak House* (1852–53) and Wilkie Collins's *The Moonstone* (1868), appeared later in the nineteenth century, following the 1842 formation of London's Detective Department of the Metropolitan police. In the 1860s, French writer Emile Gaboriau's Monsieur Lecoq stories, based on the adventures of real-life criminal-turned-detective Eugène François Vidocq, sold in huge numbers worldwide. The 1880s and 1890s, however, were the years in which British detective fiction firmly established itself as a genre in its own right and sealed its popularity with the reading public.

This appetite for detective stories doubtless is due at least in part to the emergence during this period of Arthur Conan Doyle's Sherlock Holmes novels *A Study in Scarlet* (1887) and *The Sign of Four* (1890) and short stories, which were originally published in *The Strand Magazine* (1891–92) and later collected as *The Adventures of Sherlock Holmes* (1892) and *The Memoirs of Sherlock Holmes* (1893). Whilst the Holmes novels sold slowly, the stories for *The Strand* famously captured the imagination of the late Victorian reading public straight away, elevating the magazine's already decent sales figures to over 500,000 copies per issue (Brake and Demoor 604). To put this in context, Marie Corelli's *The Sorrows of Satan* (1895), which is often called the bestselling novel of the late Victorian era, sold around 100,000 copies per year (Ferguson 67). Holmes is not the whole story of the late Victorian detective genre, however. The generic and formal features which came to dominate late Victorian crime fiction did not begin with the publication of Doyle's *A Study in Scarlet* (1887), nor were they secured fully by the *Strand* stories.

Amongst a number of 'Literary Recipes' featured in the June 1897 edition of that well-known cultural barometer, the satirical magazine *Punch*, was a formula for the modern detective story. To write such a story, the article wryly suggested, one need only, 'Take one part of [Emile] Gaboriau and fifty parts of water. Add a lady of title, a comic official from Scotland Yard, and a diamond bracelet. Strain the mixture into twelve equal parts and serve up monthly in a magazine' ('Literary Recipes'). Although *Punch*'s literary recipe does late Victorian crime fiction a great disservice, its image of the genre at that time as limited and formulaic has been remarkably hard to shake. Crime writing of this period was not a formula, however, produced simply by assembling a few stock characters and tropes cobbled together from Doyle, and evoking only one-fiftieth the intrigue of a Gaboriau story. Rather, the vast corpus of crime and detective fiction which appeared in the period before, during and after Holmes's popularity was a hugely varied body of work which rehearsed a wide range of moral and formal positions and spoke to many of the issues and anxieties that troubled late Victorian society. Sadly, much of this fascinating work is now all but forgotten. One of the broad primary interests of this study, therefore, is to situate Doyle's detective fiction in relation to a number of other obscure and overlooked, yet significant, contributions to the Victorian crime genre which were published both before and after Holmes's success.

In her 1998 survey of scholarship on Victorian detective fiction, Anne Humpherys complained that a huge number of intriguing texts were being overlooked by scholars 'in favour of an obsessive return of critical analysis to a handful of canonised texts by three male writers – Charles Dickens, Wilkie Collins, and Arthur Conan Doyle' (259). Indeed, this type of oversight is notable in a number of otherwise valuable critical histories of the genre such as Ian Ousby's *Bloodhounds of Heaven* (1976), Peter Thoms's *Detection and its Designs: Narrative and Power in Nineteenth-Century Detective Fiction* (1998) and Lawrence Frank's *Victorian Detective Fiction and the Nature of Evidence* (2003). Ousby, for instance, claims that between the publication of *The Moonstone* in 1868 and Sherlock Holmes's appearance in 1887 'there were no major contributions to the literature of detection' (*Bloodhounds* 128).

To concentrate solely on such a small corpus of canonical Victorian crime writing is to do a disservice to a significant number of other works which play important parts in the genealogy of detective fiction. Indeed, critical assessments which concentrate only upon a handful of canonical authors fail to account for, or in some cases even acknowledge, the phenomenal success of Fergus Hume's *The Mystery of a Hansom*

Cab (1886) or Dick Donovan's Glasgow Detective stories (1887), both of which were published before Holmes's first appearance in *Beeton's Christmas Annual* in December 1887. Both were hugely popular; Hume's *Hansom Cab*, in particular, sold up to half a million copies worldwide in the year before the publication of *A Study in Scarlet*. Andrew Radford's more recent survey of scholarship on Victorian detective fiction in 2008 noted that the focus on the canonical had continued in the 2000s, with 'much more research' still needing to be done on 'those other Victorian detective writers whose fiction is not yet widely available in critical editions or anthologies' (1191). Radford singles out the detective fiction of Arthur Morrison (the subject of Chapter 5 here) as being particularly overdue for critical attention. Lucy Sussex has also recently lamented that 'much of the crime writing found in the journals of the period [the nineteenth century] remains unexamined' (3).

In *From Bow Street to Baker Street* (1992) Martin Kayman was one of the first critics who sought to revise the standard account of Doyle's central place in the late Victorian crime genre. Kayman refuted claims that crime fiction from the period before Holmes comprised only less than perfect antecedents and that crime writers before Doyle had not yet established the 'correct' conventions for the genre (105). In 'Enter the Detective' (1998) Stephen Knight also argued that the notion of the crime genre being rooted in a number of canonical texts by Poe and Doyle is more than somewhat problematic. For Knight, the fact that so many crime and detective stories appeared in the pages of periodicals and magazines means that the genre does not have 'so simple or so gratifying a genealogy ... as the classic account suggests' (11). In the last few years, an increasing number of critics have finally followed Knight and Kayman's leads by beginning to undertake the important work of uncovering and analysing the significance to the history of the genre of a number of obscure and overlooked works of Victorian crime fiction from the period before and after Doyle's success. In doing so, this scholarship is helping to dismantle the somewhat outmoded critical orthodoxy that Victorian detective fiction is a genre which pivots on Collins's, Dickens's and Doyle's oeuvres.

McLaughlin, Mukherjee, Knight (*Continent*; 'Crimes Domestic') and Reitz broaden the geographical and generic scope of work on detective fiction by considering the importance of various colonial adventure stories from India and Australia to the crime canon. Ascari, Pittard ('Real Sensation'; *Purity*) and Miller (*Framed*) have prompted reassessment of detective fiction's exchanges with neighbouring sub-genres, such as sensation fiction, the gothic and the dynamite novel. Worthington has challenged the traditional evolution of the genre by providing valuable insight into the influence of late eighteenth- and early nineteenth-century criminal broadsides and periodical literature upon later canonical or so-called 'formative' works of detective fiction. Sussex, Miller ('Trouble'; 'Shrewd Women') and Kestner (*Sherlock's Sisters*) have uncovered a vast number of female authors (and female detectives) who make a valuable contribution to the burgeoning genre, exploding the notion that detective fiction was originally only a masculine domain. Finally, Joyce, Ascari and Kestner (*Sherlock's Sisters*) have argued for the need to recognise works of Victorian crime fiction that transgress the genre's usual formal and moral conventions – where detection is inefficient, where the criminal is a heroic figure, and where justice does not triumph.

My work here builds upon the important recent scholarship outlined above, addressing the continuing need for processes of recuperation by providing new insight into the importance of a number of overlooked works of late Victorian crime fiction, many of which were first published in newspapers and periodicals such as *The Star, The Windsor* and *Pearson's* or in the cheap paperback editions which filled railway bookstalls in the 1890s. I disinter texts that have had little or no critical attention, works which have been victims of what Franco Moretti has termed the 'slaughterhouse of literature' ('Slaughterhouse' 207). I investigate in detail the features of both canonical and forgotten detective fiction of the 1880s and 1890s, challenging studies which have given undue prominence to a handful of key figures. In doing so, I hope to produce something of an alternative, and much fuller, account of the late Victorian detective genre, illuminating its scope and breadth. I demonstrate how a narrow focus on only canonical fiction, like Doyle's, results in an oversimplified analytical framework which overlooks the generic, moral and formal complexities of the nascent crime genre.

There has been a critical tendency to set up crime writing of the Victorian period – the Holmes stories in particular – as a kind of straw man whereby more recent types of crime writing are defined against an oversimplified version of what has gone before. Raymond Chandler's 1944 essay 'The Simple Art of Murder' may in part be responsible for the construction of this binary. Here Chandler defines early twentieth-century American hard-boiled crime writing in opposition to a somewhat narrowly conceived model of the British genre beforehand. Chandler conceives of a model whereby the inherently disruptive and radical crime writing of the hard-boiled tradition is set up in opposition to the perceived cosy conservatism of the classic detective fiction of the late

Victorian and Edwardian eras. He advances the theory that detective fiction of the earlier British tradition is a limited and unified moral and formal entity, and that later work radically disrupts these conventions. As Lee Horsley has pointed out, Chandler's 'exaggerated' and 'overly schematic' argument has become almost single-handedly responsible for the ensuing 'defining myth' of the development of detective fiction in which both classic and hard-boiled crime writing are seen as unified, contrasting entities with no places of overlap (*Twentieth* 68–9).

Yet many twentieth-century crime fiction critics continued to enshrine Chandler's 'defining myth' of the genre by persisting in claiming that the American hard-boiled novel of the early twentieth century constitutes a seismic rupture in the development of crime fiction and that its radical political outlook and effects are in opposition to the inherent conservatism displayed by classical crime writers like Doyle. A vast number of early critical works on Victorian crime fiction by Ernst Kaemmel, John Cawelti, Dennis Porter, George N. Dove and Ernest Mandel, amongst others, argued that certain formal features and conventions mark Victorian detective fiction as a particularly conservative incarnation of the crime genre. The features upon which critics tend to base this interpretation include a preoccupation with the reassuring effect of narrative closure and resolution alongside the redoubtable moral code of the investigator or detective.

Dove, for instance, sums up the critical belief in the reassuring effects of textual resolution, and the related assumption that this signifies conservatism. He claims that late Victorian detective fiction is 'structurally a conservative genre' and that 'any writer undertaking a tale of detection where there is no resolution would soon lose an audience composed of detection fans' (41). For Marty Roth, 'the solution is what detective fiction is all about' (163). Martin Priestman has similarly argued that, structurally, detective fiction contains 'a conservative appeal to stabilising laws and rules based on ... Aristotelian notions of unity and closure' (*Detective Fiction* 21). For Cawelti, detective fiction of the Victorian era reduces and limits crime to the status of 'a puzzle, a game, and a highly formalized set of literary conventions', and in doing so transforms the serious moral and social problems of crime into 'an entertaining pastime ... [where] something potentially dangerous and disturbing ... [is] transformed into something completely under control' (105). Likewise, for Mandel, the detective fiction which emerged in the late nineteenth century is 'soothing, socially integrating literature despite its concern with crime, violence and murder' (47). For Mandel the nineteenth-century detective story in particular is 'the realm of the happy ending' where 'the criminal is always caught. Justice is always done. Crime never pays' (47). Such critics suggest, then, that detective fiction of the Victorian era is 'a literature of reassurance and conformism' where structural formulae function to assuage the anxieties and fears of the reader (Porter, *Pursuit* 220).

A second commonplace in the study of nineteenth-century crime fiction is a focus upon the causes and effects of the rise of the detective figure. It has long since been a critical orthodoxy to assert that the late Victorian detective – Holmes in particular – emerged as a new kind of hero invented to assuage the types of fears common to a predominantly middle-class urban readership. Knight (*Form and Ideology*), Porter (*Pursuit*), Moretti (*Signs*) and Mandel all examine the coinciding emergence of the detective in crime fiction alongside the evolution of the modern police force and the creation of the modern bureaucratic state. They suggest that because detective fiction flourished after the establishment of the police force, the cultural work it performed helped to reproduce values and subject positions maintaining the societal status quo. For these critics, by portraying the law as natural, even benevolent, the detective genre reflects the beliefs and views of the dominant ideology. Mandel, for example, states that, in nineteenth-century literature, the bandit hero is superseded and replaced by a 'new hero' who is 'yesterday's villainous representative of authority', the detective or the law (46). In Mandel's assessment, the detective figure wholly replaces the criminal as the hero in late nineteenth-century crime fiction, and he argues that this is evidence both of the securing of hegemony by the bourgeoisie at that time and of the genre's ultimate conservatism. The emergence of the detective hero – particularly Holmes – is attributed by Mandel to a specifically Victorian desire, in the face of the changes attendant with burgeoning capitalist society, for social and epistemological order.

Critics who focus on the rise of the detective hero in late Victorian crime writing largely argue that the trustworthiness of the detective functions to comfort and reassure readers. For Kaemmel, for instance, the 'success of detective literature' derives from its comforting assurances that the detective 'can correct the mistakes and weaknesses of the social order' (58). For Knight, too, Holmes's acumen reassures his readers that the increasingly complex and threatening nineteenth-century city can easily once again become understood and ordered (*Form and Ideology* 74). The milieu of the nineteenth-century detective, then, 'may be a dangerous world, but it is still a world of moral certainty' (Stafford 29). In such assessments the most reassuring convention of the late

Victorian detective story is the fact that readers trust completely the detective's skill, moral code, and conceptions of duty and justice. As Watson frequently remarks, and many of the above critics seem to agree, Holmes is 'a benefactor of the race' – the guardian of the moral principles by which society should operate (Doyle, 'Red-Headed League' 468). For Cawelti, both Holmes and Watson 'strongly affirm most of the values of traditional British culture' embodying a combination of 'solidity' and 'morality' central to the late Victorian ideal (277).

To some extent of course these readings are correct – late nineteenth-century crime writing did elicit a new kind of hero in the figure of the detective, an alternative to the criminal-hero of earlier criminal broadsides and *Newgate Calendars*.[3] Along with this new kind of hero came the possibility of an ensuing new kind of political perspective for crime fiction. This new type does not simply or wholly replace what went before, however, or mark the late Victorian crime genre as unproblematically conservative and reassuring. Even in its first incarnations the fictional detective was a more ambiguous figure then these sorts of interpretations allow. With *Bleak House*'s Inspector Bucket, for instance, Dickens introduced 'the first significant detective in English literature' (Penzler, Steinbrunner and Lachman 15). Even at this early stage in the incarnation of the literary detective, however, Dickens emphasised the uncertain status of the detective in the social order – Bucket is a figure who stands halfway between respectable society and the criminals he investigates. Likewise Poe's Dupin is distinguished from his rivals in the regular police force by a marked bohemianism. His mixture of rational and decadent personae sees Dupin operate outside and above the law he professes to defend and his interest in solving crime is motivated by aesthetics rather than morals.

Even stories that operate within a highly formalised and stylised set of conventions and rules – like Doyle's Holmes stories – still contain a considerable amount of flux and uncertainty. There are instances, for example, where Holmes does not catch the criminals ('A Scandal in Bohemia', 'The Five Orange Pips' and 'The Yellow Face'); is prepared to break the law in pursuit of a case ('A Scandal in Bohemia' and 'The Illustrious Client'); fails to save his client from being murdered ('The Five Orange Pips'); lets the guilty party go free ('The Boscombe Valley Mystery' and 'The Adventure of the Blue Carbuncle'); demonstrates gaps in his knowledge (*A Study in Scarlet*); shows great admiration for the criminals he is investigating ('The Red-Headed League' and 'The Final Problem'); goes on cocaine binges (*The Sign of Four* and 'A Scandal in Bohemia'); or just doesn't work very hard ('The Man with the Twisted

Lip' and 'The Red-Headed League'). As even the most cursory analysis of these canonical characters demonstrates, then, Mandel's unidirectional 'dialectical somersault' in which the picaresque rogue hero is wholly replaced in the nineteenth century by a new kind of authoritarian hero in the figure of the detective is somewhat reductive and needs reconsideration (48). Roles clearly do not simply become reversed, and the reader's sympathy does not simply decisively shift from championing the criminal rogue early in the nineteenth century to an unquestioning endorsement of law and order later in the century attendant upon the emergence of the detective hero. Neither is the late Victorian detective genre as straightforward a repository of hegemonic values as many critical interpretations allow.

Indeed, when one goes on to examine a broad range of crime stories outside the canon, it quickly becomes apparent that there are a huge number of works of late Victorian detective fiction which 'confute every idea about detection and order ever conceived' (Kestner, Review 551). An examination of a wider range of Victorian crime fiction showcases the formal diversity and thematic ambiguity present in some of the detective genre's earliest incarnations from the pivotal period shortly before, during and after Sherlock Holmes's emergence. Constraints of time and space mean that it's not possible to look at more than a handful of overlooked works in detail.[4] Therefore, in this book I concentrate on the stories which particularly well illustrate the late Victorian detective genre's possibilities for narrative and moral complexity. I study in detail works such as Arthur Morrison's *The Dorrington Deed-Box* (1897), Israel Zangwill's *The Big Bow Mystery* (1891) and Guy Boothby's *A Prince of Swindlers* (1897), where the detectives are criminals or murderers, and the criminals are heroes, demonstrating how they contribute to, stretch and invert the burgeoning rules and conventions of the developing genre in a number of fascinating and important ways. These stories illuminate the often wholly overlooked formal and moral diversity of crime writing in the 1880s and 1890s, forcing us to reassess dominant ideas about what the late Victorian detective genre is and what it does.

Studying these neglected works alongside foundational works of detective fiction illuminates a number of important yet underexplored issues underpinning the burgeoning late Victorian crime genre. These stories elucidate the nascent genre's interchanges with the gothic, sensation fiction, the dynamite novel and the imperial adventure story. They draw attention to the perhaps surprisingly large amount of late Victorian transgressor-centred crime stories which consciously invert the model of detective-as-hero, where detection is incomplete, partial or absent, where the criminals are heroes, or go free.[5] Relatedly, they demonstrate that even investigation-centred stories from this period often offer partial, problematic or failed resolutions to the crimes that they portray, where the story's questions remain unanswered, where detectives are implicated in the crime, are unsuccessful, or even criminal. I also draw attention to instances of such uncertainty in canonical works, like Doyle's Holmes stories, and works by Robert Louis Stevenson, E.W. Hornung and Oscar Wilde. In examining these alongside a number of neglected stories, I begin to reveal the overlooked scope of the late Victorian crime genre. In doing so, I help advance a necessary challenge to reductive and essentialist accounts of the formal, generic and moral complexity of the burgeoning crime genre of the 1880s–1890s.

This study's broad textual remit elucidates not only the overlooked range of formal and generic diversity contained within the nascent genre but also its ideological tensions. The types of late Victorian anti-heroes and morally ambiguous detectives resurrected in this study therefore augment recent challenges to the monological Marxist (Porter, *Pursuit*; Moretti, *Signs*; Mandel, *Delightful Murder*) and Foucauldian (Jann 'Sherlock'; *Adventures*; Leps) critical paradigms that dominated 1980s and 1990s scholarship of detective fiction, which conceived of the crime genre's formal and thematic properties as repressive and almost unproblematically conservative. This type of viewpoint is becoming increasingly outmoded, with later critics such as Pepper, Joyce, Mukherjee, Reitz, Horsley (*Twentieth*), Ascari and Pittard ('Real Sensation') arguing for a more flexible reading of the crime genre as an ideologically complicated body of work. This study's dialogic approach follows this recent scholarship in taking issue with the Marxist notion of the detective genre as a carrier of ideology, and the ensuing Foucauldian repudiation of the detective story's capacities for resistance or opposition. This flexible theoretical approach more easily accommodates the range of ideological positions with regard to agency, justice, power and control opened up within the detective fiction of Doyle, Morrison, Boothby and others. Late Victorian crime fiction is thus shown to be much more than a 'formulaic', 'conservative' and 'comforting' genre, incapable of moral ambiguity and formal variety (Pyrhönen 47–9).

My broadly historicist approach examines these works of late Victorian crime fiction alongside a broad range of cultural artefacts including advertisements, periodical articles, reviews, newspaper exposés and works of criminal anthropology. The discussion therefore also demonstrates the ways in which these are not simply superficial works of formula fiction, as the *Punch* 'Literary Recipes' article suggests, but rather speak to a range of late Victorian social and political events and cultural anxieties. Over the course of this study I examine the ways in which crime and detective fiction from the 1880s and 1890s engages with: scandals featuring respectable gentlemen criminals and sexual tourism; anxieties about the links between hard work, money and morality; the relationship between London's social geography, class and criminality; ideas about race and class which informed notions of criminality and policing in the imperial outposts of Australia and India; sensational press reportage and the creation of crimes as media events; the status of authorship for writers of crime fiction; and the debased reputation of the police following the botched investigation into the Whitechapel Ripper murders of 1888.

In my first chapter I argue for the importance of Stevenson's bestselling shilling shocker *Strange Case of Dr Jekyll and Mr Hyde* (1886) to the genealogy of detective fiction. While neither obscure nor overlooked – indeed according to the Longman annual accounts of 1886, the publisher produced and sold 43,000 copies of the novel in the first six months of its release (running to seven editions) and by June 1889 had printed and sold a further 29,000 copies, reaching the novel's sixteenth edition – *Strange Case of Dr Jekyll and Mr Hyde* nonetheless has frequently been omitted from histories of the detective genre. I suggest, however, that the novel contributes greatly to the establishment of some of the formal and thematic features that would later define much canonical (and non-canonical) detective fiction. Chapter 1 reveals the important role that the fiction of Stevenson and his followers can play in our understanding of shifting late Victorian conceptions about the social class of criminal types, specifically fears about criminality within the middle and upper-middle classes. Chapter 2 examines in detail Hume's phenomenally commercially successful Australian murder novel, *The Mystery of a Hansom Cab* (1886). I argue that Hume maps geographically specific details of local colour on to more universal representations of upper-class criminality and urban squalor in a way calculated to appeal to both Australian and British readers.

Chapter 3 explores Doyle's Sherlock Holmes short stories, suggesting that they were not perhaps as bourgeois and reassuring as is often claimed. I examine the ways in which the stories present a recurring trope of respectable men gone wrong, which finds expression through the themes of work and professionalism. The chapter demonstrates how *fin-de-siècle* codes and anxieties about hard work, the status of professional writing and the production of low literature influenced Doyle's depiction of immoral or lazy behaviour. Chapter 4 concentrates upon

Israel Zangwill's *The Big Bow Mystery* (1891), arguing that the novel offers insight into the manifold links between crime, poverty, policing and the press that troubled London's East End in the years after the Jack the Ripper murders. Chapter 5 illuminates the ways in which Arthur Morrison's post-Holmes *Dorrington Deed-Box* (1897) consciously broke with the genre's impulses towards formula and resolution, in an attempt to expose the reality of poverty and criminality in late Victorian London. Finally, Chapter 6, focusing on Guy Boothby's *A Prince of Swindlers* (1897) collection, reveals how Victorian detective fiction's domestic themes of investigation and disorder are mapped onto wider interrogations of identity construction and safety across national and global boundaries, thus illuminating *fin-de-siècle* anxieties about the New Imperialism.

The important ways that the 'Shadows of Sherlock' who are the subjects of this study rehearse and illuminate a range of late nineteenth-century social and cultural concerns stretch the narrative and moral conventions of the emerging detective genre, and anticipate the types of amoral and anti-heroic criminal protagonists who would later become such ubiquitous figures in contemporary popular culture, then, means that they boldly assert the need for a critical re-evaluation of the late Victorian crime genre as merely conservative and cosy formula fiction.

1

'Ordinary Secret Sinners': Robert Louis Stevenson's *Strange Case of Dr Jekyll and Mr Hyde* (1886)

Dr Jekyll is rather a worse kind of fellow than Mr Hyde.
Andrew Lang, 'Modern Man: Mr R.L. Stevenson.'
Scots Observer 20 Jan. 1889: 264

This chapter focuses on *Strange Case of Dr Jekyll and Mr Hyde* (1886),[1] a 'Christmas crawler' produced by Robert Louis Stevenson in answer to his publisher's request for something sensational for the 1885 Christmas literary marketplace (Stevenson, *Jekyll and Hyde* xvii). The novel, recounting a respectable doctor's transformation into a hideous criminal, was published in January 1886. Early reviews were extremely positive – writing in the *Saturday Review*, Andrew Lang called the novel 'excellent and horrific and captivating'; likewise, for *The Times* it was a 'finished study in the art of the fantastic' comparable to classic works such as 'the sombre masterpieces of Poe' (Lang, 'Stevenson's New Story'; 'Strange'). Indeed, it created an immediate sensation – selling over 40,000 copies in its first few months and running to seven editions. By February 1886, just one month after publication, it had already been parodied by that up-to-the-minute cultural barometer, *Punch*. The magazine ran a pastiche story 'to make your flesh creep' featuring 'Mr Hidanseek', a character with 'an acquired taste for trampling out children's brains and hacking to death ... Baronets' ('The Strange Case of Dr T.'). In the spring of 1887 a stage adaptation opened in Boston and New York, soon moving to London, where it ran for almost two years. By June 1889 a further 29,000 copies had been sold in the UK alone and the novel had reached a sixteenth edition.

Jekyll and Hyde has since become one of the canonical texts of late Victorian literature and its story of divided selves has become so frequently retold that almost everyone feels they know the novel and all that it is supposed to symbolise. In fact, despite having taken on the quality of a 'modern myth', *Jekyll and Hyde* is an endlessly perplexing, morally and formally ambiguous generic hybrid of sensation, gothic and detective fiction which still offers much to chew on (Luckhurst vii). In this chapter I argue that the story plays a pivotal role in the development of the tropes and themes that would come to dominate later Victorian crime fiction. In particular, I focus on how Stevenson co-opted a number of contemporary late Victorian anxieties about middle- and upper-middle-class villainy, based on true crime cases such as 'The Maiden Tribute of Modern Babylon' (1885) that were scandalising readers in the years before *Jekyll and Hyde*'s composition. Specifically, Stevenson developed the tropes of both the gentleman criminal hiding behind his outward appearance of respectability – and emanating from a familiar, respectable location – and the morally ambiguous, corrupt or compromised detective which came to dominate detective fiction of the 1890s, such as Arthur Conan Doyle's Sherlock Holmes stories, E.W. Hornung's Raffles gentleman-criminal tales, and works by popular, if less enduring, crime writers such as Arthur Morrison, Israel Zangwill and Guy Boothby.

Despite the widespread critical enthusiasm with which *Jekyll and Hyde* was received, early reviewers were often uncertain what to make of its generic status, since the novel came from the pen of a rising literary star but was marketed as a lowly 'shilling shocker'. *The Times*, for instance, opined that *Jekyll and Hyde* 'strongly impressed us with the versatility of his very original genius', but remarked also on its lowly publication in a 'sparsely printed little shilling volume' ('Strange'). On a similar note, the January 1886 issue of *The Academy* complained that the novel's 'paper cover' and 'popular price' marked *Jekyll and Hyde* as one of the lowest literary forms – a penny dreadful of the type that Stevenson describes in the pages of the novel itself, sold alongside 'twopenny salads' in a dingy Soho shop adjoining a gin palace (Noble 55; *Jekyll and Hyde* 8). Its 'appearance', then, much like the protagonists within, was 'deceitful', misleadingly suggesting that *Jekyll and Hyde* belonged to 'a class of literature familiarity with which has bred in the minds of most readers a certain measure of contempt' (Noble 55). The *Pall Mall Gazette* commented upon the relationship of *Jekyll and Hyde* to the burgeoning detective genre, decreeing that Stevenson's novel was 'not only too sensational but too literary to rank among detective stories so called' ('Function' 3).

Indeed, *Jekyll and Hyde*'s confusing conflation of high and low genres and forms continued to trouble some of the most esteemed writers and critics of the twentieth century. Most famously, in a lecture on the novel delivered at Cornell University in March 1951, Vladimir Nabokov passionately implored his students to 'completely forget, disremember, obliterate, unlearn, consign to oblivion any notion you may have had that *Jekyll and Hyde* is some kind of a mystery story, [or] a detective story' (Nabokov, Bowers and Updike 171). For Nabokov, Stevenson's novel belonged to the canon of great literature and to categorise it merely as detective fiction debased its elevated literary status. Detective fiction and so-called 'low' forms of literature have been valid objects of academic enquiry for more than 30 years, yet the generic status of *Jekyll and Hyde* remains critically contentious. It is largely accepted as playing a pivotal role in histories of the gothic and horror genres, but it is still often neglected by historians of the detective genre, who consider it an 'impure' and perplexing hybrid of generic forms (Dryden, Arata and Massie 54). Julian Symons's *Bloody Murder*, for instance, suggests that Stevenson 'hovered on the brink' of detective fiction, but concludes that he never fully committed or contributed to the genre (62). Likewise, Stephen Knight argues that the 1880s was 'a period of rapid expansion in both the numbers and the kinds of crime fiction published' for which Stevenson was 'a model' with works such as *The Suicide Club* and *The Dynamiter* (1885) (*Crime* 54; *Form and Ideology* 68). He concludes, however, that Stevenson 'wrote no specifically detective stories' and remained more interested in 'identification with the criminals' (*Form and Ideology* 69; *Crime* 63). Similarly, the novel doesn't feature in Ian Ousby's genealogy of nineteenth-century crime literature (*Bloodhounds*), in which he argues that no significant advances were made in the Victorian detective genre between the publication of Wilkie Collins's *The Moonstone* in 1868 and the first appearance of Sherlock Holmes in 1887.

In the novel, however, Stevenson does employ many of the structuring features of the nascent detective story. As its full title signals, Stevenson's *Strange Case of Dr Jekyll and Mr Hyde* is formally constructed as a mystery that in many ways resembles works of pivotal importance to the burgeoning detective genre, such as Edgar Allan Poe's ratiocinative story 'The Murders in the Rue Morgue' (1841) or Wilkie Collins's sensation novel *The Moonstone* (1868). The medico-legal term 'case' itself links Stevenson's novel with earlier pioneering works of crime fiction such as the bestselling *Leavenworth Case* (1878) by 'founding mother of the detective genre', Anna Katherine Green, and later canonical crime works such as Arthur Conan Doyle's *Case-Book of Sherlock Holmes* (1927) (Sussex 2). Its epistolary format, complete with letters, diary entries and legal documents, recalls Collins's *The Moonstone* and *The Woman in White*, and prefigures Hume's *Mystery of a Hansom Cab* (1886). As Gordon Hirsch has also pointed out, the 'three elements' which together comprise 'the formula for the detective story' are all present in Stevenson's novel – there is a mystery, the story is structured around an enquiry into this mystery and some of the concealed facts are made known at the end (229). In fact, at *Jekyll and Hyde*'s heart are a number of mysteries and at least two crimes. Eight of its ten chapters are concerned with unravelling the mystery of the baffling circumstances surrounding Jekyll's will and uncovering the nature of the puzzling relationship between the respectable doctor, who is 'the very pink of the proprieties', and Mr Hyde, 'a really damnable man' (9). The narrative is also punctuated by two of Hyde's 'monstrous' crimes – the 'trampling' of a young girl and the bludgeoning of Sir Danvers Carew, an 'aged and beautiful gentleman' (60).

Detection is also central to the narrative. Early in the novel, Jekyll's lawyer and close companion, Mr Utterson, takes on the role of amateur sleuth, embarking on an investigation into the nature of the malign Hyde's relationship with his friend: 'If he be Mr Hyde ... I shall be Mr Seek' (14). After the Carew murder, Utterson's amateur (and largely unsuccessful) enquiries are augmented by an (also unsuccessful) investigation conducted by Inspector Newcomen of the Metropolitan police. Despite their lack of success in 'solving' any of the novel's crimes, and the novel's disarmingly ambiguous ending, where Jekyll (or is it Hyde?) commits suicide, some of the previously concealed facts *are* made known at the end of the novel. We know, for instance, that Hyde was Carew's murderer and that he was Jekyll's alter ego, brought into being by a scientific experiment. Even the titles of the chapters themselves – 'The Carew Murder Case', 'Search for Mr Hyde', 'The Incident of the Letter' and 'Remarkable Incident of Dr Lanyon' – foreground the importance of clues, details and crimes, as well as the practices of searching and detecting, and in doing so prefigure the common features of later detective fiction.

Part of the reason that many critics have such trouble considering *Jekyll and Hyde* a work of detective fiction, however, may be that, despite its adherence to some of the characteristics later taken to conceptualise the genre, the novel also repeatedly disavows and disrupts some of its nascent conventions – particularly with regard to narrative resolution and the appearance of a successful, heroic detective. Despite the fact that Utterson conducts enquiries, his motivations seem misguided. He is not motivated by a neutral quest for the truth, but rather by the desire to see his friend escape scandal. Although his investigation is augmented by that of Scotland Yard's Inspector Newcomen, the police detective's investigations are characterised by an almost total lack of success. Newcomen drops unceremoniously out of the narrative early in the proceedings and Utterson fades away at the novel's close. The 'Full Statement of the Case' is thus provided by way of the criminal's (or is it the victim's?) epistolary confession, rather than through a flourish of deductive skill and an exposition of the full story of the crime. In doing so, it prefigures the shock ending of Agatha Christie's most morally and formally subversive novel, *The Murder of Roger Ackroyd* (1926), in which the narrator is revealed to be the murderer. However, the closure provided at the novel's end is partial at best – Jekyll's 'Full Statement of the Case' is ironically named, being marked by a distinct lack of fullness. Many of the novel's central questions therefore remain unanswered or ambiguous at its close – what, for instance, are the 'undignified' and 'monstrous' activities that Jekyll has always enjoyed? Why did Hyde trample a child and kill Sir Danvers Carew? Did Jekyll commit suicide or was he killed by Hyde? Overall, then, this is a novel which firmly resists the impulses towards closure and resolution often read as so characteristic of the burgeoning detective genre. It seems, therefore, perfectly to illustrate Stevenson's ambivalence to the genre, detailed in the preface to *The Wrecker*, where he admitted that he was both 'attracted and repelled by that very modern form of the police novel or mystery story' (589).

In the last few years, a growing body of scholarship has begun to challenge ideas about the 'accepted (but overly schematic) development of detective fiction as a genre' put forward by early historians of crime fiction (Pittard, *Purity* 24).[2] Many early critics had argued that detective fiction was developed through a small number of canonical works featuring certain common generic features, such as a heroic detective and a satisfying resolution in which the case is solved and the status quo is restored. More recent work on detective fiction, however, has argued for the importance to the history of the crime genre of works that do not conform perfectly to these previously prescribed 'rules' about genre and form. In this chapter, I join a number of recent crime fiction scholars who make particular claims for the importance of *Jekyll and Hyde* to the genealogy of the nineteenth-century detective genre.[3]

In this chapter, I build upon this body of work, continuing to redress the omission of *Jekyll and Hyde* from studies on the detective genre, by providing a detailed demonstration of the impact of Stevenson's novel upon the establishment of some of the formal and thematic features that would later define much of the canonical (and non-canonical) crime fiction that came to popularity in the 1890s. In particular, I suggest that the very features that make Stevenson's novel so problematic for many historians of the detective genre (respectable criminal protagonist, unsuccessful/immoral detectives, lack of resolution) in fact link it strongly to much of the crime and detective fiction that appeared later in the century. It is important to remember that, with *Jekyll and Hyde*, the already popular Stevenson sealed his place as respected member of the literary establishment; it therefore makes sense that later fledgling crime writers would attempt to emulate one of his biggest critical and commercial successes by employing and pushing further the tropes and characterisations which structured that novel. Indeed, the ambiguous formal and moral features of *Jekyll and Hyde* can be traced in later works such as Morrison's *The Dorrington Deed-Box* (1897), Zangwill's *The Big Bow Mystery* (1891), Boothby's *A Prince of Swindlers* (1897) and many of Doyle's Sherlock Holmes stories, where crimes emanate from the middle classes, from geographically respectable areas, where criminals escape, commit suicide or go free, and where the detectives may be unsuccessful, or even implicated in the crimes.

Specifically, I read Stevenson's novel in relation to changing late Victorian perceptions about the social class of criminals which had developed in light of a number of scandals featuring middle- and upper-middle-class offenders. I examine how not just Hyde but all of the novel's group of respectable gentlemen share a penchant for sexual tourism with the protagonists of W.T. Stead's 'Maiden Tribute' exposé. I unpick the related cultural contexts for the novel's depictions of blackmail, slumming and sexual crime. I consider how the novel's crimes were re-evaluated in light of the Ripper murders in 1888, and the ways in which its portrayal of respectable criminality was employed to bolster theories that the Ripper was a member of the middle or upper classes, perhaps even a doctor. Lastly, I examine the consequences of Stevenson's ambivalent portrayal of detection in the novel. In particular, I read the proto-detective Utterson's desire to subvert justice and protect his friend against dominant ideas about the moral uprightness of the Victorian detective.

In an early review of the novel, the poet and critic Andrew Lang – a great friend of Stevenson – noted what for him was the most striking feature of his associate's latest work: 'he has chosen the scene for his wild "Tragedy of a Body and Soul", as it might have been called, in *the most ordinary and respectable quarters of London*' and 'his heroes (surely *this* is original) are all successful middle-aged professional men' (emphases in original) ('Stevenson's New Story' 55). In Lang's view, then, the novel was just as much about the respectable middle-class Jekyll and his circle as it was about the degenerate criminal Hyde. Indeed, *Jekyll and Hyde* opens with Stevenson repeatedly foregrounding the respectability of Jekyll and the wider group of gentlemen with whom he associates. Their professional and bourgeois sensibilities could hardly be more clearly delineated: Gabriel Utterson, we are told, is a 'reputable' lawyer, Jekyll is an 'honourable and distinguished' doctor of both medicine and law with a string of academic qualifications – 'M.D., D.C.L., LL.D., F.R.S., &c.' – Hastie Lanyon is a 'great' doctor, Mr Guest is 'a man of counsel,' and the other unnamed members of the social circle are 'all intelligent, reputable men' (6; 55; 11; 12; 29; 19).[4] As Lang's review recognised, if *Jekyll and Hyde* is a discourse on a number of late Victorian anxieties about crime and degeneracy, then Stevenson emphatically situates those concerns in the 'ordinary and respectable' yet immoral and hypocritical world of middle-class London men (Lang, 'Stevenson's New Story' 55). Indeed, as Lang was later to put it, 'Dr Jekyll is rather a worse kind of fellow than Mr Hyde' ('Modern Man' 264).

Stevenson had already begun to explore the themes of duplicity and the types of criminality found in the respectable world in earlier works such as 'The Suicide Club' (1878), 'The Body Snatcher' (1884) and 'Markheim' (1885). The middle- and upper-class gents who are members of 'The Suicide Club', and who draw lots to decide which of their number will be murdered and which will commit the crime, serve as a reminder that criminality is not only the provenance of London's lower classes. Likewise, in 'The Body Snatcher', Stevenson's fictional reworking of the Burke and Hare murders produced for the 1884 Christmas edition of the *Pall Mall Gazette*, the story's criminals are all outwardly respectable doctors and medical men. Medical student Fettes's 'roaring blackguardly' behaviour by night is hidden by 'unimpeachable' daytime professionalism and industry (79). And whilst his accomplice, the murderer Dr Wolfe Macfarlane, is 'clever' and 'agreeable', he is also 'dissipated, and unscrupulous to the last degree' (80). In *Jekyll and Hyde*, Stevenson once again situates criminal appetites within the home and body of an outwardly respectable medical man. Jekyll enjoys 'disgrace[ful]' and disreputable 'pleasures' in private but wishes to 'carry ... [his] head high', remaining 'honourable and distinguished' in public (55). Thus he creates a potion that allows his 'wicked' and 'honourable' sides to be 'housed in separate identities' (56; 55; 56).

In the pages of Jekyll's extraordinary confession, Stevenson takes care to foreground for the reader the notion that Jekyll has always enjoyed disreputable 'pleasures' (55).[5] The transformation from Jekyll to Hyde, then, is not simply a process by which a good doctor is overtaken by an evil doppelganger, as popular reimaginings of the tale often have it. Rather, Jekyll deliberately formulates the potion that calls forth Hyde in order to create a persona in which he can 'la[y] aside restraint', 'plunge in shame' and indulge in the unspecified 'evil' activities that he has always enjoyed, without being 'exposed to disgrace and penitence' (56). As Stevenson repeatedly makes clear, Hyde indulges in no vices that Jekyll himself did not enjoy. The difference between the two is that Jekyll enjoys these vices shamefully, fearful of damage to his good name whereas Hyde is able to enjoy them openly. After seeking out Jekyll's 'undignified' or even 'monstrous' pleasures, Hyde can 'pass away like the stain of breath upon a mirror' and there in his place is 'quiet' and 'good' Henry Jekyll – a man who appears to be 'the pink of the proprieties' and 'who could afford to laugh at suspicion' (59; 60).

Stevenson takes great care also to foreground the notion that the doctor's duplicity is not uncommon. In the pages of his confession, Jekyll terms himself merely an 'ordinary secret sinner' (55; 65). He links his behaviour to that of numerous men in the past and the future, telling the reader that 'men have before hired bravos to transact their crimes, while their own person and reputation sat under shelter' and that 'others will follow, others will outstrip me on the same lines' (60; 56). When attempting to gauge the nature of Jekyll's predicament, Utterson also reflects that, 'few men could read the rolls of their life' without fear of 'the ghost of some old sin or the cancer of some concealed disgrace' (17). Stevenson seems to be suggesting that it is the 'ordinary' condition of not only Jekyll but many, or even all, outwardly respectable men to appear upright but to sin in secret and to hide these disreputable sins (55). Lang's review of the novel again seems to endorse this view. Somewhat casually, he notes that 'every Jekyll among us is haunted by his own Hyde' ('Stevenson's New Story' 55).

In concentrating on the criminality found in the respectable world, Stevenson, of course, was drawing upon the established literary tradition of situating criminality behind respectable façades found in the gothic and sensation genres where, in Winifred Hughes's phrase, 'things are not what they seem, even – in fact especially – in the respectable classes and their respectable institutions' (36). One thinks, for instance, of the handsome and popular philanthropist fraudster Godfrey Ablewhite, who features in Collins's *The Moonstone*. However, in situating criminality in the body of a respectable doctor, Stevenson was also drawing upon a number of contemporary anxieties about the changing nature of crime and criminality that were circulating in the press in the years before the novel's composition. As the matter-of-fact way that Lang relates Jekyll's predicament to the lives of 'every' contemporary man endorses, at the time of *Jekyll and Hyde*'s publication it was increasingly becoming thought of as commonplace for respectable late Victorian gentlemen to seek out 'undignified' or even 'monstrous' pleasures in secret and to conceal these pleasures from public view (*Jekyll and Hyde* 60).

Whilst this may perhaps seem surprising, the last two decades of the nineteenth century in fact ushered in a number of changing ideas about the social class of London's criminals. As Martin Wiener has demonstrated, in the 1880s and 1890s there emerged a new preoccupation with the possibility of burgeoning yet hidden levels of crime and criminality within London's respectable classes. In the second half of the nineteenth century, the relatively newly established Metropolitan police force began to achieve control over the chaotic and crime-infested London streets, moving in upon 'rough and dark' parts of the city, setting up new stations and 15-minute foot patrols (Wiener 215). Thus by the 1870s, 'more stringent standards of public order were established' and a 'new sense of public security began to emerge' (216). In *A History of Crime in England* (1876), L.O. Pike – one of the first historians of crime – observed that during the 1870s, in comparison to previous decades, 'the sense of security is almost everywhere diffused' (480). Official statistics seemed also to support this claim. There was a particularly dramatic fall in the estimated numbers of the 'criminal classes at large' between 1870 and the late 1880s, from almost 78,000 in 1869 and 1870 to 31,000 in 1889 and 1890 (Wiener 216).

One consequence of this new sense of security about street crime was that suspicion and surveillance turned inward from the unruly lower classes to 'persons and scenes of apparent respectability' (Wiener 244). The previously dominant image of criminality as the province of the slum-dwelling classes thus began to be augmented and overtaken by concerns about 'criminality hidden within the respectable world' – crimes that 'depended upon the appearance of respectability and character' (245). Questions began to be raised about what might lie behind the closed doors and respectable façades of persons and locations that a patrolling police force was ill suited to detect or deter. Concerns emerged that there might be many crimes not coming to light: sexual crimes, murders, and crimes like poisoning, identity theft and blackmail, that were hidden by – and in fact depended upon – the appearance of respectability. As one pamphlet writer of the late 1880s speculated, 'murders nowadays are very easy of concealment, and probably ... more frequent than anybody has hitherto believed. In a very material sense it is deemed possible that there may be, roughly speaking, a "skeleton in every house"' (qtd in Kalikoff 59).[6]

These concerns, however, were not merely a matter of perception. As Rob Sindall's study of the calendars of prisoners appearing before London's Quarter Sessions and Assize Courts reveals, after 1870, 'middle-class crime was on the increase' and 'the middle classes show a greater tendency to commit indictable offences than ... the lower classes' (23–4). More specifically, the statistics show that men belonging to 'Social Class I' – that is the upper and upper-middle classes, including doctors, bankers and lawyers – committed the majority of the most serious 'violence for fun' crimes, including assault and indecent assault (Sindall 26–7).[7] This high percentage of assaults and indecent assaults – as opposed to 'acquisitive' crimes like fraud or robbery – committed by men in 'Social Class I' suggests that for many well-to-do late Victorian men, satisfaction of physical desires and impulses was more important than the acquisition of goods and money which, as their social position would imply, they were probably capable of acquiring by non-criminal methods (Sindall 27–8). In the autumn of 1888, of course, as I discuss in more detail below, fears about this type of offender coalesced around theories that the Whitechapel Ripper might not be a denizen of the London slums but rather 'a homicidal maniac of the upper-class of society' – a doctor or a nobleman – 'with quite sufficient control of himself and of his faculties ... to mix in respectable society unquestioned by a single soul' (Winslow 6; 'A Possible Clue' 1). In particular, *The Star*, a Radical East End paper, advanced several theories that the murderer was 'respectable, and the last man one would suspect' ('Points About the Murders').

The ten years or so before the publication of *Jekyll and Hyde* were also rife with media exposés concerning the secret lives of outwardly respectable upper-middle-class men, which helped to disseminate to the reading public the idea that respectable exteriors often masked immoral or criminal behaviour. The year 1875 saw the sensational trial of Colonel Valentine Baker, a soldier with 'an exceptionally distinguished record', who was convicted of indecently assaulting a young single woman in a public railway carriage (Wyndham 31).[8] 'The Career of Colonel Baker', an anonymous pamphlet about the Baker case, made overt links between the outward respectability of men, their 'filthy desires', and their opportunities to commit serious crime, suggesting that 'the greater the social opportunities and advantages of a man, the more heinous his offence' (qtd in Diamond 128). The year 1881 saw the conviction in Chicago of Scottish-born doctor Thomas Neill Cream for multiple murders by poisoning. After his release in Chicago, Cream returned to London where he had trained as a surgeon, and went on to become one of Victorian England's most notorious serial killers, the Lambeth Poisoner.[9] The year of *Jekyll and Hyde*'s publication also saw two sensational sex scandals surface in the Divorce Courts, featuring cabinet ministers Colin Campbell, son of the Duke of Argyll and brother-in-law to Princess Louise, and Radical politician Charles Dilke.[10] Newspaper reports and pamphlets on the Dilke case pruriently detailed the nature of the politician's numerous acts of adultery and his penchants for 'not only adultery' but moreover 'the last outrages of depraved and unnatural French vice' (Stead, *Has Sir Charles Dilke* 15).

Reportage on cases like these not only helped to disseminate to the reading public the notion that seemingly respectable gentlemen harboured disreputable desires and were often responsible for sensational crimes, but also fed their appetite for tales of scandal in high life. The British reading public had always been fascinated by the macabre as a *Pall Mall Gazette* review of the stage version of *Jekyll and Hyde* bemoaned, 'Scratch John Bull and you find the ancient Briton who revels in blood, who loves to dip deep into a murder, and devours the details of a hanging. If you doubt it, ask the clerks at Mr Smith's bookstalls, ask the men and women and boys who sell newspapers in the street. They will tell you' ('Nightmare at the Lyceum' 5). As Richard Altick has pointed out, however, in the late nineteenth century the mass readership brought up on penny dreadfuls, sensation fiction and prurient newspaper reportage of famous crimes had developed a particularly voracious appetite for narratives of a criminal nature 'in respectable society' featuring middle- or upper-middle-class offenders (*Presence of the Present* 57).

In the year before the publication of *Jekyll and Hyde*, probably the most notorious and voraciously consumed scandal of the late Victorian era broke. Over the course of four nights in July 1885, 'The Maiden Tribute of Modern Babylon' (hereafter 'Maiden Tribute'), a series of articles written by *Pall Mall Gazette* editor W.T. Stead, exposed the 'abominable, unutterable' details of London's child prostitution trade (Stead 'Notice'). Building upon the work of earlier Victorian urban anthropologists like Henry Mayhew (*London Labour and the London Poor* 1851), James Greenwood (*Low-Life Deeps* 1876) and Andrew Mearns (*The Bitter Cry of Outcast London* 1883), Stead had spent four weeks immersed in London's underworld, investigating and documenting all the protagonists involved in the procurement of girls as young as nine for sex.[11] Stevenson's private letters reveal that he was just one amongst the thousands of readers who eagerly consumed this sensational fare.

The articles were part social commentary, part sensational melodrama, introducing readers of the *Pall Mall Gazette* to a full cast of heroes and villains. The characters ranged from the 'innocent' violated girls to their 'cunning' procuresses, and from 'unprincipled' doctors and nurses who certified virginity, to the 'evil and stalking' predators who deflowered them ('Maiden Tribute III' 3; 5; 6). The real targets of Stead's exposé, however, were the well-to-do and respectable men who visited the poor quarters of the city in order to arrange sex with young girls and those who covered these crimes up or looked the other way. Stead, a social reformer with links to the emerging London Socialist movement, revealed in detail the nature of the crimes which he claimed were being both perpetrated and suppressed by members of the comfortable classes – 'princes and dukes, ministers and judges' ('We Bid' 1). Girls as young as nine, he claimed, were daily being 'served up' to these men 'as dainty morsels to minister to the passions of the rich' ('Maiden Tribute I' 2). Stead's politically motivated objective in exposing this trade, he claimed, was to 'rouse the nation' by exposing 'vices of the rich' ('Maiden Tribute I' 2). The articles also provided excellent journalistic copy, however. W.H. Smith banned the articles from their newsstands, citing obscenity, but crowds of would-be readers soon stormed the offices of the *Pall Mall Gazette*, demanding copies of the paper.

Although in reality Stead's articles didn't expose any princes, dukes or judges, they did feature prurient details of the secret lives of a number of respectable upper-middle-class doctors and clerks. These men were travelling into low quarters of London on a daily basis to engage in sexual tourism. One of the main predators was the 'London Minotaur', a wealthy doctor from the prosperous West End, 'clad as respectably in broad cloth and fine linen as any bishop', who devoted himself to the 'ruin of three maids a night' ('Maiden Tribute III' 5). Also featured were 'the clerk in a highly respectable establishment' whose 'villainous amusement [was] to decoy and ruin children', and 'Dr D' – another 'wealthy man' – who boasted that he had ruined 2000 girls ('Maiden Tribute III' 2; 5). Stead railed that transactions like the Minotaur's were allowed to go on 'unnoticed and unchecked' because of the social class of the men involved ('Maiden Tribute III' 5). He suggested also that although these acts were against the law they were 'certainly practised by some legislators and winked at by many administrators of the law' ('Maiden Tribute III' 5). An examination of some of the statements made by parliamentary members during the debates on the ensuing

Criminal Law Amendment Bill (to raise the age of consent from 13 to 16) appears also to confirm Stead's initial accusations about the tendencies of the lawmakers and their peers to cover up these crimes or to look the other way. One member of the House of Lords points out that 'very few of their Lordships ... had not, when young men, been guilty of immorality', and cautions members to 'pause before passing a clause within the range of which their sons might come' (qtd in Walkowitz 103–4). This statement seems remarkably close to Utterson's observation about Jekyll's morality and the morality of his wider social circle: 'He [Jekyll] was wild when he was young,' and his admission that 'few men could read the rolls of their lives' without admitting that they had done 'many ill things' (17).

Regardless of Stead's own political motivations for reading sex exploitation as class exploitation, one of the most shocking consequences of the 'Maiden Tribute' was the vast amount of correspondence sent to the *Pall Mall Gazette* which freely confirmed the 'Maiden Tribute' articles' accusations about the scale and widespread nature of these behaviours amongst middle- and upper-middle-class men. Thanks to his policy of the 'universal interview', which attempted to incorporate a range of voices and opinions into the print media, Stead encouraged men to write in to defend themselves in a section of the *Pall Mall Gazette* entitled 'What the Male Pests have to say for Themselves'. Perhaps surprisingly, many men availed themselves of this opportunity, openly admitting to and defending their liberty to partake in such practices. One of the most blatant responses came from a self-styled 'Saunterer in the Labyrinth' who coolly disdained the hysteria over the 'Maiden Tribute' stating that 'no good will be done by railing against the "base appetite"' ('Musings' 2). He went on to suggest that, 'men do not really regard the appetite as base at all' and that practices like those outlined in the 'Maiden Tribute' articles were 'compulsive and compulsory' amongst the middle and upper classes ('Musings' 2). The 'Saunterer' went on wryly to thank Stead for putting 'the notion of buying a virgin into the heads of a great many men who never entertained it before' and for usefully supplying details about where to go and how much it would cost ('Musings' 2).[12] In an 'Occasional Note' published on 14 August 1885, Stead admitted that the *Pall Mall Gazette* had been 'overwhelmed' with complaints about his decision to publish the Saunterer's correspondence (3). He reminded readers, however, that his articles and the letters that followed had simply exposed the ubiquity of these criminal and immoral activities, pointing out, 'Whilst no doubt the Saunterer's moral code is revolting ... [it] represents the morality of the *average man* of the world' (emphasis added) (3).

Another reader's response to the 'Maiden Tribute' articles strongly prefigures Jekyll's revelations about his struggle to contain certain shameful pleasures. A Mr F. Gore-Brown wrote to the *Pall Mall Gazette* to express his dismay that the 'Maiden Tribute' exposé 'do[es] more harm than it will ever do good' 'by suggesting impure thoughts to the hearts of many who find the attempt to be good a hard struggle' ('Public Opinion on the "Modern Babylon" Exposures' 6). Mr Gore-Brown's struggle to suppress his impure desires, of course recalls Jekyll's admission that for years he 'regarded' and 'hid' his 'irregularities ... with an almost morbid sense of shame' (55). In a letter to Stevenson, poet and critic John Addington Symonds made a similar complaint about the effect of *Jekyll and Hyde* upon readers, warning Stevenson: 'as an allegory, *it touches one too closely.* Most of us at some epoch of our lives have been on the verge of developing a Mr Hyde ... your Dr Jekyll seems to me capable of loosening the last threads of self-control in one who should read it while wavering between his better and worse self' (emphasis in original) (Symonds 120–1).[13] What seems evident from the various types of response to the Stead exposé and Stevenson's novel, is that many men of a certain well-to-do background routinely visited poor districts of the city in order to commit sexual acts with the self-assured conviction of their prerogative to do so. It also illustrates that, like Jekyll, many more late Victorian men found it a struggle to suppress these and other 'undignified' or 'monstrous' urges (*Jekyll and Hyde* 60).

Stevenson's private papers show that he read the 'Maiden Tribute' articles at the time that he was writing *Jekyll and Hyde* and it seems entirely likely that Stead's exposé influenced the themes of duplicity and dishonourable pleasures in the comfortable classes, which are so central to the novel.[14] The editor and poet W.E. Henley had forwarded Stevenson the instalments of the 'Maiden Tribute' articles on 9 July 1885, a couple of days after the story first broke. In the accompanying letter he breathlessly asks: 'have you received the three copies of the *PMG*? For Monday, Tuesday, & Wednesday? There was never such indignation before as over this new feat of Stead's ... You shd have seen the posters: "Virgin Victims", "Horrible Revelations", "London's Vice".'[15] On the one hand, Henley scoffs at 'the rush for all this twaddle', describing how the offices of the *Pall Mall Gazette* were 'all but stormed by a crowd of hawkers'. On the other hand, however, his letter demonstrates that he shares the crowd's appetite for the article's sensational secrets, enthusing: 'What we all want to know is who's Dr D – the hero of the three maids per fortnight? and who, O who! is the Minotaur, the devourer of the 2000 virginities at five pounds apiece?' In a way that appears to confirm the belief that gentlemen regularly harboured unpalatable secrets, Henley also speculates, 'Somehow I don't think the government can or rather will interfere. If Stead really has been exploring, he has probably got hold of facts which would upset a good many of their applecarts.' Henley's observation that the government is unlikely to interfere and that this information could upset 'a good many' respectable men's 'applecarts' once again seems to confirm the perception of endemic levels of this type of behaviour within the upper-middle-class male sphere of late Victorian London. The matter-of-fact manner of his observation also suggests the extent to which this seems to have been an accepted part of late Victorian London life.

While Stevenson seems not to have replied to Henley about the 'Maiden Tribute' articles, the somewhat suspect or deviant practices alluded to in the novel strongly suggest that Stevenson had the London Minotaur and the Saunterer in the Labyrinth in mind in his characterisations of Jekyll and his circle. Certainly, we know that he was working on the novel at the time when the story broke. In drawing upon the story, he would have been working within a well-established tradition of plundering sensational news stories for the plot details of crime novels. In a now notorious attack on the sensation genre, published in the *Quarterly Review*, Henry Mansel had disparaged this process. He acerbically advised the aspiring novelist of his day, 'Let him only keep an eye on the criminal reports of the daily newspapers, marking the cases which are honoured with the especial notice of a leading article, and ... he has the outline of his story not only ready-made, but approved beforehand' (Mansel 501). Indeed, the Road Hill Murder case (revisited in 2008 by Kate Summerscale with *The Suspicions of Mr Whicher*) provided Collins with the inspiration for *The Moonstone*. So too the Burke and Hare case had inspired Stevenson's own 'The Body Snatcher', published just over a year before *Jekyll and Hyde*.

The opening scenes of *Jekyll and Hyde* strongly foreground the notion that the novel's circle of gentlemen protagonists engage in the type of sexual tourism exposed by Stead in the 'Maiden Tribute' articles. The novel opens as Utterson, the lawyer, and his 'distant kinsman' Richard Enfield are on one of their frequent 'excursions' into the London streets at night (6). As Roger Luckhurst has pointed out, even Stevenson's seemingly innocuous description of Enfield as a 'well-known man about town' would have signified for Victorian readers a 'certain sexual behaviour', or one belonging to the shady side of town life (184 fn.).

Stevenson tells the reader that both Enfield and Utterson counted their nightwalking expeditions as 'the chief jewel of each week', though in one of the first of many unanswered questions which pepper the novel, it is not revealed why they enjoy this time so much or where exactly they go to on these 'excursions' (6). As the men stroll, Enfield recounts another recent walk where he had been coming 'home from some place at the end of the world' at three in the morning, through streets where one 'begins to long for the sight of a policeman' (7). In this disreputable place, Enfield encountered Hyde, also out walking.

Enfield's late night walk in a low part of the city echoes the walk which he and Utterson are presently on, and this is further paralleled by Hyde's late night ramble. This, in turn, is mirrored by the walk Carew is on at the time he is murdered by Hyde. In a novel which repeatedly presents more questions than it does answers, the reasons for the men's repeated late night excursions into low and unnerving areas of the city are not disclosed, but the mystery shrouding the details of the walks offers a strong suggestion that they are engaged in some sort of 'mashing' or sexual tourism.[16] This shared spatial practice thematically and morally aligns almost all of the novel's gentlemen protagonists – Jekyll, Carew, Utterson, Enfield – with Hyde, as well as with Stead, Stead's Minotaur and the Saunterer in the Labyrinth. It is only the first of the many connections, however, that Stevenson continues to draw between Hyde, the wider circle of the novel's respectable protagonists and the Minotaurs featured in Stead's exposé.

Returning from their evening ramble, Utterson and Enfield pass a doorway that reminds Enfield of an incident involving Hyde that he witnessed some weeks ago. The doorway is 'blistered and distained' and bears 'the marks of prolonged and sordid negligence'; its poor state and the tramps who 'slouch in its recess' mark it as the entry to a disreputable home (6). Enfield tells Utterson that a couple of weeks ago, near this door, he watched as Hyde 'trampled' a little girl (7). This trampling, he tells his companion, left the girl 'screaming on the ground', 'was hellish to see' and marked out Hyde as 'a really damnable man' (7). Since the novel's first publication, the possibly coded meaning of the trampling incident has been a matter of great debate. Reading the novel shortly after its publication, Gerard Manley Hopkins famously speculated in a letter to friend and fellow poet Robert Bridges, dated 28 October 1886: 'the trampling scene is perhaps a convention: he [Stevenson] was thinking of something unsuitable for fiction' (Hopkins 243).[17] Although Hopkins is as ambiguous as the text in specifying what exactly he believes the trampling to signify, it seems likely that he was suggesting that it was a metaphor for the child rape exposed by Stead's 'Maiden Tribute' less than a year before. An early review of *Jekyll and Hyde* for *The Court and Society Review* drew more explicit links between the novel's trampling scene and the gentlemen who were exposed in the 'Maiden Tribute' articles, suggesting to readers that 'Hyde, it is probable, was a kind of "Minotaur"' (Review of *Jekyll and Hyde* 6).[18]

Whilst Stevenson deliberately left the nature of the crimes unspecified in order to allow for the many interpretative possibilities that they suggest – 'others must look for what is meant' – the gentlemen who gather at the scene employ a threat which again appears to draw upon a practice which sprang up after the 'Maiden Tribute' scandal broke, suggesting that Stevenson had the case in mind (Stevenson, *Letters*, vol. V, 211). Enfield and a doctor ask Hyde for monetary compensation for the child's family and threaten to 'make such a scandal ... as should make his name stink' if he does not comply with their demands to pay (8). Stevenson seems here to be referencing one of the reported consequences of the 'Maiden Tribute' in a way that would have suggested the links between Hyde and men like Stead's Minotaur to contemporary readers. The *Pall Mall Gazette* had reported how as 'a remarkable consequence of the recent revelations' of the 'Maiden Tribute' articles, gentlemen accused of sexual assault now often offered to 'square the matter' by offering a sum of money of 'no less than £5 as a solatium for wounded honour' ('Assaults on Women and Children' 10). The 'Saunterer in the Labyrinth' who wrote to the *Pall Mall Gazette* after the 'Maiden Tribute' articles also described what he ironically called 'a "very touching case" where a young girl was ravished by an officer of the guards (a married man) at a brothel in the North of London' ('Musings' 1). The Saunterer noted that before Stead's exposé, the family of the girl 'might possibly have got £50', but that now the man was 'willing to make any settlement demanded' rather than face publicity and possible prosecution ('Musings' 1).

We know that Stevenson had been following the 'Maiden Tribute' articles; he seems to have been thinking of these items from the *Pall Mall Gazette* in having Enfield and the doctor demand that Hyde pay compensation to the 'trampled' child's father. Like the gentleman in the Saunterer's story, Enfield recounts that Hyde was extremely anxious 'to avoid a scene' and so told the girl's family 'name your figure' (8). For Stevenson's readers, the disproportionately large sum of one hundred pounds which Hyde eventually pays – around £8000–10,000 in today's terms – suggests that what Enfield witnessed was probably not a literal 'trampling', and was much more likely to have been the type of sexual assault being discussed daily in the pages of the newspapers.[19]

Angus McLaren's study of the Victorian serial killer Dr Thomas Neill Cream argues that 'blackmail was a product of the unprecedented importance nineteenth-century society attributed to "reputation"' (*Prescription* 91). The nineteenth-century middle classes' preoccupation with the creation and policing of rigid boundaries between public and private spheres created a world where blackmail flourished. As Mr Justice Phillimore, Justice of the High Court, put it in 1905, 'England, with all her pretended virtues, is home of the blackmailer' (qtd in Ives 355). In Victorian England, the blackmailer's 'most potent threat' was to publicise some disreputable secret – often sexual – and thus 'ruin the offender's respectable reputation, especially among his peers, business associates, and others in a position to harm or reject him' (Feinberg 248). As McLaren points out, the reputations of men in 'sensitive positions' such as 'doctors and politicians' were particularly 'important and fragile' (*Prescription* 92). As a result of this contemporary phenomenon, blackmail plots hinging on the control and release of hidden information are a recurring motif in canonical Victorian fiction, including *Bleak House* (1852–53), *Middlemarch* (1874), *The Way We Live Now* (1875) and *Daniel Deronda* (1876).[20]

In *Jekyll and Hyde*, 'The Story of the Door' is structured around two separate but overlapping instances of blackmail or assumed blackmail. After being apprehended at the trampling scene, Hyde recognises that the threat of blackmail is one against which he is powerless: 'If you choose to make capital out of this accident ... I am naturally helpless. No gentleman but wishes to avoid a scene' (8). He agrees to pay the child's father one hundred pounds but does not have enough cash on his person. Therefore, he enters the building with the 'blistered and distained' door and returns minutes later with a cheque signed by the eminent and well-known Dr Jekyll (6). To Enfield the 'business' of Hyde having another man's cheque seems 'apocryphal' and he speculates that for 'a gentleman' to 'walk into a cellar door at four in the morning and come out of it with another man's cheque for close upon a hundred pounds' indicates some sort of a sordid secret or bond (8). He therefore assumes that Hyde is blackmailing Jekyll by threatening to disclose details of 'some of the capers of his youth' (9).[21] As a result, Enfield christens the building with the door 'Blackmail House' (9).

When Enfield tells Utterson about 'Blackmail House' the lawyer reveals that he has long since been concerned about Jekyll's will, in which the doctor leaves his fortune to Hyde in the event of his death or disappearance. Now that Utterson has been told that Hyde is a disreputable character, he begins to fear that the conditions of the will are not precipitated by 'madness', as he had previously suspected, but rather by 'disgrace' (11). Building upon Enfield's blackmail suspicions, Utterson recalls that Jekyll 'was wild when he was young' and thus automatically infers that the doctor's connection with Hyde must concern the latter's knowledge of 'the ghost of some old sin' or 'the cancer of some concealed disgrace' (17). In what is referred to as the 'Printer's Copy' of the text, the earliest draft of the novel, Stevenson is more explicit about the form that Utterson's suspicions took. He appears to entertain two hypotheses – that Hyde is blackmailing Jekyll or that Hyde is Jekyll's illegitimate son.[22] Despite making this suggestion more ambiguous in the final text, Utterson's somewhat casual and natural disclosure that Jekyll has indulged in sinful or disgraceful behaviour and that he is being made to pay for previous misdeeds still underlines Stevenson's emphasis upon the prevalence of immorality amongst respectable men. Indeed, when Utterson fears that Jekyll is being 'punished' for some 'old sin' he 'brood[s] awhile on his own past ... lest by chance some Jack-in-the-Box of an old iniquity should leap to light' (17). And whilst he evaluates his past to be 'fairly blameless' he is all the same 'humbled to the dust by the many ill things he had done, and raised up again in a sober and fearful gratitude by the many he had come so near to doing, yet avoided' (17).

What is particularly noteworthy about this opening scene and the conversation that arises as its result is that Enfield, whilst happy to suspect Hyde of blackmailing Jekyll, seems oblivious to the blackmail which he and the other gentlemen at the trampling scene enacted upon Hyde. The witnesses' extortion of money from Hyde, and the freedom from scandal which this buys him, however, strongly foreshadows the hold that Enfield believes Hyde has over Jekyll, and thus ties Enfield to Hyde. The theme of blackmail in fact emphatically blurs the boundaries between Hyde and Enfield, criminal and innocent, accused and accuser in a way that would continue throughout the novel. In *Jekyll and Hyde's* opening chapter, then, the gentlemen to whom Stevenson introduces us are more interconnected than they may at first seem and their lives are shown to be beset by secrets, blackmail and fears of threats to reputation. 'The Story of the Door' with its various unspecified acts of nocturnal encounter, its 'hellish' trampling committed by Hyde, its revelations about Jekyll's past and his will, as well as the blackmail committed by Enfield, moreover, raises serious questions not only about Hyde but about the whole group, and by extension about the secret behaviours of all 'ordinary and respectable' late Victorian gentlemen (Lang, 'Stevenson's New Story' 55).

At the centre of *Jekyll and Hyde* are two violent crimes – the trampling of the young girl and the Carew murder. These crimes bring two detectives – Inspector Newcomen of the Metropolitan police and, later, Jekyll's lawyer, Utterson – and two separate acts of detection. As Newcomen's name – with its play on the word 'newcomer' (signalling late arrival or novice) – connotes, he comes late to the novel. Despite this, the Metropolitan detective is optimistic about solving the Carew murder – after a quick inspection of Hyde's room in which he finds half of Jekyll's walking stick and a burned cheque-book, he tells Utterson confidently: 'You may depend upon it ... I have him in my hand ... We have nothing to do but wait for him' (24). The case is 'not so easy of accomplishment' as he had hoped, however, and he is soon confounded in his attempts to progress the investigation (24). Like the many bumbling policemen in fiction both before and after – Poe's Prefect of the Police, Collins's Superintendent Seegrave and Doyle's Inspector Lestrade – the ineffectual Newcomen soon drops unceremoniously out of the investigation and the narrative. In this novel, however, there is no super-detective waiting in the wings to solve the mystery or catch the murderer. Rather, the novel's acts of detection thereafter are undertaken by a deeply compromised and ultimately unsuccessful amateur sleuth – Jekyll's friend and lawyer Utterson, the self-styled 'Mr Seek', a character with which Stevenson simultaneously suggests but also resists or subverts what were becoming the conventionalised characteristics of the detective in fiction (14).

Stevenson immediately offers the reader a somewhat unusual detective-figure in that he seems naturally disinclined to ask questions about the behaviour of his middle-class peers – even if it seems likely that they are involved with a criminal. At the novel's outset, Stevenson carefully foregrounds Utterson's unwillingness to pry into others' affairs. In the story's opening lines, he makes explicit Utterson's 'approved tolerance for others' (5). Inclined to what the narrator describes as 'Cain's heresy', Utterson places great store in giving others privacy to behave as they please (5). As he puts it: 'I let my brother go to the devil his own way' (5). In other words, it seems that he is aware that his reputable companions may harbour disreputable secrets, or be implicated in crimes, and he is content with this as long as their secrets stay buried and their reputations remain intact.

Utterson's initial reluctance to investigate seems then to be based on prevailing nineteenth-century notions about the impropriety of peering into the middle-class home. This reticence may be related to prevalent attitudes of mistrust towards the relatively new practices of plainclothes detection resembling the 'detested French policing model of governmental spies and informers' (Joyce 116). When the Detective Department of Scotland Yard was created in 1842 – comprising just two inspectors and six sergeants – its use of plainclothes officers was immediately met with distrust and suspicion. Although the public was largely comfortable with the idea of uniformed constables policing the streets, and thus controlling the so-called criminal classes, there immediately was considerable discomfort surrounding the idea of this body of policemen who were authorised to penetrate middle- and upper-middle-class homes. A *Times* editorial on the formation of the detective branch, for instance, warned readers of the impropriety of these new modes of policing, opining 'there was and always will be something repugnant in the bare idea of espionage' and warning that 'the powers it intrusts often to unworthy hands are liable to great abuse' ('It Is Much to Be Regretted').[23]

Collins's *The Moonstone* and Braddon's *Lady Audley's Secret* provide perhaps the best illustration of the impact of these concerns upon the burgeoning detective genre. Braddon's amateur detective Robert Audley is appalled at the investigation of his uncle's household that he must perform in order to get to the bottom of his friend George Talboys' disappearance. As Braddon tells the reader, 'his generous nature revolted at the office into which he found himself drawn – the office of the spy, the collector of damning facts that led on to horrible deductions ... the crooked byway of watchfulness and suspicion' (156; 163). This kind of attitude towards the detective police actively impacts upon the success of the investigations conducted in Collins's *The Moonstone*. Despite his impeccable credentials, the 'celebrated' Sergeant Cuff – of whom, 'when it comes to unravelling a mystery there isn't the equal in England' – is met with tremendous resistance in the Verinder household (94). Indeed, whilst at the Verinder home, he is entirely confounded in his attempts to solve the mystery of the moonstone's disappearance. As Heather Worthington has pointed out, it is only 'once the case moves beyond the bounds of domesticity' that Cuff is able to get to the bottom of the mystery (172).

Although Stevenson's *Jekyll and Hyde* appeared some 20 or so years after these sensation novels, the mistrust of the detective police and the practice of surveillance portrayed by Braddon and Collins continued well into the late nineteenth century.[24] As Haia Shpayer-Makov's recent study of the history of nineteenth-century policing has shown, the

1877 trial of four senior members of Scotland Yard's detective branch for fraud and helping criminals to evade capture did little to enhance the reputation of detection.[25] *Jekyll and Hyde*'s opening sequence illustrates this contemporary resistance of the well-to-do to the practices of detection or enquiry. On the nightwalking expedition that follows Utterson's pronouncements concerning privacy and tolerance, Enfield recounts the story of the trampling. Like Utterson, it seems that Enfield also has, as he puts it, 'a delicacy' about 'putting questions' (9). Despite the 'hellish' nature of Hyde's assault on the little girl, Enfield tells Utterson how he had therefore decided not to make enquiries about the relationship between Hyde and Dr Jekyll (9). He resolves instead to follow what he calls his normal 'rule' of looking the other way (7). 'The more it looks like Queer Street,' he tells Utterson, 'the less I ask ... it partakes too much of the style of the day of judgment' (9). Utterson agrees, stating not once but twice, that he believes this a 'good rule' (9). Despite the involvement of their friend Jekyll in Hyde's crime, both men concur that it is best not to ask questions, not to get involved, and to look the other way – 'Here is another lesson to say nothing' (10). The pair agree to forget the incident and 'shake hands' to seal their promise 'never to refer to this again' (10). Given the 'hellish' nature of the assault described, these repeated promises to keep quiet are striking. Indeed it is difficult not to interpret this vow of silence as in some way again emphasising the 'unspeakable' nature of Hyde's crime.[26]

Despite this agreed code of silence, Utterson finds that he is 'besieged by questions' and gripped by 'almost an inordinate curiosity' about the nature of Hyde's hold over Jekyll (13; 16). The lawyer's imagination becomes 'enslaved' by the story of Hyde's trampling and his dreams are 'haunted' by visions of the act being replicated across the whole of London (13). He pictures Hyde running amok in the city and 'at every street corner crush[ing] a child and leav[ing] her screaming' (13).[27] His eventual decision to investigate the connections between Jekyll and Hyde, however, stems not from a disinterested desire to see the law upheld, or a detached interest in the artistry of crime. Rather, like Braddon's Robert Audley, Utterson becomes an amateur detective in order to come to the rescue of a friend. But whereas Audley had taken up his investigation in a crime where George Talboys was the victim, Utterson turns detective in order to investigate a crime in which his friend is intimately associated with the perpetrator.

The 'objective and disinterested stance' of the detective is one of the conventions on which the pre-hard-boiled detective genre, from Poe onwards, has traditionally been seen to depend (Thomas, *Detective*

Fiction 37). In 'The Guilty Vicarage' (1948), his study of the genre, W.H. Auden was one of the first critics to argue that the ideal fictional detective should have no complicity in the crime, or vested interest in the outcome of his investigation. He should be 'the official representative of the ethical' and his 'motive for being a detective' should only be 'a love of the neutral truth' (1). He should therefore not be 'involved in the crime', should not be 'motivated by avarice or ambition' and should certainly not be 'a friend of one of the suspects'.[28] More recently, a number of critics have similarly expressed the view that the detective in fiction should have 'no worldly stake in the outcome of the action' (Cawelti 95). As Ian Ousby has put it, the detective is 'a moral hero and a figure of power', who works simply to 'restore the order which has previously been threatened', rather than because of any personal involvement with the crime (*Bloodhounds* 21).

Disinterested ratiocination and a love of the practices of detection in no way motivate Utterson, however; instead he is propelled by an agenda to protect his friend and the wider group. After hearing the 'hellish' story of the trampling, Utterson's only concerns are about Jekyll's connection with Hyde and the damage that this may do to the reputation of his friend (9). Utterson is acutely aware that an association with a criminal would particularly damage Jekyll's reputation and he refers repeatedly to his desire to prevent his friend's 'good name' being 'sucked down in the eddy of a scandal' (28). He visits Jekyll, not to admonish his friend, but rather to help the doctor avoid implication or punishment, stressing: 'I make no doubt *I can get you out of it*' (emphasis added) (20). Utterson decides that he will set about blackmailing Hyde himself in order to free Jekyll from the man's hold, speculating that Hyde 'must have secrets of his own: black secrets' which would make Jekyll's secrets look 'like sunshine' (18). This activity of blackmail, of course, pairs Utterson with Enfield, Jekyll and Hyde himself, once again blurring the boundaries between the criminal and the novel's other protagonists.

Just as Sherlock Holmes later would, Stevenson's 'Mr Seek' sets great store in the positivist powers of sight and observation to elucidate the mystery (14). When he sets out to investigate, he decides firstly just to get a look at Mr Hyde, believing that 'if he could once but set eyes on him [Hyde] ... the mystery would lighten and perhaps roll away altogether' (13). Therefore, he elects to undertake some of the investigative practices of surveillance commonly associated with the detective genre. He decides to 'haunt the door' of Hyde's property 'by all lights and at all hours' in order to see the man and take note of his habits and demeanour (14).

The thematic links between eyesight and deduction, and their combined ability to restore order, of course, were established at the outset of the detective genre as we know it. In Poe's 'The Purloined Letter' (1844), for instance, 'observing machine' Dupin hides his enquiring eyes behind green spectacles but detects the missing letter which is hidden in plain sight, yet is invisible to everyone else. In Dickens's *Bleak House* (1852–53), Inspector Bucket's skill, likewise, is frequently attributed to his powers of sight. He is a 'mechanism of observation' who 'throws his light' on mysteries and appears 'to possess an unlimited number of eyes' (593; 280; 281). And later in the century, in Sherlock Holmes's first *Strand Magazine* adventure, the detective responds to his partner's demands to explain how he has solved the mystery by asserting, 'I see it, I deduce it,' and counselling Watson to learn to 'see' and 'observe' ('A Scandal in Bohemia' 430; 431).

In *Discipline and Punish*, Michel Foucault suggested that in the nineteenth century, 'surveillance', 'investigation', 'assessment' and 'classification' became part of the state apparatus for policing behaviour (217; 227; 220). Since then it has become something of a critical orthodoxy in studies of crime fiction to note that the detective's skill often relies heavily on his powers of sight. D.A. Miller's seminal *The Novel and the Police* (1988) is particularly influential in this regard. Drawing on Foucault's work on discipline and the panopticon, Miller argues that detective fiction is 'always implicitly punning on the detective's brilliant *super-vision* and the police *supervision* that it implies. His intervention marks an explicitly bringing-under-surveillance of the entire world of the narrative' (emphasis in original) (25). A large number of critics have followed Miller in noting the importance of sight, surveillance and regulation in the detective genre. Ronald R. Thomas, for instance, has noted that 'the detective's unique talent is an uncanny ability to see what no one else can see' ('Making Darkness Visible' 134). Stephen Knight, too, has argued that the detective conventionally works within 'a materialistic model, which can read off from physical data what has happened and what will happen' (*Form and Ideology* 74). For Martin Kayman, Sherlock Holmes polices legal, marital, economic and imperial issues solely 'by invigilation and surveillance' (*Bow Street* 81). In these accounts of the genre, then, the materialist markers of the crime are fairly easily spotted and decoded by the superior vision of the detective protagonist, who employs this visual data in arriving at his solution to the crime.

A large body of scholarship has focused on the significance of Hyde's 'troglodytic' and 'detestable' physical appearance, arguing that 'in Edward Hyde, Stevenson's first readers could easily discern the lineaments of [Cesare] Lombroso's atavistic criminal' (Arata, 'Sedulous' 233). Yet, there is a 'troubled relation between the "text" of Hyde's body and the interpretive practices used to decipher it' (236). Indeed, this is an aspect of the novel which has gone largely unexplored. In Utterson's investigation, however, Stevenson ultimately disavows the links between detective '*super-vision*' and the ability to solve mysteries or interpret criminal bodies, as Utterson is confounded by his practices of surveillance and powers of sight (Miller, *Novel* 25). An inability to read, interpret or even describe Hyde's face troubles Poole, Enfield and Lanyon – in fact almost everyone that he encounters. So, too, when the novel's unofficial detective – Utterson – does eventually catch sight of Hyde, his visual powers, unlike those of Dupin or Holmes, are little use in helping to clarify matters. In his dreams Hyde had 'no face, or one that baffled him' (13). So too, in reality, Hyde's face 'melted before his eyes' and proves impossible to read or decipher, beyond some vague and unnamable 'impression of deformity' (16). Rather than elucidating the mystery, his visual encounter with Hyde leaves Utterson only more 'disquiet[ed]' and 'perplexed' (16).[29] Stevenson's disaggregation of sight and deduction from power and authority here constitutes an intriguing challenge to the links between surveillance and law often shored up in crime fiction. He seems to be suggesting that, as Utterson fails to interpret the visual data presented to him, the forces of investigation in this novel will operate with questionable skill or authority. This, however, is just one of a number of methods by which Stevenson's investigator references but ultimately disrupts the conventional characterisations of the detective that structured the burgeoning genre.

It has been suggested that Utterson is 'a Mr Seek who does not in fact wish to find' (Hirsch 233). Utterson does want to seek, however, but crucially he wants his findings to remain buried. This detective is motivated by a vested interest in keeping the truth buried; he is acutely aware that by following the threads of this mystery he may well uncover the truth about his friend's involvement in Hyde's crimes and thus unravel the whole fabric that holds his respectable circle together. Whilst pre-hard-boiled-era detectives such as Dupin, Bucket, Holmes and Cuff are conventionally read as being motivated by a need to 'uncover the truth' and their narratives are structured by a move towards bringing details into the open, Utterson appears to be driven by quite the opposite desire (Panek 42). Because he is anxious to protect the reputation of his friend, Stevenson's detective often acts in a duplicitous manner, at times obstructing the investigations of the Metropolitan police, and even more frequently suppressing evidence or asking people to keep quiet about what they know.

Throughout his investigation, Utterson suppresses or hushes up any incriminating evidence that he finds in an attempt to protect Jekyll, and the novel is peppered with his pleas for silence. Despite the hideous nature of the trampling crime and the blackmail that occurred as a consequence, he and Enfield agree 'never to refer' to the story of the trampling again and 'to say nothing' (10). When Utterson accompanies Inspector Newcomen of Scotland Yard to the scene of the Carew murder, he neglects to inform the officer that the murder weapon which they find is the cane that he gave as a present to Jekyll years ago (22). When he visits Jekyll after the Carew murder the men agree that 'this is one of those affairs that cannot be mended by talking' and thus to 'let it sleep' (20). Utterson later tells his clerk that he shouldn't 'speak of' the note from Hyde which he shows him and that the matter 'is between ourselves' (29). When Guest's analysis of the note suggests that Hyde has 'forge[d] for a murderer', Utterson again does nothing and tells no-one (30). When Jekyll disappears soon after this, Utterson and Lanyon somewhat bizarrely agree that 'nothing can be done' and to 'keep clear' of the 'accursed topic' of the murder (32). Most striking of all perhaps, is the occasion in which Utterson and Enfield catch sight of Jekyll at the window of his cabinet when they are out walking. They 'glimpse' on Jekyll's face an expression of 'abject terror and despair' before he pulls down the blind – it seems that they have witnessed the beginnings of his physical transformation into Hyde. Both men, we are told, are 'pale' with fright and have 'horror' in their eyes, but they leave the window 'without a word' (36). Twice in as many sentences, Stevenson points out that they continue to walk 'in silence' and say nothing about the incident (36). And finally, after finding a note from Jekyll near the dead body of Hyde, Utterson warns Poole, the butler, to 'say nothing of this paper' and to wait for a few hours before calling the police (47). He believes that Jekyll may have 'fled' or be 'dead' and hopes that he may still be able to prevent this information from leaking out, thus managing to 'at least save his [Jekyll's] credit' (47).

In many of Dupin's and Holmes's investigations, the detective's role is to uncover and vocalise the secrets and suppressions which constitute the text's mysteries – to see and then to tell his sidekick, and the reader, what has really been going on. The formal structure of the Holmes adventures strongly reinforce these links between detection and speaking or telling a story; at the start of practically all the tales the client is asked by Holmes to tell his or her story, and not to omit any detail. The adventures close with a retelling of this story in which Holmes fills in all of the blanks, silences and suppressions for the benefit of Watson, the client and the reader. In *Jekyll and Hyde*, by contrast, Utterson appears to be motivated by exactly the opposite desire – to ensure that the mysteries remain quiet. The motifs of voice and silence, thus, work throughout to thematise this detective's unusual motivation to suppress the mystery. The reader of *Jekyll and Hyde* is left to negotiate an investigation full of silences, gaps and suppressions.

Later in the novel, Stevenson once again foregrounds Utterson's departure from the moral characteristics which – even at this early stage in the genre's history – were usually associated with the character of the detective in fiction. After Utterson realizes that Hyde is responsible for the 'shocking murder' of Sir Danvers Carew, the detective seems bizarrely unconcerned by the crime itself or the bringing to justice of the perpetrator (28). Despite the fact that the victim, Carew, was also his client and friend, Utterson expresses his hope that Hyde will not be caught. When he confronts Jekyll and attempts to force him to reveal his connections to the murder, he displays a level of complicity not usually found in the detective genre at this time. He tells Jekyll that he is concerned about his involvement with the murderer merely because 'if it came to trial, your name [Jekyll] might appear' (27). He is pleased to hear about Hyde's subsequent disappearance, as this removes the possibility of scandal from Jekyll's life. As he coolly tells the doctor: 'You have had a fine escape' (28). He shows no sign of pursuing Hyde or giving any information to the police; in his own cold logic, 'the death of Sir Danvers was, to his way of thinking, more than paid for by the disappearance of Mr Hyde' (31).

It is generally accepted that the implication of the detective in the corruption of his milieu did not appear in crime fiction until the early twentieth century (Cawelti 146; Malmgren 135). In the US hard-boiled incarnation of the genre, exemplified by the novels of Raymond Chandler and Dashiell Hammett, the detective often becomes embroiled in the crime, is frequently 'unstable', 'incapable of truth' and 'caught up in duplicity' (Malmgren 148). Stevenson's characterisation of Utterson, however, seems to prefigure the collapse of the detective/ criminal relationship that would become a key feature of later detective fiction. At the time when the genre was just developing, Stevenson, then, was already using the framework of the detective novel to interrogate the form's reassuring or bourgeois tendencies and assumptions. There is no such thing as a disinterested detective, Stevenson seems to suggest, or a detective with an overarching desire to protect the public or see justice prevail. Rather, his detective's foremost interest is in see-ing the reputation of his group maintained. Stevenson implies that if seemingly respectable investigators like Utterson choose to look the other way or to suppress the evidence before them in order to protect the wealthy and powerful, the forces of law more broadly – the purpose of which is to operate in the best interests of, and protect, the public as a whole – operate with questionable impartiality. Thus, the notion that everyone is equal under the law – a key premise of liberal thought – is shown to be deeply problematic.[30]

Appearing in a decade that saw class conflict proliferate, Stevenson's novel appears to have influenced later indictments of respectable men for the city's bloodiest crimes. Retroactive readings of the text, two years after its publication and following the Whitechapel murders, drew clear associations between the activities described in *Jekyll and Hyde* and the Ripper's crimes, marking it as a blueprint for the brutality and criminal-ity of the outwardly respectable. Filtered through an appraisal of Dr Jekyll as representative of a new kind of upper-middle-class offender, speculations arose about a respectable Ripper. These speculations helped to solidify the views of those on the left (particularly *The Star* and the *Pall Mall Gazette*) who held London's comfortable classes responsible for all of the city's ills. In 'Another Murder and More to Follow?' – an article for the *Pall Mall Gazette* appearing the day of the discovery of the Ripper's second victim – W.T. Stead invoked *Jekyll and Hyde* as a psychological model for the Whitechapel murderer (1). Making direct comparisons between the Ripper and 'Mr Hyde', Stead suggested that 'we should not be surprised if the murderer in the present case should not turn out to be slum bred' ('Another' 1). A few days later Stead clari-fied this thought in his latest speculations on the crimes, adding: 'It is to be hoped that the police and their amateur assistants are not confining their attention to those who look like "horrid ruffians". Many of the occupants of the Chamber of Horrors look like local preachers, Members of Parliament, or monthly nurses' ('Occasional Notes' 4). Stead finished his article by reiterating that social status and respectable appearance can easily hide deviant, even criminal, behaviour, reminding readers that John Williams, the Ratcliffe Highway murderer of 1811, was 'a man of benevolent aspect, of gentlemanly bearing' and that 'the Marquis de Sade, who died in a lunatic asylum at the age of seventy-four ... was an amiable-looking gentleman, and so, possibly enough, may be the Whitechapel murderer' ('Occasional Notes' 4).

Theories that the Ripper was a respectable-looking gentleman, rather more like Jekyll than Hyde, proliferated after the publication of these articles by Stead. After only the second Ripper murder – Annie Chapman on 8 September 1888 – other publications and social commentators began to lend support to the respectable Ripper theory. A few days later, Dr L. Forbes Winslow of Cavendish Square, London – a leading authority on medical insanity, who later offered his services in the Ripper investigation – wrote to the editor of *The Times* to share his theory that the murderer was almost certainly not a member of the lower classes. According to Winslow, the murderer was much more likely to be 'a homicidal maniac ... of the upper-classes of society', looking 'sane on the surface' (Winslow 6).[31] A couple of weeks later, an editorial from the *East London Advertiser* definitively stated that 'the murderer is ... a man with a maniacal tendency, but with quite sufficient control of himself and of his faculties to impose upon his neighbours, and possibly to mix in respectable society unquestioned by a single soul' ('A Possible Clue' 1). The message of this type of letter and article is clear – that police and Londoners should stop looking out for a visible incarnation of evil, like the 'troglodytic' Mr Hyde, and start mistrusting the respectable appearances of gentleman like Jekyll (*Jekyll and Hyde* 42).

Indeed, widespread speculation ensued that the Ripper was really a respectable gentleman who was using his social position to shield himself from suspicion. A number of high-profile upper-middle-class gentlemen emerged as suspects, including the director of the Bank of England, philanthropist Dr Thomas John Barnardo and even Liberal leader William Gladstone (Curtis 29).[32] A few of the suspects even drew explicit links between the Ripper murders and *Jekyll and Hyde*: a number of medical men emerged as strong suspects – Dr Francis J. Tumblety and Dr Thomas Neill Cream – and were detained and questioned about the murders. And, in a yet more fantastic turn of events, Richard Mansfield, the actor who played Jekyll in the 1888 London stage production of the novel at the Lyceum, was forced to cancel his run after only ten weeks as theatre-goers repeatedly contacted the police to report that they believed he was the Ripper (Curtis 78).[33]

Stevenson's novel had speculated about the freedom that respectable men had to undertake criminal activities and suggested that this sort of behaviour was endemic within bourgeois society, thereby offering an implicit critique of middle- and upper-middle-class values and morality.[34] The developing genre was heavily influenced by Stevenson's rendering of criminality within respectability and the morally ambiguous detective, and these themes and tropes would continue to appear to greater or lesser extents in detective fiction as the genre burgeoned towards the *fin de siècle*. In the best-known detective stories of the

1890s, the *Adventures of Sherlock Holmes*, crimes almost always emanate from the respectable classes. And Doyle, who was a great admirer of Stevenson's work, may have had *Jekyll and Hyde* in mind with Holmes's assertion that 'when a doctor does go wrong he is the first of criminals. He has nerve and he has knowledge' (Doyle, 'The Speckled Band' 574). Elsewhere, the figure of the corrupt detective who is implicated in the crime and the outwardly respectable criminal appeared again in novels and collections such as in Morrison's *The Dorrington Deed-Box* (1897), Allen's 'The Great Ruby Robbery' (1892) and *An African Millionaire* (1897), Zangwill's *The Big Bow Mystery* (1891), Boothby's *A Prince of Swindlers* (1897) and Hornung's *Raffles: The Amateur Cracksman* (1899), amongst others. Indeed, we might say that as the century continued and the genre developed, Stevenson's 'Strange Case' becomes not so much strange as *exemplary* in terms of how it establishes some of the central features that would define detective fiction as a genre: not necessarily as reassuring and formally conservative but rather as potentially subversive and certainly unsettling of conventional mores and values.

2
'The Most Popular Book of Modern Times': Fergus Hume's *The Mystery of a Hansom Cab* (1886)

This chapter focuses on the book that has been called '*the* bestselling detective novel of the nineteenth century' – a novel, like the others in this study, which also illustrates the often overlooked formal and ideological complexity of the nascent Victorian detective genre (Davies, *Shadows* 16).[1] Perhaps surprisingly, the bestselling detective novel of the nineteenth century is not by Charles Dickens, Wilkie Collins or Arthur Conan Doyle. Rather, the first crime novel to sell over half a million copies was New Zealand lawyer Fergus (Ferguson Wright) Hume's literary debut – *The Mystery of a Hansom Cab* (1886), a murder mystery set in Melbourne, that's now all but dropped out of the crime fiction canon. In the year before the publication of the novel often taken to be the first significant work of late Victorian detective fiction – Arthur Conan Doyle's *A Study in Scarlet* (1887) – Hume's novel was published in Australia and sold more than 25,000 copies in just three months. Before the turn of the century, *The Mystery of a Hansom Cab* had become a global hit: it had been republished in the UK, France and America; it had been turned into a successful stage play in London, Melbourne and New York (running for over 500 performances in London). Bizarrely, it had even inspired a copycat murder in Manchester in 1889.[2]

In this chapter, I examine the reasons why it has been overlooked, in spite of its huge commercial success. I suggest that the novel has been elided from the canon of Victorian fiction (in spite of its phenomenal contemporary success) precisely for the reason that should make it fascinating to any contemporary devotee of the crime genre. Specifically, with its compromised investigators and crimes featuring the middle classes, it once again showcases the formal diversity and moral ambiguity present in late nineteenth-century detective fiction, a period that is often erroneously read as producing only a particularly reassuring and conservative incarnation of the genre.

Bored with the law and determined to make a name for himself as a playwright, the young barrister Hume set out to write a novel simply 'to attract local attention' (Hume 'Preface'). As the author later put it, 'I was bent on becoming a dramatist, but, being quite unknown, I found it impossible to induce the managers of the Melbourne Theatres to accept, or even to read a play. At length it occurred to me I might further my purpose by writing a novel. I should at all events secure a certain amount of local attention' (Hume 'Preface'). Thus inspired, Hume astutely decided to write a novel specifically designed to appeal to the appetites of local readers. As he explained it,

> I enquired of a leading Melbourne bookseller what style of book he sold most of. He replied that the detective stories of Gaboriau had a large sale ... I bought all his works – eleven or thereabouts – and read them carefully. The style of stories attracted me, and I determined to write a book of the same class; containing a mystery, a murder, and a description of low life. (Hume 'Preface')

The bookseller had advised Hume well; Emile Gaboriau's 1866 crime novel, *L'Affaire Lerouge*, featuring amateur detective Tabaret and method-ical police detective Monsieur Lecoq, had established the Frenchman as one of the most widely read authors of the nineteenth century. Over the next few months, Hume constructed a story very much in the Gaboriau mould – like *L'Affaire Lerouge*, *The Mystery of a Hansom Cab* features amateur and professional detectives, family scandal, scenes of low life, mystery and murder.

In spite of Hume's hopes, the novel had a rather inauspicious start – in the summer of 1886 it was rejected by George Robertson, the leading Melbourne publisher at the time, on the grounds that 'no colonial could write anything worth reading' (Hume 'Preface'). Therefore, in October 1886, Hume had 5000 copies of the novel printed and published at his own expense. According to the *Illustrated London News*, this edition of the novel sold out in spectacularly quick time: 'in seven days after its publication not only 500 but 5000 copies were sold in Melbourne' ('The Author of Madame Midas' 410). A second and third printing followed 'until in three months 25,000 copies were disposed of, a circulation unexampled in the history of the colony' (410). A few months after its Australian debut, Hume sold the rights to the novel for 50 pounds to a group of London-based speculators who promptly rebranded themselves the 'Hansom Cab Publishing Company' (Hume 'Preface'). The first London printing of the novel followed in November 1887, with the subtitle 'a startling and realistic story of Melbourne social life'. In Britain, as in Australia, readers were swept away by *Hansom Cab*, where it soon enjoyed further tremendous sales. As J.W. Trischler of the Hansom Cab Publishing Company advised the *London Evening News* in a January 1888 interview, which was reprinted in a number of New Zealand newspapers,

> On 3rd December [1887] we published an edition of 50,000; early in January a further edition of 25,000; at the end of the month an edition of 50,000, of which we have only 7000 left; and now there is another edition of 50,000 in the hands of the printers, who are working night and day. We can't supply the trade fast enough. ('An Australian Author' 5)

In May 1888, the *Inquirer and Commercial News* advised readers that 'the Hansom Cab Publishing Company, Ludgate Hill, have already sold 200,000 copies and their present steady sale is at the rate of 3,000 daily' ('Our Adelaide Letter'). In October 1888, just 11 months after the novel was first published in the UK, the *Illustrated London News* reported that sales were now well in excess of 300,000 copies, declaring the novel to be a 'startling' and 'unparalleled success' and 'the most popular book of modern times' ('The Author of Madame Midas' 410). Indeed, so remarkable was the novel's international success that numerous newspapers and magazines across the globe reported on its extraordinary sales figures – in August 1888 the *New York Times* divulged that *Hansom Cab* had sold 300,000 copies in the UK alone, as did English magazines the *Athenaeum* and *The Graphic*, and Australian newspapers *The Argus* and the *Launceston Examiner* ('Brevities'). To put this in context, Marie Corelli's *The Sorrows of Satan* (1895), the book widely believed to have been the bestselling novel of the nineteenth century, sold around 100,000 copies per year (Ferguson 67). As Hume's 1932 obituary in *The Times* summed up *Hansom Cab*'s popularity, 'everybody read it eagerly, and in fact it went all over the world' ('Obituary' 17).

One might imagine that this level of global popularity would surely establish the novel as one of the most significant and enduring works of late nineteenth-century crime fiction. This, however, is not the case. For a start, despite its tremendous popularity with nineteenth-century readers and its impressive sales figures, Hume's novel was not well received by contemporary critics. Many early reviewers disparaged the novel's style, terming it a 'very ordinary piece of shilling fiction' that was 'from a literary point of view, valueless' and 'without any pretence of literary style' ('New Novels' 19; Sharp 438; 'Theatres' 8). Another fledgling crime writer who took time to peruse the novel shared the critics' assessment of its lack of merit. In a letter to his mother dated 1 March 1888 – just a few months after the lukewarm response to the publication of his own first detective novel in *Beeton's Christmas Annual* 1887 – Arthur Conan Doyle deemed Hume's novel, 'One of the weakest tales that I have read and simply sold by puffing', exclaiming petulantly, 'What a swindle "The Mystery of a Hansom Cab" is' (Stashower, Lellenberg and Foley 250).

Although Doyle's view doubtless reflected his disappointment over the performance and sales of his own detective novel, scholars of crime fiction have also tended to regard *Hansom Cab* as something of an anomaly rather than an important early addition to the burgeoning detective genre. Many pioneering works on the genealogy of the detective genre mention the novel only to remark upon its sales figures, without subjecting the work itself to any analysis. For instance, in the very first critical history of the crime genre – *Murder for Pleasure* (1941) – Howard Haycraft terms Hume's novel 'scarcely readable' and suggests that it belongs 'among the famous "freak books" ... mentioned here for ... historical interest only' (63). For Haycraft, the 1870s and 1880s more broadly are simply 'In Between Years', treading water between Collins and Doyle (chapter 2, title). Likewise Ian Ousby ignores *Hansom Cab's* success, terming the period between *The Moonstone* (1868) and *A Study in Scarlet* (1887) 'an interregnum', featuring no significant additions to the genre (*Bloodhounds* 136). He and other historians of the genre, he claims, are 'at a loss to explain why *The Mystery of a Hansom Cab* should have been a bestseller' (*Crime* 37). Julian Symons similarly suggests that 'it is customary to say that the book is without any kind of merit' and deems it merely 'a curiosity because of the enormous sales it achieved' (63).

More recent work on the crime genre, however, has begun to challenge the somewhat outmoded belief that late Victorian detective fiction pivots solely upon the success of Doyle's oeuvre. In the last few years an increasing number of critics have begun to undertake the important work of uncovering and analysing the significance to the history of the genre of a number of obscure and overlooked works of Victorian crime fiction from the period before, during and after Doyle's success.[3] Critical discussion of *Hansom Cab* is still limited, however, and this chapter provides one of the first sustained analyses of the novel.[4] In this chapter, I examine the disconnection between the novel's contemporary and enduring popularity. I probe the reasons for the novel's contemporary success in Australia and globally. I unpick the reasons why, despite its tremendous appeal at a time when the detective genre was just beginning, Hume's novel has been elided from the canon of Victorian detective fiction, and question why it is glossed over in critical histories of the genre. I suggest that *Hansom Cab* has been overlooked for the very reasons that should make it fascinating to any scholar or devotee of the crime genre; namely, that it showcases some of the formal diversity and moral ambiguity present in some of the earliest works of detective fiction. In the novel, as with the other works analysed in this study, criminality emanates from geographically respectable locations, detection is inefficient and corrupt, and justice does not prevail.

My approach to Hume's novel combines close textual analysis with a broader social and cultural approach which relocates *Hansom Cab's* depictions of criminality, detection and justice within the context of various late nineteenth-century Australian debates and anxieties about class, policing and crime. I examine the impact of contemporary concerns and social unrest concerning Australia's landowning class – the elite 'squattocracy' – and I read Hume's characterisation of the novel's detectives alongside a number of reports and letters detailing widespread public mistrust of the Melbourne police following a number of high-profile corruption scandals in the 1800s. These examinations will illuminate the ways in which, throughout the novel, Hume offers up social critiques of powerful and corrupt institutions, in a way deliberately designed to target and appeal to the views of the mainly lower-middle-class local audience of shilling shocker fiction. Hume then maps these geographically specific details of local colour on to more universal representations of upper-class criminality and urban squalor which would have been all too familiar to late nineteenth-century readers of British journalism or popular fiction. In the novel, then, details of the local and the global combine to evoke for the foreign reader a 'topsy-turvy world', at once exotic, but also familiar and entertaining to a global audience of crime fiction readers (Hume 7).

Over the course of the nineteenth century, Australia's population shifted from the rural to the urban, as gold-rush towns became modern cities. Australian newspaper *The Argus* had termed the Melbourne of 1835 'a primitive village' ('Unnamed Melbourne' 6). By the early 1880s, with a population approaching half a million (making it bigger than San Francisco), however, the city was now 'the metropolis of the Southern hemisphere' (Twopeny 2).[5] Journalist and noted chronicler of London life George Augustus Sala visited the city in 1885, dubbing it

'Marvellous Melbourne'. For Sala, it was an impressive and prosperous city 'teeming with wealth and humanity ... a really astonishing city with broad streets full of handsome shops, and crowded with bustling, well-dressed people' (Sala 7) (see Figure 2.1). As in England, however, where exposés such as Andrew Mearns's 'The Bitter Cry of Outcast London' (1883), George R. Sims's *How the Poor Live* (1883) and W.T. Stead's 'Maiden Tribute of Modern Babylon' (1885) provided bourgeois readers with vicarious access to the inhabitants of the city's poorest quarters, so too in Melbourne journalists and urban anthropologists were eager to document the disorderly side of life in the slums of the Australian metropolis. Australian journalist Marcus Clarke became famous for his journalistic exposés of Melbourne slum life, which featured in local newspaper *The Argus*. In 'A Melbourne Alsatia' – Alsatia being one of Victorian London's most notorious rookeries – Clarke detailed the depravity of life on Little Bourke Street in the same kinds of spatial and moral terms found in the work of Sims, Stead and Mearns on London. For Clarke, in Melbourne's slums, 'The miserable lanes, and filthy courts and houses, are the last strongholds of ruffianism, and it resists all attempts to dislodge it. The wretches who inhabit this sink of infamy seem to have no regard for time. Noonday or midnight, dawn or dusk, all times are alike to them. They sleep when it suits them, eat when it suits them, and steal drink and fight at all hours' (Clarke, 'Alsatia' 125–6).

With this divided city as backdrop, *The Mystery of a Hansom Cab* was one of the first novels to forge a connection between the Australian crime genre and urban life. In the novel's richly textured descriptions of Melbourne, Hume relies heavily on these well-documented geographical and moral contrasts between the city's 'magnificent town house[s]' and 'the squalid labyrinths of the slums' (34; 173). The reader is given the thrill of vicarious access to the drawing rooms of Melbourne's most salubrious suburbs and the denizens of its most dreadful slums, with Hume yoking an urban mystery in the style of Gaboriau or Poe onto a set of distinctly local concerns about the links between criminality, identity and the burgeoning Australian metropolis. From the outset, *Hansom Cab* is structured around the hidden connections between the inhabitants of the city's seemingly morally and geographically divided rich and poor quarters. Hume's novel opens with a newspaper report detailing a murder which occurred on a drunken cab journey 'in a public conveyance and in the public street ... within a short distance of the principal streets of this great city' (10; 7). An unknown gentleman in evening dress has been killed in a hansom cab on its journey from his club on

Figure 2.1   *Collins Street – Looking East. Melbourne.* By Alfred Martin Ebsworth, 1886

Melbourne's prosperous Collins Street – a street which 'corresponds to New York's Broadway, London's Regent Street and Rotten Row, and to the Boulevards of Paris' (Hume 59). The gentleman and an unknown companion – presumed to be the murderer – were travelling across the city from the fashionable 'Block' to the affluent beachside suburb of St Kilda, an area populated with 'mansion[s]' and 'magnificent town houses[s]' which 'would not have been unworthy of Park Lane' (34). All that is known about the murderer is that, like the victim, he was fashionably dressed in evening clothes, specifically a light-coloured coat and a soft hat – a costume that does little to identify the man personally, but which clearly marks his elevated social class. This outfit, Hume tells us, is worn by 'nine out of every ten young fellows in Melbourne', including most of the novel's urbane male protagonists, and thus locates the crime and the criminal firmly in the Melbourne of wealth (61).

The investigation of the crime leads us from Melbourne's elite to the Little Bourke Street slum, where, as Hume's 1898 preface to the novel makes clear, he 'passed a great many nights ... gathering material' ('Preface'). This area, Hume explains, is 'so like that of the Seven Dials in London' that any visitor 'kept as closely to the side of his guide as did Dante to that of Virgil in the Infernal Regions' (100). Hume's descriptions of the area rely heavily upon what Judith Walkowitz has called a 'well-established moral and visual semiotics' of the slum whereby nineteenth-century chroniclers of urban life identified 'the social character of streets' as either 'rough or respectable' (34). Rough or low areas were typically characterised by 'children playing in the streets', 'open doors, broken windows' and 'the presence of prostitutes and thieves' (35). Hume's Little Bourke Street is 'narrow', dark' and 'ill-smelling' with 'rats squeaking and scampering away on all sides'; there are 'children playing in the dried-up gutter', 'a woman with disordered hair and a bare bosom' leans out of a broken window and 'an open door' reveals 'Mongolians gathered round the gambling tables' (99–101). In his descriptions of this slum, Hume is working within the tradition described by Peter Stallybrass and Allon White, whereby nineteenth-century literature rendered the slum as 'a locus of fear, disgust and fascination' 'for the bourgeois study and the drawing-room' (191). Hume gives the reader vicarious access to the thrilling dirt and depravity housed in the den of brothel-keeper Mother Guttersnipe and – more importantly – to the secrets contained within and their manifold connections with the Hansom Cab murder.[6]

As the narrative progresses, the relationship between the two seemingly disparate spheres becomes increasingly complicated and entangled. As the novel's epigraph, published on the title page of the 1886 edition, puts it: 'As marine plants floating on the surface of waves appear distinct growths yet spring unseen from a common centre, so individuals apparently strangers to each other are indissolubly connected by many invisible bonds and sympathies which are known only to themselves.' Figuratively and literally – by way of gossip, newspaper reports and various cross-class/cross-city journeys – the story gradually reveals the full implications of connections made in the opening scene between metropolitan Collins Street, suburban St Kilda and the Little Bourke Street slums. Fascination with the story of the crime, we are told, soon also crossed the city's boundaries of geography and class: 'It was talked about everywhere – in fashionable drawing-rooms at five o'clock tea, over thin bread and butter and souchong: at clubs over brandies and sodas and cigarettes; by working men over their mid-day pint, and by their wives in the congenial atmosphere of the back yard over the wash-tub' (75). Solving the mystery and quieting the public discord that it has incited involves uncovering the hidden connections between the city's wealthiest and poorest quarters; the true identity of the victim, the murderer and a number of other characters must be uncovered and their links to the city's disparate spaces must be ascertained.

The action of the novel and the unravelling of its mysteries pivot around the dissolution and disturbances that occur within a loosely connected group of well-to-do urban gentlemen who live in Melbourne's affluent suburbs. At its centre is wool merchant Mark Frettlby, 'the wealthiest man in the colonies' (34). The murder victim is Oliver Whyte, a 'rich young ... swell', and suitor to Frettlby's daughter, Madge (33). The main suspect is 'one of the most fashionable young men in Melbourne', Brian Fitzgerald, an Irish absentee landlord with 'royal blood', who is engaged to Madge Frettlby (66; 74). And finally, the murderer is eventually revealed as Whyte's closest friend, the 'strikingly aristocratic' man-about-town Moreland (29). All the men are linked by their good looks, their fashionable dress and their social lives. They are patrons of the Melbourne Club, they attend the theatre and elite social gatherings, and they promenade on Melbourne's Collins Street 'Block'. Their clothes and appearances are strikingly similar too; they are all 'good-looking', 'charming' and 'respectable', they have light hair and moustaches (115). All dress in the latest fashion of light-coloured evening coats and soft, wide-brimmed hats – a costume worn, as Fitzgerald tells us, by 'at least a dozen of my acquaintances' and most of Melbourne's elite (61). As such, all of the main characters fit the description of the murderer and their similarities facilitate a number of misdirections involving mistaken identity (115).

Despite their outward respectability, the novel's crime and chaos is centred around a number of 'startling revelations in high life' concerning the disreputable secrets harboured by Frettlby and the gentlemen of the Melbourne of wealth (66). The members of the Frettlby circle are linked by 'Melbourne secrets and Melbourne morals' – in other words, their dishonourable pasts or disreputable behaviours (17). Frettlby is haunted by 'the sins of his youth', Fitzgerald's 'morals are no better than those of other young men' and the lawyer Calton states that 'in questions of morality, so many people live in glass houses, that there are few nowadays who can afford to throw stones' (193; 77; 177). As Fitzgerald gothically puts it, all the men of the group are haunted by 'The ghosts of a dead youth – the ghosts of past follies – the ghosts of what might have been'; and 'these are the spectres which are more to be feared than those of the churchyard' (155). In this sense, Hume was very much building upon the tradition of Australian crime writing which, owing to the huge influx of new inhabitants precipitated by the discovery of gold in Victoria and New South Wales and the legacy of penal colonisation, was beset with anxieties about the links between crime, background and identity. In early works of Australian crime writing, such as Ellen Davitt's *Force and Fraud: A Tale of the Bush* (1865), there was always a sense of the colonial landscape as 'a place populated by ... a shifting, itinerant population ... [and] freely circulating criminals ... a fluid, transient place where characters continually slip out of view, changing their identities and sometimes disappearing altogether' (Gelder and Weaver 3–4). Hume's *Hansom Cab* works strongly within this tradition, expressing a number of anxieties about the Frettlby circle's possible pasts, suggesting that these wealthy, supposedly respectable citizens might be nothing of the sort. Over the course of the novel, the full implications of a number of 'Melbourne secrets' and 'ghosts of past follies' are gradually uncovered and explored (Hume 17; 155).

In doing so, Hume was also working in line with a tradition which had long since structured popular fiction. Revelations about the dark secrets at the heart of wealthy society were very much the stuff of British Victorian crime literature, in particular. One thinks, for instance, of the murderous aristocrat Sir John Herncastle and the fraudulent philanthropist Godfrey Ablewhite in what was termed by T.S. Eliot 'the first and greatest of English detective novels' – Collins's *The Moonstone* (1868). So too in 'The Body Snatcher' (1884) and *Dr Jekyll and Mr Hyde* (1886), Robert Louis Stevenson explores the murderous criminality

found in the homes of middle-class and respectable medical men like
Jekyll, Fettes and MacFarlane. In the detective stories upon which Hume
based his novel – Gaboriau's Monsieur Lecoq novels – the villain is often
an aristocrat who abuses his class privileges. And, as Franco Moretti has
correctly and astutely observed, Doyle's Sherlock Holmes stories almost
always take place in *'the London of wealth'* (emphasis in original) (*Atlas*
136). As the editor of *The Bookseller* described it, Victorian crime literature seemed always to suggest 'temptation and immorality were only
to be found in wealthy neighbourhoods, and lewd thoughts were the
special and particular property of noblemen and "swells" with rent rolls
of ten thousand a year' ('Literature of Vice' 122). Indeed, in his preface
to the 1898 edition of the novel, Hume revealed that in his first draft of
Hansom Cab he had made Frettlby the murderer, but 'on reading over
the M.S.' decided that his decision to make the novel's wealthiest and
most respectable character the murderer was *'so obvious'* that he 'wrote
out the story for a second time, introducing the character of Moreland
as a scape-goat' (Hume 'Preface').

Of course, as has frequently been observed, these types of characterisations in fiction were most probably a calculated construction
designed to flatter and appeal to the lower-middle-class readers who
were popular fiction's most voracious consumers. As Martin Priestman
has explained, aristocrats and the wealthy were frequently rendered as
'the chief enemy of bourgeois order' (*Detective Fiction* 84). Aristocrats'
'monopoly on wealth and power' was 'the focus of middle-class resentment', and thus 'implying that they were morally unworthy of their
privileges was an effective way to advance middle-class claims for their
own superiority' (Jann, *Adventures* 78). Although he does not explicitly
address his reasons for doing so, in situating criminality at the heart of
wealthy Melbourne society, Hume seems to be strategically targeting
the appetites of lower-middle-class readers and feeding their appetites
for narratives illuminating the immorality and criminality to be found
at the heart of outwardly respectable society. Indeed, when Fitzgerald
is on trial for the Hansom Cab murder, Hume self-reflexively refers to
the insatiable public appetite for crimes in high society, spelling out
that the accused's high status has attracted a large crowd. As he puts
it, 'the popular character of the prisoner, his good looks, and engagement to Madge Frettlby ... had raised the public curiosity to the highest
pitch, and consequently, everybody who could possibly manage to gain
admission was there' (113). And, with what must be tongue-in-cheek,
Hume offers further insight into the public appetite for scandal by way
of an aside from Felix Rolleston – one of the public in court for the

spectacle of the trial who, we are told, has 'secured an excellent seat' – 'puts me in mind of the Coliseum and all that sort of thing you know ... Butchered to make a Roman Holiday' (114). In the ensuing narrative, however, Hume is deeply complicit in feeding this public appetite for high-class crime; as the novel progresses, the dark and unsavoury secrets harboured by all the members of the Melbourne Club circle are lavishly and repeatedly detailed and dissected.[7]

Perhaps surprisingly, the first gentleman whose immoral hidden life is uncovered is the *victim* of the Hansom Cab murder. Armed only with the gentleman's expensive evening clothes – a 'well-cut and well-made dress coat' and a silk pocket handkerchief bearing the initials 'O.W.' – detective Gorby identifies the victim as Oliver Whyte of Possum Villas, St Kilda (18). By the mid 1800s, it was normal for Melbourne's elite to live outside the city, and at this time the fashionable suburb of St Kilda was the premier choice for the wealthy. The pretty bayside area's 'commodious and elegant mansions and villas' were thought to provide a 'refuge away from the turmoil, the daily battle, the busy bartering of Melbourne' (Briggs, *Victorian Cities* 280). Despite Whyte's expensive evening clothes, his prestigious address and the fact that he paid his rent regularly, 'like a respectable man', his living quarters soon reveal potential immorality behind his respectable façade (25).

Whyte's apartment is 'luxurious' and 'well-furnished', but for detective Gorby its furnishings mark him as 'a man who would have friends, and possibly enemies, among a very shady lot of people' (26). Its walls, decorated with 'pictures of celebrated horses and famous jockeys', and its racks of pipes and piles of 'sporting newspapers', mark Whyte as 'fast' and a 'spendthrift' (28). More worrying still are the numerous 'plush frames' showcasing pictures of 'hussies', 'London actresses' and 'burlesque stars' and the bookcase filled with 'Zola' and other 'French novels' with 'bad ... reputation[s]' (28–9). As it has become a critical orthodoxy to observe, in the nineteenth century, 'all French novels were considered to be a danger to good conduct' – one need only think of the character of Dorian Gray, whose downfall accelerates after he is 'poisoned' by a French book (Maia 176; Wilde 124). Indeed, Zola's books were the subject of intense anxiety in nineteenth-century Australia to the extent that they were targeted by the State of Victoria Customs Department and banned by a large number of libraries (Heath, *Purifying Empire* 101). As the Victorian *Daily Telegraph* hyperbolically put it, French novels were 'a plague of obscene literature, resemb[ling] for both offensiveness and abundance, the plague of frogs which once afflicted Egypt' (qtd in Heath, *Purifying Empire* 103).[8] For nineteenth-century readers, then, Whyte's choice of reading material alone would have marked him as a dangerously decadent and potentially immoral character. Indeed, as part of the narrative's denouement, Whyte is revealed to have been far from the gentleman of first appearances; rather, he was a 'masher' – a fashionable dandy and ladies' man – and 'a confounded cad' (159; 39).

As the murder investigation progresses, we discover that Whyte, 'a stranger in Melbourne', originally came from London, where he 'went the way of all flesh', turning aside his boring life as a city clerk and taking Australian burlesque actress 'Musette of the Frivolity' as his mistress (18; 159). More surprisingly, it is discovered that Whyte's disreputable past as a masher and his mistress link him to Melbourne millionaire Mark Frettlby, one of Melbourne's most respectable citizens. Frettlby is introduced as a sober and respectable character; he is 'the wealthiest man in the colonies' and the so-called 'Wool King' of Melbourne (210; 34). As the narrative progresses, however, it is revealed that in his young days, like Whyte, Frettlby had been 'a swell' and a 'philanderer' (176). He led a 'riotous, feverish' life of 'profligacy and dissipation' where he 'spent money freely' (210; 212; 176). With the help of 'di'monds and gold', Frettlby had won the affections of the young burlesque star Rosanna Moore, with whom 'all the young fellows ... were madly in love' (176; 210). The couple married and had a daughter together; however, Rosanna ran away to London shortly afterwards, leaving their daughter with her grandmother in the Melbourne slums and allowing Frettlby to believe that she and the girl were dead.

The significance of this marriage lies in the fact that it was never dissolved, meaning that Frettlby's subsequent second marriage was bigamous.[9] More scandalously still, this means that his second daughter, Madge – a respectable belle of Melbourne society – is illegitimate. Of course, it turns out that Rosanna Moore is Musette – the same burlesque actress whom Whyte later meets in London. The plot hinges on her knowledge about the disreputable past of one of Australia's most 'respected' citizens (212). Armed with this valuable information, Whyte persuades Rosanna to return to Melbourne to blackmail Frettlby. Posing as a 'rich young man with ... a letter of introduction', Whyte goes to Frettlby's mansion, where he produces Rosanna Moore's marriage certificate (32–3). He threatens the millionaire 'in the coolest manner' that he will expose his second marriage as bigamous and his second daughter as illegitimate, if he is not given a 'large sum of money' and Madge's hand in marriage (214). Concerned with protecting his 'respected' reputation and preventing the public proclamation of his daughter's illegitimacy,

Frettlby reluctantly agrees to Whyte's requests (212). Shortly afterwards, Whyte is found murdered.

In the nineteenth century, the blackmailer's power relied on the 'ideology of respectability' – that is, the importance that all citizens placed on reputation and their 'good name' (Feinberg 248). The blackmailer's 'most potent threat', then, lay in their ability to publicise 'embarrassing facts', thus ruining the offender's respectable reputation, 'especially among his peers, business associates, and others in a position to harm or reject him' (248). Hence, blackmail and threats to reputation are pivotal plot points in a number of late Victorian crime novels such as Wilde's *The Picture of Dorian Gray* (1891) and Stevenson's *Dr Jekyll and Mr Hyde* (1886). Like Stevenson's Jekyll, Hume's Frettlby is a man to whom reputation is all important. He is 'looked up to and respected by [his] fellow citizens' and is 'famous' throughout the land for his 'honesty, integrity, and generosity' (212; 194).

Frettlby is clearly a member of what is often termed the 'squattocracy' (a play on the English aristocracy) – the group of early nineteenth-century Australian settlers who claimed and 'squatted' on unoccupied rural land, building large pastoral empires farming thousands of acres. Sheep were particularly profitable for these early pastoralists and, throughout the nineteenth century, Australia's economic growth was based almost entirely on the sale of fine wool – hence Frettlby's title 'Wool King' (34). Despite the fact that they had no legal title to the land – aside from being the first Europeans to settle on it – these squatters came to be some of the wealthiest and thus the most powerful men in Australia. As an *Illustrated Sydney News* article put it,

> we have the lordly wool merchant of the present day, inhabiting a stately chateau, fitted with every luxury that fancy can suggest; and wealth procure ... [he is] ... the occupant of a handsome city mansion ... His sons graduate at universities, and are found in the army and navy and liberal professions; his daughters are amongst the belles of society. ('Squattocracy, Past and Present')

Like the members of the squattocracy described in this article, Hume tells the reader that Frettlby has 'worldly wealth, domestic happiness, and good position ... a charming wife ... a charming daughter ... a splendid income; a charming country house ... and a magnificent town house in St Kilda, which would not have been unworthy of Park Lane' (34). To a much greater extent than Whyte, then, Frettlby's public persona is that of an eminently successful and respectable man. As the novel progresses, however, we see his respectable exterior begin to unravel – we discover that he is a bigamist with a slum-born wife (now dead from alcoholism), he has one daughter who is a 'fallen woman' living in a Little Bourke Street brothel and another that is illegitimate; he goes on to become a victim of blackmail; near the end of the novel he is unveiled as a murder suspect; and eventually he dies (a heart attack brought about by the shock and shame of his belief that Madge has found out that she is illegitimate), leaving behind a confession detailing his previous immoral life (141).

Alongside designs to emulate the broad nineteenth-century literary trends for aristocratic immorality already discussed, there is also a more local class context for Hume's decision to locate the novel's central disruption in the Frettlby home. As a wealthy wool magnate, Frettlby may on the surface have represented the cream of Melbourne society. However, Australia's squattocracy were considered by many to be opportunistic land-grabbers who had become wealthy by immoral or illegal means and who harboured disreputable or criminal pasts. As Rev. W. Pridden put it in his nineteenth-century study, *Australia: Its History and Present Condition*, 'the squatter has been converted into a respectable settler. But this is too bright a picture to form an average specimen ... Unfortunately, many of these squatters have been persons originally of depraved and lawless habits, and they have made their residence at the very outskirts of civilization a means of carrying on all manner of mischief' (323). Relatedly, many working-class Australians resented the squatters' monopoly of agricultural land in the colonies and their control of the legislative assemblies of New South Wales, Queensland and Victoria (Dryzek 120). As a result of this resentment, the period 1840–85 was marked by a 'huge class struggle' between the wealthy landowners and the working classes over land rights (O'Malley 275). So furious was this conflict that John Pascoe Fawkner – one of the founding fathers of the city of Melbourne – warned of the very real possibility of 'anarchy and bloodshed' in Australia if 'the squatters' arrogance is not curtailed' (qtd in Gollan 36). As a result, in the 1860s, the legislative councils of all four states passed Selection Acts that opened up the crown land to all citizens, in theory ending the squatters' monopoly. The Acts were 'primarily intended to help establish middle class values and institutions in place of the patriarchal or planter type of society of the squatters' (Baker 166). In practice though, as John Dryzek points out, the extent of squatters' wealth and power – combined with their propensity to offer bribes – meant that they managed to retain control of the best land, and thus tensions between the squattocracy and the lower classes rumbled on throughout the nineteenth century (120). One of the most famous consequences of this class conflict, of course, was the elevation of bushranger Ned Kelly to the status of folk-hero, and spokesperson for the plight of Australia's oppressed poor at the hands of its rich and corrupt elite.[10]

In situating immorality at the heart of the home of one of Melbourne's most eminent members of the elite squattocracy, Hume was implying that Frettlby – and by extension the squattocracy more broadly – were morally unworthy of their positions of privilege and respect. This surely must be read as part of Hume's strategy to 'attract local attention' and appeal to local readers of crime and detective fiction (Hume 'Preface'). For Hume's first readers – members of the Australian urban working and professional middle classes – *Hansom Cab*'s revelations about the illicit past and downfall of its most pre-eminent citizen, would have appealed to and underlined their own political views.

Scholarship traditionally sees detective fiction – and Victorian detective fiction in particular – as offering comfort to a predominantly middle-class urban readership by the delivery of various narrative and moral resolutions. For Ernst Kaemmel, for instance, the 'success of detective literature' derives from its comforting assurances that the detective 'can correct the mistakes and weaknesses of the social order' (58). Likewise for Stephen Knight, Sherlock Holmes 'assuage[s] the anxieties of a respectable London-based, middle-class audience' by his ability to bring to order 'an uncertain and troubling world' (*Form and Ideology* 67). In such assessments, the most reassuring convention of the late Victorian detective story is the fact that readers trust completely the detective's skill, moral code and desire to see justice delivered. As Joseph Kestner has correctly pointed out, however, there are a number of overlooked works of late Victorian crime fiction that 'confute every idea about detection and order ever conceived', owing to the fact that they feature morally compromised or unreliable detectives (Review of *Detection and Its Designs* 551). These works – of which Hume's novel is just one example – tend to be overlooked as they do not fit neatly into prescribed notions about the nineteenth-century crime genre, but offer fascinating insight into the ways that the nascent genre unsettles just as often as it reassures.

At the centre of Hume's novel are two mysteries – the Hansom Cab murder and the Frettlby family secret. These mysteries bring about two forms of detection, carried out by two officers of the Victoria state police. Hume's mystery negotiates a complicated, perhaps contradictory, range of positions on the status and effectiveness of the detectives involved. On one hand, it reproduces a number of the formal and moral conventions of what we might call the investigation-driven detective story – at the novel's heart is a murder and a family secret and much of the narrative tension derives from the drive to uncover the truth about both. In the opening chapters, therefore, we see Melbourne police conduct an investigation and correctly ascertain a number of details about the victim of the Hansom Cab murder. Hume's novel does not adhere unproblematically to this investigation-driven formula, however, as its investigations are undertaken by a pair of unpalatable detectives, who prefigure the types of detective anti-heroes that would come to prominence in early twentieth-century hard-boiled crime fiction.

The first detective on the case – Gorby – is naïve and incompetent; the second – Kilsip – is reasonably skilful, but self-interested and untrustworthy. The pair are joined in their investigation by the dashing young lawyer Calton (a natural successor to Mary Elizabeth Braddon's Robert Audley), described as 'a man that can't leave well alone' (164). However, Calton too inverts the conventional motivation and morality of the detective investigator. Firstly, he blatantly admits his purely self-interested reasons for taking up the case: 'he foresaw that ... the trial for murder would cause a great sensation throughout Australia and New Zealand [and] therefore determined to take advantage of it as another step on the ladder which led to fame, wealth, and position' (68). And, as both Pittard and Dixon have correctly noted, while on the surface of things Calton and Kilsip work towards uncovering the truth, Calton ultimately persuades his fellow investigator to suppress his findings in order to protect the reputation of the wealthy family involved.

Such unreliability from the novel's detectives may speak broadly to the fact that the prestige of the detective police was generally low in the nineteenth century – at this time there was still a great deal of resistance to the idea of outside intrusion of the domestic sphere as the detectives themselves were often of a lower class than those they investigated (Clausen 114; Worthington 172).[11] Gorby's incompetence and Kilsip's corruptibility also have a more specific local historical resonance, however. Hume's characterisations are shaped entirely by the two main problems that nineteenth-century Melbournians had with their local police – incompetence and corruption. From its inception, policing in Melbourne was beset with charges of ineptitude and corruption. Whilst Melbourne was founded (as Port Phillip) in 1835, the city and state had no official force until the statutory formation of the Victoria police in 1853. From 1835 to 1852, therefore, policing for the area was 'uncoordinated' and undertaken by 'drunkards' and 'former convicts' who were 'untrained, issued with no set of instructions, unequipped with staves or arms, and not in uniform' (Haldane 5; 10). In September 1836, the year after the city's foundation, Melbourne's first three police officers arrived from Sydney, where all three had previously been sacked for drunkenness. By 1837, all three had also been sacked from their new billets: one for repeated drunkenness, one for repeated absence and one for bribery ('Past Patterns' 16). In 1838, Chief Constable Henry Batman – son of John Batman, one of Melbourne's founding fathers – was also dismissed for bribery. Over the next 12 years, no fewer than six Chief Constables were engaged and subsequently let go.

It was not until 1853 that 'An Act for the Regulation of the Police Force' was finally passed. By this point the police force was failing in its attempts to control the social disruption and disorder caused by the gold rushes – many serving police officers had also deserted their jobs for the gold fields. The Act (and the related Police Regulations Manual) set out to curb police inadequacy and misconduct by laying down entry requirements and guidelines for police recruitment and duties, as well as detailing a list of statutory offences – including accepting bribes, desertion, gambling, drunkenness on duty and assisting prisoner escape. Despite this legislation, however, corruption and criminality continued to dog the force, so much so that a special 'police prison' had to be built at Richmond, Melbourne in 1854 (Haldane 49).

By the 1880s, when Hume was researching and writing *Hansom Cab*, the inadequacies of the Melbourne police force continued and had become a hot topic of public debate. In a force with such an inauspicious history, Chief Commissioner Frederick Standish's stewardship of the Victoria police from 1858 until the early 1880s was markedly disastrous and thus subjected to fierce and frequent criticism from press and politicians alike. Born in England, Standish was the son of the aristocratic Lancashire MP and companion of George IV, Charles Standish ('Death of Captain Standish'). Frederick Standish started his career in the Royal Artillery and at 23 was appointed to be aide-in-waiting to the Lord Lieutenant of Ireland. However, as a keen devotee of horse-racing and a heavy gambler, Standish was forced to flee Ireland for Australia in 1852 in order to escape moneylenders. After arriving in Australia under an assumed name, he started colonial life as a 'sly grog' (unlicensed liquor) seller at the Ovens Goldfield. Standish managed to work his way up quickly, however, and in 1857 he secured an appointment as Assistant Gold Fields Commissioner at Sandhurst, a position he held until transferring to the post of Chief Commissioner of the Victoria police in 1858. This rise was nothing short of miraculous; as

Paul de Serville puts it, Standish was 'a man who had left England under a cloud, using an assumed name, who had sold sly grog [and who] was now, six years later, the Chief Commissioner of Police' (*Pounds* 52). This ascendency amply demonstrates the carry-over of the early nineteenth-century English notion that well-bred gentlemen – however dubious – were natural leaders of the country, or indeed of the empire.

Whilst Commissioner of Police, however, Standish's pursuit of pleasure was 'the talk of the town' and he became an object of scandal and rumour in Melbourne ('Fracas' 3). In 1858, the same year that he was appointed police commissioner, Standish was elected to the prestigious Melbourne Club (the private gentleman's club featured in the *Hansom Cab* story) and subsequently became 'universally identified with that elitist institution' (Haldane 56). During the early years of his stewardship, he once again built up large gambling debts and became well known for drunkenness. Stories of all-night gambling sessions and drunken quarrels with other Melbourne Club members soon filled the pages of local newspapers. In one notorious and well-documented incident, reported in *The Age* and reprinted in numerous regional newspapers, Standish was 'severely horse-whipped' by Captain Robert Machell (another Melbourne Club member) in a drunken quarrel over a card game ('Fracas' 3). At this time, Commissioner Standish also became well acquainted with the Melbournian *demi-monde* on both a personal and a professional level. Indeed, he famously entertained Queen Victoria's second son Prince Alfred, Duke of Edinburgh, during his 1867–68 tour of Australia, by taking him first to the Melbourne Club and then to Mother Fraser's high-end brothel in the Little Lon district of the city (Frances 128). He also became well known for his dinner parties where male guests were accompanied by nude prostitutes who sat on black velvet chairs – 'the better to show off the whiteness of their skin' (De Serville, 'Double' 120).[12]

Needless to say, this reputation for hedonism did little to ingratiate Standish with Melbourne citizens, politicians or the local press. To an even greater extent than in his personal life, however, Standish's professional reputation was marred by impropriety and incompetence. Standish was brought before three separate Government Select Committees during his reign, focusing on accusations of favouritism, moral laxity, corruption and maladministration ('Past Patterns' 18). In the words of Chief Superintendant John Sadleir, a high-ranking officer who served under Standish, 'He was too much a man of pleasure to devote himself seriously to the work of his office, and his love of pleasure led him to form intimacies with some officers of a like mind, and to think less of others who were much more worthy of regard. From the first, this led to trouble, and lowered the tone and character of the service' (267). One favourite protégé of Standish's – Detective Superintendant Fred Winch – was investigated and eventually forced to retire for his involvement in organised corruption, including the embezzlement of police funds and running of a sly grog shop in the Police Hospital at a time when the force was supposed to be involved in purging the country of these establishments (Haldane 57). Another favourite was Thomas Lyttleton, a renowned breeder of fighting birds who held cockfights on the grounds of police stations in his district. Standish brought Lyttleton in to replace the ageing Superintendent Samuel Freeman as the Superintendent in Charge of the Melbourne District. After his demotion, Freeman committed suicide by slashing his throat with a razor.

As a result of these and numerous other incidents of scandal and maladministration, there were repeated calls for Standish's dismissal and the disbanding of the service. One parliamentary committee of 1870 found that Standish and the men that he had promoted were 'wholly unfit, as regarded either moral courage or any other qualifications to hold the position which they occupied' (Victoria Parliamentary Debates 541). Nonetheless, Standish and the force managed to hold on. Years later, the memoirs of Chief Superintendent John Sadleir revealed the reason for the preservation of the Commissioner and the force:

A high officer of the State in those evil days, a man notoriously of unclean life, was found late at night under ambiguous circumstances on the private premises of a gentleman residing in one of the suburbs. The owner of the premises did not wait for an explanation. He took the law into his own hands and severely punished the intruder, finally kicking him out of the place. Partly to safeguard himself, this gentleman called early on the following day on the Chief Commissioner of Police, related the circumstances and sought advice as to what proceedings he should take. Then followed such negotiations and interventions of friends as might have been expected, with the result that the matter was hushed up. The high official recognised, of course, that it was the intervention of the head of the police service that saved the situation. It saved also the police department, for when the schedule for the disbanding of the service came before him he promptly vetoed it. (180)

It is an interesting irony that a man with such a reputation for impropriety saved the police force by covering up the immoral behaviour of one of Melbourne's political elite. Moreover, the anecdote illustrates the pervasiveness of corruption and cover-ups in nineteenth-century Melbourne high society and thus goes some way, perhaps, to explaining Hume's decision to situate scandal within Melbourne's elite when writing a novel strategically designed to appeal to the tastes of local readers.

Despite the temporary reprieve facilitated by his ability to cover up this shady affair, Standish found it impossible to withstand criticism following his force's botched handling of the capture of notorious bushranger Ned Kelly and his gang, during which three policemen were killed (Haldane 56). Rumour had it that Standish suspended the hunt for the Kelly Gang when the weights for the Melbourne Cup were declared, although there seems to be no evidence to support this claim. Nonetheless, over the course of the Kelly Gang affair, 'lives were lost, careers ruined, and the innermost workings of the force made the subject of public scrutiny, debate and ridicule' (Haldane 73). Even Kelly himself criticised the corruption of the Victoria police under Standish in the famous Jerilderie letter – a document which has now entered the canon of Australian historiography. In the letter, Kelly scathingly described the police force under Standish in class terms as 'sons of Irish Bailiffs or English landlords who some call honest men' (Kelly 43).

The 1881 Royal Commission on the Police, which investigated the Victoria police's handling of the hunt for the Kelly Gang, also found the ethics and morality of the force lacking. According to the commission's report, Standish's stewardship of the force, both during the affair and more broadly, was 'not characterized either by good judgement, or by that zeal for the interests of public service which should have distinguished an officer in his position' and the detective branch under his command was a 'standing menace to the community' ('Royal Commission on the Police' 3). Thus, Standish retired in relative disgrace in 1881, leaving the Melbourne police force in a state of disarray and dishonour, characterised by endemic incompetence and corruption. He died of cirrhosis of the liver a short time later in poverty and disgrace. Even his obituary in *The Argus* could not avoid acknowledging the man's flawed reputation as police commissioner: 'he evidenced a lack of firmness which resulted in the police force falling into a state of disorganization. This became painfully manifest during the Kelly outbreak, when the conduct of the pursuit was carried out in a manner which led to severe reflections being cast on the officers of the force' ('Death of Captain Standish' 6).

Hume had moved to Melbourne from New Zealand in 1885. At this time, the debased state of the Victoria police force following Standish's commissionership was still being hotly debated almost daily in the pages of Melbourne's newspaper press. As a leader in *The Argus* put it, 'The condition of the police force demands the serious and immediate attention of the Government. There can be no doubt that the Victorian constabulary is thoroughly demoralized ... and disorganized ... and it cannot continue in its present state without becoming a positive nuisance to the community' ('Condition' 6). This article drew many letters of agreement from concerned citizens, including one from 'an observer ... having some knowledge of the subject' who suggested that the force had 'degenerate[d] into a state of universal corruption' and was now 'looked upon with contempt and loathing' ('To the Editor of *The Argus*' 5). Whilst it is impossible to say with any certainty that Hume followed the story of Standish, he was an educated man, working in Melbourne as a barrister, and thus it seems altogether likely that he would have read the local press and been well informed on local politics and matters of law and order. It does seem that in his characterisation of the Victoria police, through the characters of Gorby and Kilsip, Hume crystallised many of the pervading local concerns and anxieties about corruption and incompetence in the Victoria police.

The first representative of the Victorian police force to whom the reader is introduced is Detective Gorby, the policeman officially assigned to the Hansom Cab murder case. As his name – a play on both 'gorb' and 'gobble', meaning greedy and gluttonous – suggests, Gorby is a corpulent and slow-witted character. Despite conducting an initially fruitful investigation which leads him to discover the identity of the Hansom Cab murder victim, thereafter the 'kindly and apparently simple' detective is wrong-footed at nearly every turn (91). He interviews Moreland – the victim's companion and the murderer – and is completely persuaded by the man's feigned anguish at the news of his friend's death. Gorby is 'touched by his evident distress' and thenceforth questions the man in 'a sympathetic tone' (31). Completely distracted by Moreland's grief, as well as his charming and 'strikingly aristocratic' demeanour, Gorby allows himself to be convinced by a red herring suggested by the murderer (28). Moreland tells the detective that Oliver Whyte had a love rival – Brian Fitzgerald – and that the pair frequently quarrelled, including an argument on the night of the murder. Almost immediately, Gorby declares 'I don't think that [this] is a very difficult manner' and sets out to arrest Fitzgerald (33). Fitzgerald, of course, is innocent and in court is soon cleared of the charges against him. At this point, the 'complacent and self-satisfied' Gorby drops unceremoniously out of the narrative and is rarely mentioned again (91). Clearly,

Gorby is no detective hero and as such is assumed to be as unimportant to the reader as he had been to Hume. What is most significant about Gorby's botched investigation, however, is that the reader had initially been told that Gorby was 'one of the cleverest of Melbourne detectives' (43). If the lumpen Gorby is one of the detective branch's cleverest and most successful members, this creates a distinctly worrying impression of the skill and efficacy of the nineteenth-century Melbourne police force as a whole.

Of course, even at this early stage in the genre's development, the unsuccessful and unimaginative police detective was something of a crime fiction staple – one thinks for instance of Collins's inept Superintendent Seegrave or Poe's Prefect of the Police. In Hume's *Hansom Cab*, however, there is no super-detective waiting in the wings to take up the investigation. Rather, after Gorby disappears from the narrative, much of the subsequent detecting is undertaken by his rival police constable, Kilsip. Despite his relative success, however, Kilsip is equally as unpalatable as the ineffective Gorby. Hume's characterisation of Kilsip focuses strongly on his appearance – the detective is 'a tall, slender figure', his 'complexion' is 'quite colourless' and 'his hair jet black', he has 'brilliant black eyes', 'a hooked nose' and 'a hawklike face' (92). Underpinning the popular late eighteenth- and nineteenth-century interest in the science of physiognomy, which followed the publications of studies by Johann Kaspar Lavater (1775–78) and Cesare Lombroso (1876), was the widespread belief that all people should be able to ascertain the moral character of a person from their outward appearance and facial features. As an article in the prestigious *Quarterly Review* entitled 'Physiognomy of the Human Form' reminded readers, 'Everyone is in some degree a master of the art which is generally distinguished by the name Physiognomy and naturally forms to himself the character or fortune of a stranger from the features and lineaments of his face' (453). Therefore, 'upon our first going into a company of strangers, our benevolence or aversion, awe or contempt rises naturally towards persons before we have heard them speak a single word' (453). Lavater and Lombroso's works were reprinted many times throughout the nineteenth century and popular physiognomic pocket guides such as Henry Frith's *How to Read Character in Features, Forms, and Faces: A Guide to the General Outlines of Physiognomy* (1891) traced the history and practice of the science, detailing the ways in which 'our good and evil tempers, our besetting sins, habits and so on, mark our faces' (7). As William Greenslade puts it, in the late Victorian era, 'scrutinising the face' was 'a game that anyone could play' (100).[13]

Much critical work on the Victorian crime genre argues that late nine-teenth-century authors drew heavily on physiognomic theory in their descriptions of criminal characters. Stephen Arata, for instance, suggests that 'in Edward Hyde, [Robert Louis] Stevenson's first readers could eas-ily discern the lineaments of Lombroso's atavistic criminal' ('Sedulous' 233). And for Ronald Thomas, Arthur Conan Doyle's characterisation of the criminal Tonga in *The Sign of Four* strongly references Lombrosian ideas about the links between criminality and race ('Fingerprint'). For Hume, however, it is not the criminal but rather the detective whose appearance is instinctively threatening. In a playful inversion of the ways in which Victorian crime fiction conventionally appropriates popular contemporary theories about the links between physiognomy and criminality, Hume applies this pseudo-science to his descriptions of Kilsip. We are told that he is 'hardly a pleasant object to look at' and that 'once he appeared personally on the scene his strange looks seemed to warn people [off]' (92). Like Sherlock Holmes, Kilsip is frequently rendered in animal terms, but whereas descriptions of 'relentless, keen-witted ... sleuth-hound' Holmes are designed to inspire trust, Kilsip's inherent slipperiness of moral character and his danger is indicated for the reader in his frequent evocations as 'a sleek cat' or a 'snake ... seek-ing prey' (Doyle, 'Red Headed League' 461; Hume 108; 92). Thus, when he conducts an investigation, 'every one shut[s] up like an oyster' or 'retire[s] promptly into his or her shell like an alarmed snail' (92). As Hume puts it, in Kilsip, 'the student of Lavater' could easily identify the worrying physical markers of immorality and untrustworthiness (92). Rather than straightforwardly reproducing physiognomic constructions of criminality, then, Hume employs the science rather playfully to dem-onstrate the potential for criminality and untrustworthiness within the rank and file of the Melbourne police.

The immorality connoted by Kilsip's unpalatable appearance is borne out in Hume's descriptions of the detective's motivations. For animal-istic Kilsip, his 'prey' is not only the criminal that he is pursuing, but also any rival that gets in his way (92). After Moreland is caught, for instance, it is not the murderer's capture but rather the definitive proof that rival detective Gorby is wrong, which inspires Kilsip to 'purr to himself, in a satisfied sort of way, like a cat who has caught a mouse' (92; 216). Indeed, with Kilsip, Hume creates an investigator entirely unmotivated by ratiocination and a love of the practice of detection – conventions on which the characterisation of the detective, from Poe onwards, is traditionally seen to depend (Thomas, *Detective Fiction* 37). Rather, Kilsip is wholly motivated by professional jealousy and personal hatred for Gorby. When Gorby is handed the Hansom Cab case, Kilsip is 'devoured with envy', and when Fitzgerald is arrested 'he writhed in secret over the triumph of his enemy' (92). Thus, when he receives a note from the lawyer Calton asking him to assist in the investigation for Fitzgerald's defence, he is 'determined to devote himself, heart and soul, to whatever Calton wanted him to do, if only he could prove Gorby wrong' (92).

In the detective genre, particularly in its burgeoning nineteenth-century incarnation, a client usually requests the assistance of a detective (either an official policeman like Collins's Cuff or an unofficial consulting detective like Poe's Dupin) in order to help solve the mystery or catch the criminal. In *The Moonstone*, for instance, despite some resistance to Sergeant Cuff's presence in the Verinder home, the detective is summoned because 'when it comes to unravelling a mystery, there isn't an equal in England of Sergeant Cuff' (73). In *Hansom Cab*, however, in yet another surprising inversion of the burgeoning conventions of the nascent detective genre, the reader learns that it is Kilsip's jealousy, warped motivation and lack of professional reputation which inspired Calton to ask him to take on the investigation. In this instance, the slick lawyer has correctly assessed that the jealous and egotistical Kilsip's primary motivation is to snatch the Hansom Cab case from Gorby under any circumstances. He ventures that Kilsip's lack of objectivity in this regard will allow him to manipulate the detective into achieving an outcome which will be in the best interests of his client, even if this involves covering up the truth or suppressing evidence. Thus, he summons Kilsip to his office, plies him with expensive whiskey and cigars, and compliments him on his reputation in the force: 'knowing that Kilsip had that feline nature which likes to be stroked and made much of, he paid him these little attentions, which he well knew would make the detective willing to do everything in his power to help him' (94–5).

The lawyer's strange motivations for taking on an easily corruptible detective are more blatantly unveiled later in the novel when Frettlby dies and leaves behind a letter of confession, which Calton believes will expose the millionaire as the Hansom Cab murderer. When Frettlby's executors, who are gathered for the reading of the confession, question why Kilsip is there, Calton coolly answers, 'Because I want him to hear for himself that Mr Frettlby committed the crime, *so that he may keep it quiet*' (206). It turns out, however, that Frettlby's letter instead exposes Moreland as the murderer and a blackmailer. It also reveals the novel's other mystery – the Frettlby family secret – along with details of the millionaire's disreputable past. At this point, Calton again appeals to

Kilsip to 'keep silent on the subject' in order to protect the Frettlby family's reputation (223). Despite the fact that this suppression goes against what should be the detective's motivation to see information brought to light, Kilsip is easily persuaded to allow the details of the Frettlby secret to be withheld. He does this, we are told, as long as he can be guaranteed the honour of being 'always looked upon as the man who had solved the mystery of the famous hansom cab murder' and thus of being 'ranked far above Gorby' (223; 219). This concealment, of course, and the career fulfilment that it facilitates, also recalls the cover-up undertaken by Commissioner Frederick Standish which saved both his job and the disbandment of the Victoria police force.

In a curious coda to the story, however, Hume advises the reader that because of 'the good service' Kilsip had given the Frettlby family, Fitzgerald bestowed upon Kilsip 'a sum of money which made him independent for life' (223). It is difficult to pinpoint exactly what this 'good service' could be, apart from the suppression of the Frettlby secret. It is difficult also to interpret the cash that Kilsip is paid as anything other than a bribe, and while this is never spelled out explicitly by Hume, the transaction occurs in a chapter entitled simply 'Hush Money'. Whilst this chapter title is intended to refer to the money sought from Frettlby by Moreland, the cash that Kilsip receives certainly strongly echoes the various acts of blackmail or attempted blackmail which structured the novel's plot and precipitated the Hansom Cab murder. It is employed to buy Kilsip's silence and his suppression of Frettlby's entanglement with the Hansom Cab murder. By way of this 'hush money', the detective is linked strongly with the novel's criminal protagonists. Both the money and Kilsip's motivations, then, forcefully undermine the conventional characterisation of the detective as an 'objective and disinterested' investigator with 'no worldly stake in the outcome of the action' (Thomas, *Detective Fiction* 37; Cawelti 95). Kilsip, by contrast, is motivated by envy and is happy to see the truth buried. He accepts money to ensure that the wealthy family at the heart of Melbourne society are not dislodged from their powerful position. Hume, therefore, seems to be suggesting that the forces of law and detection in Melbourne are easily bought and altogether disinterested in seeing criminals brought to book and justice delivered – conventions on which the character of the detective is often seen to depend. Local readers familiar with any recent newspaper stories about their own police force, however, would have had no problem recognising these dubious qualities.

In the characters of Kilsip and Gorby, then, Hume is creating a crystallisation of nineteenth-century Melbournians' main concerns about their local police. The incompetent and ineffectual Gorby arrests and charges the wrong man, fails to spot the murderer, and is unceremoniously dropped from both the case and the novel. The malign Kilsip is untrustworthy and unscrupulous and eventually accepts a large sum of money to keep quiet about certain matters involving the Melbourne elite. In the novel, the detective/criminal binary is emphatically blurred, but for local readers, the corruption and incompetence embodied in Hume's detectives would have been all too realistic and familiar. Just as Hume's focus on the immorality found at the heart of the aristocratic Frettlby circle can be interpreted as a calculated construction designed to flatter and appeal to the lower-middle-class readers, then, so too his rendering of a corrupt and ineffective local constabulary seems designed to appeal to readers all too familiar with the iniquities of their police force and unlikely to be persuaded by fictional representations of detectives as avatars of heroism, morality and success. Whatever the reason, this negative characterisation of the Melbourne police doubtless once again underscores the critically overlooked tendency for extremely popular and widely read works of late Victorian crime fiction to unsettle as well as shore up the conventional links between the detective, restoration of order, and morality. The detectives in Hume's novel then represent a link between the characterisation of the police in the Victorian and US hard-boiled crime genres, which has been largely overlooked or ignored because it unsettles orthodox accounts of the development of the genre.

In situating the locus of the novel's crime and immorality in the home of one of Australia's most respected citizens, Hume anticipates some of the tropes that would structure the later hard-boiled and noir detective fiction which would emerge in early twentieth-century America. In the US hard-boiled novels of the 1920s and 1930s, there is always 'a secret' representing 'an occurrence or desire antithetical to the principles and position of the house (or family)' which haunts the narrative (Skenazy 114). They are structured by what has been termed a 'gothic causality', where the outwardly affluent and respectable present is threatened by the disclosure of unpalatable past events (Skenazy 114). In Raymond Chandler's *The Big Sleep* (1939), for instance, the affluent Sternwood mansion harbours a number of unpalatable secrets and crimes. Just as the Californian hard-boiled crime novel would later delineate, Hume also suggests that wealth and success in a land of new beginnings are often founded on dark and disreputable hidden pasts. Predating *The Big Sleep* by more than 50 years, Hume's *Hansom Cab* is haunted not only by the Hansom Cab murder itself but also by the Frettlby family secret's manifold connections to the crime. As such, the novel represents a largely unexplored link between the nascent detective genre and the range of moral and formal positions contained within what is often taken to be its far more 'uncertain', 'deviant' and 'morally ambiguous' hard-boiled incarnation (Haut 8).

Hume's novel also anticipates the ways in which the noir and hard-boiled crime novels of the early twentieth century would implicate the detectives in the criminal milieus that they are charged with investigating. It has become something of a critical orthodoxy to observe that the hard-boiled detective is often 'incapable of truth' and 'caught up in duplicity', and that his interventions could only ever be 'partial and limited' (Malmgren 148; Pepper 10). So too in *The Mystery of a Hansom Cab*, Hume's detectives are not wholly successful, they are often wrong-footed and they are easily corrupted. Again, this dubious morality necessitates a re-evaluation of interpretations of crime writing which focus on the rather schematic differences between the morality of detectives from the genre's beginnings and golden age and those that appeared in its later hard-boiled incarnations.

The novel ends on a curiously downbeat and ambiguous note – Frettlby's legitimate daughter Sal is deprived of her birthright and Frettlby's illegitimate daughter Madge leaves Melbourne with the inheritance to which she is not entitled. Corrupt policeman Kilsip establishes himself as a private detective with the hush money he received in order to keep the details of the case quiet, and Moreland, the criminal, commits suicide in jail, thus escaping the conventional channels of justice. In this novel, then, the oft-cited touchstones of nineteenth-century detective fiction – success, justice, morality and resolution – are shown by Hume to be deeply problematic and inapplicable to a late Victorian Melbourne suffused with anxiety about class conflict and police corruption. As with the hard-boiled crime novels that would appear in the early twentieth century, crime is depicted less as a product of occasional and aberrant tears in the social fabric, but rather as the inevitable consequence of urban modernity.

It is likely on account of the ways in which *Hansom Cab* does not fit easily into models of the genre, which were developed later and applied retroactively, that (in spite of its extraordinary contemporary success) the novel has been dropped from the crime canon. For today's critics and readers, however, its transgressive features constitute a fascinating foreshadowing of the hard-boiled detective genre and the growing number of respectable murderers and corrupt detectives that would come to prominence in twentieth- and twenty-first-century popular fiction and culture. It is because of these important ways in which *The Mystery of a Hansom Cab* stretches the narrative and moral conventions of the emerging detective genre that the novel deserves to be reinstated to the canon of nineteenth-century crime writing. And it is to the most canonical of late Victorian detective stories that I turn in the next chapter, which examines Doyle's Sherlock Holmes stories, attempting to ascertain whether these too contain any of the unsettling or ambiguous moral or formal features found in Hume's overlooked novel.

3

'L'homme c'est rien – l'oeuvre c'est tout': The Sherlock Holmes Stories and Work

This chapter focuses on the late Victorian detective genre's most famous and canonical incarnation – Sherlock Holmes.[1] Arthur Conan Doyle's detective stories are now so well known, so frequently studied and so often reimagined in popular culture that it perhaps seems there cannot be much new to say about them. In fact, despite the stories' popularity and mythic status, the Holmes of the popular imagination is often little more than an agglomeration of vague (and sometimes inaccurate) details gleaned from later adaptations – hansom cabs, fog, Baker Street, murder, deerstalker hats, drug addiction, and 'bromance' with Watson.[2] The stories, however, are 'more lively, more varied, and interesting than the usual remembered model' and they still offer much to consider (Knight, *Form and Ideology* 75).

In this chapter, I trace the impact of late Victorian debates and anxieties about the professionalisation of authorship upon the depiction of work in Doyle's detective fiction. I suggest that a large number of the Holmes stories foreground debates and ideas about the literary marketplace, professionalism, and the problematic relationship between work, money and morality. In particular I focus on how connections between labour, value and morality are repeatedly addressed in the stories with clients, criminals and Holmes himself anxiously interacting with issues of work ethics, payment and labour capital. I suggest that an examination of Doyle's shifting attitudes to work, professionalism and respectability within the stories is a productive way of illuminating the often overlooked moral and ideological complexity of the Holmes canon.

It was while the 20-year-old medical student Arthur Conan Doyle was undertaking a surgical apprenticeship in Birmingham that he received the news that he was to have a story published for the first time. In his memoirs, Doyle later recalled his wild delight that he might be able to give up the relatively boring medical profession for a career as a writer, as he put it 'that shillings might be earned in other ways than by filling phials' (*Memories* 23). 'After receiving that little cheque,' he said, 'I was a beast that had once tasted blood ... I had proved that I could earn gold, and the spirit was in me to do it again' – this 'red in tooth and claw' image illustrating the combative approach necessary for survival in the often Darwinian late Victorian literary marketplace (Stoker 1). After the acceptance of this story, however, Doyle was to struggle for success on what he called 'the real field of battle' of the literary marketplace for almost another ten years without success (*Memories* 80). In 1886 the aspiring author finally decided to set about what he called the 'fresher, crisper and more workmanlike' task of producing a piece of detective fiction inspired by the work of Emile Gaboriau, Robert Louis Stevenson and Edgar Allan Poe (*Memories* 62).

Doyle's detective made his first appearance in the novella *A Study in Scarlet*, published in *Beeton's Christmas Annual* 1887, after none of the big publishing firms would take it on. Surprising as it may now seem, this first Sherlock Holmes story caused barely a ripple of interest with either critics or the reading public. Indeed, the detective could have remained a one-book novelty had it not been for a now-famous luncheon hosted by the American publishing house Lippincott's in September 1889. Perhaps prompted by the recent spectacular sales of Fergus Hume's *Mystery of a Hansom Cab* (1886), the managing editor of the publishing house invited Doyle and fellow author Oscar Wilde each to submit a 'spicy' crime story for the first English edition of *Lippincott's Magazine* (Davies, 'Introduction' x). Wilde's contribution was to be one of his most famous and controversial works, *The Picture of Dorian Gray* (1891), the Faustian story of a young man's downfall into a life of decadence and crime. Doyle's offering was *The Sign of Four*, a second outing for Holmes.[3] Once again, however, Doyle's detective fiction failed to cause a stir.

In fact, it was not until his reappearance in the July 1891 edition of the popular new family magazine *The Strand* that Holmes finally caught the public's attention. The magazine had been founded in 1890 by the editor of *Tit-Bits* magazine and pioneer of the New Journalism, George Newnes. With his first successful periodical publication, *Tit-Bits*, Newnes had demonstrated that he understood how to 'develop and exploit the concept of a community of readers' targeting the readers of penny papers (Jackson, *George* 30). With *The Strand*, Newnes hoped to reconfigure the middle ground of the magazine market, targeting the middle-class, white-collar commuters who frequented railway bookstalls. *The Strand* was available at these bookstalls for sixpence, and provided a cheap, entertaining assortment of light, short articles and stories perfect for the commuter's journey. Newnes had chosen for the magazine the name of Victorian London's main East–West thoroughfare – the Strand – as a geographical metaphor for the publication's content. As he put it, 'it is through the Strand itself that the tide of life flows fullest and strongest and deepest' (qtd in Blathwayt, 'Lions' 170).

To read *The Strand*, then, was to experience the 'tide of life' of the city. Combining biographies of famous and important men, crime and adventure stories, factual articles on various interesting professions, and features for women and children, the *Strand*'s contents were strategically designed to appeal to the middle-class, yet aspirational, professional male and his family. As Reginald Pound, employee and biographer of *The Strand*, puts it, 'the middle classes of England never cast a clearer image of themselves in print than they did in *The Strand Magazine* ... it faithfully mirrored their tastes, prejudices and intellectual limitations' (Pound 7). A self-made man, Newnes clearly identified himself with his target audience and designed the magazine with his own tastes in mind, claiming, 'I am the average man. I don't have to put myself in his place. I am in his place. I know what he wants' (qtd in Pound 25). Doyle agreed, observing that Newnes had provided 'average men' with 'just the class of literature which ... interested them, elevated them, and did them good' (Doyle, 'Tribute' 2).

From the outset the magazine also showed a preoccupation with crime and detection. Its first issue contained an article on the Thames river police, while its second number featured 'Jerry Stokes', a detective story by Grant Allen, inaugurating the magazine's relationship with the crime genre. Early in 1891, Doyle approached the *Strand*'s literary editor Herbert Greenhough Smith with a proposal to revive his detective in a series of short interconnected stories which would 'engage the attention of the reader' and 'bind that reader to that particular magazine' (*Memories* 80–1). After reading the first two Holmes stories, Smith reportedly ran to Newnes's office to tell him that he had discovered 'the greatest short-story writer since Edgar Allan Poe' (qtd in Jackson, *George* 103). Smith's enthusiasm for the idea was soon endorsed by the reading public. From the publication of the first Holmes story for *The Strand*, the magazine's already impressive sales figures soon boomed at well over 500,000 copies per issue (Brake and Demoor 604). Indeed, in his biography of the magazine, former *Strand* employee Reginald Pound describes how libraries opened late on the *Strand*'s publication day, the third Thursday of every month, specifically to cater for eager Holmes fans (Pound 92). The commercial and cultural success of *The Strand* and the Holmes phenomenon, then, was particularly contingent upon the mutually beneficial 'culturally symbiotic' relationship between the two – the perfect marriage between the author of a low literary product who wanted to be a serious writer and a middle-market publisher with high cultural ambitions (McDonald, *British* 159). As Doyle himself put it, in a 1921 letter to Greenhough Smith about Holmes, 'if I am his father, you were the "accoucheur"' (Hollyer, 'My Dear Smith' 24).

In this new popular format and location, the Holmes stories ran for just two series of 12 monthly instalments, however, before the detective's 'death' in 'The Final Problem' in December 1893.[4] Indeed it was in a letter dated 11 November 1891, when the stories had been running in *The Strand* for only five months, that Doyle first made clear the nature of his feelings about the place of the Holmes stories in his literary hierarchy and expressed his desire to kill off the detective. In this letter he wrote the now famous lines, 'I think of slaying Holmes ... and winding him up for good and all. He takes my mind from better things' (Stashower, Lellenberg and Foley 300). From this date, Doyle continued to plan Holmes's demise; in his memoirs he describes how a holiday at Reichenbach Falls with his wife sealed Sherlock's fate. Doyle felt immediately that this 'terrible place' would make 'a worthy tomb for poor Sherlock', even if, he added wryly, 'I buried my bank account along with him' (*Memories* 84). And so before long, in a struggle with his arch-rival, Professor Moriarty, Holmes disappeared over the Reichenbach Falls, swallowed up in a 'dreadful caldron of swirling water and seething foam' ('The Final Problem' 846). Although the detective was resurrected in 1901 and again in 1903, at the time of 'The Final Problem''s composition Doyle firmly believed that the hero was dead and that this would be the last Holmes story. He considered Holmes as 'a lower stratum of literary achievement' and felt that he could now capitalise on his elevated reputation and attract an audience for what he termed his 'highest ... conscientious, respectable' work, his historical fiction (*Memories* 84; Stashower, Lellenberg and Foley 301).

A cartoon penned by Doyle in 1930, not long before his death, emphasises that even years later the writer still did not place Holmes at the pinnacle of his personal and professional hierarchy (Figure 3.1). The sketch shows a flea-bitten workhorse pulling a heavy baggage cart inscribed with the name 'Life Work Carriage Co.' A pile of cases weighs the cart down; and indeed each of these bears the label of a different aspect of Doyle's life and work. 'Medical practice' jostles alongside 'historical novels', 'elections' rests on top of 'psychic research'. The case marked 'Sherlock Holmes' is not the largest, the heaviest or the most prominent, and on first inspection is even quite difficult to spot, resting inconspicuously between '500 lectures' and 'Australia 1921'. In the mind of Doyle, it seems, Sherlock Holmes was just one amongst many of his life's burdens and accomplishments.

Despite the lowly status of the Holmes stories in Doyle's literary hierarchy, Holmes is now considered to be *the* canonical Victorian detective, alongside which all others pale in comparison. Indeed, Holmes's position as detective 'apotheosis' is so dominant that analysis of Doyle's novels and stories often forms the basis of arguments about the entire Victorian crime genre (James 114). A large number of critical studies on the Holmes stories and novels focus on the ideological import of the rise of the 'super-detective' and the reassuring effect of a figure able to read, decode and solve the moral and semiotic mysteries of the massifying

Figure 3.1 'The Old Horse.' By Arthur Conan Doyle. *Sir Arthur Conan Doyle: Centenary*, 1859–1959 (1959): 23

urban environment (Priestman, *Cambridge* 68).[5] A number of other major critical works on the Victorian crime genre focus on the Holmes stories' formal properties, arguing that their formulaic problem-setting and problem-solving structure, combined with ingenious and economical construction, provide various narrative satisfactions (Kayman, 'Short Story' 48). For John Cawelti, for instance, Doyle's Holmes stories reduce and limit crime to the status of 'a puzzle, a game, and a highly formalised set of literary conventions', and in doing so transform the serious moral and social problems of crime into 'an entertaining pastime ... [whereby] something potentially dangerous and disturbing ... [is] transformed into something completely under control' (104–5). Likewise, for Ernest Mandel, the Holmesian detective story in particular is 'the realm of the happy ending' where the detective always triumphs, and crime is shown never to pay (47). Such critics suggest that the Holmes stories offer a 'pleasing, comforting world-view' where a focus on narrative and moral resolution functions to assuage the anxieties and fears of the reader about crime in late Victorian London (Knight, *Form and Ideology* 5).

Likewise for most Foucauldian critics of the detective genre the emergence of the detective as hero reads as both a cause and an effect of the triumph of disciplinary society.[6] For these critics the processes of surveillance, taxonomy and diagnosis infuse the Holmes canon. For Rosemary Jann, for instance, the Holmes stories disseminate certain late Victorian codes of behavioural conduct. Reading the stories thus causes readers not only to identify with the rule of law but to discipline themselves (Jann, 'Sherlock' 685–90). Such readings of the Holmes stories also tend to focus on the ways in which the knowledge and technologies of sight associated with Bentham's panopticon operate on a more literal level. Sight, surveillance and classification allow the detective to read and decode both the physiognomy of the true criminal and the mysteries of the streets. Holmes's skill, for instance, is to observe a 'system of signs' and transform these random signs into 'a text identifying the malefactor' (Stowe 368). Thus Holmes functions as a kind of super-detective or *ur*-policeman (particularly with regard to his powers of sight or supervision) who sees and rectifies all problems he encounters.

A number of more recent critics of crime fiction, however, have pointed out that the Holmes stories' relationship with discipline and the dominant ideology is more ambiguous and problematic than is often claimed.[7] For Caroline Reitz, for instance, critics writing in the wake of D.A. Miller's *The Novel and the Police* (1988) 'still provide a too-tidy explanation of the rise of the detective figure' in which the detective is 'almost effortlessly panoptical' (xxii). As Reitz astutely points out, however, Holmes 'chafe[s] against social boundaries' just as often as he defends them (65). Indeed, he seems always to be 'straddling the very boundaries that Foucault has discipline policing' – mad/sane, dangerous/harmless and normal/abnormal (xxii). Simon Joyce also argues that many Foucauldian readings of the Holmes stories (and Victorian detective fiction, more broadly) depend upon an 'overvaluation' of various structural and thematic devices, such as 'closure', 'linear ... mystery plots' and the 'omniscience and omnipotence' of the detective (130). For Joyce, Miller's work in particular displays a tendency towards 'premature totalisation and theoretical conspiracy' whereby power and discipline are always shown as triumphant (77). This type of assessment of Victorian detective fiction, then, blindly overlooks the occasions when the burgeoning genre 'transgresses a number of these conventions' (Joyce 130). In this chapter, I build upon this recent body of scholarship in claiming that an examination of the complexities of Doyle's representation of work illuminates the ways in which the stories are less comforting, less reassuring and less representative of bourgeois ideology than is often claimed.[8]

In the Victorian era, '*everyone* proclaimed that man was created to work' (emphasis added) (Houghton 189).[9] Thomas Carlyle is the figure credited with disseminating the early Victorian version of the doctrine of hard work (in which he invoked God as the origin of the compulsion to work). By the late Victorian period, however, and based upon the continuing popularity and influence of Samuel Smiles's bestselling treatises *Self-Help* (1859) and *Life and Labour* (1887), the compulsion to work was defined as a moral issue and a question of character. As Smiles expressed it:

> The life of a man in this world is for the most part a life of work. In the case of ordinary men, work may be regarded as their normal condition. Every man worth calling a man should be willing and able to work. The honest working man finds work necessary for his sustenance, but it is equally necessary for men of all conditions and in every relationship of life. (*Life and Labour* 1)

The attitudes to work espoused by Smiles were taken up and spread 'as efficiently and fervently as any of the great nineteenth-century missionary enterprises' (Briggs, *Victorian People* 118). Following Smiles's popularity, the motivation to work became thought of as 'less a divine order than a discipline that originated within the subject' (Danahay 8).

In the late Victorian period, in particular, the ideals of the Smilesian work ethic found their expression in 'an emphasis upon self-discipline, self-denial and hard work' (Danahay 7).[10] Refusal to work or laziness, therefore, was taken as an indicator of some sort of 'moral and social sin' (Houghton 189).

In a culture that so defined itself in relation to work, therefore, any late Victorian individuals perceived to be passive or non-productive – the upper classes, drug addicts, the poor, men who worked from home and intellectual workers – were open to suggestions of impropriety (Danahay 23). Because their work was both passive and conducted from the home, writers were therefore particularly frequently accused of pursuing an idle profession (Lund 23).[11] John Stuart Mill, for instance, attacked Thomas Carlyle's characterisation, in *Heroes and Hero Worship* (1843), of authorship as a heroic occupation. Mill argued that this passive intellectual work bore no comparison to the 'exhausting, stupefying toil' of what he termed 'real labour' (qtd in Danahay 25). Owing to these sorts of criticisms, Walter Besant, in his role as president of the Society of Authors, found it necessary publicly to defend the work ethic of the professional author. In his 1899 essay *The Pen and the Book*, Besant reminded readers that the 'modern man of letters ... goes to his study every morning as regularly as a barrister goes to chambers' and that 'he makes an income by his labour which enables him to live in comfort and to educate his children properly' (Besant 24). Here, Besant defended the writer's labour against suggestions of ease by deliberately linking the work of the modern author with the older, resolutely respectable and hardworking profession of the law.

Neither was the late nineteenth century a good time for an author with serious literary ambitions to write what was still perceived as the lowly genre of detective fiction.[12] In particular, certain influential guardians of established culture were beset with anxieties about the debased quality of literature as a result of the professionalisation of writing and the idea that demands of the literary marketplace were augmented by questions about the morality of producing literature to order and for payment. This purist literary elite, exemplified by the figure of *National Observer* editor W.E. Henley and his circle, repeatedly and vociferously let it be known that they were particularly offended by any relations between literature, work and money. For Henley, writing in 1891, 'the man of letters' should not produce work based on the demands of the 'many-headed monster' of the reading public and the literary marketplace ('Literature and Democracy' 528). 'If once he listen to the voice of the great public, or yield to the tinklings of its shillings,'

Henley continued, 'he is a traitor to his art, and henceforth a stranger to literature' (528).

Perhaps unwisely, given these sorts of debates, Arthur Conan Doyle frequently referred to money as a motivating factor in his writing career. In a speech given at an honorary dinner hosted by the Author's Club in late June 1896, for instance, he openly admitted, 'I would like to say that I was led into the field of letters by a cheering ambition, but I fear it is more correct to say that I was chased into it by a howling creditor' ('A Dinner to Dr Doyle' 79). Doyle's memoirs and letters from the 1880s and 1890s also frequently employ language which indicates his awareness and complicity in debates about the inherent status and value of different writing jobs and publications. In a number of letters to his mother, Doyle speaks with relative disdain about his 'low key' writing for publishers and magazines which were 'easy of admittance, comparatively, and pay quite well' (Stashower, Lellenberg and Foley 358; 226). This writing is juxtaposed with his historical novels, which he terms his 'highest' and most 'conscientious' work (301).

In giving up medicine for writing, Doyle's own career had progressed from a profession associated with hard work to one which constituted 'less visible labour' (Jaffe 109). As a result, he was particularly 'anxious about his own literary standing' in light of contemporary concerns about the work ethic of the passive professional author, and anxious to emphasise the solid, monotonous, conscientious quality of his work (McDonald, *British* 121). And yet, Doyle's beliefs about the nature of literary value and hierarchy appear to have actively impacted upon his working habits at this time. He seems to have devoted considerably less time and energy to his detective fiction than to what he considered his 'higher work' (Stashower, Lellenberg and Foley 302). His letters and pocket diaries from 1891 attest that the Holmes adventures were produced extremely briskly and in rapid succession.[13] During an unproductive lull in his newly established oculist's practice, based near London's Harley Street, where 'not one single patient ever crossed the threshold', he wrote the first six of the *Adventures of Sherlock Holmes* series (Green, 'Conan' 23). His diary indicates that he sent off 'A Scandal in Bohemia' to A.P. Watt, his literary agent, around the end of March. 'A Case of Identity' was dispatched on 10 April; he sent 'The Red-Headed League' on 20 April, followed by 'The Boscombe Valley Mystery' on 27 April. On 4 May Doyle was struck down by influenza, which delayed the fifth Holmes story, 'The Five Orange Pips', until 12 May. The sixth story, 'The Man with the Twisted Lip', was delayed until Doyle had fully recovered and was not received by Watt until August.

The illness inspired a decision by Doyle to quit his ill-paying medical career and devote himself to full-time writing: 'I saw how foolish it was to waste my literary earnings in keeping an oculist's room in Wimpole Street, and I determined with a wild rush of joy ... to trust for ever to my power of writing' (Stashower, Lellenberg and Foley 294). By September he had given up the practice and his Russell Square lodgings and moved to suburban South Norwood to work from home as a full-time writer.

By 14 October 1891, less than six weeks into his career as a full-time professional writer and less than four months after the first of the Holmes stories was published by *The Strand*, Doyle was evidently already tiring of the Holmes stories and of this mode of literary production. He wrote to his mother: '*The Strand* are simply imploring me to continue Sherlock Holmes ... The stories brought me in an average of £35 each, so I have written ... to say that if they offer me £50 each *irrespective of length* I may be induced to reconsider my refusal' (emphasis in original) (Stashower, Lellenberg and Foley 296). This request, which he feared 'high-handed', however, was quickly and easily granted by the editors at *The Strand* who were well aware of the stories' effect on the magazine's sales figures of around 500,000 copies per issue (296). Doyle's letters to his mother over the next few weeks indicate the surprising speed with which he produced this next batch of the commissioned stories. On 29 October 1891 he writes to tell Mary Doyle that he has written two in the last week (301). In November 1891 his diary documents that he has written another four in the last fortnight (Green, 'Conan' 23). As the Holmes stories are, on average, around 8500 words in length, this suggests that Doyle was writing approximately 17,000 words per week, or over 2500 words a day.

These sorts of pecuniary references and the speed at which he dashed out the work may in part be responsible for the frequent accusations of a profiteering sensibility which dogged Doyle's career from the outset. A satirical review of the first edition of *The Adventures of Sherlock Holmes* for Henley's paper, the *National Observer,* for instance, openly drew links between the detective genre, the literary marketplace and Doyle's profiteerism. The review concluded with a faux-interview with Holmes in which the detective makes the following deduction about this edition of Doyle's stories:

> this book is large and expensively brought out; moreover it is issued by a publisher who caters for the million ... Dr Doyle must have heard of me, through Watson or the police ... he saw I should suit his game (which is money); and having invented spurious stories about

me hit upon a publisher similarly unscrupulous. ('The Real Sherlock Holmes' 606)

On a number of occasions Doyle strongly refuted accusations of mercenariness, pointing out that his work was not characterised by sporadic bursts of industry followed by periods of leisure but instead was relatively steady, monotonous and laborious (*Memories* 83; 106). The brisk manner in which he produced the Holmes stories, however, rather suggests the opposite. Thus, even one of Doyle's most recent (and generous) biographers suggests that Doyle always considered writing as 'a business rather than as a calling' (Stashower 31).

As a *Strand* reader, Doyle would have been well aware that the magazine's editorial policy demonstrated a preoccupation with articles and tales about work and professionalism. Indeed in most of its articles, even if they were not specifically about work, *The Strand* enshrined a dominant mid-Victorian value system that regarded hard work as an indicator of morality. Editor Newnes was himself the epitome of the Victorian Smilesian self-made man or captain of industry, founding a vast publishing empire from nothing. He established some of the most successful magazines of the 1880s and 1890s, including *The Strand and Sunday Strand*, *Tit-Bits*, *The Westminster Gazette*, *The Wide World Magazine* and *Woman's Life*, and in the process became known as one of the founding fathers of the New Journalism. In the words of one of his biographers, Newnes was a tireless worker, always 'all business and bustle' – a man who 'put his feet up only at the end of a twelve hour day' (Pound 20). Indeed, one of his obituaries drew explicit links between Newnes and the mid-Victorian heroic captains of industry lauded in *Self-Help*, observing: 'Sir George Newnes, had he lived fifty years earlier, might well have sat for one of the characters in Smiles's "Self-Help", since he was in every respect a self-made man, who carved his way to fame and fortune by persistent industry' ('Sir George Newnes').

Newnes valorised the gospel of hard work and evidently believed that reading articles about the industry of others would be suitably entertaining yet improving for his readers. From its first issue, the magazine therefore displayed an enthusiastic preoccupation with examining the world of work. Interwoven amongst its many strands were articles on myriad aspects of London working life. Its factual features show a preoccupation with defining, knowing and theorising the professional, with a number of recurring series providing hidden insights into the arcane world of numerous types of work. The first volume (Jan.–June 1891) alone has articles on work at the Metropolitan Fire Brigade, Great

Ormond Street Children's Hospital, the Thames river police, the Royal Veterinary College, the currency mint, the law courts and a gardening co-op, alongside articles on child workers in London, how novelists write for the press and how an East End photographer spends his day. Even a later article – 'Thieves v. Locks and Safes', about the technology of keys and safes – casts safe-breaking as a profession, referring to how criminals are always 'at work' to get something 'without paying for it' ('Thieves v. Locks' 497).

Through its articles on work and professions, the *Strand*'s readers were exposed to a constant underscoring of the links between morality and work by way of recurring focus on professional expertise. The article in the magazine's first issue which follows the Thames river police, for instance, strongly affirms the industriousness, skill and dedication of the men. The correspondent informs readers that when the *Princess Alice* sank in 1878, 'the men of the Thames river police were on duty for four or five nights at a stretch' ('A Night with the Thames Police' 125–6). And an observation about the knowledge of the Thames police strongly prefigures the type of panoptic expertise often attributed to Sherlock Holmes himself: 'These river police know every man who has any business on the water at night. If the occupant of a boat was questioned, and his "Yo-ho!" did not sound familiar, he would be towed to the station' (128). A June 1893 article on illustrator Harry Furniss, which formed part of the *Strand*'s series on the work of eminent Victorians, and which was published in the same volume as Doyle's 'The Adventure of the Reigate Squire', makes clear the continuing editorial focus on the links between industriousness and moral character. Despite the fact that Furniss's work is passive, based on knowledge capital rather than physical labour, and is conducted from the home, the article vigorously underscores his strong work ethic. Talking about Furniss's apprenticeship, interviewer Harry How reminds readers:

> It had meant a hard struggle for young Furniss. He was loaded down with clerical work, but in his own little room, when the day's labours were done, he would sit up till two and three in the morning [working on illustrations]. There was no quenching his earnestness. Work with him was a real desire. It is so to-day. To rest is obnoxious to him. (How 580)

The article's reverential tone and repeated references to the comfort and happiness of Furniss's domestic life further underline the fact that to work hard is to be successful and respectable.

An earlier *Strand* article in this informal series on professions of interest reverentially takes the reader inside the offices of *The Strand Magazine* itself, allowing access to editor Newnes's 'sanctum sanctorum' ('A Description' 594–6). His workspace, we are told, was positioned to be 'secure from casual interruption', thus emphasising the sanctity of his work (595). The large and detailed accompanying illustration shows Newnes at his desk, head bowed, engrossed in manuscripts and surrounded by books, pens, letters and all the various instruments of his trade. Indeed all of the illustrations which accompany the article depict the *Strand* employees – from literary editor Greenhough Smith to the printers and delivery boys – in the milieu of the workplace, as if momentarily interrupted from their labour, or even at work, as if too busy to stop and pose (Figure 3.2). The article and illustrations, as with the earlier articles on the Thames police and Harry Furniss, work hard to underscore *The Strand Magazine*'s endorsement of the Smilesian gospel of hard work. In the same volume even the advertising material appears to espouse this reverence for industry, with an advertisement for Sunlight soap advising readers that, 'Good work makes you feel good' and that 'Sunlight Soap does good work.'

MR. NEWNES'S OFFICE.

Figure 3.2   Strand editor George Newnes at work. 'A Description of the Offices of *The Strand* Magazine.' *The Strand Magazine* July–Dec. 1892: 595

A small number of critics have focused upon the correlation between the politics of the Holmes stories and their publication in *The Strand*.[14] On the whole, these scholars tend to argue that Doyle's detective stories are ideologically in alignment with the magazine's editorial policy, in that they seem to be about crime but in fact underscore Victorian bourgeois values. For Paula J. Reiter, for instance, Holmes represents 'a professional fantasy of complete competence, public service, independence, and spectacular occupational excitement' (74). Likewise, for John Cawelti, Doyle's detective fiction is 'deeply Victorian' and Holmes strongly embodies many of the dominant 'values of traditional British culture' – 'solidity' and 'morality' (277). Indeed, at first glance, the Holmes stories may appear to be ideologically in alignment with the *Strand*'s emphatically bourgeois moral and political stance on work and professionalism – that is, they appear to share its fascination with the importance of hard work.

On further inspection, however, the Holmes stories do not wholeheartedly shore up bourgeois ideology and are frequently not as conservative and ideologically in sync with *The Strand* as many critical interpretations suggest. In Doyle's stories, Holmes frequently behaves in ways which at the very least problematise readings of the detective as an uncomplicated 'comforting reliable hero', wholly successful and dedicated to his work (Knight, *Form and Ideology* 92). In 'A Scandal in Bohemia', 'The Five Orange Pips' and 'The Yellow Face', for instance, Holmes fails to catch the criminals. In 'A Scandal in Bohemia' and 'The Illustrious Client' Holmes breaks the law in pursuit of a case and speculates about what an excellent criminal he would have made. In 'The Red-Headed League' and 'The Man with the Twisted Lip' he scorns his clients and the police, instead admiring the work of his criminal adversaries. In 'The Boscombe Valley Mystery', 'The Man with the Twisted Lip' and 'The Adventure of the Blue Carbuncle' he lets the guilty party go free. In *The Sign of Four* and 'A Scandal in Bohemia' he blithely indulges in cocaine binges. In *A Study in Scarlet* and 'The Man with the Twisted Lip' we see the gaps and failings in his knowledge. And in 'The Man with the Twisted Lip' and 'The Red-Headed League' we see that Holmes is lazy and often doesn't work very hard. Rather than an uncomplicated avatar of bourgeois norms and codes, as is often claimed, Holmes is a complicated character, a law unto himself. As he puts it on more than one occasion: 'I am the last court of appeal' (Doyle, 'Five Orange Pips' 507).[15] As such, work in the Holmes stories is less about spectacular and unblemished professional success and more about the complex ways in which late Victorian males – clients, criminals, the official police and even Holmes himself – interact with dominant discourses of late Victorian professionalism.

From the outset, Doyle's Sherlock Holmes narratives are preoccupied with issues relating to work and professionalism. The first novella, *A Study in Scarlet* (1887), opens with Watson 'endeavouring to unravel' the mysterious nature of Holmes's work and finally discovering that his mysterious new acquaintance has 'a trade' as 'a consulting detective ... the only one in the world' (23). This is quickly followed by the first instance of what would become a staple Holmesian device – Holmes correctly deduces someone's occupation after only the briefest observation. The detective works out that Watson is 'clearly an army doctor' who has recently returned from Afghanistan (21).

Holmes's fascination with the professions of others was famously inspired by Doyle's medical school tutor Dr Joseph Bell. Doyle had been impressed by Bell's dazzling ability to read the 'sign-manuals of labour' and 'stains of trade' from the appearances of patients (Green, *Uncollected Sherlock* 364). In an interview for *The Bookman*, Doyle recounted that 'a slight callus, or hardening on one side of his forefinger, and a little thickening on the outside of his thumb' was a 'sure sign' for Bell that a man was either a cork-cutter or a slater (Blathwayt, 'A Talk' 50). In the first Holmes novella, Watson tells the reader that, like Bell, the detective believes that a man's calling is 'plainly revealed' by his 'fingernails, by his coat-sleeve, by his boot, by his trouser-knees' (22). And, in practically every following Holmes story, we see the detective deduce a person's job from their appearance. In the first short story, 'A Scandal in Bohemia', Holmes explains to Watson that 'a black mark of nitrate of silver upon the right fore-finger' and a bulge on the side of a top hat mark an active member of the medical profession (431). In 'A Case of Identity', Mary Sutherland is revealed to be a typist by the 'dint of a pince-nez' on her nose (477). In 'The Norwood Builder', an untidy sheaf of papers signifies that the bearer is a solicitor (867). And in 'The Red-Headed League', Jabez Wilson's hands, tattoos and sleeves mark him as a sailor and a freemason who has recently done a lot of writing (450–1).

The stories' preoccupation with the work of Holmes's clients does not end there, however. Rather, the conflict between the desire to earn money easily and by working at a job where the salary offered is disproportionate to the value of their labour is a problem that structures a significant number of the first two series of Holmes stories. This problem troubles the proprietor of a pawnbroker's shop in 'The Red-Headed League', an engineer in 'The Engineer's Thumb', a governess in 'The Copper Beeches', a clerk in 'The Stockbroker's Clerk' and a journalist in

'The Man with the Twisted Lip'. In each of these stories Holmes's clients are seduced into ill-advised activities which promise an opportunity to earn money quickly and easily but which ultimately turn out to be shameful, harmful or criminal. These are members of the lower-middle and professional classes, like Doyle and the *Strand*'s typical reader, with the same desires for wealth and status, and fears of poverty and social disgrace, which would have motivated both the young Doyle and his readers. The clients all succumb to the temptation of the easy money and the stories offer a fascinating insight into the effects of greed in the context of certain dominant late Victorian moral and ethical codes of behaviour regarding money and work. The Doyle who had recently accepted the well-paid but low-status Holmes commissions for *The Strand* is also clearly paralleled.

The first of the Holmes stories to explore in detail tensions about work, morality and earnings is 'The Red-Headed League' – only the second of Doyle's commissions for *The Strand*, which was first published in August 1891. The story perfectly encapsulates the long-held critical observation that 'striking' and 'bizarre little problems' contribute as much to the storylines of the Holmes canon as does actual crime (Jann, *Adventures* 72). At the same time, it rehearses the various ways in which lower-middle-class men, exemplified in this case by Holmes's client, interact with and deviate from late Victorian professional and moral ideals exemplified by the Smilesian work ethic. The story is a parable of the temptation by easy money of Jabez Wilson, a cash-poor, time-rich, lower-middle-class shopkeeper. Wilson, the red-haired owner of a none-too-successful pawnbroker's business, is enticed into a money-making scheme which seems, and ultimately is, too good to be true.[16] Wilson, whose description of his ill-paying business recalls Doyle's memories of his unprofitable time spent as a consulting oculist, is persuaded to take a second job with the mysterious Red-Headed League in order to earn some extra cash. The Red-Headed League, which is brought to Wilson's attention by his recently appointed assistant, Vincent Spalding, offers extremely well-paid positions for red-haired men to undertake menial work. Wilson applies, and is duly offered the job with the Red-Headed League. In his duties for the League, Wilson has to copy out the *Encyclopaedia Britannica* for four hours a day at the League's London offices. For this work he is paid four pounds a week. In today's terms, Wilson's weekly salary of four pounds equates to around £350.[17] At the start of his eighth week of work, Wilson arrives at the offices of the Red-Headed League to find them abandoned and a note advising him that his services are no longer required. It is Wilson's reluctance to lose this well-paying position which motivates him to consult Holmes. He hopes that Holmes will be able to uncover the mystery of the Red-Headed League's disappearance and discover why his opportunity for easy money has been removed.

In this story, however, Wilson is presented by Doyle as naïve and greedy; indeed, his inability to recognise the potential immorality suggested by his over-valued labour brings him Holmes's scorn and reprimand. After Wilson outlines his problem, Holmes surveys the pawnbroker's 'rueful face', and he and Watson rather uncharacteristically 'burst into a roar of laughter' (457). Holmes's light-hearted tone changes moments later to one of acerbic reprimand when he reminds the offended Wilson that his sense of injustice at the dissolution of the league has no validity: 'I do not see that you have any grievance against this extraordinary league. On the contrary, you are, as I understand, richer by some thirty pounds, to say nothing of the minute knowledge which you have gained on every subject which comes under the letter A. You have lost nothing by them' (458). The inference is that the 'not over-bright' pawnbroker is lucky to get away with his foolishness without greater reprimand and may have benefited as much from the small amount of detailed knowledge gleaned in the fulfilment of his duties as from the 32 pounds payment he received (455). Duly admonished, Wilson disappears from the narrative, evidently equally as expendable to Doyle as he had been to Holmes and the Red-Headed League.

As Holmes quickly discovers, the Red-Headed League job was simply a fool's errand devised by Wilson's recently appointed shop assistant (professional arch-criminal John Clay, in disguise) so that he could remove Wilson from the premises every day and thus tunnel from the pawnbroker's basement into a neighbouring bank vault. As soon as Holmes makes this discovery, Wilson disappears from the story and his search for John Clay takes over the rest of the narrative. Clay (the criminal) mirrors Wilson, however, by way of a similarly distorted relationship between labour and payment. Where Wilson's work for the Red-Headed League sees him performing 'purely nominal' duties for a large wage, Clay's labour inverts this formula; Holmes discovers that Clay had secured the job at the pawnbroker's by offering to work for 'half-wages' under the pretext of learning the trade (456; 452). In a capitalist society, as Franco Moretti has pointed out, 'suspicion often originates from a violation of the law of exchange between equivalent values' and thus 'anyone who pays more than a market price or accepts a low salary can only be spurred by criminal motives' (*Signs* 139). Indeed, Holmes finds it 'perfectly' and 'obvious[ly]' suspicious that any potential employee would underprice their own labour – and it is these suspicions that alert him to Clay's true identity and criminal intentions (456). Wilson's failure to acknowledge the suspicious nature of this 'violation of the law of exchange between equivalent values' not once, but twice, in the story (with his over-valued labour and Clay's under-valued labour) marks his naïveté and the reason for Holmes's contempt (Moretti, *Signs* 139). The overpriced labour which Wilson undertakes, of course, also recalls Doyle's own request and subsequent acquisition of an exorbitant sum for his second batch of *Strand* stories – a commission which he dashed out in a short space of time.

'The Engineer's Thumb', the ninth story in the *Adventures* series, published by *The Strand* in March 1892, is strikingly similar to 'The Red-Headed League' but more forcefully underlines the perils of being tempted by easy money. Like Jabez Wilson, Victor Hatherley, a self-employed consulting engineer, is offered a disproportionate amount of money for a small job. Unlike Wilson, however, Hatherley is not merely a patsy who needs to be distracted in order for a crime to be committed. Instead he is actively involved in the crime itself. A criminal gang has persuaded Hatherley to fix a mechanised press which they use in the counterfeiting of coins. Hatherley agrees to take on this work for a fee of 50 guineas – a large sum equivalent to around £4500 in today's terms. The crime in this story operates on a number of figurative levels; counterfeiting, of course, devalues the inherent worth of money – the currency on which capitalism depends. Similarly, Hatherley's overpriced employment disrupts the relationship between labour and reward.

As a professional engineer, Hatherley would have belonged to a higher stratum of the middle class than shopkeeper Jabez Wilson. His occupation would have categorised him as belonging to what the Registrar General's survey of 1921 termed 'Social Class I' or 'the professions', alongside doctors, lawyers and journalists (qtd in Sindall 23). The engineer therefore would have been expected to possess what Matthew Arnold termed the 'fine and governing qualities' of the 'professional class' (qtd in Perkin 83). Thus he would have been expected to have been well aware of the social and moral error of accepting work with the coining gang.[18] His higher professional status and his greater involvement in the crime therefore suggest that Hatherley has committed a greater mistake than Wilson. Thus the punishment enacted on Hatherley by Doyle is necessarily more severe. After he has completed his work on the coining press, the criminal gang try to murder Hatherley. Whilst trying to escape from the room containing the counterfeiting press, Hatherley traps his hand in its machinery and he loses a thumb. It is fitting here that it is the very machinery of his profession that gravely injures the engineer. Seeking treatment for this injury leads Hatherley to Dr Watson. The injury is described in uncharacteristically visceral terms by Doyle – 'It gave even my hardened nerves a shudder to look at it,' says Watson, 'there were four protruding fingers and a horrid red spongy surface where the thumb should have been. It had been hacked or torn right off from the roots' (580). The shocking violence of the punishment and the sensationally bloody nature of its description by Doyle are unusual in the Holmes canon, again emphasising the gravity of Hatherley's error.

Perhaps surprisingly, given the serious nature of the injury, Holmes coolly dismisses Hatherley's predicament. When the engineer laments: 'I have lost my thumb and I have lost a fifty-guinea fee, and what have I gained?' Holmes 'laugh[s]' and advises Hatherley that he has gained 'experience' (595). In other words, he has learned a harsh lesson about the importance of adhering to the usual moral codes concerning the links between money and labour. 'The Engineer's Thumb' and 'The Red-Headed League', then, illustrate the ways in which Doyle's characterisations of the moral and ethical failings of Holmes's middle-class clients, who suffer the consequences of their un-Victorian desire to earn well without having to work hard, comprise an important element of the stories' ideological power. This has led scholars such as Knight (*Form and Ideology*) and Jann ('Sherlock'; *Adventures*) to suggest that the Holmes stories unproblematically disseminate middle-class behavioural codes and values.

However, 'The Man with the Twisted Lip' (*The Strand* Dec. 1891) – only the sixth story in the *Adventures* series – constitutes a more radical examination of anxieties about money, labour and productivity, in which the work ethic of multiple characters, including Holmes himself, comes under scrutiny. As such, this tale illustrates the ways in which Doyle's detective fiction is not always as unquestioning in its dissemination of dominant Victorian values as is often argued. The story involves a journalist who poses as a beggar during the day because he can earn more in that manner than by working honestly.[19] This story opens with a rescue mission which sees Dr Watson forego a cosy domestic evening with his wife and travel to a 'vile' opium den 'in the farthest East of the city' in order to retrieve Isa Whitney, the husband of one of his wife's friends ('Twisted Lip' 522). Whitney is on an opium binge and has not returned home for days – his insalubrious slumming recalling the nocturnal adventures of the male protagonists in Stevenson's *Strange Case of Dr Jekyll and Mr Hyde* (1886). Despite the unsavoury nature of his present predicament, Whitney's respectable credentials are strongly foregrounded from the story's outset. He is a university graduate, his brother is the principal of a theological college and he is married to one of Mrs Watson's closest school companions. By giving himself over to self-indulgent 'orgies' of opium consumption, however, Whitney has betrayed and forsaken his respectable position (522). Despite being a figure of good social standing, he is now 'the wreck and ruin of a noble man' who is 'an object of mingled horror and pity to his friends and relatives' (521).

After being found, reprimanded and dispatched home by Watson, Whitney disappears from the rest of the story, yet his predicament haunts the remainder of the narrative. Whitney's association with the opium den, his debased social status and the neglect of his roles as respectable middle-class gentleman and husband foreshadow the events surrounding the disappearance of Neville St Clair. The story continues to play with connections made in this opening scene between the opium den, the metropolis, the workplace and the comfortable bourgeois home. Deducing the nature of a number of male protagonists' involvement with these various spaces is a key structuring element which underpins the narrative. All of the story's main protagonists – Watson, Whitney, Holmes and Hugh Boone/Neville St Clair – are linked by their encounters in various domestic and urban spaces and by the themes of work and counterfeit identities, resulting in a blurring between criminal, client, detective and victim. Roles, professions and identities overlap and collide in one of Doyle's most thematically and ideologically complex stories.

Whilst in the opium den, Watson meets Holmes disguised as an old opium eater. Holmes is so immersed in his environment that Watson passes him twice before noticing him: 'It took all my self-control to prevent me from breaking out into a cry of astonishment ... there, sitting by the fire and grinning at my surprise, was none other than Sherlock Holmes' (524). Given that the earlier novels showed that Holmes has a penchant for cocaine injections, his appearance in an opium den is a potentially troubling indicator of further drug use. Indeed, Holmes's greeting underscores the extent to which drug use is an assumed part of his life: '"I suppose Watson," said he, "that you imagine that I have added opium-smoking to cocaine injections and all the other little weaknesses on which you have favoured me with your medical views"' (524). It is quickly revealed, however, that Holmes is at the opium den to work on the case of Neville St Clair, who he believes has been murdered in one of the den's upstairs rooms. These links between Whitney,

Holmes and drug use re-emerge again, however, when Holmes returns from the den. Once back at Baker Street, Holmes recreates the milieu of the opium den in order to work on solving the case. Watson describes how, with a number of pillows, Holmes 'constructed a sort of Eastern divan, upon which he perched himself cross-legged, with an ounce of shag tobacco and a box of matches laid out in front of him' (535). On this eastern divan Holmes sits 'in the dim light' with 'an old brier pipe between his lips' and 'his eyes fixed vacantly upon the corner of the ceiling, the blue smoke curling up from him, silent, motionless' (535). The blue smoke, the vacant eyes, the lethargic demeanour and the 'dense tobacco haze' which still hangs in the air on the following morning reinforces the blurring of distinctions between Whitney, the opium smoker on a binge, and Holmes whilst working (535).[20]

The case was brought to Holmes by St Clair's wife. Whilst shopping in London, the lady had passed the opium den and was alarmed to catch sight of her husband at the window, shrieking, and apparently being grabbed from behind. Hugh Boone, a disfigured beggar, the eponymous 'Man with the Twisted Lip', is found hiding in an adjacent room at the opium den and is arrested for St Clair's murder. Unusually, Holmes is in agreement with the police – like them he is (wrongly) convinced that St Clair has been murdered by Boone. Despite his belief that St Clair is dead, Holmes has been employed by Mrs St Clair to discover what her husband was doing in the opium den, what happened to him when there and why Hugh Boone murdered him (530). We later discover that St Clair's shriek was precipitated merely by his alarm at being spotted by his wife in the disreputable environs of the opium den, rather than having signified an attack on his person. The truth is that journalist Neville St Clair and vagrant Hugh Boone are one and the same and St Clair has been masquerading as the beggar for some years now. In the course of an investigation on beggary in the metropolis for one of the evening newspapers, St Clair had discovered that he could earn significantly more in a day 'working' as Boone than he could in a week as a reporter. He duly left his job and embarked on a double life, travelling each day to London by train dressed like thousands of other commuters and transforming himself into Boone in rooms above the opium den. When the police arrived at the opium den, St Clair had quickly dressed as Boone and subsequently allowed himself to be arrested and to remain in jail for murder dressed as Boone, rather than have this secret double life revealed to his wife.

The story's structural pairing of the deception of two wives – Mrs Whitney and Mrs St Clair – and the illicit activities of two husbands suggests that the themes of this case are not 'singular' or 'bizarre' events 'outside the conventions of everyday life' as are so many of Holmes's cases ('Red-Headed League' 453). Instead the similarities in the cases of Isa Whitney and Neville St Clair suggest that disreputable secrets may be common among Victorian middle-class men. Indeed, this story raises many questions about 'the degree to which any Victorian wife knows the true nature of the family paterfamilias' (Kestner, *Sherlock's Men* 96). The story therefore rehearses an anxiety common after the revelations of W.T. Stead's 'Maiden Tribute of Modern Babylon' investigation and the 1888 Whitechapel murders – that the city was a domain in which appearances could not be trusted and where dual lives, especially amongst middle- and upper-middle-class men, were common. It plays on the same fears that were responsible for the countless theories that Jack the Ripper, the most feared and notorious criminal of the era, was not a slum-dweller, but rather an outwardly trustworthy and respectable man – a doctor, a banker or even a member of the royal household.[21]

In 'The Man with the Twisted Lip', this common late Victorian theme of dual identity is inverted or twisted by Doyle. Doyle shows that an outward appearance of respectability is capable of duping everyone, including a man's own wife or a super-detective like Holmes. Just as Isa Whitney's university education and his eminently respectable brother mark his innate refinement and make his misbehaviour all the more surprising, so too St Clair appears outwardly solidly bourgeois and hence respectable. St Clair's 'temperate habits', the fact that he is 'a good husband', and the prosaic nature of his commute 'into town ... every morning, returning by the 5.14 from Cannon Street every night' mark him as a solid and respectable gentleman like countless other 'well-dressed men about town' (526). St Clair follows the same pattern of travelling to the city by day and home to the suburbs by night without anyone, including his wife, really knowing where he works and thus 'without anyone having a suspicion as to my real occupation' (526).

In a genre fascinated with exploring the ways in which the social self can be counterfeited, it is commonly held that the superior vision of the detective allows him to see through disguises and identify the true criminal. It is argued that Holmes works within 'a materialistic model, which can read off from physical data what has happened and what will happen' (Knight, *Form and Ideology* 74). To some extent this is true, but, as Jann has pointed out, Holmes's powers of observation work best when decoding the bodies of manual labourers. As she puts it, '[Holmes's] sweeping claim that a man's calling is "plainly revealed" by his fingernails, calluses and the state of his clothing is much truer of the working class than of the middle and upper classes' ('Sherlock' 691). Indeed, Holmes appears to have considerably more difficulty penetrating disguises like St Clair's because, like everyone else, he allows himself to be distracted by the cover of St Clair's apparent respectability. He enjoys staying at St Clair's 'large and comfortable' suburban villa and appears readily to accept Mrs St Clair's assessment of her husband's propriety (534). Thus, from the outset of the case of 'The Man with the Twisted Lip', Holmes is wrongly convinced that St Clair must have been murdered and he spends much of the investigation wrong-footed by this assumption. It is only when he spends a night smoking and ruminating on his Eastern divan that he recognises the true facts of the case. On realising his mistake he acknowledges, 'I have been as blind as a mole,' and suggests to Watson that he (Holmes) is 'one of the most absolute fools in Europe', deserving 'to be kicked from here to Charing Cross' for his stupidity (536; 535; 535).

Holmes's inability to penetrate St Clair's disguise as Boone for so much of the case emphasises the story's power to unsettle the links between identity and appearance so crucial to detective fiction. The scene in which Holmes finally washes off Boone's make-up to reveal St Clair works to emphasise the dialectical spiral of respectability and criminality within the social construction of identity at play in this story. Whereas St Clair's respectable life has masked a criminal one, Boone's literal mask hides 'a pale, sad-faced, refined looking man' (540). In this story, Doyle exposes a potentially widespread pathologisation of the middle-class male hidden by respectability. This is all the more troubling for the reader because of the problems that even Holmes has had in detecting it.

'The Man with the Twisted Lip' radicalises the theme of overpriced labour by presenting St Clair not simply as the victim, but also as the instigator, of the deception. St Clair himself devises the scheme of overpaid labour purely to earn more money more easily than he would have done if he were engaged in a real profession. When finally unmasked, St Clair justifies his deception in economic terms, appealing to Holmes, 'You can imagine how hard it was to settle down to arduous work at two pounds a week when I knew that I could earn as much in a day by smearing my face with a little paint, laying my cap on the ground and sitting still. It was a long fight between my pride and the money, but the dollars won at last' (539). He is not the naïve victim of a criminal conspiracy tempted by the possibility of augmenting his modest but honestly earned salary. Rather, St Clair set out consciously to deceive and defraud, thus once again blurring the story's distinctions between client and criminal, victim and victimiser. Links between the working practices of Holmes and St Clair, and the social practices of Holmes and Isa Whitney, blur the moral positions of the story's characters further still and result in a highly morally ambiguous story. The story closes with Holmes reminding Watson, and the reader, that he solved this case merely by sitting on his pillows and smoking. This emphasis on the ease of the detective's own work forms part of a larger series of tensions – between amateur/professional, interest/disinterest, hard work/languor – that recur in Doyle's characterisation of Holmes, which I explore in detail in the following section. Once again, of course, they also recall the anxieties regarding hard work, money and morality which so troubled Doyle's own fledgling career.

The Holmes stories not only foreground the professional dilemmas and immoral work ethics of Holmes's clients and the criminals he pursues, they are similarly fascinated with the work of Holmes himself. From the outset, however, Doyle's presentation of Holmes's work and professional status is replete with moral ambiguities and contradictions that undermine critical readings which argue for both the 'complete' and 'spectacular' success and the 'morality' of the detective figure in late Victorian crime fiction (Reiter 74; Cawelti 277). Holmes's skill as a detective is, of course, an important aspect of the stories which should not be dismissed. Arguments which focus solely upon Holmes's professional success, however, fail to account for much of the stories' variability with regard to the detective's character and work. In fact, Holmes operates on and against many of the moral and legal boundaries which he works to police.[22]

Indeed, right from the outset the Sherlock Holmes canon emphasises the contradictory nature of Holmes's work. In *A Study in Scarlet*, the Holmes to which both Watson and the reader are first introduced is an outsider: 'queer in his ideas', 'cold-blooded' and 'eccentric' – a man who is shown by Doyle to operate at the margins of social respectability (14–15). His acquaintance, Stamford, warns Watson that Holmes has been known to beat cadavers at the medical school morgue simply to study post-mortem bruising, seemingly oblivious to the code of ethics outlined in the Hippocratic Oath (15). In the next breath, Stamford speculates that Holmes might well be the type of person who would dose a patient with poison simply in order to observe the effects (15). His cold-blooded attitude to his medical patients prefigures his morally detached attitude to many of the clients and criminals he encounters in the course of his adventures. The uncertain nature of Holmes's status as a scientist, but not an enrolled medical student, also prefigures his uncertain role as professional, yet also amateur, detective.

Watson's strong desire to deduce the occupation of his unconventional new roommate suggests a typically Victorian belief in the importance of professionalism and a conviction that to know someone's profession is to better understand their social and moral status. Harold Perkin points out that the mid-Victorian values and beliefs of 'the professional social ideal' still held true in the 1880s and 1890s (116). The Smilesian 'true gentleman' and the 'gospel of hard work' remained indicators of respectability, and any leisured gentleman was viewed with distaste and even suspicion (Perkin 120). Watson's attempts to understand the nature of Holmes's work, however, serve only to underline the confusing nature of the detective's professional status. In spite of the precision with which Holmes defines his own occupation – 'I have a trade of my own. I suppose I am the only one in the world. I'm a consulting detective' – the detective and his work remain resistant to categorisation and are replete with contradictions (*A Study in Scarlet* 17). Holmes is categorised variously as both 'amateur' and 'professional'; early in the canon he describes relying on his detecting work for his 'bread and cheese', elsewhere he describes it as providing little more than an 'escape' from 'ennui', later still Watson describes how Holmes works more 'for the love of his art than for the acquirement of wealth' (*A Study in Scarlet* 26; 67; 87; 'Red-Headed League' 467; 'The Speckled Band' 558). Likewise Holmes's knowledge is uneven and not suggestive of a specific profession – his learning is 'profound' in some areas, such as chemistry, but 'feeble' and 'unsystematic' in others such as politics and anatomy (*A Study in Scarlet* 20–1).

Watson's observations of Holmes's everyday working patterns do little to help him deduce the nature of Holmes's profession:

> Sometimes he spent his day at the chemical laboratory, sometimes in the dissecting rooms, and occasionally in long walks, which appeared to take him into the lowest portions of the city. Nothing could exceed his energy when the working fit was upon him; but now and again a reaction would seize him, and for days on end he would lie on the sofa in the sitting room, hardly uttering a word or moving a muscle from day to night. On these occasions I might have suspected him of being addicted to the use of some narcotic. (*A Study in Scarlet* 18–19)

Part of the difficulty in specifying the nature and extent of Holmes's work is that his newly created profession, like Doyle's, and so many others at the time, produced knowledge, and thus was essentially passive, and hence 'invisible'. The work of a professional who 'professes rather than produces – whose speech, writing, or knowledge is his commodity' is by its nature difficult to assess (Jaffe 109). Like Doyle, Holmes's capital is mental rather than physical, and his work falls into a slippery category where it is often invisible or hard to see. His long periods of passivity, followed by short bursts of hard work on detecting cases, are reminiscent of Doyle's work pattern when writing the Holmes stories for *The Strand*. Because of this, Holmes's work often seems to constitute the type of intellectualism dismissed by Mill as not constituting real work. Given Holmes's appearance of languor and laziness, Watson finds it hard to ascertain what his roommate does for a living. Likewise, in 'The Noble Bachelor', the solidly working-class Captain Lestrade criticises Holmes's working methods in terms which again rehearse contemporary concerns about the invisibility of intellectual work. The policeman attacks Holmes's passive methods of deduction, finding them lazy in comparison to his own more active means of investigation. He sarcastically snipes at the detective: 'I believe in hard work and not sitting by the fire and spinning fine theories' (607).

Elsewhere, Holmes's work in both 'The Red-Headed League' and 'The Man with the Twisted Lip' again illustrates the passive nature of his profession and the ways in which his detection might be confused with laziness or languor. In both cases Holmes appears to do little more than lounge on an ottoman smoking a pipe in order to solve the mysteries. In order to crack the case of 'The Red-Headed League' Holmes needs to smoke for a mere 'fifty minutes' – the solution to the case is 'a three-pipe problem' (459). Shortly afterwards he spends 'all the afternoon' at a concert in St James Hall 'wrapped in the most perfect happiness ... his languid, dreamy eyes ... as unlike those of Holmes the sleuth-hound, Holmes the relentless, keen-witted, ready-handed criminal agent, as it was possible to conceive' (461). He solves 'The Man with the Twisted Lip' case, he claims, merely by 'sitting upon five pillows and consuming an ounce of shag' (540).

Sidney Paget's illustrations for *The Strand* also appear to reinforce the passive nature of the detective's labour. Of the 111 illustrations accompanying the *Adventures* series, 71 feature Holmes. Of these only 16 (25 per cent) depict Holmes actively working – looking for evidence, interviewing clients or examining clues. Nearly twice as many – 26 – show Holmes sitting, lounging, smoking or at leisure. The illustrations for 'The Man with the Twisted Lip' are a striking reinforcement of the ease with which Holmes solves the case, visually suggesting the similarity between the work of Holmes lounging on his pillows and Neville St

Clair's work begging in the city (Figure 3.3). The detective's languorous demeanour cuts against Smilesian and Carlylean notions about the conventional relationship between hard work and moral character. Indeed, when questioned by Watson about his thoughts on Carlyle, Holmes, perhaps ironically, goes as far as to profess complete ignorance of the mid-Victorian advocate of hard work: 'he enquired in the naïvest way who he might be and what he had done' (*A Study in Scarlet* 19). This lack of reverence for the gospel of work and for the consistent industry aligned with that doctrine once again marks Holmes's potential for deviancy from accepted norms of behaviour. This ambiguous positioning with regard to Holmes's productivity and work ethic also undermines critical readings which focus on the unmitigated 'complete success' of the nineteenth-century detective (Reiter 74).

Watson's observations of Holmes's working habits, then, serve only to emphasise the ways in which the detective's work fails to adhere to bourgeois convention: he is cold-hearted and morally detached, erratic and unproductive, he frequents low parts of the city – recalling the potentially immoral slumming expeditions featured in *Jekyll and Hyde* – and he even uses drugs. If, as Miller claims, discipline puts in place 'a perceptual grid' in which 'a division between the normal and the deviant inherently imposes itself', Holmes appears to be a figure operating on the boundaries of such a grid (Miller, *Novel* 18). Holmes's behaviours – his laziness, his drug use and slumming expeditions, the unconventional, morally detached nature of his work – suggest deviancy, rather than normalcy. This moral ambiguity unsettles critical readings which argue for the redoubtable moral code of the nineteenth-century detective hero, and Foucauldian readings of the genre which focus on the detective as the avatar of disciplinary society. The Holmes to whom we are introduced is not at all a straightforward embodiment of 'solidity' and 'morality', as has often been claimed, but rather is a borderland figure who appears to be 'straddling the very boundaries that Foucault has discipline policing', displaying elements which are at once hard-working/lazy, normal/abnormal and criminal/respectable (Cawelti 277; Reitz xxi).

From fairly early in the Holmes canon, Doyle implies that Holmes could just as easily have been a criminal as a detective. In 'The Boscombe Valley Mystery', after the criminal is identified, Holmes cryptically asserts, 'There but for the grace of God, goes Sherlock Holmes,' suggesting that the detective understands, and perhaps wrestles with, his own propensity for criminality (504). Indeed, in 'Charles Augustus Milverton', Holmes plans to commit a burglary in order to recover the

"HE IS A PROFESSIONAL BEGGAR."

"THE PIPE WAS STILL BETWEEN HIS LIPS."

Figure 3.3 Sidney Paget's illustrations for 'The Man with the Twisted Lip.' *The Strand Magazine* July–Dec. 1891: 629; 634

letters that Milverton – 'a genius in his way' – is using to blackmail his client (963). As he details these plans to Watson, Holmes nonchalantly produces 'a first-class, up-to-date burgling kit, with nickel-plated jemmy, diamond-tipped glass cutter, adaptable keys' (969) of the type described in the 1894 *Strand* article 'Thieves v. Locks and Safes'. Whilst the kit itself does not prove that Holmes has committed other burglaries, it nonetheless demonstrates that he is amply equipped to do so if he pleases. Complicating his moral position further still, he wryly tells Watson, 'I don't mind confessing to you that I have always had an idea that I would have made a highly efficient criminal' (969).

In the last story of the last Holmes volume to be published, 'The Retired Colourman' (1926), Doyle has Holmes speculate again about a potential career in crime. He tells the Scotland Yard Detective Inspector McKinnon that burglary would have been 'an alternative profession, had I cared to adopt it' (1406). Speculating on the consequences of taking up burglary as a profession, he muses: 'I have little doubt I should have come to the front [of the field]' (1406). With such characterisations, Doyle certainly seems to have relaxed his earlier priggish advice to brother-in-law E.W. Hornung that in literature the hero should never be a criminal and that criminality should never be made to appear light-hearted or gallant (*Memories* 87). Such characterisations also unsettle critical arguments which dogmatically assert that 'in every story Sherlock Holmes is the unquestioning, incorruptible guardian of the Victorian criminal and moral codes' where 'his unvarying role is that of the detector, preventer, judge and punisher of every larcenous and immoral act' (Redmond 135).

One of Holmes's most morally ambiguous characteristics, which further shores up his uncertain status between the law-abiding and criminal worlds, is his disregard for the law and his admiration and empathy for the criminals he investigates. The detective often opines that 'the days of great cases are past' and that 'criminal man has lost all enterprise and ingenuity' ('The Copper Beeches' 635). He laments the lack of 'audacity and romance' in the London criminal underworld and relishes the opportunity to come up against a challenging adversary ('Wisteria Lodge' 1089). A pattern of admiration for some of the cleverest criminals he investigates also begins fairly early in the Holmes canon. In 'A Scandal in Bohemia', the very first of the Holmes stories for *The Strand*, Holmes is 'beaten by a woman's wit', yet is full of admiration for the woman who beats him and escapes his clutches (448). For Holmes, Irene Adler's ingenuity means that she 'eclipses and predominates the whole of her sex' (429). In future she is referred to by the detective simply as '*the* woman', such is the nature of her impact upon Holmes (emphasis in original) (448).

Likewise in 'The Red-Headed League', Holmes's contempt for client Jabez Wilson's naïveté is in sharp contrast to his admiration for criminal John Clay's professionalism. The detective has been 'on his track for years' but has 'never set eyes on him' (463). Described variously as 'formidable', 'daring' and 'remarkable' (despite being a 'murderer, thief, smasher and forger'), Holmes uses the language of professionalism and the workplace to describe Clay's criminal achievements (463). The lawbreaker is reverentially noted by Holmes to be 'at the head of his profession' (463). The terms in which Holmes expresses his admiration for Clay and his claims that he would 'rather have my bracelets on him than on any criminal in London' mark the thief as Holmes's professional and intellectual equal (463). Indeed the detective and the criminal politely pay tribute to each other's professionalism, with the respect due to colleagues: '"I must compliment you." "And I you," Holmes answered. "Your red-headed idea was very new and effective"' (466). In demonstrating Holmes's admiration for Clay's professionalism, Doyle takes the late Victorian admiration for work and rather daringly inverts it. The policeman who accompanies Holmes to make the arrest, by contrast, is contemptuously dismissed by Holmes as 'an absolute imbecile in his profession' (463). Through the theme of work, then, Clay is paired with all the other characters in the story. Clay and Wilson are linked by an unhealthy desire for money and a distorted relationship between labour and payment. Clay and Jones, the investigating police officer, are linked by their status within their respective 'professions' – Clay is at the top and Jones is at the bottom (463). Finally, Clay and Holmes are linked in admiration for each other's work and their places at the heads of their professions. This story's thematic preoccupation with profession and morality is played with by Doyle to great ironic effect, with roles, professions and identities overlapping and colliding, thus blurring the boundaries between criminal, client, detective and victim.

Holmes's admiration for the criminal, Clay, also contrasts with the detective's disregard for the work of the policemen whom he encounters. Holmes's cool admiration for Clay, his cold reprimand of clients like Wilson and Hatherley, and his disgust at the incompetency of Lestrade, Gregory and Jones, however, represents an ironic reversal of the values one might expect from a representative of the law and signals his frequent lack of regard for the official disciplinary framework.[23] Holmes claims that these detectives' 'normal state' is to be 'out of their depths' (*The Sign of Four* 98). Jones is 'limited by the fact that he has no room for theories', Lestrade is bound by 'finding it very hard to tackle the facts' and Gregory 'lacks ... the value of imagination' (*The Sign of Four* 124; 'Boscombe Valley Mystery' 496; 'Silver Blaze' 669). Such buffoonery from the official police speaks to the fact that 'the prestige of the police was low when Doyle began to write', a topic that was to be exploited in a large number of post-Holmes detective stories and which I explore in more detail in the next chapter (Clausen 114).

Holmes's attitude towards Lestrade, Jones, Adler and Clay forms part of a pattern which is repeated throughout Doyle's stories where the detective dismisses the state police but admits to being 'proud to do business' with the criminals he faces ('The Priory School' 932). In considering these types of criminal worthy of professional equality, Holmes displays an appreciation of what Foucault has called the 'aesthetic rewriting of crime', the nineteenth-century phenomenon whereby crime is shown to be 'the work only of exceptional natures' (68). In Foucault's assessment, crime literature at this time became 'the exclusive privilege of those who are really great' and the focus shifted from physical confrontation and punishment to the intellectual struggle between 'two pure minds' – the criminal and the detective (69). Holmes appreciates 'the beauty and greatness of crime' in the work of these criminals whom he considers his intellectual equals (Foucault 68). In 'The Speckled Band' – the adventure which Doyle listed as his favourite Holmes story – Holmes takes very seriously the threat posed by the villainously named Dr Grimesby Roylott.[24] He explains that 'when a doctor goes wrong he is the first of criminals', because a doctor's 'nerve' and 'knowledge' equip him with the ability to excel ('The Speckled Band' 574). The detective goes on to muse that the famous doctor-poisoners Palmer and Pritchard were 'among the heads of their profession' (574). We must assume that the profession to which Holmes is referring is murder rather than medicine, as neither Palmer nor Pritchard were particularly highly regarded as doctors (Elmsley 431).

This reverence for the professional, skilful and audacious criminal of course culminates in his regard for his nemesis and 'intellectual equal' Professor Moriarty, whose 'career has been an extraordinary one' ('The Final Problem' 833; 832). Despite knowing that Moriarty means to kill him, Holmes describes how his 'horror' at Moriarty's crimes is 'lost in admiration for his skill' (833). The opening pages of 'The Final Problem' repeatedly refer to Moriarty's criminal and professional stature; he is thus variously described as: 'The Napoleon of Crime', 'a genius', 'a philosopher', 'an abstract thinker', a 'brain of the first order', 'wily', 'brilliant' and 'splendidly organised' (832–4). Moriarty is the first criminal who is explicitly named as Holmes's 'intellectual equal'; Holmes describes the master-criminal as being 'on quite the same intellectual plane as myself' (833; 838).

Moriarty's control of the city is also evoked in terms strikingly similar to descriptions of Holmes's panoptic 'complete knowledge' of London's crime (*The Hound of the Baskervilles* 302). The master-criminal sits 'motionless, like a spider at the centre of its web' knowing and feeling 'every quiver' of the web's 'thousand radiations' ('The Final Problem' 833). When tracking Holmes, Moriarty anticipated and 'saw every step which I took to draw my toils round him' (833). Moriarty thus embodies the same qualities of surveillance and diffuse power as are often attributed to Holmes himself by Foucauldian critics of the crime genre. Yet significantly, the crime for which Moriarty is responsible largely goes 'undetected' and unpunished (833). While some of his more lowly agents have been caught, what Holmes terms 'the central power' – Moriarty himself – is 'never caught' and moreover is 'never so much as suspected' (833). This ability to evade detection once again questions the efficiency of the police in Victorian London and, more significantly, also exposes the limitations of Holmes's detecting powers. The story, which details the struggle between the two great powers, of course sees our 'reassuring' and 'invincible' 'super-detective' hero killed along with Moriarty at its close (Pittard, 'Cheap, healthful literature' 17; Leps 193; Gillis and Gates 194). The downbeat and uncertain ending to what Doyle believed would be the final Holmes story certainly unsettles critical readings of Doyle's oeuvre which argue that it is the realm of reassuring textual closure and the 'happy ending' (Mandel 47).

The Holmes stories, then, published in an era fascinated with work, professionalism and morality, rather than simply shoring up hegemonic ideas about these issues, instead examine and dissect their contradictions and ambiguities. In doing so, they both reflect Doyle's own conflicted position and once again illuminate the ways in which the nascent genre was not as conservative and formulaic as has often been suggested. Rather, even the late Victorian genre's most well-known and canonical tales contain a perhaps surprising amount of formal, moral and ideological ambiguity. In the following chapters I turn to the detective stories that sprang up in the wake of Holmes's success, concentrating particularly on those stories which pushed further the genre's transgressive potential.

4
Something for 'the Silly Season': Policing and the Press in Israel Zangwill's *The Big Bow Mystery* (1891)

In this chapter I focus on Israel Zangwill's subversive and intriguing *The Big Bow Mystery* (1891), a crime novel published in the immediate wake of Arthur Conan Doyle's successful Sherlock Holmes stories for *The Strand*.[1] 'A Scandal in Bohemia' appeared in July 1891; just over a month later, on 22 August, and running in daily instalments until 4 September, *The Big Bow Mystery* was published in London's only politically Radical daily newspaper, *The Star*. At the time of the novel's publication, Zangwill – a young writer with a growing reputation for witty and political material – was the paper's literary columnist. The paper had been founded in summer 1888 by the pioneer of New Journalism T.P. O'Connor as 'the Radical evening organ for the metropolis' (*The Star* 17 Jan. 1888: 1). It soon became known for its stirring and direct editorials in support of Home Rule and the reform of Scotland Yard, and for its sensational crime reportage. The paper became particularly notorious for its prurient and sensational coverage of the Whitechapel Ripper murders in the summer of 1888, during which time its circulation soared to over 300,000 copies daily.[2] In summer 1891, the paper's editor contacted Zangwill requesting something 'original' for 'the silly season': a piece of fiction that would capture and reflect its readers' interest in crime, politics and sensation (Zangwill, 'Of Murders' 202). With 'murder in my soul', Zangwill later quipped, *The Big Bow Mystery* 'was written in a fortnight, day-by-day' (202; 204).

Zangwill's novel reached upwards of 250,000 readers daily during its serialisation in *The Star*.[3] It proved so popular that later the same year it appeared in book form, published by London firm Henry and Co., which ran to several editions. Indeed, despite its speedy composition, Zangwill felt that *The Big Bow Mystery* was 'an excellent murder story ... as sensational as most of them', but 'contain[ing] more humour and character creation than the best' ('Of Murders' 201). As Zangwill notes, the novel not only employs but also stretches and inverts the burgeoning detective fiction genre. *The Big Bow Mystery* yokes the crime fiction formula of a 'locked-room mystery', pioneered by Edgar Allan Poe some 50 years before with 'The Murders in the Rue Morgue' (1841), onto a fascinating tragicomic portrait of life in an East London slum – the type of novel for which Zangwill later would come to be known. The result is an intriguing, and often self-conscious, experiment with the conventions of genre which offers insight into the manifold links between crime, poverty, policing and the press in the East End district of Bow.

The novel tells the story of the murder of a middle-class philanthropist who has been slumming in the East End. His body is found in a locked bedroom which displays no sign of an intruder and contains no murder weapon. The list of suspects is a coterie of East End working-class residents, including a leading trade unionist, the victim's impoverished landlady, a retired detective from the Met's detective branch and a hack journalist. The surprising denouement reveals that the retired police detective is the murderer, his crime spurred on by a desire for notoriety in print. *The Big Bow Mystery* is one of the earliest crime novels to invert emphatically the 'detective as hero' model that is often read as so characteristic of Holmes-era crime fiction (Shpayer-Makov 240). It is also a witty and satirical comment on press coverage of murder and detecting, on modern policing and upon the detective genre itself. The title alone is the first indication of the novel's satirical and self-reflexive qualities: the phrase 'Big Bow Mystery' refers both to the area of East London where the murder takes place and to *The Star* and 'Pell Mell Press' newspaper headlines that feature inside, sensationally recounting any developments as 'The Big Bow Mystery Thickens' (229; 219).

This chapter illuminates the multiple ways in which *The Big Bow Mystery* consciously subverts a number of the burgeoning conventions of the nascent genre. Specifically, I begin by examining how the novel's setting and its depiction of the poverty of East End life constitutes an intriguing inversion of the genre's norms with regard to class and geography. The second half of the chapter concentrates upon Zangwill's portrayal of the detective-as-murderer and his interaction with the press, examining the ways in which this maps onto a broad critique of Scotland Yard and an attack on the growing late Victorian trend for press sensationalism in the reportage of crime. Along the way, I examine the novel's unusual 'detective-as anti-hero' feature (a topic that I explore in more detail in the following chapter).

Despite its comic tone and subversive qualities, contemporary reviewers tended to agree with Zangwill's positive assessment of the novel,
often praising its wit and ingenious plot. For *The Bookman*, 'the mystery
is a good one, kept very close till the end' ('New Books' 166). Likewise,
The Speaker found the novel 'an extremely clever tour de force, elabo-
rated in Mr Zangwill's wittiest manner' ('Fiction' 172). A number of
reviews believed *The Big Bow Mystery* to be a cut above the average crime
story. The *Athenaeum* praised especially its subversive and satirical qualities, terming the novel 'just such a "detective story" as would be written
by a young and clever writer with a hearty contempt for the ordinary
"shocker"' ('Short Stories' 400). The *Glasgow Herald* went further, terming the novel 'one of the best detective stories which have been published recently' ('Literature' 9). In light of Doyle's recent success with
the Holmes stories in *The Strand* – which had helped the magazine to
sell around 500,000 copies per monthly issue – this was high praise
indeed (Brake and Demoor 604).

In spite of its contemporary popularity, however, the novel is usually only briefly cited in histories of crime fiction as one of the first
full-length 'locked-room mysteries', in which the murder takes place
inside an apparently sealed space.[4] This type of story was pioneered
by Poe, used by Sheridan Le Fanu in *Uncle Silas* (1864) and employed
to great effect by Doyle in 'The Speckled Band' (Feb. 1892), one of his
most popular Sherlock Holmes stories.[5] Yet if *The Big Bow Mystery*'s
basic 'locked-room' framework relies upon a detective fiction staple, its
plot, setting and characterisation do not. Despite its unusual East End
setting, its engagement with socialist politics, its satire of sensationalist
press coverage of murder and policing, and the extraordinary fact that
the murderer turns out to be the police detective who found the body,
however, *The Big Bow Mystery*'s significance is still largely overlooked
in detailed analyses of the development of crime fiction.[6] This chapter
hopes to begin to redress its continuing critical neglect by scholars of
the crime genre.

At this stage it will be helpful to provide a brief overview of the plot,
as the novel is not widely known or studied. The mystery concerns the
murder of the upright-sounding Arthur Constant, who is discovered,
apparently murdered, in his bed at a Bow boarding house. 'Arthur
Constant, B.A. – white-handed and white-shirted', had been slumming
in the East End of London whilst devoting himself to the cause of rights
for the working classes and urban poor (207). Constant's landlady, the
also aptly named Mrs Drabdump, discovers his body in the company
of her neighbour, retired police detective George Grodman, whom

she asked to break into her tenant's room when he did not answer his morning wake-up call. Just as with the down-at-heel landlady, Mrs Drabdump, and the 'untiring worker for the benefit of humanity', Arthur Constant, Grodman's name too is pleasingly significant (214). In a deliciously ironic flourish on Zangwill's part, given that the character turns out to be the murderer, 'grodman' in Yiddish translates as 'upright' or 'straight' man (Rochelson, *A Jew* 49).

Constant is found with his throat slit from ear to ear, and neither the murderer nor the weapon can be found, despite the fact that the bedroom's doors and windows are all locked from the inside. A coroner's inquest rules out suicide and the case is investigated by Edward Wimp, Grodman's Scotland Yard successor and bitter rival. Wimp's investigation soon pins the crime on another of Mrs Drabdump's lodgers – union leader Tom Mortlake, the so-called 'hero of a hundred strikes' (208). When it appears that Wimp will be lauded for solving the case, Grodman visits the Home Secretary to offer his confession to the murder. He describes how he had often dreamed of committing a perfect crime that would 'baffle detection' (296). He seized his opportunity after breaking down the door and discovering that Constant was not dead but just sleeping soundly having taken a draught for toothache. He hoped that the story of this perfect crime would provide a fitting appendix to his bestselling memoir 'Criminals I Have Caught', allowing the book to run to a twenty-fifth edition.

Zangwill is now best remembered as 'the Dickens of the Ghetto', the chronicler of nineteenth-century Jewish slum life responsible for the international bestseller *Children of the Ghetto* (1892). The novel was commissioned by the Jewish Publication Society of America to function as a kind of 'Jewish *Robert Elsmere*', emulating Mrs Humphry Ward's bestselling novel of Christianity in crisis ('Israel Zangwill: A Sketch'). The resulting portrait of London East End slum life in the Jewish ghetto was drawn from Zangwill's own boyhood. The son of Jewish immigrants from Russia and Poland, Zangwill grew up in Whitechapel, considered himself a 'pure Cockney', and often boasted about being born 'within the sound of Bow Bells' ('Israel Zangwill'). At that time, Whitechapel was flooded with impoverished Jewish immigrants escaping Eastern European economic hardship and pogroms, to such an extent that the area became known as 'little Palestine' (Endelman 157).[7] The area was also a notorious site of poverty, degradation and crime, the 'quintessence of inner London poverty, the "boldest blotch on the face" of the capital of the civilized world' (Walkowitz 30).

Unlike other late nineteenth-century slum novelists, such as George Gissing or Arthur Morrison, however, whose *The Nether World* (1889), *Tales of Mean Streets* (1894) and *A Child of the Jago* (1896) were notorious for their grim portrayals of the depravity precipitated by London slum life, Zangwill depicted the East End in a more nuanced, less brutal, light. As early reviewers noted, Zangwill's tales of tenements, soup kitchens, sweatshops and strikes are told with wit and warmth. For *The Bookman*, for instance, 'the incessant interplay of fun and melancholy ... is one of the salient characteristics of the genius of Israel Zangwill' ('Six Novels of the Moment' 256). Likewise for *The Times*, *Children of the Ghetto* exhibited a 'careful distribution of shade and light' in its descriptions of 'the mean streets of Whitechapel and the rest of London Jewry'. 'Nobody but a Cockney Jew could have written the books of the Ghetto series,' it suggested, Zangwill 'shows us the niggardly closed fist as well as the open hand; the meanness and the magnanimity' (qtd in 'Zangwill' 33). So too in *The Big Bow Mystery*, the novel that would be Zangwill's only foray into the detective genre, the author creates a nuanced and tragicomic portrait of the late nineteenth-century residents of London's Bow.

The East End area of Bow is not far from Whitechapel, not only the setting for *Children of the Ghetto*, but also the site of the Ripper murders, the nineteenth century's most notorious unsolved crimes. Clearly this is an appropriate location, then, for a novel about a crime whose 'insolubility' would 'tease the acutest minds in Europe and the civilized world' (Zangwill, *Big Bow* 300). Although not far from the City and the prosperous West End, late Victorian Bow was figuratively a million miles away from the 'fancy hotels, mansions overlooking the park, [and] great banks' which form the geographical epicentre of the most famous late Victorian detective fiction, the Sherlock Holmes stories (Moretti, *Atlas* 137). Rather than banks, hotels and mansions, the area housed a large number of factories, including the Bryant and May match works; a number of flour mills, breweries and gasworks; the Great Eastern Railway; and the philanthropically funded centre of culture for the lower classes, the People's Palace. In neighbouring Bethnal Green and Mile End stood the philanthropic settlements Oxford House and Toynbee Hall, from which idealistic male university graduates sought to bring friendship, education and enlightenment to the local poor.

In Charles Booth's 1898–99 Poverty Map, Bow is coloured mainly in the purples that denote a mixture of comfortable and poor inhabitants, but is peppered also with pockets of the blacks and blues which mark the 'vicious, semi-criminal', 'poor' and 'very poor' classes. Booth's accompanying publication, *Life and Labour of the People in London* (1891), likewise notes that Bow is a 'very mixed' area, with 'tradesmen, clerks, teachers, artisans, and labourers, horsekeepers, charwomen, gas stokers and distillery employés living next door to each other' (33). 'The majority of these people belong to a fairly comfortable class of artisans, shopmen and clerks ... commercial travellers and tradesmen, some of them Jews, and a large number of labourers,' Booth explains, 'but there are many below the line of poverty through casual work, thriftlessness, or drink ... [and] others dirty and improvident' (33).

Given the poverty, the large immigrant population and the presence of liberal philanthropic institutions such as Oxford House, it is not surprising that in the 1880s and 1890s East London became known as an area of growing class agitation and socialism. Bow in particular was famously the site of the successful match-girls' strike of July 1888 at the Bryant and May factory, organised in part by prominent social reformer Annie Besant and *Star* writer George Bernard Shaw, amongst others. This successful strike encouraged the growth of New Unionism among workers at the Port of London, leading to the famous dock strikes of August 1889 and the first attempt to organise unskilled women workers into a trade union. Bow would also later become the location for the East London Federation of Suffragettes, formed by Sylvia Pankhurst in 1913 after she broke with the main Women's Social and Political Union. *The Star* had been launched as a paper that spoke to and for these social and political concerns. In O'Connor's editorial address for the first edition he spelled out that the paper was for 'the charwoman who lives in St Giles', the seamstress who is sweated in Whitechapel, the labourer who stands begging for work outside the dockyard gates in St George's-in-the-East'. 'The effect of every policy,' he added, 'must first be regarded from the standpoint of the workers of the Nation, and of the poorest and most helpless among them' (*The Star* 17 Jan. 1888: 1).

On account of this political agenda, the *Star*'s editor sought to recruit young writing staff with politically left-wing beliefs. Its staff in the years 1888–91 included a number of Fabian socialists or committed political radicals including George Bernard Shaw, Annie Besant, Ernest Parke and Sidney Webb. Its editorial focus in these years was very much on issues that affected the residents of East London – Home Rule, exposure of loopholes in the Factory Act (1878) and demands for the overhaul of Scotland Yard and the Criminal Investigation Department (CID), in light of Chief Commissioner Charles Warren's over-zealous policing of working-class political demonstrations. Like most of his fellow *Star* writers, Zangwill was a committed political activist with 'distinctly socialist and communitarian sympathies', as well as a talented literary craftsman (Glover 190). After meeting Theodor Herzl in 1895, the author became the leading British spokesman for the Zionist movement, and later went on to found the Jewish Territorial Organization (ITO), a breakaway organisation committed to the establishment of a homeland for Jewish people wherever suitable land could be found. Zangwill's political activism was not confined to Jewish issues, however. The author was also active in the pursuit of women's suffrage and a founding member of the Union of Democratic Control, a pacifist organisation which opposed Britain's involvement in the First World War.[8]

As he pointed out in 'My First Book', an 1893 article on the beginnings of his career as an author, Zangwill felt that his work should always touch on important social issues, should always contain the 'subtler possibilities of political satire' (635). His first novel, *The Premier and the Painter*, published in 1888, then, was a political satire in which the Tory Prime Minister changed places with a Radical working man from Bethnal Green. In the novel, Zangwill noted, Bethnal Green was presented with 'photographic fullness', 'governmental manoeuvres were described with infinite detail' and contemporary social events were captured in 'Female Franchise and Home Rule episodes' (637). The whole novel, he explained, was intended to offer 'nothing less than a *reductio ad absurdum* of the whole system of Party Government' (635).

Likewise, in *The Big Bow Mystery* – in theory merely a lightweight crime novel for the 'silly season' – Zangwill loses no opportunity to reflect upon the many hardships of East End slum life or to criticise the performance and motivations of London's police (Zangwill 'Of Murders' 202). A background of class conflict, poverty, police brutality and corruption haunts the narrative in *The Big Bow Mystery*, as much as does the 'wraithlike' fog which shrouds the novel's evocative opening passage (*Big Bow* 205). Therefore even a short description of a minor character like the downtrodden landlady Mrs Drabdump emphasises her tragic situation – her experience of serious illness, bereavement and poverty. She is a poignant figure 'struggling through life like a wearied swimmer trying to touch the horizon' (206). She takes in lodgers like Constant, Zangwill tells the reader, only for money and company, having lost her husband to lockjaw, and her two infant children to scarlet fever and diphtheria (206).[9] Mrs Drabdump's predicament is not unusual, however. Another minor character details the multitude of financial pressures faced daily by Bow residents like the landlady and the rest of the novel's main players: 'bread at fourpence three-farden a quarter and landlord clamourin' for rent every Monday morning almost afore the sun's up and folks draggin' and slidderin' on till their shoes is only fit to throw after brides and Christmas comin' and sevenpence a week for schoolin'!' (236). It is surely not incidental, then, that the malign Grodman is also a slum landlord who owns 'several houses' on the street where the murder occurs (210). The fact that the ex-detective draws rent from residents to supplement his already sizeable police pension – 'I had plenty of money and it was safely invested' – would surely have helped bolster his unpalatability to readers of *The Star* (296).

A more comic, but no less illuminating, representation of the local residents' hardship comes in the form of hack writer Denzil Cantercot. The character is a poet with high literary aspirations and ghost-writer of Grodman's bestselling police memoir, 'Criminals I Have Caught'. With this character, Zangwill briefly turns his satirical eye to the hardships suffered by lowly authors when trying to compete in the late Victorian literary marketplace. In 'My First Book' Zangwill had quipped that 'by dint of slaving day and night for years', the literary marketplace might provide aspirant late Victorian authors with 'fame infinitely less widespread than a prize-fighter's and a pecuniary position which you might with far less trouble have been born to' (641). Indeed, the penniless and unknown, yet hardworking, Cantercot would not have been out of place in *New Grub Street* (1891), Gissing's famed depiction of the exigencies of the late Victorian literary scene, which had been published only a few months before the serialisation of *The Big Bow Mystery* began. Like Gissing's Edwin Reardon, Cantercot's life is a continuous struggle to pay the pittance required for his meagre food and slum lodging. Despite the fact that Grodman's memoirs are now in their twenty-fourth edition, Cantercot earns no money from the book's success. The author scrapes by on piecemeal trade journalism for the 'Mile End Mirror', the 'New Pork Herald' and the 'Ham and Eggs Gazette' (241). In the novel, his biggest earnings come from an erroneous tip about the Big Bow murder sold to Detective Wimp for a shilling.

In the immediate aftermath of Constant's murder, Zangwill once again creates a deeply affecting image of the desperation of life for many Bow residents in an aside about the aftermath of the crime. Before the police even begin to investigate the murder, a hoard of casual workers and tramps falsely admit to the crime in order to avail of the free shelter and food that a stay in jail provides. Despite the horror of conditions in jail, 'the number of candidates for each new opening in Newgate is astonishing' (212). Zangwill's sobering inference is that, for many 'poor wretches', a false imprisonment may bring about better living conditions than life in the outside world of the East End (219).

The backstory of the murder victim that emerges after the crime is also used by Zangwill to explore the class tensions that trouble Bow, and their role in precipitating the crime. The victim, Arthur Constant, was known locally as a 'kid-glove philanthropist' – a wealthy slummer who became involved with the plight of the East End poor during a residence at Oxford House (249). After his residency at Oxford House, we are told, Constant moved to the private lodgings in Bow in accordance with his continued desire 'to live in every way like a Bow working man' and 'to share the actual life of the people' (207; 214). Along with its more well-known counterpart Toynbee Hall, Oxford House was one of a number of university settlements set up in 1884 in the midst of East London's most notorious slum districts. These institutions were primitive residential centres for idealistic male Oxford and Cambridge graduates from which they conducted charity work and attempted to form cross-class fraternal bonds with the local community. The basic nature of their domestic arrangements, 'sustained settlers' illusions that they were truly sharing the "primitive" life of Bethnal Green' (Koven 252).[10] The residents of Oxford House and Toynbee Hall, however, were not wholly admired for their sacrifices. Rather, they were often the target of intense criticism from those who 'lampooned their pretensions to become East Londoners merely by living for a few months in a slum settlement' (Koven 259).[11]

Therefore, despite his selfless actions, Constant and his fellow 'kid-glove philanthropists' are objects of satire to Zangwill and to the real East End residents of the area (249). For Mrs Drabdump, for instance, there was '[not] much practical wisdom' in Constant's wish 'to black his own boots (an occupation at which he shone but very little)', to eat 'the artisan's appanage' and to 'concern himself with tram-men' (207). Likewise, for Detective Grodman, who was 'born and bred in Bow', Constant was a foolish and naïve idealist (210). Grodman remembers the man as a 'simple-minded young fellow, who spoke a great deal about the brotherhood of man' without having had any real sense of the hardship of daily life in Bow (217). Evidently much more familiar with the often Darwinian nature of East End life, the ex-detective cynically recalls, 'I ... knew the brotherhood of man was to the ape, the serpent, and the tiger' (297).

With its East End location and scenes of working-class slum life, *The Big Bow Mystery* enacts an intriguing inversion of the genre's burgeoning norms with regard to class and geography. Franco Moretti has suggested that Victorian crime fiction generally takes place 'in the London of wealth' (*Atlas* 136). Although Arthur Conan Doyle's first two Sherlock

Holmes novels took the detective to unfashionable, working-class areas south of the Thames, these works were not particularly popular. In the later Holmes short stories published in *The Strand* (1891–93), which were 'immediately extremely popular', the location had shifted to fashionable West London (135). For Moretti, Holmes new-found success pivots on this shift in location, with which he claims 'Doyle "guessed" the right space for detective fiction' (135). As for the East End, after the adventures moved to *The Strand Magazine*, 'Holmes goes there exactly once in fifty-six stories' (135).[12] 'Urban poverty', Moretti claims, 'is a visible widespread reality, which has absolutely no mystery about it' (137). In detective fiction, by contrast, 'crime must be precisely an enigma: an unheard-of event, a "case," an adventure. And these things require a very different setting from the East End' (137).[13]

It doubtless holds true that crime and detective fiction needs to deal in exciting and sensational crimes, but it does not necessarily follow that readers (either then or now) have no interest in crimes that occur in lowly locales. Quite the opposite, in fact.[14] Neither does it mean that late Victorian crime writers entirely avoided writing about the East End or other working-class areas. In fact, when one examines a range of non-canonical late Victorian detective novels, one sees that in fact there were a number of writers – such as Zangwill, as well as Arthur Morrison and Fergus Hume – whose detectives operated within a less glamorous milieu. And, as such, these novels offer readers an unusual insight into the complicated relationship between late Victorian class, crime and policing within London's poorest areas.

As Haia Shpayer-Makov's exploration of policing in the nineteenth century shows, from the late 1870s onwards, London's police force and detective branch came under increasing attack from the press. In 1877 headlines blazoned that some of the most senior officers in Scotland Yard's detective branch were guilty of forgery, fraud, accepting bribes and warning well-known criminals of intended police action. The ensuing trials, in which three senior officers were found guilty and sentenced to two years' hard labour, were the subject of intense public interest and were covered in prurient detail by the press. The detective department and the topic of policing 'now took up greater space in newspapers and journals than ever before', but this attention was emphatically unsympathetic and 'not to the advantage of the force' (Shpayer-Makov 202). So widespread was public dissatisfaction with Scotland Yard and the CID that the ever-reliable cultural barometer *Punch* magazine soon renamed the detective unit 'The Defective Department' and 'The Criminal Instigation Department' (Pulling 92).

In the few years before the publication of *The Big Bow Mystery*, the reputation of the London police force and detective branch continued to take a battering, particularly from the Radical papers. During the first half of the 1880s, Irish extremists embarked upon a campaign of bombing public buildings on the British mainland in an attempt to force the government into sanctioning Irish Home Rule. Throughout the campaign there were at least 20 successful and attempted bombings, mainly in London, with targets including the office of *The Times* newspaper, London Bridge, the Tower of London and two underground stations. Particularly embarrassing was the attack of 30 May 1884 which detonated an explosion at the offices of the Irish Branch of Scotland Yard.[15] The press was filled with stories about the atrocities, which were read as worrying reminders of the limited ability of the police to protect society.

The force's reputation also suffered in light of heavy-handedness at a number of demonstrations by socialists and the unemployed, most particularly the protest against coercion in Ireland held on 13 November 1887, which came to be known as Bloody Sunday. In the course of the demonstration, held at London's Trafalgar Square, police attacked protesters with batons; hundreds were injured and three were killed. The *Pall Mall Gazette* (whose editor W.T. Stead was one of the protest organisers) reported the incident, in characteristically strident tones, 'London was yesterday delivered up to the terrorism of the soldiery and the police. In order to prevent the holding of a lawful meeting, ruffians in uniform were dispatched to ride down and bludgeon law-abiding citizens who were marching in procession towards the rendezvous' ('At the Point of the Bayonet'). After the events of Bloody Sunday, police incompetence became a favourite topic of *Star* editorials, not just in the ensuing months, but for the next few years. As L. Perry Curtis has noted, 'no editorial voice was more caustic about Scotland Yard and the CID than the *Star*, which could neither forgive nor forget the baton charges of Bloody Sunday' (133).

No event provoked such intense and sustained press scrutiny of the police, however, as the investigation into the Whitechapel Ripper murders of summer and autumn 1888. When the number of murders rose to four (on 30 September) and five (on 9 November) without the identification of a viable suspect, *The Star* ramped up its outrage about the force's inefficiency in a series of daily editorials entitled 'What We Think'. In one of the first of these, the paper opined, 'Whitechapel is garrisoned with police and stocked with plain-clothes men. Nothing comes of it. The police have not even a clue. They are in despair of the utter failure to get so much as a scent of the criminal.' ('Horror Upon

Horror'). As the days passed, murders increased and a culprit was not found, the newspaper's criticism of the inadequacies of the police intensified. As the leader of 18 September put it, 'Public discontent with our present detective system increases with every day that passes over without any satisfactory clue being obtained to the perpetrator or perpetrators of the latest Whitechapel horrors' ('Our Detective System'). On 1 October, with a culprit still not found, the paper declared, 'The police, of course, are helpless. We expect nothing of them. The metropolitan force is rotten to the core' ('What We Think'). The detective branch in particular was described as 'fallible and ill-armed' – a squad of 'men whose incompetence and ignorance are the laughingstock of London' ('Police Alarms'; 'What We Think' 11 Sept. 1888)

In its coverage of the Whitechapel murders *The Star* squandered no opportunity to read the lack of police success as evidence of disregard for the plight of the lower classes. In an editorial published on the night of the first murder, the paper claimed that police brutality against East End residents was a daily occurrence: 'During the last few weeks hardly a day has passed when some constable has not been convicted of gross insult and harshness to some peaceful inhabitant' ('What We Think' Aug. 1888). As the Ripper murders escalated, *The Star* increasingly read the crimes as conceptualising the nature of the class and economic divide in London at the time. As its leader on 14 September 1888 shrieked, in typically inflammatory style, 'Neighbourhoods go mad like individuals, and while the West is discussing the Whitechapel horrors over its wine, the East is seething with impatience, distrust, horror. What a situation!' ('What We Think'). The paper also often flagged up East End residents' anger at the discrepancy between the murder investigation's lack of success and the always over zealous policing of working-class political demonstrations. As the paper's leader on 3 October reported, 'At the unemployed meeting in Hyde-park yesterday a huge placard was exhibited bearing the words: – "The Whitechapel Murders. Where are the Police? Looking after the Unemployed"' ('What We Think').

Alongside this evidence that the police failure with the Whitechapel murders preoccupied the attendees at unemployment meetings, a large number of the letters published in 'The People's Post Box' also demonstrate that the *Star*'s lack of faith in the police was shared by its readers. As Shpayer-Makov points out, after the unsuccessful Ripper investigation, distrust, suspicion and public lack of confidence in London's police rumbled on for the next few years. Disgruntled members of the public often took to the letters pages to express their continuing fear and dissatisfaction; therefore, 'when a murder case was not solved quickly ...

the press was filled with letters from readers ... questioning the ability of police detectives to bring serious law offenders under control' (212). 'An Observer Waiting', for instance, advised the *Star's* editor, 'Sir – You certainly hit the nail right on the head in your Saturday issue on our detective force. The inefficiency of our detectives is quite clear' ('The People's Post Box'). Indeed, *The Star*, more than any other paper, served as 'a crude barometer' of public interest in the Ripper murders and their related feelings about the police (Curtis 59). Notably, it achieved an all-time sales high of well over 300,000 copies just after the murder of Mary Kelly, the fifth and final Ripper victim, on 9 November 1888.

It is right within this post-Ripper mood of police distrust by the lower classes that Zangwill's novel was published in *The Star*. It should come as no surprise then that, in this novel written specifically for the paper, Zangwill chose to foreground repeatedly the brutality and incompetence of the police, in what surely must be a calculated appeal to the sensibilities of the *Star* editors and readers. Tensions between the police and the public are brought to the fore in the novel in a scene of high drama as 'labour leader' Tom Mortlake is arrested for Constant's murder (253). The location of this arrest – at a working mens' club on the Whitechapel Road, where a commemorative portrait of the murdered Constant is to be unveiled – allows Zangwill to bring together the police and players from all parts of the class spectrum and to comment on the highly charged atmosphere of such cross-class events (208). The meeting is attended by Liberal leader and Home Rule supporter William Ewart Gladstone, along with 'several local M.P.'s of varying politics ... three or four labour leaders, a peer or two of philanthropic pretensions, a sprinkling of Toynbee and Oxford Hall men' and a 'densely packed' mass of East End residents (264–5). After Mortlake's shock arrest by Wimp, the polite intermingling of upper and lower classes breaks down; a number of men scale the platform and a 'conscientious constable' wallops an Irish MP 'with a truncheon' (268). As a result of this over-zealous policing, the meeting erupts into a 'fury ... black with staves, sticks, and umbrellas, mingled with the pallid hailstones of knobby fists' (268–9). Shouts rise up from the crowd, 'Boys! ... This is a police conspiracy ... Three cheers for Tom Mortlake! ... Three groans for the police!' (266–7). In the baton charge of the Irish pro-Home Rule MP which causes the breakdown of order, of course, *Star* readers could clearly discern the echoes of Bloody Sunday, a favourite topic employed by the paper in its ongoing critique of the London police.

Flagging up the disparity in how the Conservative and Radical papers interpret such politically charged events, Zangwill presents a number of pastiche headlines on the riot from the Liberal and Conservative press. In its coverage of Bloody Sunday, *The Star* had strenuously put forward that the riot was caused by over-zealous policing. *The Times*, by contrast, reported on the 'heroic' victory of police over a 'vast mob of organized ruffianism, armed with lethal weapons', which had attacked 'civilized society' (14 Nov. 1887). Likewise in *The Big Bow Mystery*, Zangwill recreates a similar disparity in how politically opposed papers interpret the events of the 'Big Bow Mystery Battle – as it came to be called' (270). The riot is denounced in the Conservative press as indicative of 'the raging elements of Bow blackguardism' and 'the pernicious effects of socialism' (287). In an interview with a Liverpool workers' paper, by contrast, 'artisan orator' Mortlake attributes his arrest to 'the enmity and rancour entertained towards him by police throughout the country' (212; 213). Zangwill tells us that Mortlake, 'had never shrunk upon occasion from launching red rhetoric at society' (212). And so, allowed by the paper to wax lyrical about the failings and corruption of the police, the man bitterly reflects on their behaviour, suggesting that the motto of the Metropolitan force is 'First catch your man, then cook the evidence' (212–13). He ends the interview with one final accusation of injustice, exclaiming, 'Tell your readers it's all a police grudge' (213).

The act of police brutality which precipitates 'The Big Bow Battle', and the corruption suggested by Mortlake, however, is not confined to this isolated incident (270). In fact the spectre of police wrongdoing haunts the narrative right from the outset. In the novel's opening pages when Mrs Drabdump calls upon Grodman to tell him 'something has happened to Mr Constant', the detective automatically assumes that the man's work as spokesman for the local tram-drivers' union has landed him in trouble with the local constabulary. He nonchalantly speculates that Constant has been 'bludgeoned by the police at the [union] meeting this morning' (210). Elsewhere, the narrative is peppered with pithy asides that undermine the authority and skill of the Metropolitan force. After the murder, Zangwill, clearly referring to the Whitechapel murders, notes that 'the Department has had several notorious failures of late' (230). Early on in the case of the Big Bow Mystery, when the investigation is floundering due to lack of evidence, Zangwill quips, 'the police could not even manufacture a clue' (219).

Zangwill's portrayal of a police fundamentally at odds with – and even dangerous to – the residents of Bow and Whitechapel must have been designed to appeal to the opinions and emotions of the *Star*'s readers. In making the police force so incompetent, corrupt and unpalatable, though, Zangwill – probably more than any other author in this study – was consciously and fundamentally inverting the still-blossoming conventions of the nascent late Victorian detective genre. Not for Zangwill the creation of the heroic avatars of the disciplinary system so often thought to conceptualise the late Victorian detective genre. Rather, he portrayed a Metropolitan force much more representative of the limited, often corrupt and often unsuccessful policing that the late Victorian working-class public experienced in their daily lives. In doing so, Zangwill's novel illustrates the hugely subversive potential of the genre even as it was still coming into being and the willingness of authors to break its burgeoning conventions for political or satirical effect. In this way, the novel begins emphatically to destabilise readings of late Victorian detective fiction that read that particular historical incarnation of the genre as 'in thrall to the existing social order' and 'committed to the restoration of the status quo' (Horsley, *Twentieth* 10).

At this stage, I want to turn to the intricate nexus of press and public opinion that structures and surrounds Zangwill's depiction of the murderer and the crime. By Grodman's own account, a desire for acclaim and publicity constitutes the motivation both for committing the murder and for his confession. From the novel's outset, then, the narrative of the crime is intimately bound up with its representation in the media. 'Within a few hours the jubilant news-boys were shrieking' about the murder and 'the leader-writers revelled in recapitulating the circumstances of "The Big Bow Mystery"' (212; 226). In an instance of even greater self-reflexivity, *The Star* itself is identified as the first paper to break the details of the crime to the public (212).[16] As it had done in Hume's *The Mystery of a Hansom Cab* (1886), the clamorous press attention surrounding the Bow murder means that the story of the crime reaches and fascinates even those outside its immediate milieu. The news story of the 'Big Bow Mystery' is consumed with equal voracity by members of all classes: 'it was on the carpet and the bare boards alike, in the kitchen and the drawing room. It was discussed with science or stupidity, with aspirates or without' (226). Jokes on the subject 'appeared even in the comic papers' and medical journals; 'the *Lancet*'s leader on the Mystery was awaited with interest' (227). Editorials on the topic appear in *The Star* and the *Pell Mell Press* and the papers' letters pages are flooded with theories about the crime. Like the morning and evening newspapers that disseminated its details, talk of the crime 'came up for breakfast with the rolls, and was swept off the supper-table with the last crumbs' (226). Very much like the Ripper murders, then, the Big Bow mystery is not simply a crime but rather a fully fledged 'cause célèbre' and 'media event' (Walkowitz 191–2).

In the novel, Zangwill goes on to foreground repeatedly this relationship between the crime and the press by embedding a large number of pastiche newspaper reports and letters to the press in the text. Specifically, the novel reproduces many of the developing conventions of sensational reportage which characterised the New Journalistic approach to crime pioneered by papers like *The Star* in the 1880s. T.P. O'Connor believed that the New Journalism practised by *The Star* should 'strike your reader right between the eyes' (O'Connor 434). Therefore, from its inception, the paper became notorious for its attention-grabbing and graphic coverage of crime, which was notably more lurid than that of its more established counterparts. After the body of the second Ripper victim was found, for instance, the *Times* headline reported mildly 'Another Murder in Whitechapel' (1 Sept. 1888). *The Star*, by contrast, led with the rather more unrestrained multiple headline: 'A Revolting Murder. Another Woman Found Horribly Mutilated in Whitechapel. Ghastly Crimes by a Maniac', and the visceral sub-head 'A Policeman Discovers a Woman Lying in the Gutter with Her Throat Cut – After She has been Removed to the Hospital She is Found to be Disembowelled' (31 Aug. 1888). Zangwill's experience as a writer for the paper doubtless helped establish the feeling of authenticity that characterises headlines in the novel such as 'A Philanthropist Cuts His Throat', 'Grodman Still Confident' and 'Horrible Suicide in Bow' (212; 289; 212). In these lurid headlines, and the novel's sensational news reports, stir the echoes of the *Star*'s prurient reportage on the Whitechapel murders just a couple of years before. Indeed, Zangwill's headlines function both as an extension and as a critique of the *Star*'s sensational techniques.

The *Star*'s lurid coverage certainly did nothing to deter readers – quite the opposite in fact. At the height of the *Star*'s coverage of the Ripper murders, the paper became a self-declared 'phenomenal success', with a soaring circulation of over 336,300 copies a day, a 'figure never yet approached by any other Evening Paper in the world' (*The Star* 3 Sept. 1891). In fact, the British reading public had long since enjoyed reading about both factual and fictional tales of murder and the macabre. Robert Louis Stevenson's gruesome *Strange Case of Dr Jekyll and Mr Hyde* (1886) had been a huge seller in the years before and after the Ripper murders. Richard Mansfield's successful adaptation of the novel for the stage was still running at the time that Zangwill's novel was published five years later. One *Pall Mall Gazette* review of the production drew explicit links between its success and the public appetite for lurid crime reportage: 'the critics may curse the morbid and the horrible, but the craving for them is deeply rooted ... If you doubt it, ask the clerks at

Mr Smith's bookstalls' ('Nightmare at the Lyceum' 5). Earlier still in the century, a broadside seller had cheerfully told Henry Mayhew, 'there's nothing beats a stunning good murder, after all' (*London Labour* 237). Later in the century, it seems, this ghoulish maxim still very much applied.[17]

Very much in the populist journalistic mode, then, Zangwill's faux news reports and headlines in the novel reproduce the type of focus on the visceral details of the crime commonly found in press reports on crime and murder – the 'cut throat', the 'blood' and the 'horror' (212; 226). Zangwill reproduces this graphic press coverage of the murder in his novel, however, not simply to emulate the contemporary press but also to criticise editors' willingness to oblige the public appetite for gory details of sensational crimes. Despite his appropriation of their sensational journalistic tropes, then, Zangwill's commentary on the press coverage of the Big Bow Murder is far from sympathetic. His ghoulish observation that, after the inquest, 'the floodgates of inkland were opened, and the deluge pattered for nine days on the deaf coffin where the poor idealist mouldered', juxtaposes the short-lived fad of prurient press attention with the corporeality of the victim's death (226). Zangwill satirises the incessant yet empty speculation of the press about cases of sensational crime in his pointed observation that, 'The tongues of the Press were loosened, and the leader-writers revelled in recapitulating the circumstances of "The Big Bow Mystery," though they could contribute nothing but adjectives to the solution' (226). It seems then that despite his employment at one of the leading organs of New Journalism famed for its attention-grabbing reportage, Zangwill held a healthy disrespect for the apparent glee with which the contemporary press covered serious crime.

Bolstering this rendering of the Big Bow Mystery as a fully fledged, and more than somewhat distasteful, media spectacle in the vein of the Whitechapel murders, the site of Constant's demise becomes a 'a shrine of pilgrimage' for the newspaper-reading public (226). In the aftermath of the Ripper murders, the sites of the crimes almost immediately became destinations of what is now called 'dark tourism' or 'thanatourism'.[18] The term refers to the phenomenon of tourist travel to sites of famous crimes or disasters. According to Curtis, after only the second murder, the Whitechapel murder sites were being visited by Londoners from all social classes. Indeed, several papers from the time carried the Central News report of 'a night tour through the brightly lit thoroughfares and dark alleys of Whitechapel' to visit the scenes of the crimes (129).[19] Likewise in the case of the Big Bow crime, eager consumers of the story came to observe the site of the crime: 'From all parts of town, people came to stare up at the bedroom window and wonder with a foolish face of horror' (226).

Another component of the media spectacle that attended sensational late Victorian crimes committed in the age of the New Journalism was the involvement of readers by way of the newspaper letters pages. Over the course of the nineteenth century, 'the expansion and institutionalization of letters to the editor in the mainstream press' had opened up the pages of national newspapers to the public creating 'a putatively free forum for debate' (Brake and Demoor 359). In the wake of the press coverage of sensational crimes like the Ripper murders, therefore, readers flooded papers with letters voicing their theories, experiences and solutions. The 'great and the good' – writers, politicians, doctors, police chiefs and lawyers – as well as everyday working-class readers, shared their thoughts on the case. For the newspaper editors, to 'reflect and to accommodate the opinions of the reading public' was 'a great selling point' (Brake and Demoor 360). For George Earle Buckle, editor of *The Times* from 1884 to 1911, for instance, readers' letters were 'the most valuable "free copy" in the world' (Kitchin 57). 'Whenever anything happens anywhere, or any topic of interest is being discussed,' he noted, 'the most distinguished authorities in the land will write to *The Times* about it' (57).[20]

From the readers' point-of-view, 'Letters to the Editor' columns presented an opportunity to become 'active respondents ... in dialogue with the publication they read and with other readers' rather than simply 'passive consumers of print' (Brake and Demoor 260). In the wake of the Ripper murders, an avalanche of letters descended upon various London papers, as well as upon the police themselves. A small percentage of this correspondence claimed to be from the killer, boasting about past and future deeds. The vast majority of these letters, however, simply proffered theories about motive or identity and advice for – or criticism of – the police. One particularly prolific correspondent was Dr Lyttleton Forbes Winslow, one of the country's leading experts in criminal insanity, who ran an asylum in London's Hammersmith. From the case's outset, Winslow used the letters pages of a number of papers including the *New York Herald*, *The Times* and *The Lancet* to urge the police to take him on as a consultant. He boasted that his experience with the criminally insane meant that he could surely catch the murderer within a fortnight. By writing to the papers in this manner, reader-correspondents like Winslow 'wrote themselves into the Ripper story' and in the process offered 'clues about their own desires, fantasies, and fears' (Curtis 239). Indeed, so eager was Winslow to project himself into the case that police briefly suspected him of being the Ripper himself (Walkowitz 213).

Just as with the Ripper murders, in *The Big Bow Mystery* Zangwill documents how 'the papers teemed with letters' from readers eager to put forth ideas or solutions about the crime (226). Employing terminology which precisely echoes his editor's request for a sensational crime novel for *The Star*, Zangwill notes that these letters constituted 'a kind of Indian summer of the *silly season*' (226).[21] Zangwill has great fun producing a number of pastiche readers' letters and satirising the types of far-fetched solutions proposed within them. In a doubtless self-conscious acknowledgement of his novel's similarity to Poe's locked-room mystery, Zangwill has the first correspondent – a 'professional paradox-monger' – point out the 'somewhat similar situation in "The Murder in the Rue Morgue"' and suggest that 'Nature had been plagiarising' (227). A 'Constant Reader' responds, suggesting that an organ-grinder's monkey could indeed have climbed down the chimney and committed the crime. In turn, this theory creates 'considerable sensation' and results in a flurry of serious responses on the monkey's methods (227). 'The contest raged so keenly,' we are told, 'that it was almost taken for granted that a monkey was the guilty party' (227).

Also detailed are a variety of 'scientific explanations', involving 'powerful magnets' and window panes removed using diamonds as cutters (228). The theory that Constant's room could be accessed by 'trap-doors and secret passages', we are told, was raised by readers so many times that it was 'as if ... No 11 Glover Street ... were ... a medieval castle' (228). Zangwill's fairly gentle satire on the far-fetched nature of these readers' letters culminates with the more pointed observation that 'Those papers that couldn't get interesting letters stopped the correspondence [on the case] and sneered at the "sensationalism" of those that could' (227). Here, he was doubtless referencing the criticism from more established and 'serious' evening papers of the *Star*'s prolonged exploitation of the Ripper murders as a topic of public debate.

The reason that retired 'great detective' Grodman commits murder is itself strongly related to the intricate relationship between policing, press, public opinion and power that structures much of the novel. In a highly satirical piece of plotting, Grodman confesses that a desire to provide 'an appendix to the 25th edition ... of my book "Criminals I Have Caught"' was his 'sole reason' for committing the murder (295). In the 1880s and 1890s, alongside the vogue for detectives in fiction, a trend emerged for the publication of real detectives' memoirs as full-length books.[22] Well-known examples of the genre popular at the time when

Zangwill was writing *The Big Bow Mystery* include Andrew Lansdowne's *A Life's Reminiscences of Scotland Yard* (1890) and Inspector Maurice Moser's *Stories from Scotland Yard* (1890). This literary genre persisted in popularity right into the twentieth century, with later famous examples including G.H. Greenham's *Scotland Yard Experiences* (1904), Francis Carlin's *Reminiscences of an Ex-Detective* (1920) and Percy Savage's *Savage of Scotland Yard: The Thrilling Autobiography of Ex-Superintendent Percy Savage* (1934). As the titles foreground, the majority of these memoirs were written not by everyday officers but rather by retired high-ranking detectives who had served in the prestigious detective branch of London's Scotland Yard.

For Shpayer-Makov, detectives' motives for producing these memoirs were often a mix of 'self-promotion' and the opportunity to set the record straight about the often mundane and unsuccessful reality of detective work (285). In Zangwill's cynical and politically motivated account, however, this literary genre is clearly motivated only by an opportunity to brag, a desire for money and a need for fame. The 'famous ... sleuth-hound' Grodman had been 'known to all the world' during his stellar career; since his retirement, however, the man has been merely 'a sleeping dog', of no consequence, marginal and unimportant to the police force and the public (296; 208).[23] Desperate not to let his renown diminish, Grodman spends the months following his retirement preparing his book along with ghost-writer Cantercot. The book's title, 'Criminals I Have Caught', is unpleasantly egotistical, foregrounding the arrogant Grodman's singular focus on the successes of his career, hearkening back to his glory days as Scotland Yard's premier investigator. The ex-detective makes 'plenty of money' from the publication, but reneges on a deal to share the profits with Cantercot the writer – one of the first indications of his dishonourable nature (296). Sales eventually slump, however, and Grodman passes time rereading his book obsessively, revelling 'over and over again' in his 'ancient exploits' (296). Zangwill's foregrounding of this mercenary quality to Grodman's character was doubtless once again designed to appeal to the working-class readers of *The Star*. The paper's working-class East End readers would have responded well, one feels, to Zangwill's implication that the publication of police memoirs represented a galling money-making opportunity for members of the already well-paid but often brutal and negligent members of the force.

Perhaps inspired by the dual detective dynamic at the heart of Hume's recent bestseller, *The Mystery of a Hansom Cab* (1886), a fierce rivalry between Grodman and his successor structures the narrative and sets in motion its action. After his retirement, Grodman's role as foremost criminal investigator for Scotland Yard was swiftly overtaken by the splendidly named Edward Wimp, whose cognomen immediately marks him as weak and whining.[24] In his descriptions of the young pretender, Zangwill foregrounds Wimp's similarities to super-detectives of the past and present. In contrast to Grodman's 'slow, laborious, ponderous' methods of detection, Wimp's technique is strikingly Holmesian (243). His skills lie in the field of 'circumstantial evidence' – collecting 'dark and disconnected data' and 'putting two and two together to make five' (243). Over this data, Wimp casts 'the electric light of some unifying hypothesis' and as a result solves most of the crimes he investigates (243). Zangwill here is employing 'one of the commonest metaphors' used to connote skill in detective fiction: that of 'throwing light onto darkness, illuminating what had previously remained hidden' (Pittard, *Purity* 24). In the crime fiction of many of Zangwill's predecessors – Poe, Dickens, Collins and Doyle, amongst others – 'sight' and 'light' are key parts of the detective's armoury, with the detective often presented as 'an expert interpreter of a textualized visual world' (Smajic 6). As Ronald Thomas has noted in his discussion of detection in *Bleak House*, for instance, Bucket is often depicted employing his 'impressive visualizing powers', armed with a bull's-eye lantern and 'casting his light and his gaze upon ... scenes of urban blight' (*Detective Fiction* 131).

So powerful are Wimp's powers of sight and deduction that his reputation threatens 'to eclipse the radiant tradition of Grodman' (243). As Grodman lays out in his confession, he was so consumed with jealousy for the man 'who had been blazoned as my successor' that he decided 'to commit a crime that should baffle detection', solely to dislodge Wimp's stellar reputation and to reinstate his own (296). Yet, despite his exalted reputation, Wimp's professional performance in the Bow murder case in fact falls far short of super-detective status (300). Rather, the young detective unknowingly blunders at every turn of his investigation of the Big Bow Mystery and as a result is the target of biting satire from Zangwill. 'By dint of persistent blundering', and ingrained political bias against the union agitator, Wimp comes wrongly to suspect Mortlake and arrests him for the crime (301).

Despite the fact that this arrest is 'an egregious [and] colossal blunder', however, Mortlake is convicted and both Wimp and the public come for a short time to think of this 'successful' solution to the case as the highpoint of the detective's career (267). Incensed by Wimp's wrongful acclaim, Grodman uses the medium of the press to begin to tarnish Wimp's reputation. The ex-detective taunts Wimp in a series of letters to the editor of the *Pell Mell Press*. This fictional organ is clearly a thinly veiled version of the *Pall Mall Gazette*, the paper in which editor W.T. Stead had pioneered the 'universal interview'. By means of this new journalistic practice, Stead had published the multiple perspectives of readers on sensational events like the 'Maiden Tribute' affair in sections such as a letters column entitled 'What Male Pests Have to Say for Themselves' (*Pall Mall Gazette* 30 July 1885). In his letters to the paper, Grodman draws attention to the CID's 'several notorious failures of late' and cautions Wimp not to make a similar mistake with the Bow case (229). In particular, the ex-detective singles out Wimp's embarrassing inability to catch the Whitechapel murderer, who is 'still at large' (229). Once again, Zangwill's pastiche follows a well-trodden path in recent newspaper critiques of Scotland Yard over its failure to identify the Ripper – the topic had featured incessantly in *The Star* in the three years since the murders and still proved popular with its readers.

If the current detective branch does not 'pay more attention' to its investigation of the Big Bow Mystery, Grodman hyperbolically opines, 'one of the foulest and most horrible crimes of the century will for ever go unpunished' (230). 'It is impossible that I should ever know a day's rest till the perpetrator of this foul deed is discovered,' he closes (230). Therefore the ex-detective urges 'anyone who shares my distrust of the authorities' to get in touch with him rather than Scotland Yard (230). In these letters, not only does Grodman play on the East End's lack of confidence in the police in the aftermath of the Ripper murders, he also self-constructs a persona as a super-detective. His letters are intended to suggest to the public that it is he – and not Wimp – who possesses the superior skills and ability needed to solve the case. In a short letter signed simply 'Scotland Yard', Wimp retorts, declaiming the 'incredible bad taste of Mr Grodman's letter in your last issue' (232).

Once again drawing attention to the extent of the complex relationship between the press and modern crime-fighting, this unprofessional public slanging match between the two detectives in the pages of the press underscores the novel's deeply critical portrayal of the police. The exchange does achieve Grodman's desired effect, however, of reminding the reading public in the novel of his once legendary status. Eager to reacquaint themselves with the detective's successes, the public soon clamours for his memoir, *Criminals I Have Caught,* and the book quickly 'passes from the twenty-third to the twenty-fourth edition' (217). Now a fully fledged media celebrity, the old detective's appearance at the inquest into Constant's death soon thereafter 'excited as keen a curiosity as the reappearance "for this occasion" of a retired prima donna' (217).

Before long he is being interviewed for the evening papers and starring in headlines such as 'Grodman Still Confident' (289). When he visits the Home Secretary's office in the final scene of the novel, the crowd gathered outside cheer and chant his name, 'Grodman! Hurrah!' (291).

What is deeply satirical about this press and public attention, however, is that Grodman of course is not merely an interfering old crime-fighter lending his expertise to the floundering Scotland Yard. Rather he is the murderer, arrogant and complacent enough to insert himself into the case and the media spectacle of the crime, secure in his belief that he will not be caught. Once again, then, this ostensibly comic piece of plotting underscores the novel's much more serious and sustained critique of the arrogance and corruption of the London police, who are presented as more interested in money and acclaim than the mundane work of catching criminals. This critique also takes in the press, however, as Zangwill seems to be suggesting that the current vogue for sensational crime reportage and detective memoirs has set in motion the possibility for ineffectual and corrupt members of the police to become lauded and sought-after celebrities.

In *The Big Bow Mystery*, of course, there is no true super-detective waiting in the wings to solve the case correctly. The real solution is revealed only by the murderer's confession. It is once again Grodman's inability to let Wimp enjoy wrongful credit for solving the crime that precipitates his final desperate confession. In the office of the Home Secretary, Grodman outlines that the 'sole reason' for his confession is the 'unexpected' acclaim that Wimp has achieved for wrongful 'success' in arresting Mortlake for the murder (300). As the old detective tells it:

> Mortlake was arrested and condemned. Wimp had apparently crowned his reputation. This was too much. I had taken all this trouble merely to put a feather in Wimp's cap, whereas I had expected to shake his reputation by it ... that Wimp should achieve a reputation he did not deserve, and overshadow all his predecessors by dint of a colossal mistake, this seemed to me intolerable. (300–1)

In the novel's final scene, Grodman discovers that his confession has been unnecessary. A letter has just arrived which provides an alibi for Mortlake and which therefore also disproves Scotland Yard's ill-conceived theory. As the Home Secretary puts it – with 'grim humour' – 'Mr Wimp's card-castle would have tumbled to pieces without your assistance. Your still undiscoverable crime would have shaken his reputation as you intended' (302). In one final poignant reminder of the intricate relationship between the press and the story of the crime, the 'shrill voices of newsboys' float up from outside: 'A reprieve of Mortlake! Mortlake reprieved' (301). 'Those evening papers are amazing,' notes the Home Secretary laconically, 'I suppose they have everything ready for the contingency' (301). The novel closes on a subdued note with Grodman's suicide, after which his body is borne away by some of Mortlake's supporters gathered outside the office. The downbeat ending here is yet another way, of course, in which Zangwill's novel resists the impulses towards resolution and restoration which are so often read as characteristic of the late Victorian detective genre.

In his article on 'The Future of Journalism' (1886), W.T. Stead makes a direct equation between 'the "personal" mode of journalistic address and the ideological function of the newspaper as an instrument of democratic social change' (Salmon 118). In Stead's populist account of the role of the New Journalism, 'the journalist appears as an heroic figure: a "leader of the people," accountable to his followers, but opposed to the constituted authority of the state' (Salmon 119). It is fitting then that in his crime story written for one of the foremost Radical organs of the New Journalism, Zangwill used the opportunity to offer a forceful critique of the recent poor performance of the police and a broader reflection on the daily hardships of poverty and social inequality incurred by residents of the East End. What is more surprising perhaps is that he also uses the opportunity to comment upon the role of the press in exciting fear and hysteria over crime. Given how ruthlessly *The Star* exploited the Whitechapel murders as an editorial topic, this seems a particularly daring move. The inclusion of these audacious criticisms, however, demonstrates that Zangwill did not intend *The Big Bow Mystery* to be read merely as a frothy novel for the 'silly season' (202). Rather, it should be viewed as a crime novel that makes a serious attempt to capture some of the intricacies of the complex relationship between crime, policing, publicity and the press in late Victorian Britain. In doing so, Zangwill's novel anticipates the work of much later crime writers such as James Ellroy or David Peace, whose LA Quartet and Red Riding Quartets, respectively, offer grim meditations on the relationship between police wrongdoing and crime reportage. It also once again undermines claims that it was not until the emergence of the hardboiled mode of crime fiction in 1920s America that the genre became 'a tool to dissect society's flaws and failures' (Messent 17). Rather, the 1890s detective novel was very much capable of powerful and thought-provoking social critique.

5
Tales of 'Mean Streets': The Criminal-Detective in Arthur Morrison's *The Dorrington Deed-Box* (1897)

In this chapter I focus on Arthur Morrison's *The Dorrington Deed-Box* (1897), a collection of six short stories published in the wake of Sherlock Holmes's 'death', which push the burgeoning Victorian crime genre's transgressive potential to its furthest extreme. After Holmes disappeared over the Reichenbach Falls in December 1893, apparently never to return, many magazines were desperate to poach the readers who had developed a voracious appetite for Arthur Conan Doyle's crime fiction. A vast number of Holmes 'clones' and inversions sprang up in the pages of family magazines such as *The Windsor, The Idler, Pearson's* and in *The Strand* itself (Greenfield 18). Indeed Morrison's tubby, affable – and somewhat dull – detective Martin Hewitt was the *Strand Magazine*'s own swift replacement for Holmes, appearing in March 1894. The Hewitt stories were the first foray into the detective genre by Morrison, a fledgling writer, who would later become known for his grim slum novels. Early reviews of the Hewitt collection were reasonably favourable, yet tended to emphasise Morrison's indebtedness to Doyle's detective stories and the similarities between Holmes and Hewitt. The *Leeds Mercury*, for instance, generously suggested that Morrison's Hewitt tales were 'the only stories worthy to succeed Dr Conan Doyle's "Adventures of Sherlock Holmes"' ('Magazines and Reviews' 3). The *Times* review of the collected stories more bluntly concluded that Hewitt was simply 'a second Sherlock Holmes' (Review of *Martin Hewitt, Investigator* 15).[1]

Morrison's Dorrington stories, however, published in 1897, amplified and took much further the formal, moral and political ambiguity found in the Holmes canon and in earlier detective fiction. Holmes, of course, had provocatively asserted on more than one occasion that he believed he would have made 'a highly efficient criminal' (Doyle, 'Charles Augustus Milverton' 969). Horace Dorrington, a 'private enquiry agent' from the firm Dorrington and Hicks, takes this notion to its furthest extreme being simultaneously both a private detective and a criminal (Morrison, *Dorrington* 18).[2] He is always on the lookout for an 'opening for any piece of rascality by which he might make more of the case than by serving his client loyally' and, throughout his adventures, lies to, steals from, poisons, blackmails and attempts to kill various clients and criminals (65). The clients Dorrington meets are themselves self-serving, corrupt and often criminal, and the Metropolitan police are almost entirely absent. The result is a disturbingly chaotic and unsettling portrait of a late Victorian London pervaded by greed and crime.

While it may seem surprising that the character of Dorrington overturns many of the narrative and moral codes of the burgeoning detective genre, *The Windsor Magazine*, in which the Dorrington stories were first published, set out from its first issue to 'loosen the collar' of moral censoriousness which defined the editorial policy of magazines like *The Strand* (Ashley 223). The foreword to the *Windsor*'s first number sets out its ideological departure from the mid-Victorian values of *The Strand* quite clearly:

> There is no moral necessity for a home magazine to be tedious, to regale the wife with solemn precepts when she wants to be cheered, and the husband with little tales which never touch the strong currents of life ... So the chief purpose of the *Windsor* magazine is to illuminate the hearth with genial philosophy, to widen its outlook ... to make it crackle with good humour which is born of true tolerance, and puts to flight the exaggerated self-consciousness of aggressive virtue. ('Foreword' 1–3)

A feature of the *Windsor*'s fiction, then, was that it should be 'lively and exciting' and that it need not concentrate on the activities of the virtuous. And in 1895 the magazine enjoyed its first 'runaway success' with Guy Boothby's highly sensational stories about dastardly master-criminal Dr Nikola (Ashley 224). The magazine's foreword had also taken a swipe at the identikit nature of the hordes of Sherlock Holmes imitators which were being churned out by periodicals at the time, wryly commenting: 'the world is not yet so completely cured of marvels that every novelist is reduced to evolving analytic significance from the buttons of the heroine's shoe' ('Foreword' 3). It was clear, then, that any crime fiction featured in the magazine would need to present a marked departure from the Holmes analytical-detective model. The Dorrington stories, however, with their frequent touches on 'the strong currents of life' and their highly ambiguous moral position, represented just such a departure and were perfectly in alignment with the magazine's somewhat daring editorial policy and the fiction with which it enjoyed immediate commercial success ('Foreword' 1). Despite this, however, they did not prove a hit. Morrison's only biographer, Peter Keating, has described the stories as an 'unusual, if hardly successful' addition to the corpus of late Victorian detective fiction; and indeed they have all but disappeared from critical accounts of the genre (33).

In the three years between the publication of his first and second detective collections, Morrison gained a reputation as a brutally pessimistic chronicler of London slum life with works such as *Tales of Mean Streets* (1894) and *A Child of the Jago* (1896). The son of a dockland engine-fitter, born in the poverty-stricken area of Poplar, Morrison had ample first-hand experience of East End life. His first job was a secretarial role at the philanthropically funded centre of culture for the lower classes, the People's Palace on the Mile End Road, less than a mile from the sites of the Jack the Ripper murders. This too provided Morrison with the opportunity to study at close hand the living conditions of the East End poor. Three years later, in 1889, he became assistant editor of the centre's magazine, the *Palace Journal*, under its idealistic founder Walter Besant, where he made use of his deep knowledge of the East End. Indeed, one of his first commissions for the *Palace Journal*, a series of sketches of London's East End entitled 'Cockney Corners', published in 1889, show the beginnings of what would become Morrison's characteristically unflinching mode of portraying East End slum life. In 'Whitechapel', published on 14 April 1889, the area is rendered as a 'horrible black labyrinth ... its every wall, its every object, slimy with the indigenous ooze of the place; swarming with human vermin whose trade is robbery and whose recreation is murder' (Morrison 'Cockney').

Morrison left the *Palace Journal* in 1890 to pursue journalism full-time. For the next few years he worked as a typical late Victorian hack of the type described in George Gissing's *New Grub Street* (1891), publishing articles and pot-boiler stories in numerous newspapers and magazines in an attempt to establish himself as a more serious writer. During 1891–92 his comic children's series 'Zig Zags at the Zoo' appeared in *The Strand*, alongside the Sherlock Holmes adventures. He was also a key figure in one of the famous prize competitions run by George Newnes's other publication, *Tit-Bits*. Morrison wrote the detective story 'Hidden not Lost', about 500 buried gold sovereigns, in which the twist was that the money really was hidden in a field outside London. Hulda Friedrichs's biography of Newnes emphasises the lowly status of such hack work, describing how it was Morrison himself who travelled to the field, dug the hole and buried the coins.[3]

The year 1891 saw the publication of Morrison's first book, a now all-but-forgotten collection of supernatural stories entitled *The Shadows Around Us* which caused barely a ripple of interest with either critics or readers. In this year he also enjoyed his first real literary success with the appearance in *Macmillan's Magazine* of 'A Street', a 'quietly despairing' article on the 'mean streets' of East London, which showcased his disillusionment with the idealistic philanthropic work undertaken at the People's Palace (qtd in Keating 20). The article attracted the attention of the influential *National Observer* editor, W.E. Henley, who invited Morrison to expand 'A Street' into a series of short stories. The result was *Tales of Mean Streets*, published serially in the *National Observer* throughout 1893 and in book form the following year.[4] The book capitalised on the public appetite for tales of urban exploration and sensational exposés of the London poor documented in recent bestselling treatises such as Andrew Mearns's *The Bitter Cry of Outcast London* (1883), W.T. Stead's 'The Maiden Tribute of Modern Babylon' (1885) and William Booth's *In Darkest England and the Way Out* (1890). As a result, *Tales of Mean Streets'* semi-autobiographical stories about the squalid lives of 'Outcast London' were an immediate commercial and critical success, with the collection running into several editions and establishing Morrison as one of the leading lights of British realism.

The success of *Tales of Mean Streets* led Reverend Arthur Osborne Jay, rector of the local parish church of one of London's worst slums, the Old Nichol, to invite Morrison to visit the area and write about its hardships. The Old Nichol was an area of 30 streets or so located just off the East End's Shoreditch High Street. It comprised a 'district of barely mapped alleyways, sunless cellars, tunnels and courts, cul-de-sacs, stables, barrows, and sheds', where poverty, disease and crime proliferated (Miles ix). Inside the Old Nichol the mortality rate was twice as high as in the surrounding area of Bethnal Green, in which the mortality rate was itself four times higher than in London as a whole. Morrison agreed to Jay's invitation and the result of his research there was the author's second successful work of slum fiction, the brutally pessimistic *A Child of the Jago* (1896). In the novel the Old Nichol is fictionalised as the 'useless, incapable, and corrupt' criminal ghetto, the Jago (Morrison, *Jago* 11). Morrison's friend and former editor W.E. Henley termed it 'a dreadful book' – not an aesthetic judgement, but rather a sober reflection on its power in conveying the 'dreadful' reality of the slum (Henley, 'Some Novels' 258).

The novel was a kind of brutal late Victorian inversion of Charles Dickens's *Oliver Twist* (1837–38). Dickens had defined his novel as an illustration of 'the principle of Good surviving through every adverse circumstance' (Dickens, *Oliver* vii). *A Child of the Jago*, by contrast, describes in grim detail 'the corrupting effect of heredity and environment on a slum child' (*Jago* 123). The novel's protagonist, Dicky Perrott, born to alcoholic, abusive parents, has 'no reasonable chance of living a decent [life]' – as Morrison puts it, he is 'born foredamned to a criminal or semi-criminal career' (*Jago* 39). Perrott's father hangs for murder and Dicky himself becomes a petty thief who is stabbed to death in a street fight. As with Morrison's later novels, *To London Town* (1899) and *The Hole in the Wall* (1902), the central question around which *A Child of the Jago* is structured is how a slum-born child may escape a life of brutality and crime to become a decent citizen. Morrison's emphatic answer in all these novels is that they cannot.

What's clear from *A Child of the Jago*, as well as contemporary interviews with the author about his work, however, is that Morrison was in no way a radical or 'socialist' writer, as some critics have claimed (Priestman, *Crime* 17). Nor were his slum novels meant to function as a platform for the philanthropic rehabilitation of London's poor and criminal classes. Rather, his representation of the lifestyle, values, physiques and morality of the East End poor reveals 'distaste and a deep scepticism towards possibilities of their amendment, rehabilitation, or redemption' (Miles xxiv). Indeed, Morrison harboured some disturbingly eugenicist views on how to deal with the problem of London's slum dwellers, involving emigration, penal settlements and sterilisation. As he chillingly outlined in an interview on *A Child of the Jago* for the *Daily News*,

> The majority of Jago people are semi-criminal ... Look at these long lists of families going back to the third or fourth generation and all criminals or lunatics ... for my part, I believe ... in penal settlements [for the poor] ... Why not confine them as lunatics are confined? Let the weed die out, and then proceed to raise the raisable. That is why I killed Dicky Perrott. He could not escape from his environment, and had he lived, would have become perforce, as bad as his surroundings. ('Children of the Jago')

On the face of it, *The Dorrington Deed-Box*, a series of post-Holmes short detective stories published in light-hearted family magazine *The Windsor*, should perhaps have little in common with the unflinchingly grim 'mean streets' of the author's slum fiction. Like Dicky Perrott, however, private investigator Dorrington is East End slum-born and seems inexorably drawn to a life of criminality. The six stories in the collection detail the desperation and amorality of Dorrington's milieu, charting, in reverse order, his rise from East End petty criminal to respected and successful, but deeply corrupt, West End professional detective. Dorrington may have escaped the geographic confines of the East End, but his story is not one of heart-warming bad-boy-made-good. He is no heroic avatar of the disciplinary system and his detective consultancy does not provide a reassuring service to the imperilled citizens of London. Rather, it affords him the misleading appearance of middle-class respectability and the attendant opportunity to exploit, cheat or even kill his clients if it profits or pleases him to do so. As such, Morrison's Dorrington stories, like Israel Zangwill's *The Big Bow Mystery* (1891) before them, in which the detective is himself a vicious criminal, forcefully destabilise readings of the late Victorian detective genre which argue for it as an uncomplicated disseminator of bourgeois morality and bourgeois values and for the detective as a wholly successful and reassuring type of hero.[5] In Morrison's stories, the detective's skills are put to malignant, self-serving uses, the detective/criminal binary becomes blurred and the rule of law is almost totally absent, emphatically destabilising the genre's reassuring nature and readers' conception of trust, morality, justice and the way that society operates.

It's difficult to determine exactly why Morrison chose to transgress so many of the burgeoning rules of the emerging detective genre by creating a world inhabited with corrupt private detectives, self-serving (and often criminal) clients and absent official police. He was an almost inordinately reticent and private figure who gave very few interviews in comparison with fellow late Victorian crime writers like Doyle or Boothby. A letter that has recently come to light shows Morrison refusing an interview with a book reviewer on the grounds that, 'I prefer my private concerns not to be written about,' adding cryptically: 'a man has only to make a very small success to make a great many enemies, and the less they know of him, the less harm they can do' (qtd in Newens 37). The author also worked hard to obscure his humble origins, repeatedly misleading census enumerators and interviewers about his East End place of birth and working-class family background. In 1897, he informed *Who's Who* that he was born in Kent, the son of a professional man, and had been educated at private school – information erroneously reproduced in the *Times* 1945 obituary for the author. Perhaps related to this desire for privacy and misdirection, Morrison left instructions for his personal papers to be destroyed after his death. Sadly, these instructions were carried out and we are left with only a tiny amount of Morrison's correspondence and manuscripts.

Whatever the reason, however, the originality and complexity of the Dorrington stories' moral, ideological and formal effects means that they deserve further critical attention. I suggest that their rehabilitation into the canon of late Victorian crime writing could play an important role in the ongoing and necessary critical re-evaluation of schematic or reductive interpretations of the detective genre at this time. This chapter provides one of the first sustained analyses of the Dorrington stories.[6] It charts in detail the multiple ways in which the Dorrington stories invert the nascent conventions of the late Victorian detective short-story genre and examines the effects of these inversions. Specifically, I look at the unusual and unsettling ways in which Dorrington functions both as the source of the stories' crimes and as the supposed provider of solutions to the crimes. Along the way, I examine the stories' depiction of class, crime and geography in relation to their East End location and slum anti-hero. I illuminate the ways in which the Dorrington stories interact with, and at times invert, various theories and ideas concerning the moral character of London's neighbourhoods, fears about appearance and disguise in the late Victorian city, and the mythology of the detective hero as popularised by Holmes. I consider how Morrison's unusual decision to make his detective a criminal fundamentally upsets what are read as the formal and moral conventions of the genre. Finally, I consider the extent to which the stories' generic inversions affected their contemporary reception and sealed their disappearance from the canon of crime fiction.

In the opening lines of the first story in the Dorrington collection, narrator James Rigby introduces himself as a wealthy but naïve young man whom the detective had befriended a few years earlier. Rigby's reliability as a narrator is immediately foregrounded – we are told that he is an 'intelligent' young man who benefited from an 'exceptional upbringing' (3). The reader, therefore, accepts his word about the terrifying stories and revelations to follow. Much of the early action of the story involves Rigby recounting how he had met Dorrington on an ocean liner from Australia to England. Only later do readers discover that Dorrington had approached Rigby as part of an elaborate plan to enlist him as a client, murder him and steal his inheritance. Rigby, then, makes a strikingly unusual narrator in that he is Dorrington's victim rather than his trusty sidekick. With this character, Morrison inverts one of the successful narrative strategies of the burgeoning detective short-story genre – that of the neutral sidekick-narrator. Like Watson, Rigby has first-hand experience of the action, but, as victim, he is much more implicated in the story of the crime than Holmes's partner had been, up to this point.[7]

In his seminal analysis of the formal properties of the crime genre, *The Poetics of Prose* (1977), Tzvetan Todorov famously characterises detective fiction in terms of the use and occurrence of two competing and opposing narrative points of view – the 'story of the crime' and the 'story of the investigation'. These two separate yet overlapping narrative strands can be explained as the story of 'what really happened' and the story of 'how the reader (or the narrator) has come to know about it' (45). Todorov argues that the dangerous action of 'the story of the crime' conventionally takes place before either the detective or the narrator is involved (45). The pages that separate the discovery of the crime from the revelation of the criminal 'are devoted to a slow apprenticeship: [where] we examine clue after clue, lead after lead' (45). The second story, the story of the investigation, 'is often told by a friend of the detective who explicitly acknowledges that he is writing a book' (45). This guarantees the 'immunity' of the narrator who deals only with the dynamic, but ultimately safe, 'story of the investigation' (47). Because the crime has already occurred, the characters in the story of the investigation are insulated from the dangerous narrative space containing the actual crime. As Todorov puts it: 'Nothing can happen to them' (44). In 'The Narrative of Mr James Rigby', by contrast, the narrator is also the victim and is dangerously physically and emotionally embroiled in the 'story of the crime' itself. Investigation plays no part in this first story of the collection – instead the bizarre nature of the crime perpetrated against him is simply documented and narrated by Rigby.

At the start of the story, the friendship between the two men seems innocent and Dorrington appears entirely trustworthy. The ship's passengers all find Dorrington to be 'a most pleasant acquaintance' whose 'manners' are 'extremely engaging' (14–15). Grateful for the company and friendship, Rigby also finds Dorrington 'altogether the most charming person I had ever met', and the pair soon become friends, swapping stories about their backgrounds (15). Dorrington divulges that he is a 'private enquiry agent' who is 'pretty well known' and 'stands as high as any – if not a trifle higher' in the trade than other private detectives, again cementing his appearance of respectability (18–19). Rigby divulges that he is an orphan and that his father killed a robber, who happened to be a member of the Sicilian mafia, on a trip to Italy 20

years ago. He confides in Dorrington that his father was in turn murdered by the vengeful Camorra a short time later.

The full-page illustration by Stanley L. Wood displayed on the facing page of *The Windsor* that accompanies these initial revelations
depicts the exact moment of Rigby's father's crime (244). The dynamic
illustration shows Rigby's father with revolver drawn; the gun emit-
ting a puff of smoke and flame, evidently having just been fired. The
Camorrista is depicted with knife in hand, falling dead to the ground,
his face distorted with pain (Figure 5.1). This bloody and sensational
narrative detail, and the visceral nature of the accompanying illustration, seems to exemplify Stephen Knight's assertion that much post-
Sherlock Holmes crime literature begins to show 'an increased interest
in the grisly and sensational', whereby 'the mid-century obsession with
property as the core of respectable life had shifted towards a central
importance of the identity of the self, and threats towards it' (*Crime* 67).
The graphic nature of the illustration and the anecdote more generally,
combining threats against both property and body, suggests that these
stories will certainly push the burgeoning detective genre into bolder,
more shocking terrain.

Learning about the manner of the father's death, Dorrington advises
Rigby that he fears that the Camorra may still want revenge. When,
on their return to England, Rigby is followed and finds the 'sign of the
Camorra' outside his hotel room door he consults Dorrington (37).
Dorrington proposes that the two men swap identities under the pretext
of protecting Rigby. Rigby is taken to the respectable suburban home of
the Croftings, a 'very trustworthy' couple employed by Dorrington (38).
Believing himself to be safe, Rigby retires to his room with some of Mrs
Crofting's 'excellent' coffee and falls asleep (46). At this point, the grisly
and sensational threats against the body, which had been foreshadowed
by the visceral description of Rigby's father committing murder, suddenly come to the forefront of the narrative. Rigby awakens abruptly in
surprising and dangerous circumstances:

> I woke with a sensation of numbing cold in my right side, a terrible
> stiffness in my limbs, and a sound of splashing water in my ears. All
> was pitch dark, and – what was this? Water! Water all about me. I was
> lying in six inches of cold water, and more was pouring down on top
> of me from above. My head was afflicted with a splitting ache. But
> where was I? ... And then the conviction struck me with a blow – I
> was in a covered iron tank, and the water was pouring in to drown
> me! (47–8)

"His assailant fell dead on the spot."

Figure 5.1 Stanley L. Wood's illustration for 'The Narrative of Mr James Rigby.'
The Windsor Magazine Jan. 1897: 245

In this story, then, far from possessing the 'immunity' postulated by Todorov, our narrator has been drugged, tied up, dumped in a water cistern and left to drown by Dorrington's accomplices (44). The threats from the Camorra had been an elaborate ruse fabricated by Dorrington in order to force Rigby into hiding so that he could be killed and his inheritance stolen.

In the first story in this unusual collection, various inversions of Todorov's ideas on form in detective fiction have occurred. The story of the investigation plays no part in 'The Narrative of Mr James Rigby', instead the bizarre nature of the story of the crime perpetrated against him is simply documented by the narrator. The dangerous action of the crime, which Todorov claims usually takes place before the detective or the narrator is involved, is violently present in this story. The narrator, who is also client and victim, has had an attempt on his life made by the story's detective, who is also the criminal. In 'The Narrative of Mr James Rigby' no character has the immunity proposed by Todorov, and both the detective and the narrator are deeply embroiled in the story of the crime. Rigby, of course, does not die. He goes on to describe his escape and his trip to Dorrington's office accompanied by the police. Finding the office abandoned, he discovers the detective's 'deed-box' containing his casebook and files. Dorrington, however, is on the run and during the course of the collection, he is never caught (52). 'Months have passed,' Rigby tells us, since the crime occurred, 'and neither Dorrington, his partner Hicks, nor the Croftings have been caught' (52). The fact that the police have been unable to catch the criminal-detective and that the law is not mentioned again further works to reinforce the emphatic absence in these stories of the forces of justice and resolution often associated with late Victorian detective fiction.

Until the narrative turning point with Rigby's attempted drowning, readers of *The Dorrington Deed-Box* are unaware that Dorrington is not only a detective but also a criminal. Contemporary reviews of the Dorrington stories, such as the one for *The Times*, suggested that 'people who ... pine for more of Sherlock Holmes with a difference will find what they want in *The Dorrington Deed-Box*' ('Recent Novels' 4). At the point of discovery that Rigby is not only the narrator but also the victim and that Dorrington is not only a detective but also the criminal, however, the expectations of the reader hopeful for 'more of Sherlock Holmes' are shockingly confounded. Rather, the collection pushes the moral ambiguity found in the Holmes stories to its furthest extreme. The ensuing stories continue to provide readers with further insight into the horrors of Dorrington's past. From the detective's abandoned deed-box, Rigby pieces together and narrates some of Dorrington's greatest cases and crimes. Roles and identities further blur and overlap, with the detective, Dorrington, now a fugitive, and Rigby, the victim-narrator, turning detective to piece together Dorrington's past. The resulting five stories reconstructed by Rigby are in themselves a meta-story of Rigby's investigation into Dorrington's past, yet their overall narrative trajectory moves not towards the restoration of order nor to the apprehension of Dorrington and his accomplices. Instead, the stories outline the shocking amorality of Dorrington's universe, charting, in reverse order, his rise from East End bagman to respected and success-ful, but deeply corrupt, professional detective. The stories detail both real detective work alongside Dorrington's attempts to outwit, cheat, steal from and occasionally kill the various clients and criminals with whom he deals along the way.

Early reviews of the stories tended to focus on the collection's simi-larities to and departures from the expected narrative and moral con-ventions of the nascent short-story detective genre. Similarities to the Holmes adventures, then, were generally taken to add to the stories' appeal. On the other hand, however, differences from the Holmes sto-ries, specifically the appearance of more serious crimes and the crimi-nalisation of the detective hero, were found by almost all reviewers to detract from the appeal of Morrison's Dorrington tales. The *Pall Mall Gazette*, for example, initially found that 'the idea of a private enquiry agent who, when it suits his ends, turns round and bites the hand that feeds him, is distinctly ingenious' ('Bran-Pie'). However, in the end, the review objected to the stories' dubious morality and argued that the stories were 'marred by the futile attempt at murder which is dragged in by the shoulders'. The reviewer laments, 'Mr Morrison is always sac-rificing his constructive skill to the demands of cheap sensationalism' ('Bran-Pie'). In the *Saturday Review*, H.G. Wells similarly lamented that Morrison's literary talents were being wasted on a lowbrow medium: 'Just as we have admired Mr Morrison for his "Lizerunt"; we have dis-liked him for his despicable detective stories' (573). The *Times* review of *The Dorrington Deed-Box* solemnly complained that whilst 'the mas-ters of criminal romance ... lighten and brighten their dark webs with threads of pure love and chaste mutual flames ... Mr Arthur Morrison does nothing of this work in *The Dorrington Deed-Box*' ('Recent Novels'). Morrison's detective, the review opines, 'does not ... rescue endangered virtue and demolish crime. He is a criminal himself, and murders or steals, or otherwise infringes the Decalogue, for his own hand.' 'Hence,' the review concludes, 'these ingenious but deplorably shabby romances are hardly sympathetic' ('Recent Novels').

Franco Moretti has noted that, 'in times of morphological change, like the 1890s for detective fiction ... no one knows what will work and what won't' ('Slaughterhouse' 215). For Moretti, then, it is readers, rather than writers, who determine the success of genres by opting for certain forms, and it is the marketplace that settles on those forms that last and those that die away. This argument seems particularly applicable to the fate of the Dorrington stories, which enjoyed many fewer reprints than Morrison's slum novels and Martin Hewitt stories, and have been completely out of print since 1901. Contemporary reviewers were evidently unhappy with Morrison's deliberate inversions of the moral and formal conventions of the nascent detective short-story genre. It appears that late Victorian readers may have felt the same way.

The Dorrington Deed-Box's second episode, 'The Case of Janissary', employs a slightly different narrative strategy from the collection's opening story. On first inspection, therefore, the story appears to be addressing some of the problems that reviewers had with Dorrington's dubious morality, by following a case in which Dorrington has resolved to work honestly. This complex story involves the theft of racehorses, the work of an illegal betting ring and the mysterious death-by-drowning of a number of customers of a bookmaker. Dorrington is asked to investigate the deaths by the owner of the promising racehorse, Janissary. Rigby, the narrator once again, explains that in this instance Dorrington 'could see no opening for any piece of rascality by which he might make more of the case than by serving his client loyally' and that the detective therefore resolves to serve the client honestly (65). As such, it initially appears that this story will follow a narrative and moral structure that more closely adheres to the burgeoning conventions of the detective genre.

Indeed, early in the story, we see Dorrington engaged in more familiar 'real' detective work – he is approached by the client and takes on the case, he then pores over cuttings about the crime from the local newspaper, as Sherlock Holmes often does, and draws upon his valuable store of esoteric knowledge about the racing world (87). Suspecting the bookmaker of drowning customers in order to avoid paying their winnings, Dorrington sets out to watch the man's house. Like Doyle's Holmes, Charles Dickens's Bucket or Wilkie Collins's Cuff, it seems that Dorrington possesses a super-detective's skills of unseen observation and deduction – he is extremely 'skilled at watching without drawing attention to himself' (88). As D.A. Miller has famously pointed out, detective fiction often turns on the importance of the practices of watching and observing: it is 'always implicitly punning on the detective's brilliant *super-vision* and the police *supervision* that it embodies. His intervention marks an explicit bringing-under-surveillance of the entire world of the narrative' (35). More specifically, Miller argues, the detective's skill is his ability to deduce the importance of small, seemingly inconsequential details, 'the ordinary "trivial" facts of everyday life' (35). In *The Moonstone*, for instance, Sergeant Cuff's investigation turns on his ability to recognise the importance of a tiny smear in the paintwork of Rachel Verinder's freshly lacquered door. Likewise, from Dorrington's observation of various unremarkable everyday practices – lights being switched on and off, blinds being drawn and the dismissal of a servant girl despite the fact that there is a dinner guest – Morrison's detective deduces that a crime is about to take place: 'Dorrington thought for a minute, and then suddenly stopped, with a snap of his fingers. He saw it all now' (91). By showing Dorrington engaged in genuine detecting work, and by more closely emulating the narrative formula of investigation-driven detective fiction, Morrison appears to be attempting to make his murdering-detective protagonist more palatable to the reader. However, just as with 'The Narrative of Mr James Rigby', the story's morality ultimately turns out to be deeply ambiguous.

After Dorrington deduces what is happening with the case, and despite his resolution to work honestly, the detective breaks into the criminals' house. Once there, he finds the bookmaker and his wife in the act of drowning their victim. Dorrington does not apprehend the criminals, however, but rather congratulates them on their enterprise:

> that isn't a bad idea in its way, that of drugging a man and drowning him in your cistern up there in the roof, when you prefer not to pay his winnings. It has the very considerable merit that, after the body has been fished out of any river you may choose to fling it into, the stupid coroner's jury will never suspect it was drowned in any other water but that ... as I say, your notion was meritorious. (95)

He then confides, 'I may as well tell you that I'm a bit of a scoundrel myself by way of profession,' before informing the couple that he will not turn them over to the authorities because their water tank is 'too useful an invention to give away to the police' (95). Instead, he blackmails the couple into becoming his partners in crime, musing, 'you and your tank may come in very handy from time to time' (95).

Of course, this is the husband and wife who had tried to drown Rigby in *The Dorrington Deed-Box*'s opening story. In a story that had initially suggested that it might follow a more conventional detecting case, then, the detective engages in blackmail and burglary, overlooks murder, lets the criminals go free and plans to commit future murders. The tale ends with Rigby's unsettling observation that 'The Case of Janissary' occurred three years before the Croftings attempted to drown him in their tank. 'In the meantime,' Rigby asks readers, 'how many people, whose deaths might be turned to profit, had fallen victims to the murderous cunning of Dorrington and his tools?' (97). We are not given the answer to this chilling question. Despite the initial suggestion that this Dorrington adventure may be more palatable than the first story, then, it ends up almost surpassing it in terms of its moral depravity.

Within the context of the 1890s detective genre, already so replete with the counterfeiting and duplication of identities, the Dorrington collection's opening two stories offer an intriguing problematisation of the boundaries between detective, victim and criminal, and between 'the story of the crime' and 'the story of the investigation' – a pattern that continues throughout the collection (Todorov 45–7). The four remaining Dorrington stories – 'The Case of the Mirror of Portugal', 'The Affair of the Avalanche Bicycle and Tyre Co., Limited', 'The Case of Mr Loftus Deacon' and 'Old Cater's Money' – continue this destabilising narrative strategy, as well as further crystallising the collection's recurrent patterns of blurred roles and identities. These stories also give the reader a greater insight into Dorrington's work as a private detective and the manner in which he came to be set up in that profession.

At this point it is useful to jump forward to the collection's final two stories, as these deal with Dorrington's past and the breakthrough case that sealed his reputation as a detective. Only at this late stage does it become clear that Dorrington does not share Sherlock Holmes's cultured and educated background. Instead, these stories chart the ways in which Morrison's criminal-detective has been compelled to better himself unconventionally by employing ingenuity, cunning and criminality. The last story in the collection, although the first chronologically, 'Old Cater's Money', illuminates Dorrington's beginnings as a lower-class ruffian. The story is set in London's Deptford, just across the Thames from Poplar where Morrison was born, where the young Dorrington is working 'at very cheap rates' as a collector for a 'two hundred percent money-lender' (282; 260). When Charles Booth visited Deptford in July 1899 to survey the area for his social map of the city, he classified it as inhabited by the 'poor', 'very poor', and 'vicious and semi-criminal', coded as light blue, dark blue and black on the finished map. In his memoir of life as a Detective Inspector of the Metropolitan police, Joseph F. Broadhurst likewise classified late nineteenth-century Deptford as 'the blackest spot in London at the time' (20).[8] The story outlines the nature of Dorrington's disreputable work – in this case, his attempt to steal the will of the eponymous 'Old Cater' (another moneylender) for his boss. Although the reader is not told the precise details of his upbringing, Dorrington's need to take on this type of criminal work for such 'wretchedly ill pay' assuredly indicates the desperation of his personal circumstances and the effect of his poor background on his opportunities for respectable employment (258).

'Upwardly mobile' Morrison worked his way out of the poor area of his birth and for the rest of his life was eager to obscure his humble beginnings (Gagnier 123). Many of the characters that featured prominently in the naturalistic slum fiction with which he achieved such critical acclaim, however, were depicted with neither agency nor options. In *A Child of the Jago*, for instance, Morrison depicts the situation of the residents unflinchingly and without optimism – the forces of Victorian self-improvement, philanthropy, education and the police make no impact upon the amoral and closed world of the Jago, or the characters trapped within. The novel's central character, Dicky Perrott, is the child of both a petty-criminal alcoholic father and of the Jago streets themselves; as such he is heir to 'a black inheritance' (Morrison, *Jago* 133). His tragic life is wholly determined by his amoral Jago surroundings, which he never leaves and which drag him down into criminality and ultimately to self-destruction and untimely death.

Morrison's representation of Dorrington's slum background in 'Old Cater's Money' represents an intriguing twist on that of his brutally pessimistic slum novels, however. In the final *Dorrington Deed-Box* story, we learn that Dorrington's criminality and cunning (an inevitable product of his corruptingly poor East End upbringing) are employed as necessary methods of social mobility, which facilitate his escape from his slum surroundings. One might view Dorrington as a second Dicky Perrott – but a Dicky who manages to escape (geographically, if not morally) his criminal background. Dorrington's criminality, in 'Old Cater's Money', and the opportunity to escape the drudgery of his life of poverty that it provides, then, represents a kind of worrying inversion of the Smilesian 'self-help' so common in Victorian fiction. This in turn plays upon common middle-class anxieties about the social and geographical mobility of London's lower classes following the Bloody Sunday Riots of the late 1880s, where East End demonstrators marched on Pall Mall and Piccadilly, throwing stones and chanting, as horrified members of the middle and upper classes looked on from the barricaded windows of fashionable West End gentleman's clubs. Likewise, Dorrington's ability to obscure his slum background and pass himself off as a respectable member of the middle classes once again speaks to the same fears about social deception turning on the heterogeneity and anonymity of the modern urban experience which had structured Robert Louis Stevenson's *Jekyll and Hyde* and many of Doyle's Holmes stories.[9]

The next story chronologically – 'The Case of Mr Loftus Deacon' – emphasises the extent of the social and geographical mobility offered to Dorrington by the criminal act depicted in 'Old Cater's Money'. The story opens with Dorrington already comfortably operating as a private detective very much in the Holmesian mould. He has emulated Holmes in making his professional base in the prosperous West End of London, with consulting rooms in Bedford Street, a real street just off the Strand. On Booth's 1898–99 Poverty Map, the area surrounding Dorrington's office is coloured wholly in red – marking it as a solidly 'middle-class' and 'well-to-do' area, emphasising again the extent of Dorrington's social advances.[10] The location just off the Strand is pertinent for another reason, however. The Strand was the city's main East/West artery, uniting socially diverse areas of East and West London that were conventionally considered 'as separate entities with carefully delimited boundaries and distinctive characteristics' (Joyce 36). The office's location here is highly significant, then, suggesting Dorrington's figurative straddling of London's high and low areas and his ability to operate successfully in both.

The story opens as Dorrington is visited at his office by Mr Henry Colson, a retired lawyer, who calls the detective to Bedford Mansions in London's affluent St James to investigate the murder of his friend, Loftus Deacon. The location of the crime – at the heart of the wealthy and prestigious West End – as well as the respectable profession of the client and even the victim's name connote gravity and respectability. Loftus suggests loftiness or elevated status, and a deacon, of course, is a figure of authority in the Christian church. The 'Case of Loftus Deacon', we are told, was the job 'that had helped to give Dorrington much of that reputation which unfortunately too often enabled him to profit far beyond the extent to which his clients intended' (201). Dorrington's successful resolution of the case, a rather conventional locked-room murder mystery of the sort pioneered by Edgar Allan Poe in 'The Murders in the Rue Morgue' (1841), gave the detective 'one of his best advertisements' (201).[11] It is significant, then, that this is the only story in the collection where Dorrington works completely honestly. In this case, which occurred a 'few' years ago, 'there was such a stir at the time over the mysterious death of Mr Loftus Deacon', that 'it well paid Dorrington to use his utmost diligence in an honest effort to uncover the mystery' (201).[12]

The fact that Dorrington works honestly on the case only partially explains why it helps to secure his reputation as a professional consulting detective. The location and status of the crime more closely emulate the Holmesian model: as Moretti has astutely noted, despite the tendency to remember Sherlock Holmes as having had frequent associations with the underworld of Victorian London, the crimes that the super-detective investigates are almost always situated in London's wealthiest and most respectable areas. 'The epicentre' of *The Adventures of Sherlock Holmes*, Moretti points out, 'is clearly in the West End' (*Atlas* 134). 'As for the East End,' he notes, 'Holmes goes there exactly once in fifty-six stories' (134). It is significant, then, that East End Dorrington emulates Holmes in forging his professional reputation with a case in the West End's St James.

Unlike Holmes, however, who rarely leaves his home environment of London's West End, Dorrington is also comfortable and accepted at the other 'End' of the social and geographical spectrum. Indeed, Dorrington seems to be able to negotiate, and flourish in, both low and high areas of the city. In 'Old Cater's Money', he takes on and beats the criminals and lowlifes of his native East End. In 'The Case of Loftus Deacon', he is equally comfortable negotiating with respectable clients, fraternising with Deacon's upper-class acquaintances and ultimately penetrating the mysteries harboured in a prosperous West End villa. The mobility that allows Dorrington to flourish in two such diverse social settings, however, is only used positively in one story – 'The Case of Loftus Deacon'. Elsewhere in the collection, it is employed for the furtherance of the detective's malign plans. As such, the social mobility that might in other circumstances have signalled Dorrington's panoptic powers and success as a detective instead represents a worrying challenge to the possibility of knowing and fixing his social identity. For the socially conservative Morrison, this criminality off-the-leash is what happens when someone from the East End slums moves above his station.

In 'The Case of the Mirror of Portugal', arguably the most interesting and complex of the Dorrington collection, Morrison continues to show the detective's mastery over both respectable and low parts of London, particularly in relation to the ways that he interacts with and exploits his clients. According to W.J. Reader, in the late 1800s, there were still only four safely 'respectable professions': state service, the church, the law and medicine (8–10). 'The root of the matter', claims Reader, 'appears to lie in the feeling that it was not fitting for one gentleman to pay another for services rendered' (37). Indeed, as many critics have observed, the figurative equation between selling one's body for sex and selling one's body for other services deeply troubled the concept of Victorian professional earnings.[13] Doyle worked hard to foreground Holmes's exacting professional ethics, discretion and pecuniary disinterest in light of these anxieties. Watson frequently comments on 'the discretion and high sense of professional honour which have always distinguished my friend', carefully noting the occasions on which Holmes works without charge and does his best to protect the reputations of his clients (Doyle, 'The Veiled Lodger' 1374). In having his narrator do so, Doyle went some way to creating the image of the private detective as a trustworthy expert at a time when the integrity of the police and the detecting profession more broadly was a matter of some anxiety.[14] Throughout 'The Case of the Mirror of Portugal', Dorrington leads clients to believe that he possesses the same skills and operates to the same ethical standards as had super-detective Holmes, but, unlike Holmes, he seeks to gain clients' trust in order to manipulate it so as to serve his own malignant ends. As such, the story goes some way to reignite readers' anxieties about the respectability of the detecting profession, unsettling readings of the post-Holmes detective as a figure of trust.

Doubtless influenced by both Collins's *The Moonstone* (1868) and Doyle's 'The Adventure of the Blue Carbuncle' (1892), 'The Case of the Mirror of Portugal' involves the theft of a priceless diamond of Indian origin – the eponymous Mirror of Portugal – which until recently has been in the possession of French cousins Jacques and Leon Bouvier, who live in London's Soho. The diamond was stolen by their grandfather during the French Revolution, and both the cousins and their fathers have argued since over its ownership. When the gem is stolen, the Bouviers, each believing that the other cousin is the thief, both visit Dorrington to ask him to steal back the stone. The real thief, however, is a third man – a corrupt diamond trader who has learned about the gem from the cousins.

The story opens with Jacques Bouvier's visit to Dorrington's office to seek the detective's help in recovering his stolen diamond and continues throughout to move between Dorrington's respectable office on Bedford Street, the cousins' dingy residence in Soho, the Pimlico home of the actual thief and the diamond market at Hatton Garden, mapping the hidden connections between the inhabitants of these diverse urban spaces. The detective notices the out-of-place 'poorly dressed' Frenchman hanging around the entrance to his prosperous office and employs Lombrosian physiognomic theory in reading the appearance of the man (105). For Dorrington, the client bears what the influential nineteenth-century criminal physiognomist Cesare Lombroso termed the 'stigmata' of poverty and criminality (300). Bouvier's face, Dorrington observes, is 'of a broad, low type, coarse in feature and small in forehead' (105–6). His clothes are 'thin and threadbare, and he has no overcoat' despite the cold weather (106). For the detective, then, Bouvier's appearance provides clear 'evidence' of a number of easily readable physical characteristics that mark him as resident of London's Soho (106). Once a respectable residential area, Soho was vacated after a cholera outbreak in the 1850s and later in the century became a haven for the city's immigrants. On Booth's Poverty Map the area was shaded completely in the blues and blacks of poverty and criminality. In fiction, of course, Soho had been home to one of the late nineteenth century's most famous criminals – Robert Louis Stevenson's Mr Hyde.[15]

Despite Dorrington's own slum beginnings, the physical descriptions of the potential client and the detective emphasise the apparent class contrast that now exists between the two. Dorrington is a 'tall, well-built ... handsome fellow' with a 'military moustache' (14–15). The illustrations (Figure 5.2) that accompany the story also work to foreground the respectability of Dorrington's dress and physiognomy – with his well-groomed moustache and gentleman's tweed morning suit he is reminiscent of Holmes's eminently respectable narrator, Dr Watson, or even Arthur Conan Doyle himself. In this story, then, the technologies and skills of criminal physiognomy that feature so often in the crime genre are employed but are rendered unhelpful as the links between appearance, location, respectability and class are repeatedly blurred and inverted.[16] Morrison presents the reader with an atavistic-looking yet innocent client and a respectable-looking yet criminal detective. That the detective himself disrupts the means of discerning links between appearance and morality so often employed in detective fiction, makes the stories all the more radical in their disruption of the conventions of the genre.

Morrison's treatment of Dorrington's interview with the prospective client references, but once again subverts, the idea of the trustworthy and discreet detective embodied in the figure of Holmes. Once inside

Figure 5.2 Stanley L. Wood's illustration of Dorrington for 'The Affair of the Avalanche Bicycle and Tyre Co., Limited.' *The Windsor Magazine* Dec. 1897: 593 (left). Sidney Paget's illustration of Dr Watson for 'Silver Blaze.' *The Strand Magazine* Jan.–June 1892: 646 (right)

the office for his consultation, Jacques Bouvier explains the diamond's history and requests that Dorrington steal the stone back from his cousin, whom he believes to be the thief. He stipulates that the police must not be involved and that he will reward Dorrington for his service with one-quarter of the gem's value. The client's request implies that Dorrington has a reputation for working outside or against the parameters of the law. Dorrington, however, leads Bouvier to believe that he is deeply offended by his request, and that he in fact operates to the same high ethical standards as had Holmes. The detective hides his displeasure that Bouvier is unable to pay his fee by pretended offence at the client's request that he commit a crime. Dorrington's feigned offence is couched in terms which parodically recall Sherlock Holmes's stern admonishments of foolish or greedy clients:

> You have no money, and you offer no guarantee of your bona fides, and the sum of the thing is that you ask me to go and commit a theft ... and then give you three-quarters of the proceeds. No my man, you have made a mistake. You must go away from here at once, and if I find you lounging about my door again I shall have you taken away very summarily. (112)

The criminal-detective, of course, is not really offended. He has sent the client away simply because he has no money, but Dorrington still very much plans to investigate the crime and to keep the diamond for himself. The narrator outlines Dorrington's planned deception:

> Dorrington was quite ready to steal a diamond, or anything else of value ... but he was no such fool as to give three-quarters of his plunder – or any of it – to somebody else ... the politic plan was to send Jacques Bouvier away with the impression that his story was altogether pooh-poohed and was to be forgotten. (114)

Without respectable status or wealth, Jacques is quite without agency and thus has no power to question the ethics, motives or actions of the outwardly respectable detective. Indeed, despite the fact that he has brought the case to Dorrington, Jacques at this point drops unceremoniously out of the narrative and is not mentioned, apprised or consulted again.

When the second of the cousins – Leon – arrives at Dorrington's office shortly after Jacques Bouvier leaves, Dorrington uses the information that Jacques had previously provided to put on a show of detecting knowledge and mastery designed to dazzle the potential client. Making a pretence of consulting a bulging file, Dorrington regales a bamboozled Leon with information about both his family history, the history of the diamond and details of its recent theft. In doing so, Dorrington leads the potential client to believe that he is imbued with the super-detective's characteristic panoptic knowledge of the city. Following D.A. Miller's seminal work on detective fiction and the panopticon, critics of the crime genre have frequently returned to the 'all-seeing' aspect of Holmes's character (Miller, *Novel* viii). Stephen Knight, for example, attributes Holmes's success to both his 'supreme knowledge' and his 'special and amazing powers' of sight (*Form and Ideology* 72). Evoking these impressive Holmesian demonstrations, Dorrington loftily tells the impressionable Leon:

> It is my trade to know everything. My agents are everywhere. People talk of the secret agent of the Russian police – they are nothing. It is my trade to know all things. I see that you are astonished. Very likely. Very few of the families whose dossiers we have here are aware of what we know. (119–20)

The demonstration of detecting knowledge recalls the impressive acts of deduction often performed by Sherlock Holmes when meeting a new client. Owing to anxieties and concerns surrounding professionals whose capital was invisible, part of the professional's armoury was to demonstrate their respectability, their knowledge and their necessity to the client (Perkin 16). The recurring impressive demonstrations of skill performed by Holmes when meeting a new client, then, might be read as a clever act of self-propaganda consciously enacted to iterate his professional necessity and his worth. In Dorrington's case his ersatz display of detecting skill is not enacted, as was Holmes's, solely to impress or reassure the client, or to demonstrate his all-pervasive knowledge, but rather to legitimise his request for a 20-guinea fee for his work, which he is duly paid. Dorrington is knowingly, but deceptively, emulating the knowledge and skills of the super-detective in order to manipulate and steal from a trusting client.

Dorrington's fake detecting skill, however, is quickly followed by a display of impressive real detective work in which he examines the scene of the robbery, questioning witnesses, comparing footprints to various characters' shoes, and picking up clues from tiny pieces of previously unnoticed broken glass and other detritus. With this scene, Morrison supplies the 'fix' of clue-puzzle-based detective fiction for which readers had developed an appetite with the Holmes stories. The scene closes, however, with Dorrington reverting to criminal rogue. The detective's questions have revealed that Leon shares an office with a trader who can be found at the diamond market on most days. After correctly deducing that the other diamond trader is the thief, Dorrington tells the client that he will recover the gem from the diamond market the next day. Of course, he has no intention of returning the diamond to Bouvier. Walking away from the client for the last time in the story with his 20-guinea fee, Dorrington congratulates himself for easily tricking and stealing from his trusting customers, thus placing readers in a position of complicity:

The stony-faced Dorrington could not repress a smile and something like a chuckle ... the simple Frenchman, only half a rogue – even less than half – was now bamboozled and put aside as effectively as his cousin had been. Nothing stood between Dorrington and the absolute possession of that diamond but an ordinary sort of case such as he dealt with every day. And he had made Bouvier pay a fee for the privilege of putting him completely on the track of it! Dorrington smiled again. (131–2)

When Dorrington confronts Hamer, the real thief, the dialectical spiral of roles and identities in the story shifts again and Dorrington the criminal comes to the fore. Dorrington shows admiration for Hamer's theft, and in contrast to his dealings with the Bouviers, treats Hamer with the respect due to an equal. Hamer confesses, describing how he had tracked and followed Bouvier, turning detective in a way that further complicates and blurs the roles and identities of this story's protagonists. Michel Foucault's famous contention that late nineteenth-century crime writing concentrated upon 'the intellectual struggle between criminal and investigator' is significant here (69). The overlaps between Hamer and Dorrington, however, emphatically destabilise the rigidity of Foucault's schema as the signifiers *detective* and *criminal* become blurred and overlap. When Hamer appeals to Dorrington, saying that they are both criminals and should share the stolen goods, Dorrington reverts from criminal to detective. He explains how the respectable cover of his profession automatically refutes impropriety and trumps Hamer's position as a thief. He scornfully reminds Hamer of his lower status: 'Pardon me, but we are *not* in the same position, by a long way. You are liable to an instant criminal prosecution. I have simply come, authorised by my client ... to demand a piece of property which you have stolen. That is the difference between our positions, Mr Hamer' (140).

With the balance of power re-established, the pair journey to Hamer's home in the prestigious London suburb of Pimlico to recover the diamond for Dorrington. Pimlico was an area firmly coloured either red or gold on Booth's Poverty Map – denoting middle- and upper-middle-class wealthy residents. In a collection that so often disrupts assumptions about the links between geography, class and appearance, the location of the diamond thief here once again foregrounds the idea that criminality is often hidden behind the most respectable of façades. Once at the house, Hamer and his wife make a desperate attempt to offer Dorrington a drugged drink – which, of course, recalls Rigby's drugging in the collection's opening adventure. Dorrington is much less naïve than Rigby, however. Suspecting their murderous intentions, he refuses the drink, threatening to call the police if they do not hand over the diamond immediately. They walk to a nearby bridge on the (somewhat unbelievable) pretext that it is hidden there, but when they arrive Mrs Hamer suddenly produces the diamond from her pocket and casts it into the River Thames.[17] In *The Windsor Magazine* the accompanying full-page illustration on the facing page depicts the moment of the diamond's final disappearance (470). The illustration works to reinforce the shocking lack of narrative closure, which is so often read as characteristic of late Victorian detective fiction. The story ends with Dorrington impassively shrugging his shoulders and walking away, unruffled, and ready to take on his next case and exploit his next client.

Once again, as with previous tales in the Dorrington collection, this story closes with a troublingly amoral vision of late Victorian London. The characters in this story are all criminal to some extent: resolution, justice and the law play no part, and nastiness and self-interest are all-pervasive. It could be argued that the downbeat ending of the story legitimises the status quo by demonstrating that crime does not pay, a suggestion that has been made in relation to the Dorrington collection (Knight, *Crime* 71). Yet in this story and in the collection more broadly, Dorrington does not really lose – he keeps any fees or profits and he manages always to evade the law. He is assuredly better off than the Bouviers and the Hamers, whose low status and taint of criminality prevent them from reporting Dorrington or retaliating against him in any way. The story, then, presents readers with an unsettling view of the metropolis. Appearances cannot be trusted and the story's outwardly most respectable characters – the detective and the suburban diamond trader – are its most deceptive and amoral. The respectable office at the Strand and the prosaic villa in Pimlico harbour vicious criminals ready to steal, blackmail and murder for their own ends. The lower-class characters – the Bouviers – may have connections with the crimes of the past yet have little or no agency to help themselves and they end up being robbed, exploited and dumped by the detective in whom they placed their trust. Law and the police are also absent and irrelevant – unable to prevent Dorrington's criminal enterprises or protect the victims of his crimes.

In his discussion of the late nineteenth-century detective genre, Moretti has suggested that *'fictional crime [takes place] in the London of wealth; real crime [takes place] in the London of poverty'* (*Atlas* 136). In order to be successful, therefore, detective fiction should focus on 'an *enigma*: an unheard-of-event, a "case", an "adventure"' (137). Fans of detective fiction, Moretti claims, want to read about crimes concerning 'fancy hotels, mansions overlooking the park, great banks, diplomatic secrets ... the old London of privilege', rather than the humdrum and depressing criminality of everyday life (137). For Moretti, Sherlock Holmes – perhaps the most popular fictional detective of all – owes his success entirely to the West End location of the majority of his *Adventures*; Doyle '"guessed" the right space for detective fiction' (135).

As one might expect from the author of acclaimed naturalist fiction dealing with the reality of life in London's worst areas, Morrison, by contrast, refuses to ignore crimes associated with the London of poverty. In the Dorrington stories, he follows Doyle in depicting a number of crimes, clients and criminals emanating from the wealthy West End of London. But alongside these, he sets a number of his stories in its poor East End and his detective anti-hero is a slum-born criminal. In doing so, Morrison creates a collection of stories that, although still often sensational in tone and subject, acknowledge some of the grittier, more unsavoury realities of crime in late Victorian London. Alongside the diamond robberies, revenge plots, and threats of stolen inheritance and identity which had provided the intrigue in so many of Holmes's cases, Dorrington's adventures also touch on some of the realities of poverty, environmental determinism and class exploitation that had suffused Morrison's critically acclaimed slum novels.

In doing so, however, Morrison sealed the fate of his Dorrington detective stories to become significantly less popular and ultimately less enduring than Doyle's. Morrison's depiction of the brutality involved with lower-class crimes and criminals within the traditionally entertaining genre of detective fiction seems to have made the collection unpalatable for late Victorian readers. The lack of popularity and their virtual disappearance from the canon of detective fiction, however, is contingent precisely on the factors that make the stories so fascinating and illuminating for twenty-first-century critics and devotees of crime fiction. The Dorrington collection exposes the world as unfair and exploitative. For clients such as Rigby, hard work and correct behaviour are not rewarded with success. For Dorrington, by contrast, disloyalty, criminality and exploitation provide him with a comfortable living and an appearance of respectability. Clients, detectives and members of the public from across a wide social spectrum are all shown to be devoid of moral values and tainted with criminality. Readers are thus left with a troubling vision of the late Victorian metropolis pervaded by crime, greed and self-interest. The official forces of law are absent and the most successful private detective in London is deeply corrupt. For today's

readers, the stories therefore provide a fascinating fictional representation of the brutal, Darwinian struggle for survival in late Victorian
London and an interesting inversion of the genre's conventions.

Ultimately, however, it was most likely Morrison's decision to make
his protagonist, Dorrington, both a detective and a criminal that may
have caused the collection's omission from the canon of crime literature.
Many of the earliest critics of the crime genre 'selected and canonized'
only the stories that shored up their own 'normative' and prescriptive
view of what the genre was (Ascari 3). In particular, they disregarded
works with supernatural, transgressive or unconventional elements. Yet,
for today's readers, the transgressive quality of Morrison's Dorrington
collection appears as a fascinating foreshadowing both of the emergence of the hard-boiled detectives early in the twentieth century and
the popularity of a growing number of amoral anti-heroic detectives
in late twentieth- and early twenty-first-century fiction, television and
film. One is reminded of the corrupt detectives in Jim Thompson's *The
Killer Inside Me* (1952), James Ellroy's LA Quartet or the eponymous 'Bad
Lieutenant' in Abel Ferrara's 1992 movie.

In his seminal 1944 essay on crime fiction, 'The Simple Art of Murder',
Raymond Chandler used the term 'mean streets' to define Hammett's
fictional world.[18] This world, as George Grella would later expand, is 'an
urban chaos, devoid of spiritual and moral values, pervaded by vicious-
ness and random savagery' (110). In this world, no-one is what they
pretend to be: criminals wield political power, police are corrupt and
caught up in criminality, and justice is hardly ever served. 'It is not a
very fragrant world,' Chandler claimed, 'but it is the world you live in'
(236). Whilst Chandler and a number of later critics of detective fiction
might disagree, this hopeless and amoral urban milieu did not originate
with Hammett, however, or even in the twentieth-century American
crime genre. Rather, this too is the unfragrant world that Morrison,
the author who rose to fame with his unflinchingly grim portrayals
of urban slum life and who popularised the expression 'mean streets',
evokes in his Dorrington stories, published at a time when the detective
genre was coming into being. It is because of these important ways in
which *The Dorrington Deed-Box* stretches our understanding of the development of the narrative and moral conventions of the emerging detective genre and anticipates the type of criminal protagonists who would
become such ubiquitous figures in contemporary popular culture that
the collection deserves reconsideration within the crime fiction canon.

6
'A Criminal in Disguise': Class and Empire in Guy Boothby's *A Prince of Swindlers* (1897)

> The London criminal is certainly a dull fellow ... This
> great and sombre stage is set for something more wor-
> thy than that.
> Arthur Conan Doyle, 'The Bruce-Partington Plans',
> 1146

In this chapter, I concentrate on Guy Boothby's *A Prince of Swindlers*[1] – a contemporarily popular, yet now critically overlooked, collection of six short crime stories set in Calcutta and London, which appeared in 1897, the year of Queen Victoria's Diamond Jubilee.[2] Boothby's collection was serialised from January to September 1897 in *Pearson's Magazine*, one of the many *Strand*-inspired family magazines that grew up in the 1890s. The following year it was issued in book form by Ward, Lock, and Co., the publisher renowned for *The Windsor Magazine* (where Arthur Morrison's Dorrington stories appeared), as well as popular late Victorian crime novels such as Arthur Conan Doyle's *A Study in Scarlet* (1887) and Oscar Wilde's *The Picture of Dorian Gray* (1891). Boothby's stories detail the adventures of Simon Carne, an English master-criminal and master-of-disguise based in India, who travels to London at the time of the city's Jubilee celebrations to commit a series of high-profile robberies.

Carne may well have been the first late Victorian rogue hero: the character predates Ernest W. Hornung's more well-known gentleman thief Raffles by more than a year. Somewhat bizarrely, Carne also has an alter ego in the form of super-detective Klimo, who investigates and 'solves' a number of Carne's robberies (therefore profiting from both the robbery and the fee) and various other cases.[3] The collection follows Carne through the planning stages in India to the execution of various robberies and cases he takes on as Klimo while in London. At the collection's close, Carne fears the police may be on his trail, and escapes back to the imperial outpost. Apart from this brief mention of the police, and Klimo's faux-detection, the forces of law, order and detection are largely absent from this collection. Like the other collections and novels in this study, then, Boothby's Carne/Klimo stories once again unsettle accounts of the late Victorian crime genre that suggest 'the criminal is always caught. Justice is always done,' and 'Crime never pays' (Mandel 48). In this chapter, I illustrate the multiple ways in which Boothby's stories illustrate the often overlooked formal and ideological complexity of the burgeoning late Victorian detective genre by examining how the collection maps domestic Victorian detective fiction's themes of investigation and disorder onto wider interrogations of identity construction and safety across personal, but also national and global boundaries.

The crime and detective genres, as John MacKenzie and others have correctly observed, burgeoned at the historical moment in which the internal conflicts contained by the concept of nation were externalised onto the larger field of the empire (204–5). As a consequence of the shared historical genesis of detective fiction and the imperial project, it has therefore been claimed that crime writing is 'often the first voice to respond to new social and cultural encounters generated by the colonial situation' (Knight, *Continent* 25). Indeed, the thematic links between criminality and empire made by crime writers are evident from the very beginnings of the detective genre. In Edgar Allan Poe's 'The Murders in the Rue Morgue' (1841), C. Auguste Dupin attributes murder to an orang-utan brought to Paris from Borneo by a sailor. And in what is arguably the first English detective novel, *The Moonstone* (1868), Wilkie Collins interrogates the malign impact of imperial expansion upon the British domestic world as a 'quiet English house' is 'invaded by a devilish Indian diamond' – the diamond itself having been seized in an act of colonial rapacity (47).

There is, of course, a familiar critical narrative about the Victorian *fin de siècle* that characterises the era as a particularly fraught period 'of mounting complexity and contradiction' with regard to empire (Dixon 2). The Berlin Conference of 1885, the failure of British troops at the Siege of Khartoum, the so-called scramble for Africa, the undermining of Britain's steel manufacturing superiority by German and American competition, and the decline of the Royal Navy relative to the navies of France, Germany, Russia and Italy all underscored the fragility of British imperial dominion.[4] As Patrick Brantlinger puts it, 'After the mid-Victorian years the British found it increasingly difficult to think of themselves as inevitably progressive; they began worrying instead about the degeneration of their institutions, their culture, their racial "stock"' (*Rule of Darkness* 230). As a consequence, popular fiction at this time is 'saturated with the sense that the entire nation – as a race of people, as a political and imperial force, as a social and cultural power – was in irretrievable decline' (Arata, 'Occidental' 622). In some of the most popular and enduring novels and stories of the 1880s and 1890s anxiety about the decline of imperial might is betrayed by a preoccupation with the vulnerability of the centre of the British Empire to various types of invasion, miscegenation and degeneration. In Rider Haggard's *She* (1887), Arthur Conan Doyle's *A Study in Scarlet* (1887), Bram Stoker's *Dracula* (1897), H.G. Wells's *The War of the Worlds* (1897) and Richard Marsh's *The Beetle* (1897), amongst others, distances between imperial centre and periphery collapse as problematic figures repeatedly travel (or plan to travel) from various outposts to wreak havoc upon London.[5] In these works, London comes under attack from a fantastic and gothic assortment of invaders – including cannibals, vampires, aliens and Oriental shape-shifting insects – in which a variety of contemporary anxieties about race, gender, crime and degeneration is fused.

Stephen Arata has termed these types of fictions 'narratives of reverse colonization' (*Fictions of Loss* 108). For Arata these reverse colonisation narratives express late Victorian Britain's colonial fear and guilt. The fear is that the civilised world is on the verge of being attacked by primitive forces, a product of the 'cultural guilt' of a 'troubled imperial society' where 'British culture sees its own imperial practices mirrored back in monstrous forms' (108).[6] Arata does not consider crime writing in his study, yet many of the detective stories of the late Victorian period share reverse colonisation fiction's anxieties about the links between criminality, race, nationality and border transgression. Despite Arthur Conan Doyle's enthusiastic personal support of the British imperial project, for instance, his Sherlock Holmes stories and novels clearly betray anxieties about both the possibility of 'going native', and the instability of distances between the empire's domestic core and foreign periphery.

In the opening lines of the first Holmes novel, *A Study in Scarlet* (1887), Doyle strongly articulates an anxiety about the permeability of national boundaries. Before the super-detective is even introduced, Watson famously describes the London to which he has returned as 'that great cesspool into which all the loungers and idlers of the Empire are irresistibly drained' (Doyle, *Study* 14). London is characterised by Doyle, then, not as the stable and impenetrable heart of the empire but rather as a dirty, deregulated space, easily, almost automatically, permeable to foreign substances and things. The newly permeable imperial metropolitan space resists the possibility of maintaining control of, or policing, the movement of bodies and things across personal and national boundaries. The project of empire, here, is culpable in opening up London to a new type of criminal element – the foreign criminal.

Indeed, Doyle repeatedly returned to this imperial theme in the later Holmes tales; a common feature of stories such as *The Sign of Four*, 'The Speckled Band', 'The Boscombe Valley Mystery' and 'The Crooked Man', for instance, is the appearance of an Englishman who has experienced moral decline in the colonies, becoming more like the savage natives that surround him. This tainted colonial figure then returns to the imperial centre, where his criminal urges or past cannot be suppressed and where he therefore threatens the peace. In these stories, Holmes's work involves the identification of the invader and his attempts to minimise their threat to the existing social order.[7] Boothby's *A Prince of Swindlers* collection, which was doubtless designed in part to capitalise on post-Holmes appetites for short-story detective fiction, builds upon and takes further Doyle's anxious imagining of crime facilitated by the spatial links between the imperial core and periphery. Rather than following a detective's attempts to catch the colonial criminal, thus restoring order to the imperial centre, however, Boothby's stories are much more overtly morally ambiguous as readers instead follow Carne's arrival in the homeland and the successful accomplishment of his crimes.

This chapter follows significant contributions to scholarship on nineteenth-century canonical crime writing and empire in examining the complex and shifting relationship between constructions of nationality, criminality and imperial ideology in Boothby's collection.[8] My analysis focuses on how representations of the colonial outpost, and the related ways in which the stories reproduce or disavow imperialist rhetoric with regard to race and gender, variously conform to or disrupt the usual paradigms by which crime stories explain criminality. I consider how the stories' representation of Carne's criminality engages with a number of contemporary late Victorian theories regarding criminal anthropology, class and race. Finally, I examine how representations of patriotism and nationality work within the stories at times to reinscribe and at times also to unsettle dominant ideologies with regard to national identity.

Often critically lambasted for his 'rough', 'simple-minded', 'careless' and 'unconvincing' production and style, Australian-born Boothby was nonetheless one of the most popular and commercially successful writers of late Victorian genre fiction (Review of *A Prince of Swindlers* 676; 'After Grant Allen' 4). Following his arrival in London from the then British colony of South Australia in 1894, the rise of Boothby's literary career was meteoric. In 1894, Ward Lock published his first novel *In Strange Company; A Story of Chili and the Southern Seas*, which enjoyed modest success. On the strength of this promise, Ward Lock published three more of Boothby's novels the following year. One of these, *A Bid for Fortune*, starring exotic master-criminal Dr Nikola, was wildly successful. The publishers and public demanded sequels, which quickly were supplied, and within a couple of years Boothby was established as a popular and prolific author. An 1896 interview with *The Windsor Magazine* confirms that, after only two years as a professional writer, 26-year-old Boothby was living in a luxurious country house and working on his seventeenth novel ('The Creator of Dr Nikola' 131). The interview describes how, on an average day, Boothby started work at five a.m. and completed six thousand words, dictating the work onto a wax-cylinder phonograph which was then typed by a bank of secretaries. Elsewhere, the author unashamedly admitted to having 'finished one novel in the morning and begun another in the afternoon' ('Obituary: Mr Guy Boothby').

Boothby died in 1905 at only 37, yet in his short lifetime he had managed to 'pump out' more than 50 'delightful shilling shockers' that were tremendously popular with the reading public ('London Theatrical Talk' 7). As an article on literary fashions for *Blackwood's* magazine put it, 'He [Boothby] discovers the demands of the public and hastens to supply them' ('Fashion in Fiction' 533). His most successful and enduring fiction, typified by the Dr Nikola novels, opportunistically blended elements of the popular detective, adventure and gothic genres, and took in crime, exoticism and the occult whilst tracing criminal exploits across various discursive spaces of the empire.[9] As the *New York Times* observed, Boothby's 'favourite locale' was Asia and his 'favourite' types of protagonist were 'persons of tremendous prowess, profound learning and terrible depravity' ('A Guy Boothby Operetta' 4). An article on his Nikola stories that featured in *The English Review*, and which unsurprisingly was quoted in much of Ward Lock's promotional material, claimed that with this strategy Boothby had managed to climb 'ahead even of Mr Cutcliffe Hyne and Mr Conan Doyle' in the reading public's estimation and 'may be said to have topped popularity's pole' (qtd in Warden 318). In a 1901 interview with the *Westminster Review*, also frequently reproduced in advertisements for Boothby's latest work, Rudyard Kipling similarly attested to the author's popularity, stating that 'Boothby's name is large upon hoardings and his books sell like hot cakes' (qtd in 'Contemporary Literature' 712). Indeed, alongside Marie Corelli and Mrs Humphry Ward, Boothby was one of the ten most popular writers of the late Victorian era with a number of his novels and short stories appearing on 16 of the *Bookman's* monthly bestseller lists in the period 1896–1900 (Bassett and Walter 211). While Boothby had his biggest commercial success with the Nikola novels, the *Bookman* records for August and September 1900 show that *A Prince of Swindlers* was 'the best selling five shilling novel' in those months, some two years after the collection's first release in book form ('Monthly Reports').

Whilst his novels were tremendously popular with the reading public, members of the literary establishment tended to focus on Boothby's reputation for quantity rather than quality. In Andrew Lang's 1902 novel *The Disentanglers*, a woman novelist tells guests at a dinner party that she is manufacturing a dozen books simultaneously. A fellow guest's remark, 'Why, you are the Guy Boothby of your sex,' is met with uproarious laughter (27). Boothby's obituary in the *New York Times* likewise underlines the author's reputation for inexhaustible productivity rather than work of high quality: 'Books from his pen appeared with bewildering frequency, and among English authors it has been a standing joke that he invented a machine by which he turned them out' ('Death of Guy Boothby'). Indeed, an unpublished letter from Boothby to fellow author Bram Stoker makes clear that he was aware of his reputation for quantity rather than quality. Boothby enquires of Stoker: 'When are we going to have a new book? Surely it's about time for one,' and, referring to his own literary output, jokingly adds: 'As you may have had the misfortune to observe, I'm still pumping 'em out!' (Boothby, Letter to Bram Stoker 12 Nov. 1905).

It is most likely because of Boothby's rough, careless and uneven style that much of his work, the *Prince of Swindlers* collection included, has until now been overlooked in critical accounts of crime writing. The *Prince of Swindlers* collection, however, capitalises upon the appetite for short detective fiction with both a domestic and an imperial flavour which followed the tremendous success of Doyle's Sherlock Holmes stories. Indeed, this parallel was foregrounded in advertising for the collection and by contemporary critics. *Punch's* review of the collection notes that, 'In *A Prince of Swindlers*, Mr Guy Boothby has taken a hint from Sherlock Holmes' ('Our Booking Office' 110). An advertisement for the January 1897 *Pearson's Magazine* also deliberately plays up the connections between the adventures of Carne and Holmes, advising potential readers that Carne's 'mysterious schemes bid fair to rival the adventures of the now defunct Sherlock Holmes' (Advertisement for *Pearson's* 3). Drawing overt connections between the *Prince of Swindlers* collection and the Sherlock Holmes adventures was most likely a canny marketing ploy on the part of *Pearson's* to attract readers who had developed an appetite for Doyle's detective fiction, but one that was not totally without foundation, despite the fact that the collection's main focus is on a criminal protagonist who evades the law.

Despite the stories' central focus on Carne and his crimes, Boothby also manages (albeit somewhat awkwardly) to insert a number of the formal and moral conventions of what we might call the investigation-driven detective story and to suggest links between the *Prince of Swindlers* collection and the Holmes stories, by giving Carne an alter ego in the form of super-detective Klimo. Klimo, who Boothby tells us, 'has won for himself the right to be considered as great as Lecoq or even the late lamented Sherlock Holmes', is often called in to solve Carne's robberies and other prominent cases, including one in which he saves metropolitan London from a potentially devastating terrorist attack orchestrated from the imperial outpost. While the inclusion of Klimo is undoubtedly a more than somewhat far-fetched plot device (of the type for which Boothby received critical scorn), the author doubtless included the detective alter ego in the collection to broaden its appeal, providing readers addicted to Doyle's detective fiction a 'fix' of this tremendously popular type of story.

Unlike Sherlock Holmes, however, whose character and actions were often ambiguous but who mostly acted out of a desire to see justice delivered and order restored, Klimo is not motivated primarily by any such desire to see justice done. His chief functions are to allow Carne to benefit from both the spoils of the robbery and the detective's fee, to make sure that the police are not called in to investigate Carne's crimes – he refuses to take a case if the police are already involved – and to ensure that Carne gets away with his crimes completely unsuspected. Boothby therefore complicates the reader's anticipated moral alignment with the detective as they are instead made complicit in the crimes by their awareness from the outset that Carne is the thief and that Klimo, the detective, is a fake.

In the collection's opening two stories – 'A Criminal in Disguise' and 'The Den of Iniquity' – which are set in Calcutta, India is repeatedly cast by Boothby as a place where the European self is in danger of becoming morally tainted by contact with its low racial Others. 'A Criminal in Disguise' opens in northern India, where the narrator, the Earl of Amberley, is in his last term of office as Viceroy. As Morrison had done with the Dorrington collection, Boothby also makes the unusual decision of having the stories narrated by Amberley, who would go on to be one of Carne's victims. The collection's subtitle – 'the viceroy's protégé' – draws attention to the pivotal importance of Amberley's complicity in and facilitation of Carne's crimes: it is Amberley who introduces Carne to many of the high-profile Londoners that become the victims of his robberies and the viceroy suffers grave social embarrassment when the identity of the thief is revealed. This in turn foregrounds Boothby's accusation that the project of empire facilitates metropolitan crime, more broadly. The role of viceroy, in real life, entailed being the Queen-Empress's personal representative in India and 'in practice the most powerful ruler in Asia' (Seaman 346).[10] That Carne makes one of the most powerful representatives of empire in India 'complicit' in 'a series of felonies' perpetrated upon the empire's heart illustrates the ways in which, throughout the collection, Boothby plays on contemporary anxieties that the architecture of empire may in part be responsible for London's crime problems (*Prince* 7; 22).

The story introduces the reader to Englishman Carne, but outlines the ways that he has been assimilated into the outpost, resulting in a hybrid national and racial identity. Whilst horse-riding in the Indian jungle, the Indian viceroy becomes lost and is grateful to encounter a palace deep in its midst. Amberley is welcomed into the palace by a native servant and introduced to Carne, 'an Englishman' (8–9). Despite his Englishness, however, the self/Other boundaries upon which Edward Said and others have argued that imperial subjectivity is constructed become blurred in Boothby's initial descriptions of Carne, therefore problematising his national identity and thus raising attendant questions about his morality. We are told that Carne has a handsome, distinctly European physical beauty, yet he dresses like 'a native' (12). His home is a 'semi-European' white palace, but it is surrounded by disorientating Indian jungle (12). He lives in close contact with indigenous people, and employs a troop of Indian servants. He has a history of travel and is intimately acquainted with the geography and topography of the Indian city, slums and jungle. And finally, he has great knowledge of and admiration for native art (12). This conflation of Oriental and Occidental characteristics immediately blurs the boundaries of Carne's national identity and thus, from the collection's outset, marks him as a hybrid creature – English, but also Indian.

Mukherjee has drawn attention to the frequency with which an imperial rhetoric focused on the inherent immorality of 'criminal India' circulated in British fiction and non-fiction from 'the late eighteenth century' onwards (23). In Mukherjee's account, British citizens were led to believe in an essential Indian criminality by way of various narrative accounts written by colonialists based in the contact zone of India itself. One of the first such accounts and one which 'lay at the root of the subsequent construction of universal Indian criminality' was John Zephaniah Holwell's account of the 1756 Black Hole of Calcutta incident (Mukherjee 27).[11] Later texts such as Charles Grant's 'Observations' (1812–13) and Philip Meadows Taylor's *Confessions of a Thug* (1839) stressed to British readers that Indian criminality was essentially different, and less susceptible to reform, than the type of British criminality which was an area of concern at home. Indian criminals, Grant pointed out, 'are not like the robbers in England, individuals driven to such desperate courses by sudden wants. They are robbers by profession, even birth' (63). These native criminals, Grant argued, were not even an aberration to the norms of Indian society but instead were considered an essential and natural part of society, the result of 'naturally criminal castes' whose natural instinct was to 'murder', 'rob' and 'despoil' (58–9).[12]

In *Orientalism* (1979) Edward Said argues that such binary construction of differences between Western imperialists and the indigenous people of a colonised country is a crucial component of imperial discourse. Where Said states that 'the essence of Orientalism is the ineradicable distinction between Western superiority and Oriental inferiority' he infers that the essence of imperialism also rests upon a perceived distinction between the superiority of the coloniser and the inferiority of the colonised, a perceived division between civility and savagery (881). Gayatri Chakravorty Spivak, of course, has famously termed this process *Othering*: 'a process by which the empire can define itself against those it colonizes, excludes, and marginalizes' (107). In the *Prince of Swindlers* collection Boothby not only employs Orientalist tropes to suggest the inherent criminality of the natives but moreover to show how Carne's time in the outpost has led him to assimilate some of their characteristics, and hence their criminality.

For readers in the late 1800s, a hybrid national identity like Carne's would have been a particularly well-known and often-employed signifier of potential danger. In his study of Europeans in nineteenth-century India, David Arnold notes how at this time cross-cultural figures were figures of fear and suspicion. A 'European loafer', for example, who appeared at the Madras Vagrancy Committee in 1867, was described as being 'dressed more like a Native than a European', with 'a red fez cap on his head, and native slippers on his feet' (120). This man, and other such cross-dressed figures, Arnold points out, were perceived as scandalous and as potentially dangerous because by 'going native' they exposed the fragility of the construction of white European imperial identity and its permeability to what was believed to be the essentially inferior Indian morality and way of life (121). On this basis, Carne's native characteristics would have been an easily recognisable warning for Boothby's late Victorian audience of his absorption of the inherent immorality and criminality signified by non-Western Others. Carne is neither self nor Other but somehow simultaneously both, and straddles the clearly defined boundaries and binaries upon which both nineteenth-century national and criminal identity were constructed.[13]

The collection's second story, 'The Den of Iniquity', opens with Carne and Amberley meeting again at the Government House of Calcutta, before Amberley's departure for England. At this meeting, Carne arranges to visit Amberley in London at the time of the Queen's Jubilee celebrations. These plans are soon revealed to be far from innocent, as the story immediately follows Carne's subsequent journey into the city's slums where he visits a prostitute. While with this prostitute – Trincomalee Liz – Carne outlines his plan to use this trip to steal from the wealth collected there for the occasion of the Jubilee. Boothby's descriptions of Calcutta's spaces throughout this story are structured by the geographical and moral contrasts between the disorderly, dirty and immoral native quarter and the quiet, clean, orderly colonial quarters. As Gail Chiang-Ling Low has pointed out, the colonial city is always composed of two separate spheres – the civil station and the native quarter. The aesthetically pleasing civil station is characterised by its order and cleanliness; streets are laid out in a 'geometric' pattern, and its public and private spaces are both 'cool' and 'clean' (Low 163; 159; 165). The native quarter, by contrast, is characterised by its dirt and disorder (Low 165).

In his descriptions of Calcutta and renderings of the Indian topography, Boothby relies heavily on these binaries, thus reinscribing the symbolic boundaries upon which common Orientalist cultural demarcations are founded. Carne's meeting with Amberley – the embodiment of British rule and order – takes place in the 'sacred precincts' of Calcutta's civil station (23). This is immediately contrasted with a lingering description of the squalor of the city's nearby native quarter. This area, Boothby explains, is the site of 'the most infamous dens the mind of man can conceive' where many 'an exhibition of scented, high-toned, gold-lacquered vice' can be found (25). Carne knows the area well, we are told, and has 'been able to master all of the intricacies' of this 'rabbit warren' of 'countless' 'dark ... lanes, streets and alleys' brimming with 'dirt', 'decay' and a 'great number of unsavoury odours' (26–7). Boothby thus creates a topography of the city of Calcutta upon which an inherent, infectious criminality is inscribed. Following what Mukherjee, Teltscher and others have termed the 'imperial mythification' of the Black Hole of Calcutta incident of 1756, the city of Calcutta played a particularly important role in the ways in which imperialists constructed the idea of a particularly Indian criminality (Mukherjee 26).[14] Teltscher notes that 'anxieties of colonial rule surface frequently in accounts of Calcutta' (199). Foremost among these is the fear of 'dirt and disease' and both physical and moral 'contamination and corruption through contact with Indians' (199).

According to Peter Stallybrass and Allon White, in nineteenth-century literature the city was often 'produced as a locus of fear, disgust and fascination' where the sewer, the prostitute and the slum were 'recreated for the bourgeois study and the drawing-room' (191). In such literature the 'bourgeois subject continuously defined and re-defined itself through the exclusion of what it marked out as "low" – as dirty, repulsive, noisy, contaminating' (191). The 'emphasis on dirt', in particular, is 'central to the discourse which traced concealed links between slum and suburb, sewage and "civilisation"' (130). This principle is illustrated by countless works of Victorian fiction and non-fiction, such as Charles Dickens's *Oliver Twist* (1837–38) and Henry Mayhew's *London Labour and the London Poor* (1851), which give readers the pleasure of safe access to the dirt and degradation of the London slums. Boothby emulates the effect of this slumming by reproducing the transgressive pleasure of a visit to, in this case, the native quarter of Calcutta. In 'The Den of Iniquity', when Boothby describes the disorder of the exotic slum streets of the native quarter, he allows the reader vicarious access to the thrilling confusion, dirt and squalor, whilst simultaneously producing some well-known tropes that signify for the reader India's inherent criminality. The threat of the disorder of the native quarter spilling over the boundaries of the civil station is mirrored by the threat of the disintegration of the boundaries between high and low, moral and immoral, self and Other. That Carne is able to navigate the high and the low, the colonial and the native quarters of the city without detection, spatially thematises the dissolution of boundaries that has occurred between his Occidental self and criminal Oriental Other.

Like Carne, Trincomalee Liz, the woman that he has come to the slums to visit, is a border creature – she is of mixed race, she is a prostitute and she is a criminal. This hybrid status and her facilitation of

Carne's crimes immediately cast her as an opponent of the order, justice and morality of the empire. Indeed, Boothby's characterisation of Liz and her surroundings evokes suggestions of danger and eroticism common to Victorian imaginings of the odalisque, an exotic and seductive woman in a harem setting, through which the orient is feminised and fetishised. The odalisque is traditionally an object not only of desire, because of her beauty and sexual availability, but also of anxiety because of the dangers of disease and miscegenation owing to her sexuality. The imperial government, in particular, feared that exotic women would prove irresistible to the British men stationed in the contact zone, and that the British military could thus be weakened by transmission of venereal disease. This fear led to the Contagious Diseases Act of 1864, which was passed in order to curb the effects of sexually transmitted diseases on soldiers stationed in garrison towns.[15] As a result, the figure of the odalisque, simultaneously desired and feared by the white male, became one of the central tropes of nineteenth- and early twentieth-century colonial fiction, such as Bram Stoker's *The Jewel of Seven Stars* (1903), featuring the beautiful but vampiric mummy of Egyptian Queen Tera, who avenges the rape of her tomb by a British archaeologist (Pal-Lapinski xvi).

Boothby rehearses anxieties about the figure of the odalisque, sexual contact and miscegenation firstly by detailing Trincomalee Liz's mixed race and describing the sexual power of her Indian mother – a courtesan herself, who 'was lovelier than the pale hibiscus blossom' and who used her charms to snare an Italian Count (28–9). The temptation of Liz's own sexuality and its inherent danger are indicated for the reader by her apartment's furnishings – with its hookah pipe 'curled up ... in a fashion somewhat suggestive of a snake' connoting both sexuality and danger, and the 'comfortable divans ... inviting repose' more blatantly suggesting the potential for sexual congress (28). The two illustrations of Liz, which appear in the periodical edition of the text, again emphasise this tension between desirability and danger. The first shows Liz poised against an exotic and luxurious backdrop, her passive stance inviting the male gaze (Figure 6.1). The second depicts her lounging indecorously on a divan next to Carne.

The dangerous consequences of Liz's sexual power are more explicitly outlined in Boothby's prurient revelation that she was 'notorious from the Saghalian Coast to the shores of the Persian Gulf' and that 'those tiny hands had ruined more men than any other half-dozen pairs in the whole of India' (28). Boothby here links the disruptive potential of Trincomalee Liz's sexual power upon the orderly lives of many Western

A second later Trincomalee Liz entered the room.

Figure 6.1 E.F. Skinner's illustration for 'The Den of Iniquity.' *Pearson's Magazine* Jan.–June 1897: 14

men with the wider disruptive power of the native upon the settler. In this story, however, Liz's power is not employed in an overtly sexual manner: instead Boothby focuses on how her power affords her the resources to obtain 50 thousand pounds for Carne by the following midday. It also enables her to find and secure the services of Hiram Singh and Wajib Baksh, 'the most expert craftsmen in India', who will accompany Carne to England to pose as servants and help him carry out his criminal plan; to evade the law herself; and to identify the law and warn Carne that it may be on his trail (32). Liz disappears from the rest of the collection before reappearing in the penultimate story where she sends Carne a telegram warning him that the law, in the figure of an Inspector Bradfield, has tracked him from India and is en route to London to perform his arrest.

The characterisations of Trincomalee Liz, and the Indian city, then, reinscribe many of the usual paradigms by which colonial crime and adventure stories explain criminality. Like Doyle's colonial detective fiction they play on contemporary fears about the mysteries and dangers that originate from the imperial outpost. In line with Doyle's detective stories, Boothby's representations of the colonial outpost and its native inhabitants reproduce many Orientalist depictions of India's inherent lasciviousness, dirtiness and criminality, and contrast these with the inherent order and morality of the English – like Amberley and the civil station. Boothby also begins to disrupt these paradigms, however. In contrast to Doyle's colonial Holmes stories, Boothby does not provide a main protagonist with the ability to bring order to the inherently criminal natives, to prevent non-natives stationed in the outpost from becoming tainted by its criminality, or to solve mysteries that originate outside national borders. Instead Boothby's hero Carne is himself an Occidental gone native, not a detective but a thief who is in cahoots with one of the most dangerous native types – an exotic and criminal female. This story therefore begins to suggest that while imperial rhetoric posits the natural superiority and civilising ethos of the colonising race, the discursive economy of the imperial project can operate in two directions. English characters, then, are just as likely to experience a moral decline while stationed in the outpost as to civilise the unregenerate natives with whom they are surrounded. The worrying implication for the stories' readers is that such characters are then free to travel to the imperial centre and to infect it with their criminality.

As Joseph McLaughlin has noted, in late Victorian fiction, 'describing people, places and experiences on the periphery of empire' is often employed as 'an effective narrative strategy for imagining the imperial centre' (1). Readers of Conrad's *Heart of Darkness*, for example, have long since realised that the novel's title refers to the darkness not just at the heart of the Belgian Congo but also at the heart of imperial London. Doyle's earlier identification of the spatial and moral relationship between the imperial centre and outpost, in *A Study in Scarlet* (1887), had been similarly negative. For Doyle, London was not the beating heart of the empire, but rather a stagnant 'cesspool' into which the dregs of the empire inevitably sank (14). As Ronald Thomas and Yumna Siddiqi have correctly observed, the Sherlock Holmes novels and stories return frequently to the theme of English characters experiencing moral decline in the colonies by becoming more like the criminal natives who surround them. In *The Sign of Four*, for instance, Jonathan Small and Captains Morstan and Sholto are tempted and embroiled in a criminal plot initiated by a pair of immoral Sikh guards (55). A common feature of the later Holmes adventures such as 'The Speckled Band', 'The Boscombe Valley Mystery' and 'The Crooked Man', amongst others, is the return of a tainted colonial figure to the imperial centre, where their criminal urges or pasts cannot be suppressed and they therefore threaten the peace.[16] In 'The Boscombe Valley Mystery', for instance, John Turner and Charles McCarthy are both men who have been corrupted by their time in the colonies. On their return to the homeland, the men are haunted by the criminality they indulged in at the outpost and cannot be assimilated into a life of lawfulness. Doyle, of course, was well known to be an enthusiastic supporter of the imperial project, a view which is borne out in his characterisation of natives as savage and in the related moral decline of English characters in the outpost.[17] Turner and McCarthy's return to the social order of the imperial centre at least equivocally, if not intentionally, however, expresses the negative consequences of time spent in the imperial outpost and the increased permeability of borders as a consequence of the imperial project.

Similarly, in the remainder of the *Prince of Swindlers* collection, the links between criminality and empire established in the collection's opening stories construct imperial London as a place vulnerable to and easily permeable by foreign criminals. In the remaining stories, Boothby foregrounds and brings together the issues of empire, nation, detection, order, invasion and crime as the reader learns about the victims and enactment of Carne's crimes in the metropolis at the time of Queen Victoria's Diamond Jubilee. The stories thus reproduce and build on Doyle's construction of imperial London as a collection point for the dregs of the empire and his motif of the return of the colonial male who has been tainted by criminality in the outpost. Rather than following a detective's attempts to catch the colonial criminal, however, thus restoring order to the imperial centre, Boothby's readers instead follow colonial criminal Carne's arrival in the homeland and the successful accomplishment of his crimes. The collection's remaining stories are structured around a series of invasions: the invasion of London by new cultures, in the form of hybrid Carne and his Oriental accomplices; Carne's burglaries of the homes of a series of millionaires; Klimo's invasion of these same homes as faux-detective; and the threat of an attack on London from a group of Irish-American terrorists.

The year of Queen Victoria's Diamond Jubilee was 'marked by considerably more introspection and less self-congratulation than the [jubilee] celebration of a decade earlier' (Arata, 'Occidental' 622). A number of critics have argued that the countless street parties, processions, balls and shows put on to celebrate the Diamond Jubilee were merely 'a gigantic confidence trick' carried out to distract from 'Britain's faltering great power status' and to attempt to boost 'flagging national morale' (Judd 140). Indeed, this was a year when even leading public figures appeared to admit, if not concede, that imperial confidence was on the wane: Kipling's 'Recessional', composed on the occasion of Victoria's Diamond Jubilee, famously suggested that 'all our pomp of yesterday / Is one with Nineveh and Tyre!' and saw 'our navies melt away' (13–15). Likewise, in his first ever political speech, given after his return from India in July 1897, a young Winston Churchill spoke about the public perception that 'in this Jubilee year our Empire ha[s] reached the height of its glory and power, and that now we should begin to decline, as Babylon, Carthage, and Rome have declined' (Churchill 774).

It is significant then that this year saw the publication of a large number of paradigmatic 'reverse colonization narratives' where distances between imperial centre and periphery collapse as a variety of cannibals, vampires and other gothic outsiders travel from various outposts to wreak havoc upon London (Arata, *Fictions of Loss* 108). In Bram Stoker's *Dracula*, H.G. Wells's *The War of the Worlds* and Richard Marsh's bestseller *The Beetle*, the imperial centre comes under attack from a fantastic assortment of invaders that rehearse a number of contemporary anxieties about race, empire and crime.[18] For Arata, these reverse colonisation narratives, which see 'the "civilised" world ... on the point of being colonised by "primitive" forces', express late Victorian Britain's colonial fear and guilt ('Occidental' 623). The fear is that the civilised world is on the verge of being attacked by primitive forces, a product of the 'cultural guilt' of a 'troubled imperial society' where 'British culture sees its own imperial practices mirrored back in monstrous forms' (623).

Despite the largely patriotic and even jingoistic nature of much of its material, *Pearson's* magazine's features and fiction from 1897 betray many late Victorian fears and anxieties about declining imperial strength through a shared thematic focus on the contemporary invasion of Britain's imperial centre.[19] Published for the first time in the same issues as the *Prince of Swindlers* collection, there is perhaps the most chilling and enduring narrative of reverse colonisation, H.G. Wells's *War of the Worlds*, which sees London attacked and destroyed by Martian invaders.[20] Besides these, the 1897 issues of *Pearson's* also contain 'Donald Penstone's Escape', a detective story by V.L. Whitchurch, which describes the attack on London and subsequent escape to Australia of a notorious Fenian dynamiter. Even a factual article on the work of the Thames river police (much in the same vein as *Strand Magazine's* earlier 'A Night with the Thames Police') is framed to focus on the potential for accelerated levels of crime in the Jubilee metropolis resulting from the increased permeability of imperial borders at London's docks.

The Thames river police article, published in January 1897, opens by describing the problems of London's 'river piracy', which results in the robbery of goods worth 'more than a third of a million per annum', mostly from West Indian merchants (Du Plat 18). It moves on to detail the prevalence of smuggling, not only of tobacco, but also of explosives, jewels and criminals. The 'worst offenders', we are told, are 'the crews of a well-known line of packets trading with such ports as Hamburg, Rotterdam, Bordeaux and Ghent' (22). The 'most sensational' recent crime facilitated by the river, however, was an 'attempt to blow up London Bridge' (23). Two suspicious men had hired a boat and a little later there was an explosion at the bridge, but no one was apprehended. The perpetrators 'disappeared' and the boat 'was never seen again', the Thames police superintendent explains (23). The unsettling implication of this article for the reader is that, owing to the flow of goods and people in and out of London's docks, many other criminal enterprises will go on unheeded and undetected.

'The Duchess of Wiltshire's Diamonds', the third episode in the collection, published in the following edition of *Pearson's*, plays on many of the same fears about foreign criminality and smuggling raised in the Thames police article. The story opens with Carne's successful penetration of the worryingly permeable boundaries of the imperial metropolis, as he arrives in Jubilee London from India by sea.[21] The imperial centre, Boothby suggests, will host many criminals wanting to prey upon the wealthy gathered in the metropolis for the Jubilee. Building upon

Doyle's imagining of late Victorian London as the 'cesspool' of empire (*Study* 14), Boothby describes how the 'joyous occasion' of the Jubilee celebrations which 'filled our hotels to repletion, and produced daily pageants the like of which few of us have ever seen or imagined' also 'attracted swindlers from all parts of the globe' (Boothby, *Prince* 7–8). The story follows Carne's penetration of Amberley's influential London social circle. Carne uses his position of trust to gain access to and steal the duchess's diamond necklace, which is valued at 50 thousand pounds, and which he has promised to Trincomalee Liz as a gift for her help with his plan.

In 'The Duchess of Wiltshire's Diamonds', Boothby demonstrates how appearances can be manipulated in order to hide criminality, to exploit the trust of clients and thus to facilitate the penetration of clients' homes and lives. Whilst in India, Carne's criminal status was highlighted by his native dress, his knowledge of local art, his familiarity with Calcutta's low quarters and his consort with local criminals. Once in the imperial centre, however, these native characteristics are replaced with Western dress, home, servants, hobbies and manners. Thus, Carne's colonial invasion of London is framed and hidden by the civilised and familiar. He mirrors the behaviours and appearances of the group he wishes to infiltrate and so assumes the trappings and demeanour of a typical wealthy English gentleman – living in a Park Lane mansion, travelling by 'luxurious brougham', buying a yacht and a racehorse, attending the opera, Jubilee balls, charity events and gentlemen's clubs, and employing a 'grave and respectable' English valet to augment his group of exotic servants (43; 40). These signifiers of an outwardly respectable London life fool his peers into believing that he should share their 'distinguished position in the social life of the world's greatest metropolis' (43). 'Within twenty-four hours' of Carne's arrival in Britain, we are told, he 'was the talk, not only of fashionable, but also of unfashionable, London' (42). Amberley and his wife are 'brimming over with praise' for Carne; likewise the Duchess of Wiltshire is 'charmed' by Carne and is 'full of his praises' (42). Yet, behind the conventional façade of his respectable outward appearance and home, Carne creates an oasis of Oriental art and craft: his Park Lane townhouse is filled with imported Eastern commodities, and is staffed by Indian servants, signifying his lingering Otherness and criminality. We, as readers, alone are privy to the fact that this lifestyle is funded by ill-gained money, obtained by a foreign prostitute in the imperial outpost, and that he harbours criminal plans. Detective fiction's common tropes of disguise and duplicity here are given an imperial and racial twist.

With this story, then, Boothby is referencing but deconstructing an important convention of late Victorian scientific discourse common to crime writing – the identification of criminal and moral deficiencies by the application of physiognomic analysis. Underpinning the new late Victorian science of criminal anthropology spawned by the publication of Cesare Lombroso's *L'Uomo Deliquente* (1876) was the widespread belief that all people should be able instinctively to recognise the physical characteristics of a criminal. J. Holt Schooling's article 'Nature's Danger-Signals: A Study of the Faces of Murderers' (1898) for the *Harmsworth Magazine*, for instance, offers just one example of the subsequent popularity of this belief. Schooling advised readers that 'when you feel a certain instinctive aversion for a face, even though your reason or your supposed self-interest gives you no warning, then I say let your instinct have its way, and take the warning that Nature is holding up to you as a danger-signal' (660). Ronald Thomas's work has been influential in demonstrating the ways in which late Victorian detective fiction often draws upon the popular science of criminal physiognomy when dealing with issues of race, identity and constructions of criminality. He notes that detective fiction – specifically the first three canonical detective novels: Wilkie Collins's *The Moonstone*, and Doyle's *A Study in Scarlet* and *The Sign of Four* – frequently evokes criminal threats originating from outside Britain. For Thomas, in the Sherlock Holmes stories, the foreigner is often rendered interchangeable with Lombroso's degenerate criminal man. In *The Sign of Four*, for instance, the murderous Andaman Islander Tonga is 'naturally hideous' with a 'misshapen head', 'small fierce eyes' and 'distorted features' (Doyle, *Sherlock* 141). The indigenous people of this area, Holmes tells Watson, are 'so intractable and fierce ... that all the efforts of the British officials have failed to win them over in any degree' (141). The murder that the foreigner commits, therefore, is simply 'the natural action bred by the "instincts" of a "savage" criminal body, the traces of which are easily discernible to the scientific eye' (Thomas, *Detective Fiction* 233). Rather than straightforwardly reproducing such constructions of foreign criminality in *A Prince of Swindlers*, however, Boothby rather daringly demonstrates the potential for such foreign invaders to be hidden behind the most English, and thus respectable, of façades.

In 'The Duchess of Wiltshire's Diamonds', Carne uses his appearance of Englishness to gain a position of trust within Amberley's circle. Without any signifier of Carne's cultural hybridity, and thus of his potential criminality, Amberley and his circle read Carne's deceptively Western physical beauty to connote nobility and respectability. Carne is lengthily described by Amberley as possessing 'one of the most beautiful countenances I have ever seen in my fellow-men', with a 'broad forehead', 'large and dreamy' eyes, 'ears as tiny as those of an English beauty' and a nose 'more [like] that of the great Napoleon than any other I recall' (13). In these beautiful features Amberley and his circle read a trustworthy moral character; that of 'a man accustomed to command' (13). It therefore goes without question that he is allowed to borrow the duchess's valuable necklace, which her ladyship plans to wear at a Jubilee ball, under the pretence of studying its intricate Eastern case.

As with Dorrington, whose criminality was masked by the appearance of respectability, Carne's delightful appearance fools his peers. Boothby, however, adds a new colonial and racial frisson to Carne's mastery of disguise. Once the necklace is in his possession, Carne has his Indian craftsmen accomplices construct a replacement case and an imitation paste necklace. He skilfully lays elaborate tracks to implicate that the robbery was committed by an outsider – he has one of his staff pose as a foreigner and visit a well-known pawnbrokers, where the man enquires about selling a diamond necklace to traders in Amsterdam. The story does not end with the successful realisation of Carne's criminal plan, however; rather, Carne suggests that the Wiltshires call in his Park Lane neighbour, the renowned detective Klimo, to investigate the robbery. It seems, perhaps, that fans of the investigative detective story genre will receive a 'fix' of their favourite type of narrative.

Indeed, in his descriptions of Klimo, Boothby openly invokes the idea of the super-detective embodied in the figure of Sherlock Holmes. Klimo is described as 'remarkably astute', 'renowned', 'famous', a 'master of his trade', who is 'the cleverest detective in the world' (38; 176; 35; 79; 63). He is 'as great as Lecoq, or even the late lamented Sherlock Holmes' (35). Owing to his combination of effectiveness and discretion, Holmes frequently was engaged by members of the aristocracy to deal quietly with their problems. Likewise, Amberley notes that 'half of' Society London had been 'induced to patronise' Klimo and that his name had recently gained popularity and acclaim in the metropolis's highest strata (35). The city, we are told, is buzzing with excitement not only about the Jubilee but also with talk of the 'now famous' super-detective (35). Indeed, one of the story's accompanying illustrations shows Klimo's services being promoted on a London billboard alongside an advertisement for that famous Victorian commodity, Pear's Soap (Figure 6.2).[22] As Morrison had done with Dorrington, however, Boothby suggests that the post-Holmes respectability and status of the detecting profession can easily be manipulated to exploit the trust of clients, by facilitating the penetration of wealthy clients' homes and lives.

Thus, when Klimo is called in to 'solve' the robbery of her ladyship's famous jewel necklace, the detective puts the Metropolitan police on the tracks of the fake pawnbroker's client, after sending the real diamonds back to Trincomalee Liz on a trading boat bound for Calcutta. At the story's close, Carne joins Amberley and the Duke of Wiltshire at an exclusive gentleman's club where they toast their great friendship and drink to Klimo's deductive skills and 'ingenuity' (63). The conventional trope of the detective's skilful ability to penetrate all levels of society and the city is employed to ironic effect in this story, then, as Carne/Klimo exploits the trust of his high-society friends and clients, benefiting from both the robbery and the reward.[23] This in turn complicates the reader's usual moral alignment with the detective as they are made complicit in the robbery by their awareness from the outset that Carne is the robber and that Klimo's detection is merely a performance.

A poster setting forth the name of the now famous detective, Klimo.

Figure 6.2   E.F. Skinner's illustration for 'The Duchess of Wiltshire's Diamonds.' *Pearson's Magazine* Jan.–June 1897: 168

Despite the rather far-fetched nature of this story, the various fears about foreign criminality, theft and crime in the city and its trading ports which 'The Duchess of Wiltshire's Diamonds' mobilises, reference the very real fears addressed in the earlier *Pearson's* article about the Thames police. Even more bizarrely, however, the events in Boothby's story foreshadow almost exactly a real imperial diamond robbery that took place later that year. Newspapers from around the globe, including the *New York Times*, reported in late May 1897 that the £300,000 'Imperial Diamond', a Jubilee gift to the Queen from the Nizam of Hyderabad, had been stolen and replaced with a paste imitation whilst en route from Calcutta to London ('Imperial Diamond Stolen' 8). It is unclear whether the diamond was ever found.

I now want to turn to 'A Service to the State', the only story in the collection which follows Klimo engaged in a genuine detecting case. In this story Carne is almost completely absent and we follow Klimo taking on a case which gives him the opportunity to save all sections of metropolitan society from a terrorist attack. Like the collection itself, the story is structured by a number of invasions across various domestic, national and personal boundaries. Carne's targeting of Jubilee London as depicted in 'The Duchess of Wiltshire's Diamonds' is contrasted here with a more dangerous threat to state security. The story opens with Klimo receiving Mrs Eileen Jeffreys, a 'frail wisp of a girl', into his consulting rooms (91). In pointed contrast to the diamond-laden aristocrats who people many of the collection's other stories, Mrs Jeffreys, the wife of a 'respectable' Bank Inspector, is 'neatly but by no means expensively dressed' and thus seems designed to parallel, and hence appeal to, the less affluent, but nonetheless respectable, readers of *Pearson's* (105; 91). Mrs Jeffreys, an Irish-American, tells Klimo that she is worried about her father who recently left America and has taken up residence with her and her husband in their Bloomsbury home. The arrival of a mysterious coded telegram from America, which is undecipherable to all but her father, has caused him great 'mental strain', to be sick with fear and to be 'seized with remorse' over its undisclosed implications (105; 93).

Like Doyle's colonial detective stories, the narrative space of 'A Service to the State' is haunted by the threat of the invasion of an old imperial secret into the modern metropolis. In this case the imperial secret at first seems only to threaten the respectable domestic London space of Mrs Jeffreys and her husband. Klimo deciphers Mrs Jeffreys's coded telegram, however, and it is soon revealed that he has uncovered a threat with repercussions beyond the domestic sphere. He has decoded a message about 'one of the biggest Fenian conspiracies ever yet brought to light' (100). A gang of Irish-American terrorists are planning a bomb attack on London during the Jubilee celebrations. The 'one aim and object' of the gang, we are told, is 'to destroy law and order in this country' (100). The telegram outlines that two men – the principal members of the terrorist organisation and old acquaintances of Mrs Jeffreys's father – are sailing to Britain with 50 thousand pounds in order to oversee and carry out the bomb plot. The men, Maguire and Rooney, have previously been responsible for 'a terrible dynamite explosion in London, in which forty innocent people lost their lives' (103). Klimo's investigation uncovers that they are blackmailing Mrs Jeffreys's father and plan to stay with the Jeffreys family while they carry out their latest bomb attack.

In the opening lines of 'A Service to the State', Boothby employs language which reminds the reader of the links between the Irish terrorists and Carne. The gang intend to take advantage of the opportunity of the Jubilee to strike at 'half the crowned heads, or their representatives, of Europe', echoing Carne's earlier plans to invade Jubilee London and target 'half the sovereigns of Europe' (100; 7). The terrorist invasion, then, recalls Carne's earlier arrival in London, yet the reader is persuaded to see that the Fenians pose a far more serious threat. Carne's imperialist rhetoric in his description of the terrorists emphasises their much greater threat to all citizens of the imperial centre. Carne terms the terrorists 'the enemies of law and order', who have taken advantage of the opportunity of the Jubilee to strike a much greater 'blow at the Government and society in general' than that of which he is guilty (100). Boothby spatially links the threat of the impending invasion with a number of London activities – the threat of the bomb, then, preoccupies Carne during a visit to 'the wife of the Prime Minister', a concert at Queen's Hall and a drive in the busy Hyde Park (97). By linking the idea of the bomb with activities which foreground both the practices of everyday life and the locus of state power in imperial London, Boothby emphasises for the reader the very grave nature of the threat posed by the Fenian terrorists and speaks to readers' own experiences of terrorist attacks in the 1880s and 1890s.

The Fenians, of course, were a real group with which Boothby's *fin-de-siècle* readers would have been familiar. The Fenians' first organised political offensive in Britain was the Clerkenwell Prison bombing in 1867, which was followed by a number of bombings and assassinations in Ireland and London throughout the 1880s and 1890s. Most famously perhaps, on 24 January 1885, Fenian dynamiters set off near-simultaneous explosions in the Houses of Parliament, the Tower of London and

Westminster Hall. No one was killed, but several tourists were badly injured. Following these events, as Elizabeth Carolyn Miller has pointed out, bombs and terrorism became 'new additions to the fabric of life in 1880s and 1890s Britain', and thus provided a historical basis for the emergence of terrorism in popular fiction (*Framed* 189). Miller has noted, however, that 'a historically incongruous aspect' of most 1880s and 1890s dynamite and invasion fiction is 'the absence of Ireland and Fenian dynamite' (214). Much late Victorian and Edwardian dynamite fiction – such as Wilde's *Vera; Or, the Nihilists* (1883), Henry James's *The Princess Casamassima* (1886) or Conrad's *The Secret Agent* (1907) – instead concentrates on the threat of terror from nihilist or anarchist organisations.[24] In focusing on an Irish terrorist threat to London, Boothby's story follows Robert Louis Stevenson's *The Dynamiter* (1885), and is one of the few works of dynamite fiction that correlates its form of political violence with the concerns of his contemporary readers. 'A Service to the State' is not *Pearson's* only story published in 1897 to deal with the Irish terrorist threat, however. In the same edition as 'The Duchess of Wiltshire's Diamonds', 'Donald Penstone's Escape', by V.L. Whitchurch, gives an account of the escape of a fictional 'celebrated Fenian', wanted in connection with 'some notorious Fenian outrages' (116).

In bringing the threat of Irish terrorism into the *Prince of Swindlers* collection, Boothby once again complicates the emerging genre's representations of colonial criminality. Locating the threat of criminality in a terrorist organisation that would have posed a real and present threat to his readers, Boothby is at variance with Victorian detective fiction's tendency to construct criminality as an unlikely aberration. In drawing upon the types of very real criminal threats which had actually disrupted the order and safety of *fin-de-siècle* metropolitan life, Boothby's engagement with terrorism would have been potentially much more unsettling to readers than those of his detective fiction forebears, which tended to concentrate on threats from fantastically aberrant colonials, such as the one-legged colonial criminal Jonathan Small, and his accomplice Tonga, the pigmy cannibal, who feature in Doyle's *The Sign of Four*. Boothby's and Whitchurch's stories, by contrast, are constructed to play upon very real contemporary fears about the inability of the police to contain criminal networks. In Whitchurch's story, for instance, the forces of detection have been powerless to prevent Penstone's escape. The story ends on a particularly unsettling note, which foregrounds the negative consequences of Britain's spatial links with the imperial outpost. Despite being 'shadowed closely' by a number of detectives, the terrorist evades capture and escapes on 'a steamer' bound for Australia (116; 120).

Conversely, in the figure of Klimo, Boothby sees that the threat from the Irish terrorists is, at least partially, diffused. Apparently without irony, Carne soliloquises that 'as a peaceable citizen of the City of London, and as a humble servant of her majesty the Queen, it is manifestly my duty to deliver these rascals into the hands of the police' (105). Boothby recreates detective fiction's drive to resolution and employs a number of super-detective-*esque* characteristics which replicate for the reader the narrative and moral reassurance of investigative-centred crime fiction. The remainder of the story, then, follows Carne as he poses as an official policeman, conducts surveillance of the criminals, arrests the terrorists at Mrs Jeffreys's home and offers the men a form of justice. In his arresting speech Carne ironically attributes his success in catching the criminals to a Holmesian panoptic knowledge of crime and the city. He tells the men that he was 'long-since' aware of their travel from America and their terrorist plot, and pretends to them that they 'have been shadowed ever since you set foot ashore' (116). Carne offers the terrorists a 'choice' between 'arrest and appearance at Bow Street, or immediate return to America': a deal which he tells the men has been 'authorised by Her Majesty's Government', although, of course, it has not (116).

In a collection which blends transgressor and investigative-centred crime fiction, this is probably the collection's most generically conventional story in its reproduction of dominant ideology, its construction of the threats posed by outsiders and its drive to narrative and moral resolution. At the same time, however, the restoration of order offered by this ending to the story is not quite as neat as much of the investigation-centred detective fiction which it emulates. For one, the terrorists have not been dispatched either officially or permanently, and the real Metropolitan police were never involved. At the story's close, Boothby also distinctly differentiates Carne's morality and motivation from those of Holmes. Boothby ironically echoes and inverts the typical Holmesian moral gesture of refusing money from respectable middle-class clients, to comic effect. Holmes had only rarely accepted fees from clients that he respected. By contrast, Carne's seemingly moral desire 'to save the girl and her father' and 'the nation' is overridden by a rather more self-interested desire to appropriate the 50 thousand pounds which the terrorists have in their possession (105). Whilst Carne professes to be happy at the prospect of playing 'policeman' and 'public benefactor', he admits that his ultimate motivation had been financial: 'If it hadn't been for the money I should have had nothing to do with it [the case] at all' (105). When Mrs Jeffreys comes to Klimo to enquire about 'the extent of her debt' he beneficently tells her 'You owe me nothing but your gratitude. I will not take a half-penny' (118). When she leaves, however, the reader sees him smile and open his pocket-book to reveal 45 thousand pounds which he has appropriated from the terrorists. 'I did not take her money,' he chuckles to himself, 'but I *have* been rewarded in another way' (emphasis in original) (118).

Despite the very real threat to late Victorian London that it depicts, then, Boothby's story ends on a comic but unsettling note with Carne admitting that money rather than morality had motivated his actions. The story, then, is complex, perhaps uneven and unconvincing, but exemplifies the ways in which Boothby experiments with different moral positions, genres and types of closure throughout the collection and the variety of positions into which the reader is projected as a result. At the story's close, Carne reverts to criminality and his invasion of Jubilee London continues. Indeed, after 'A Service to the State', Boothby's collection contains two further tales of Carne's criminal exploits in London. In the final story, 'An Imperial Finale', Carne commits one last daring robbery before fleeing on his yacht. The collection's final lines underscore his ultimate lack of morality, with Carne directly addressing the reader, saying that he has 'no regrets ... none whatever' (191). Amberley, the narrator, tells us that, since the escape, 'the police of almost every civilised country have been on the alert' to effect Carne's capture (22–3). The collection ends with one final image of uncertainty as the reader is told that Carne has thus far managed to evade the world's greatest law-enforcement agencies and remains at large.

For today's readers, the *Prince of Swindlers* stories provide a fascinating articulation of a range of late Victorian anxieties about invasion and foreign criminality that attended the end of the century and an interesting inversion of the nascent detective genre's conventions. They reveal how Victorian detective fiction's domestic themes of investigation and disorder are mapped onto wider interrogations of identity construction and safety across national and global boundaries, thus illuminating *fin-de-siècle* anxieties about the New Imperialism. In keeping with other narratives of reverse colonisation, these stories offer contemporary readers a troubling vision of a Jubilee-year metropolis that is easily penetrable by foreign criminals, terrorists and returned colonials who have gone native whilst in the imperial outpost. The open-endedness of the *Prince of Swindlers* collection suggests that the ideological and ethical contradictions which it has raised will not be resolved. The oft-cited touchstones of detective fiction – success, order, reassurance and resolution – are shown by Boothby to be deeply problematic and inapplicable to a late Victorian Britain suffused with anxiety about imperial decline.

Conclusion

This study has sought to augment recent challenges to reductive and essentialist accounts of both the genealogy and the complexity of the crime genre in the period before, during and after the emergence of Doyle's Sherlock Holmes. By focusing on Doyle's detective stories, alongside other well-known fiction by Robert Louis Stevenson, and works by critically neglected authors like Arthur Morrison, Israel Zangwill, Fergus Hume and Guy Boothby, we have seen the divergent possibilities of crime writing at the time when it was just becoming a popular and self-conscious genre. As early as the 1880s, the nascent detective genre frequently surprises and challenges the reader – with partial, problematic or limited resolutions to the crimes it portrayed, with stories where detectives are absent, implicated in the crime, or unsuccessful, or where criminals take centre stage, escape or emerge as heroes. In this study, then, the fascinating – but often overlooked – formal and ideological scope of the late Victorian crime genre has begun to be uncovered.

This study also challenges readings of late Victorian detective fiction as somehow more detached from its milieu and less gritty or 'real' than the genre's later hard-boiled or twenty-first-century incarnations, instead demonstrating just how closely late nineteenth-century narratives of crime interact with political and sociological debates and anxieties of the time. Chapter 1 reveals the important role that Robert Louis Stevenson's popular 'shilling shocker' *Jekyll and Hyde* (1886) plays in the detective genre's developing focus on the types of criminality within the middle classes being reported in the press. If in the 1860s sensation fiction brought crime fiction into the domestic world, in the 1880s Stevenson forged a connection between the genre and the contemporary middle-class urban home, which would dominate detective fiction for the rest of the century. Chapter 2 demonstrates the influence of police corruption scandals and class agitation on Fergus Hume's commercial phenomenon *The Mystery of a Hansom Cab* (1886), the bestselling crime novel of the nineteenth century. Chapter 3 shows how a number of prevalent *fin-de-siècle* anxieties about reading, the status of professional writing and the production of low literature influenced Arthur Conan Doyle's Sherlock Holmes stories. Chapter 4 illuminates the influence of corruption in the London police and the sensationalism of the press in Israel Zangwill's East End murder story, *The Big Bow Mystery* (1891). Chapter 5 showcases how Arthur Morrison's *The Dorrington Deed-Box* (1897) consciously broke with the genre's impulses towards formula and resolution, in an attempt to expose the grim reality of slum poverty and criminality in late Victorian London. Finally, Chapter 6 reveals how Guy Boothby's *A Prince of Swindlers* (1897) illuminates *fin-de-siècle* anxieties about the permeability of national boundaries facilitated by the imperial project. This study, then, demonstrates that much of the forgotten crime writing of this period is not simply cheap, throwaway fiction, justifiably omitted from histories of the genre, but instead illuminates many of the tensions and anxieties that suffused late Victorian culture and society.

Although many of these texts and authors have been dismissed and omitted from the crime canon as victims of the 'slaughterhouse of literature', they also anticipate the moral ambiguity that would become so characteristic of the later crime genre (Moretti, 'Slaughterhouse' 207). The outwardly respectable anti-heroes and corrupt or eccentric detectives that populate early twentieth-century hard-boiled fiction and film, and so much contemporary crime fiction, television and film, are present in the works of Doyle, Hume, Stevenson, Zangwill, Boothby and Morrison at the time when the detective genre was just coming into being. The detective protagonists in the stories studied here are not avatars of heroism and authority, but rather are compromised and often corrupt individuals, foreshadowing the morally ambiguous characters that populate the most popular crime fiction, television and film of today. The Guy Ritchie *Sherlock Holmes* film franchise, the BBC series *Sherlock* and CBS's *Elementary*, which reimagine Doyle's creation for the modern viewer, all revel in flaunting the *fin-de-siècle* detective's bohemian qualities flagged up in this study – his drug-taking, his disregard for the police and the law, and his moral detachment. So too in popular characters like crime investigator/serial killer Dexter Morgan, protagonist of the *Dexter* novels and Showtime television series, *Breaking Bad*'s mild-mannered chemistry teacher/drug lord Walter White, and most recently *True Detective*'s troubled detective duo Martin Hart and Rustin Cohle, stir the echoes of Dorrington, Carne, Grodman and Kilsip. These types of figures may not have been palatable to early critics of detective fiction who omitted them from the crime canon, but they are exactly the sorts of morally complex characters that delight and intrigue current fans of the genre.

Because of the important ways that the 'Shadows of Sherlock' who have been the subjects of this study stretch the moral and formal conventions of the emerging detective genre, and anticipate the types of criminal protagonists and compromised detectives who would become such ubiquitous figures in contemporary popular culture, then, these works offer much for the modern reader to chew on and enjoy. They also help demonstrate the need for a continuing critical re-evaluation of the late Victorian genre as merely conservative and cosy formula fiction. There is much more work to be done in this area, however. The need remains for further processes of re-evaluation, consolidation and recuperation which this study has begun, with potentially hundreds more valuable 'Shadows of Sherlock' languishing in the shade, as yet undetected.

Notes

Introduction

1. Howard Haycraft dates the first critical article on fictional detectives as appearing in the *Saturday Review* in May 1883. However, that article did not refer to detective fiction as a separate and distinct genre. See Haycraft 6.
2. See Smith, *Golden*, an anthology which covers the period 1891–1917. As countless critics have pointed out, the problem of definition itself provides potential pitfalls for any historian of the genre. What is the difference between a story about crime and a work of crime fiction? Can a story without a detective be termed detective fiction? In this matter I follow the modern viewpoint espoused by Knight (*Crime*), Ascari and Sussex that 'crime fiction' is the most comprehensive and flexible appellation for the genre. In my study, all of the stories I examine feature detectives of one sort or another – some are members of the constabulary, some are unofficial friends or helpers, some are privately employed consulting detectives, some are masquerading as detectives, some are successful in solving crime, some are not, some are corrupt, some lie to, steal from or even murder their clients. For this reason, I retain and employ the terms crime and detective fiction alongside each other throughout the study, emphasising the extent to which both categories can co-exist and apply to individual texts coming out of the late Victorian period.
3. For more on criminal broadsides and the eighteenth- and early nineteenth-century crime genre, see Worthington.
4. It would be impossible to attend to all the works of Victorian detective fiction which thus far have been overlooked by critics of the genre. The problem is that the corpus is just too large. Hubin lists approximately 6000 works of crime fiction published in this period alone.
5. The notion of the detective and criminal being the same person of course draws upon earlier works like the criminal biographies of the 1700s featuring thief-turned-thief-taker Jonathan Wild and French criminal Eugène François Vidocq, who became the founder and head of the French police. For more on this see, for example, Emsley and Shpayer-Makov.

1 'Ordinary Secret Sinners': Robert Louis Stevenson's *Strange Case of Dr Jekyll and Mr Hyde* (1886)

1. Hereafter, abbreviated as *Jekyll and Hyde*.
2. See, for example, Joyce; Pittard ('Real Sensation'); Ascari; Spooner.
3. Maurizio Ascari, for instance, argues that *Jekyll and Hyde*, along with *The Dynamiter*, cannot be omitted from studies of the detective genre as both novels greatly influenced Doyle's *A Study in Scarlet*. Ascari suggests that the separation of detective and gothic fiction more broadly is an artificial and

misleading project, produced by a critical investment in rationalism. For Ascari, many of the first critics of the detective genre, such as R.A. Freeman and Howard Haycraft, selectively composed the detective canon in order to confirm their view that the detective story celebrated rationalism. Therefore they excluded any 'impure' works with supernatural, sensational or transgressive elements such as criminal heroes (Ascari 1–11). In doing so, these critical works promoted and sustained an enduring and 'normative view' of 'a genre whose borders were being traced with increasing sharpness' (4).

In *Capital Offenses*, Simon Joyce likewise argues for the important place of *Jekyll and Hyde* in the Victorian crime genre. For Joyce, Stevenson's novel belongs to a group of late Victorian works featuring 'privileged offenders' of the type that had featured in novels from the earlier gothic tradition (164). Stevenson's Henry Jekyll, then, along with Wilde's Dorian Gray and Doyle's Professor Moriarty, is a reworking of the type of 'aristocratic rake and libertine' found in the novels of Ann Radcliffe and Matthew Lewis. In crime fiction of the 1880s and 1890s, these aristocratic offenders are 'taken out of European castles and country houses and transplanted into the modern metropolis' (164). The emergence of this body of privileged offenders destabilises readings of the trajectory of the Victorian crime genre, such as Ernest Mandel's, where the detective wholeheartedly replaces the criminal as hero as the nineteenth century comes to a close.

4. This and subsequent references to *Jekyll and Hyde* are taken from the 2002 Penguin edition of the text, edited by Robert Mighall, unless otherwise stated.

5. In a first draft of the text, commonly referred to as the 'Printer's Copy', Stevenson was a little more explicit about these acts, terming them 'disgraceful pleasures ... [and] vices ... at once criminal in the sight of the law and abhorrent in themselves'. For more on this, see Veeder and Hirsch.

6. See also Emsley; Shpayer-Makov.

7. Sindall uses the definitions of class based on the Registrar General's classification of 1921. As he points out, 'although the Registrar General's classifications are open to criticism they are still a widely used classification for the ordering of nineteenth-century material, and that of 1921 is the nearest comprehensive and reliable social classification to the period under review' (23). Although Sindall's study itself is now more than 30 years old, it still represents one of the fullest and most-cited studies on nineteenth-century crime and the middle classes.

8. The case inspired the 1894 pornographic novel *Raped on the Railway: a True Story of a Lady who was first ravaged then flagellated on the Scotch Express*. See Sweet.

9. For more on Dr Thomas Neill Cream, see McLaren, *Prescription*.

10. For more on late Victorian scandals see Diamond; Cohen; Garrigan; Walkowitz.

11. Bizarrely, however, in the course of his investigation, Stead procured a virgin himself and was eventually tried and jailed for this offence. As Andrew Smith has pointed out, the investigation ironically turned Stead into the type of Minotaur he sought to expose. See Smith, *Victorian Demons*.

12. The Saunterer's letters were later attributed to Harold Frederic, an American writer and journalist, based in London. See Dodge.

13. However, Symonds's responses to Stevenson have frequently been interpreted as related to the topic of homosexuality. See, for instance, Roger Luckhurst's Introduction to the 2006 Oxford World's Classics edition of *Jekyll and Hyde*.

14. In *City of Dreadful Delight*, Judith Walkowitz briefly suggests that the 'Maiden Tribute' articles influenced a number of works of 1880s and 1890s fiction, including: *Jekyll and Hyde*; *The Picture of Dorian Gray*; *Dracula*; and *The Island of Dr Moreau*. In *The Modern Gothic and Literary Doubles*, Linda Dryden has also briefly made this connection between *Jekyll and Hyde* and 'The Maiden Tribute' articles. For Dryden 'the coincidences are too compelling to ignore' (82). Dryden does not analyse the connections between the two in any detail, however.

15. This and subsequent references to this letter are from: W.E. Henley, letter to Robert Louis Stevenson, 9 July 1885. The Edwin J. Beinecke Collection of Robert Louis Stevenson, GEN MSS 664, Request Box 13, Letter number: #4841, Beinecke Library, Yale University, New Haven, Connecticut.

16. The practice known as 'mashing' – that is, a descent across space and class boundaries in search of sex or drugs – should be distinguished from the practice of 'slumming', which carries associations of benevolent intent. For more on this see Koven.

17. See also Gray, who suggests that 'although the trampling scene may well be disturbingly indicative of the abuse of children in Victorian society generally, it may also have a much more specific literary source in George MacDonald's *Phantastes: A Faërie Romance*, published in 1858' (493). In 'Psychopathia Sexualis', Stephen Heath links the trampling incident with some sort of sexual assault, and more broadly links Hyde's depravity with sexual perversion.

18. Stevenson would no doubt have protested against both accounts; in a letter to John Paul Bocock he railed against the public interest in specifying the sexual nature of Hyde's crimes, exclaiming 'the beast Hyde ... is no more sensual than another' (Stevenson, *Letters*, vol. VI, 56). Yet even this protest seems to suggest the links that Stevenson wished to draw between Hyde, Jekyll and the average late Victorian male. And as he acknowledged in another letter, the nature of Jekyll's sins remains unspecified precisely to allow for the many interpretative possibilities that they suggest. As he put it: 'I have said my say as best as I was able: others must look for what is meant' (*Letters*, vol. V, 211)

19. *Measuringworth.com*, a website containing various tools for calculating contemporary relative values of past assets and transactions, calculates that the relative value of £100 in 1885 to be between £8080.00 and £11,000.00 in 2011. *Measuringworth.com*, ed. Lawrence H. Officer and Samuel H. Williamson, 28 Jan. 2011. www.measuringworth.com/index.html.

20. For more on Victorian blackmail see McLaren, *Sexual Blackmail*; Kucich; Welsh.

21. For many critics, this blackmail suggests the homosexual blackmail which gained popularity after the Labouchere Amendment to the 1885 Criminal

Law Amendment Act, which outlawed acts of 'gross indecency' between two men. For more on this see McLaren, *Sexual Blackmail*; Showalter.

22. Perhaps suggesting that the old sin was a sexual indiscretion of which Hyde was the product. In 'The Sedulous Ape', Stephen Arata notes that the relationship between Jekyll and Hyde is suggestive of that between a father and son, as Hyde is variously referred to as 'little', 'young' and Jekyll's 'protégé'.

23. For more on this distrust of surveillance and the detective police see Summerscale; Shpayer-Makov.

24. As Worthington has suggested, it was most probably not until after Sherlock Holmes gained popularity in the early 1890s that the public's negative perceptions of the detective police began to change and improve.

25. For more on this see Shpayer-Makov, 37–9.

26. Elsewhere, on the topic of Hyde's 'unspeakable' appearance, Elaine Showalter has argued that when Stevenson's male characters 'find something *unspeakable* about Hyde' Stevenson is invoking 'the most famous code word in Victorian homosexuality' (112).

27. An image which once again seems to conjure suggestions of the 'Maiden Tribute' case.

28. As Auden himself acknowledges, however, this formula applies only to a very small number of canonical detectives – including Poe's Dupin, Doyle's Holmes and Chesterton's Father Brown. Indeed, it largely discredits the importance to the detective genre of figures like Mary Elizabeth Braddon's Robert Audley or Dashiell Hammett's Continental Op, who were (or became) in some way implicated in the crimes that they investigated.

29. Likewise, later in the investigation, when Utterson sees investigative data he is unable to assimilate it or deduce what it should be telling him. When Guest points out the striking visual similarity between Jekyll and Hyde's handwriting, Utterson agrees but goes on wrongly to extrapolate that this means Jekyll has forged for Hyde. And when he and Poole break down the door to Jekyll's cabinet, Utterson sees Hyde's dead body and wrongly assumes that either Hyde has committed suicide or Jekyll is the murderer.

30. For more on the relationship between crime fiction and classic liberal thought see McCann.

31. In an interesting turn of events, Forbes Winslow was briefly suspected of the Ripper crimes, on account of his persistent desire to become involved in the investigation of the case. See Walkowitz 213.

32. For more on Dr Barnardo and allegations of impropriety, see Koven.

33. These types of suspicions still have currency today, of course. See, for instance, Knight's *Jack the Ripper*, which theorises an elaborate alliance of politicians, doctors and freemasons covering for Prince Albert Victor.

34. It is noteworthy, however, that all of the respectable gentlemen in the novel escape apprehension or punishment and that the novel ultimately, perhaps reluctantly, ends up reinscribing their socially dominant positions within late Victorian society. In the process Stevenson fails to offer any sort of alternative to the status quo (which inevitably favoured vested interests).

2   'The Most Popular Book of Modern Times': Fergus Hume's *The Mystery of a Hansom Cab* (1886)

1. The quotation 'the most popular book of modern times' in the chapter heading is from 'The Author of Madame Midas'.

2. The victim, John Fletcher, a wealthy paper merchant and member of Lancashire County Council, was poisoned with chloral during a drunken cab journey on 26 February 1889. As the Christchurch *Star* reported it: 'It must have been with mixed feelings that Mr Fergus Hume on Wednesday morning, read of the conviction of the Manchester murderer, Charles Parton, for a crime precisely analogous to that described in the "Mystery of a Hansom Cab". There can indeed be little doubt that if Mr Hume's shilling "marrow-curdler" had never been written, the estimable but bibulous Mr Fletcher would never have been poisoned. A copy of the novelette was found in Parton's possession, and there can scarcely be room for doubt that it suggested to him his nefarious scheme' ('Murder in Manchester').

3. Stephen Knight's excellent survey of the crime genre, for instance, notes the important part that Hume's novel had in making detective fiction 'a major force' in the late Victorian literary marketplace (*Crime* 52). Christopher Pittard ('Real Sensation'; *Purity*) has also recently made a persuasive case for the important place of Hume's novel in the genealogy of crime fiction. Pittard argues that not only the novel's phenomenal sales figures but also its appropriation of a number of tropes from the sensation genre, which would continue to feature in a number of later works of crime fiction, qualify it as a more significant event in the history of the detective genre than the publication of Doyle's *A Study in Scarlet*.

4. The only other scholarly works on Hume's novel are Stephen Knight's introduction to the 1985 Hogarth Press reprint, Christa Ludlow's 'The Reader Investigates' and a chapter in Robert Dixon's *Writing the Colonial Adventure.*

5. For more on the growth of nineteenth-century Melbourne, see Davison; Briggs, *Victorian Cities.*

6. Pittard ('Real Sensation'; *Purity*), Dixon and Ludlow provide excellent analyses of Hume's depictions of the Melbourne slum and underclass in their work on the novel. For this reason, I focus on Hume's depictions of the police and upper class.

7. For more on the public appetite for crime and sensation, see Twitchell.

8. For more on the regulation of French literature in nineteenth-century Australia, see Heath.

9. Bigamy, of course, was one of the staples of the sensation genre, featuring prominently in novels such as Mary Elizabeth Braddon's *Lady Audley's Secret* (1862). For more on the links between Hume's novel, detective fiction and the sensation genre, see Pittard, 'Real Sensation'.

10. For more on Ned Kelly as folk-hero, see Seal.

11. For more on the status of police in Victorian society, see Summerscale.

12. For more on Standish's connections with the Melbourne *demi-monde* see Frances; De Serville, *Pounds.*

13. For more on the nineteenth-century fascination with physiognomy see Pearl; Pick.

3 'L'homme c'est rien – l'oeuvre c'est tout': The Sherlock Holmes Stories and Work

1. Quotation in the chapter heading from Doyle, 'The Red-Headed League' 468. This phrase translates as: Man is nothing; work is everything.
2. The term 'bromance' has been particularly associated with Guy Ritchie's film *Sherlock Holmes* (2009), with reviews entitled, for instance, 'Muscular Sherlock a Victorian Bromance with Fights'. For more on Holmes/Watson bromance, see Wynne and Vanacker; Porter, *Sherlock*.
3. Given Doyle's prominence in the field of detective fiction the publishing history of the Sherlock Holmes canon has already been well documented. Virtually all histories of the genre offer accounts of the publication history of the stories and novels, so these details need not be rehearsed again in great detail. For more details see, for example, Ousby, *Bloodhounds*; Symons; Knight, *Form and Ideology*; McDonald, *British*; Kestner, *Sherlock's Men*.
4. These stories were later collected as *The Adventures of Sherlock Holmes* (1892) and *The Memoirs of Sherlock Holmes* (1894). Of course, Holmes was later resurrected by Doyle in *The Hound of the Baskervilles* (1902), *The Return of Sherlock Holmes* (1905), *The Valley of Fear* (1915), *His Last Bow* (1917) and *The Case-Book of Sherlock Holmes* (1927).
5. Significant additions to this body of criticism include work by Knight (*Form and Ideology*), Mandel, Porter, Moretti (*Signs*), Jann (*Adventures*), Kestner (*Sherlock's Men*) and Thomas (*Detective Fiction*).
6. See Miller (*Novel*); Jann ('Sherlock'; *Adventures*); Leps; Thoms; Thomas (*Detective Fiction*).
7. See Mukherjee; Reitz; Joyce.
8. A number of scholars have offered brief observations about the significance of profession in the Holmes stories (Jann, 'Sherlock'; Knight, *Form and Ideology*; Stowe). However, discussions of the Holmes corpus have largely ignored the links that Doyle repeatedly makes between issues of morality, respectability and the ethics of work or professionalism. In particular, Stephen Knight has argued that 'The Man with the Twisted Lip' speaks to Doyle's anxieties about the ethics and effects on his professional status of quickly churning out what he perceived as a 'low' literary product (*Form and Ideology* 98–101). This chapter's argument was inspired by Knight's reading. I go further than Knight, however, arguing that Doyle's complex and often contradictory characterisation of work in a large number of the stories addresses his anxieties surrounding perceptions about the work ethic of the intellectual labourer.
9. While it is important to acknowledge that middle-class Victorian culture was not 'a monolithic structure', an 'imperative moral code' with relation to work was nonetheless 'a touchstone' of various grades and striations of the Victorian middle class. See Wood, *Violence* 36.
10. For more on Samuel Smiles, the 'Gospel of Work' and its place in Victorian middle-class ideology see Grint; Danahay; Adams; Briggs, *Victorian People*.
11. For more on relations between late Victorian authorship, work and money, see also Poovey; Robbins; Pettitt; Hack; Ruth.
12. For more on late nineteenth-century debates on literary hierarchy and value see Carey; McDonald, *British*; Brantlinger, *Reading Lesson*.

13. See, for instance, Gibson and Green; Hollyer, 'Author to Editor'; Hollyer, 'My Dear Smith'; McDonald, 'Adventures'; Green, 'Conan'.
14. See Knight, *Form and Ideology*; Pittard, 'Cheap, healthful literature'.
15. This and subsequent references to the Holmes novels and short stories are taken from Doyle, *Complete Stories*, unless otherwise stated.
16. Wilson would have been categorised as 'petty bourgeoisie' or lower-middle-class (Perkin 78). Perkin defines the late Victorian 'petty bourgeoisie' as 'shopkeepers, schoolteachers, clerks and white-collar workers' who 'generally earned less than £160 a year but still stoutly claimed middle-class status' (78).
17. According to *Measuringworth.com* (see Chapter 1, n. 19), the relative value of £4 in 1890 (the story is set in April to October 1890) was £341 in 2010. In *The Rise of Professional Society*, Harold Perkin suggests that a late Victorian shopkeeper would most likely have earned 'a good deal less than £160 a year' (78). £160 per annum equates to £3 per week. Perkin's values are based on Leo Chiozza Money's 'National Income of the United Kingdom' from *Riches and Poverty* (1904). See Perkin 75–80.
18. For more on the social status of engineers in Victorian Britain, see Perkin.
19. A probable source is 'A Day as a Professional Beggar', an article that featured in George Newnes's *Tit-Bits* magazine on 17 January 1891, in which a journalist goes undercover as a beggar, and finds that he can earn large sums of money by doing so. Although this may seem far-fetched, in 2010 a number of British newspapers reported on the court case of a former estate agent who gave up his career for professional begging, with which he earned £23,400 a year. See Smith, 'Bogus Tramp'.
20. Suggestions of addiction also recur throughout the novellas – Holmes's drug use is another characteristic with which his persona cuts against definitive late Victorian ideas about normality. In *A Study in Scarlet*, Watson observes Holmes's slumming expeditions to low parts of the city and subsequent days spent on the sofa in torpor, suggesting that the detective goes to East London to purchase opium (19). *The Sign of Four* opens more explicitly with Holmes injecting his 'seven-per-cent solution' of cocaine and with Watson revealing that he has witnessed this 'three times a day for many months' (97). While cocaine did not carry the same extremely negative connotations as opium for mainstream Victorian society, in the late 1880s and 1890s the medical and popular press nonetheless contained widespread warnings about the dangers of cocaine addiction and the links between cocaine and opiate use (Berridge and Edwards 221–4). Solidly bourgeois medical man Watson certainly is disturbed by the signs of Holmes's drug use and reads his habit as 'a pathological and morbid process' which will result in the detective's physical and moral decline (*The Sign of Four* 97).

    While Holmes's drug use is mentioned less as the stories progress, doubtless part of Doyle's stated desire to make Holmes a warmer, more appealing character, when the subject does return in one of the later adventures it is no less disturbing for Watson. In 'The Missing Three-Quarter' (1904) Watson fears that 'periods of idleness' are tempting Holmes again to consider engaging in 'that drug mania which had threatened once to check his remarkable career' (Doyle, *Sherlock* 697). To find Holmes's work, which has been termed 'a professional fantasy of complete competence [and] public service', so frequently aligned by Doyle with questions of addiction and drug-taking, suggests that the detective's professional demeanour is more complicated than some recent criticism allows and that he engages in some of the degenerate behaviours that we might expect him to police in others (Reiter 74).

21. For more on 'respectable Ripper' and 'Royal Ripper' theories see Curtis; Knight, *Jack the Ripper*.

22. Of course, real-life popular figures like French criminal-turned-detective Eugène François Vidocq and thief-turned-thief-taker Jonathan Wild had already blurred the boundaries between detective and criminal. These sorts of ambiguities were also present in many of the Victorian detective genre's canonical incarnations, such as with Edgar Allan Poe's Dupin and Charles Dickens's Inspector Bucket. For more on the overlaps between detective heroes and earlier rogue heroes see Vidocq; Rzepka 51–72.

23. Indeed, Holmes is often scornful of the petty trifles of his bourgeois clients, which seem to constitute much of his work in the *Adventures*, complaining, for instance, that his detective practice 'seems to be degenerating into an agency for recovering lost lead pencils and giving advice to young ladies from boarding schools' ('The Copper Beeches' 635).

24. In 1927 Doyle was asked to pick his top 12 Sherlock Holmes stories for an article in *The Strand*. He identified 'The Speckled Band' as his favourite and finest Sherlock Holmes story. His second favourite was 'The Red-Headed League', followed by 'The Dancing Men', 'The Final Problem', 'A Scandal in Bohemia', 'The Empty House', 'The Five Orange Pips', 'The Second Stain', 'The Priory School', 'The Devil's Foot', 'The Musgrave Ritual' and 'The Reigate Squire'. His first choice was shared by *Strand* readers who also voted 'The Speckled Band' their favourite Holmes story. See Doyle, 'My Favourite' 32.

4   Something for 'the Silly Season': Policing and the Press in Israel Zangwill's *The Big Bow Mystery* (1891)

1. The quotation in the chapter heading is from Zangwill, 'Of Murders', 202. Silly season: the months of August and September, when newspapers often publish articles on trivial topics owing to the lack of 'serious' news because of the summer parliamentary recess. The *OED* cites the first usage as an 1861 article in the *Saturday Review*.

2. In only its second number, the newspaper advertised that it had broken a world record by selling 142,600 copies of the first issue. For more on the *Star*'s sales, policies and politics see Goodbody.

3. In 1891, in one of the editions which featured *The Big Bow Mystery*, the paper proclaimed proudly the 'phenomenal growth of a phenomenal success', detailing that 'week by week the circulation of *The Star* has risen until ... the world's record was broken with 336,300 copies on a Single Day, a figure never yet approached by any other Evening Paper in the world' (4 Sept. 1891: 4). Although this figure is difficult to substantiate, the Waterloo Directory's entry on the paper lists its circulation at 280,000 daily in 1890 and 300,000 daily in 1893.

4. For more on this see Cook.

5. In March 1927 *The Strand Magazine* ran a competition for readers to guess which Sherlock Holmes story Doyle rated as his very best (see also Chapter 3, n. 24). In an article accompanying the results of the competition, Doyle presented readers with a list of his 'top twelve' Holmes stories. 'The Speckled Band' took first place in this list. A Mr R.T. Newman of Spring Hill, Wellingborough won one hundred pounds and an autographed copy of Doyle's autobiography, *Memories and Adventures* (1924), for guessing correctly. See Doyle, 'Sherlock Holmes Prize Competition'.

6. In his survey of the crime genre, Martin Priestman offers a brief assessment of the novel. He correctly observes that it contains a left-wing political thrust where 'the public are hoodwinked into looking the other way by the detective cult' (*Crime* 18). Frustratingly, though, Priestman does not go on to expand upon these claims or extrapolate their significance for the Victorian detective genre more broadly. William Scheick's 'Murder in My Soul: Genre and Ethos in Zangwill's The Big Bow Mystery' (1997) – a little problematically, for me – considers the novel as an example of the late Victorian *romance* genre, as opposed to the crime or detective genre.

   In 'The Big Bow Mystery: Jewish Identity and the English Detective Novel' (1991), which looks at the novel in the context of Zangwill's Jewish identity, Meri-Jane Rochelson has made the most astute and fullest commentary on *The Big Bow Mystery*. Rochelson correctly observes that it 'illustrates the subversive potential of the detective genre' and the ways in which 'the nineteenth-century detective novel could indeed serve as a vehicle for cultural criticism with the power to unsettle rather than reassure its readers' ('*Big Bow*' 11). Other critics tend to mention the novel in their histories of the genre simply to comment upon its unusual premise. For Stephen Knight, for instance, the fact that the detective commits the murder is 'barely credible' (*Crime* 81). Likewise, for Julian Symons, this detail of the crime is 'preposterous' (96). Symons's observation that the novel is 'much more nearly a parody than has been acknowledged' is nearer the mark in its understanding of the novel's self-conscious engagement with the detective genre's burgeoning conventions and the important role that satire has to play within it (96). David Glover has expanded upon Symons's observation, providing an excellent short analysis of the novel's satire of politics and sensational journalism – a topic which I, in turn, will further explore in this chapter. Writing in 2000, Joseph Kestner singled out four non-canonical Victorian crime novels which he claimed ought urgently 'to receive consideration': Fergus Hume's *The Mystery of a Hansom Cab* (1886), H.F. Wood's *The Passenger from Scotland Yard* (1888), Arthur Griffiths's *The Rome Express* (1896) and Israel Zangwill's *The Big Bow Mystery* (1891). For Kestner, the need for detailed analysis of Zangwill's novel was the most pressing, as, quite simply, it 'confutes every idea about detection and order ever conceived' (Review of *Detection and Its Designs* 551). Now, almost 15 years later, this fascinating early addition to the late Victorian detective genre is still ripe for reconsideration on account of its unusual subversion of that genre's burgeoning norms and conventions.

7. For more on Jewish Whitechapel, see Endelman.

8. The causes to which Zangwill became most actively involved in the period after 1906 were Zionism, pacifism and women's suffrage. See Rochelson, *A Jew*, 129–50.

9. Mrs Drabdump wonders why two political young men would lodge with her as because she has no husband she has no vote. In later life, female suffrage would be just one of the many political causes for which Zangwill would campaign tirelessly. For more on this see Rochelson, *A Jew* 129–50.

10. For more on Oxford House and Toynbee Hall, see Koven.

11. See, for example, Margaret Harkness's 1888 novel, *Out of Work*.

12. There's probably a little more to it than Moretti allows here – the stories' periodical instalment format, for instance, surely also played a large part in their respective success. That said, Moretti is correct in his observation that canonical Victorian crime fiction generally avoids 'the London of poverty' (*Atlas* 136).

13. Doyle himself appears to promulgate that view in 'A Case of Identity', only the third Holmes story for *The Strand*. Watson declares that the types of crimes reported daily in the paper – 'a husband's cruelty to his wife', for instance – are largely 'crude' and 'vulgar' and therefore 'neither fascinating nor artistic' (469).

14. One only has to look at the appetite both then and now for reports, fiction, anything at all, on the Ripper murders.

15. For more on Irish terrorism in Victorian London, see Miller, *Framed*.

16. Although this happens only in the newspaper version of the novel. In its publication in book form the name of the publication has been changed to *The Moon*.

17. For more on the relationship between crime reportage and the public, see Williams. The title of his book, *Get Me a Murder a Day!*, references the famous motto of Lord Northcliffe, founder of the *Daily Mail*.

18. For more on this concept, see Lennon and Foley.

19. Numerous tours of Jack the Ripper's London murder sites are still operating today. A Google search for 'Jack the Ripper tour' returns dozens of examples.

20. In less prestigious papers such as *The Star*, however, letters were much more likely to be from everyday inhabitants of the East End than from the well-known public figures who would write to *The Times*.

21. In his introduction to the 1895 edition of the novel, Zangwill once again draws links between the press and his novel, suggesting that during its serialisation numerous *Star* readers sent letters offering solutions to the crime (202). The paper printed no such letters, however, and neither are they apparent in any of the reams of private correspondence held at the main Zangwill archives. It seems likely that this claim itself may then be yet another instance of the playful self-reflexivity with which Zangwill surrounds the novel.

    In this introduction, Zangwill also describes a letter to the editor of *The Star* in which he claimed that the plot to *The Big Bow Mystery* was decided in response to readers' letters: 'as each correspondent sent in the name of a suspect, I determined he or she should not be the guilty party' (202). He goes on to point out that this was a joke: 'one would imagine that nobody could take this claim seriously, for it is obvious that the mystery-story is just one species of story that can not be told impromptu or altered at the last moment, seeing that it demands the most careful piecing together and the most elaborate dove-tailing' (203).

22. It is important to acknowledge, however, that there were a number of highly successful foreign police memoirs published earlier in the century,

including French detective Eugène François Vidocq's *Mémoires* (1829) and Louis Canler's *Autobiography of a French Detective from 1818 to 1858* (1862). Shpayer-Makov clarifies that 'few detectives in the British Isles published books relating to their work experience before the 1880s' (277). One of the 'rare exceptions' to this rule was the publication in 1861 of Edinburgh police detective James McLevy's *The Casebook of a Victorian Detective* (Shpayer-Makov 277).

23. Zangwill's canine metaphor here at first appears to draw upon the term with which Holmes was often described by Doyle. However, the term 'sleuth-hound' was not used by Doyle until 'The Red-Headed League' which, although written in April 1891, was not published until August 1891, the same month that Zangwill's novel was serialised in *The Star*.

24. The *Oxford English Dictionary* dates the use of the word 'wimp' as a term of insult connoting 'a feeble or ineffectual person' to 1920, some 29 years after the publication of Zangwill's novel. The *OED* does list 'wimp' as an alternative spelling to 'whimp', meaning c.1890 'to whine'. It is unclear, therefore, whether this name had the double-meaning that modern readers would detect. Given that so many of the characters in the novel have significant or ironic names, however, I am reluctant to give up on the notion that the name Wimp was not used deliberately by Zangwill to connote either a weak or a whining person. Thanks to the good people of the VICTORIA listserv – particularly Meri-Jane Rochelson, David Latané, Timothy Stunt, Malcolm Shifrin and Judith Flanders – for their help in tracing the origins and usage of this word.

5   Tales of 'Mean Streets': The Criminal-Detective in Arthur Morrison's *The Dorrington Deed-Box* (1897)

1. As Christopher Pittard has noted, however, 'The Ward Lane Tabernacle', the final story in the third Hewitt collection, 'ends on a note of uncertainty unusual in detective fiction', with an inquest where parts of the crime go unsolved (*Purity* 103). This, of course, overturns what is read as the usual formal structure of detective fiction and thus anticipates Morrison's more morally and formally ambivalent – and hence much more interesting – second foray into the detective short-story genre, *The Dorrington Deed-Box* (1897).

2. Unless otherwise noted, this and subsequent references to *The Dorrington Deed-Box* are taken from the 2002 edition.

3. See Friedrichs 94–5.

4. The phrase 'mean streets', of course, would later famously be employed by Raymond Chandler in his seminal essay 'The Simple Art of Murder' (1944), securing its association with the crime genre.

5. It has become something of a commonplace in the study of crime fiction for critics to argue that the late Victorian detective emerged as a new kind of hero invented to assuage the types of fears common to a predominantly middle-class urban readership. Ernest Mandel, for example, has claimed that:

> the detective story is the realm of the happy ending. The criminal is always caught. Justice is always done. Crime never pays. Bourgeois legality, bourgeois values and bourgeois society always triumph in the end. It is soothing,

socially integrating literature despite its concern with crime, violence and murder. (47)

In other words, despite late Victorian detective stories' preoccupation with crime and criminality, they present the city as an ultimately 'benevolent and knowable universe' – a world that may contain confusion or chaos but that can be rectified by the superior vision of the detective (Grella 101). For many critics, however, an even more reassuring convention of the late Victorian detective story is the unshakeability of the detective's moral code and his adherence to duty and justice. For John Cawelti, for instance, Sherlock Holmes in particular embodies and upholds the best and most upstanding Victorian values – 'solidity' and 'morality' (277). As previously discussed, this type of reading is becoming increasingly outmoded, however, as a number of more recent critics uncover lost detective stories which confound all arguments for the reassuring nature of the Victorian crime genre.

6. The first full-length academic article on the Dorrington stories was my own 'Horace Dorrington, Criminal-Detective: Investigating the Re-Emergence of the Rogue in Arthur Morrison's The Dorrington Deed-Box (1897)'. Elsewhere, for one of the fullest and best analyses of the collection, see Horsley, *Twentieth* 32–4. For other brief descriptions see Knight, *Crime* 71; Priestman, *Detective Fiction* 114; Binyon 166; Thesing 135; Panek 111; Greene, *Detection* 24; Kestner, *Edwardian Detective* 46; Greene, *Rivals* 126; Nevins and Moorcock 252. Greene reprints 'The Affair of the Avalanche Bicycle and Tyre Co., Limited' in *Rivals*. There is an entry on Arthur Morrison in Herbert 135. This entry, however, quite wrongly concludes that, with Dorrington, Morrison 'conformed to the status quo, working smoothly within established tradition without breaking new ground' (135).

7. In a number of the Holmes stories published after Dorrington, however, Watson's moral position becomes more ambiguous. In 'Charles Augustus Milverton', for instance, Watson burgles a flat with Holmes and does not reveal the identity of Milverton's murderer. And, in 'Abbey Grange', Watson and Holmes let the murderer go.

8. For more on the social history of Deptford, see Bullman, Hegarty and Hill.

9. For more on anxiety about social deception in Victorian London, see Nead.

10. See Booth.

11. For more on the development of the locked-room mystery, see Cook.

12. The story is not without sensational details; Loftus Deacon's corpse is graphically described and depicted in a visceral full-page illustration. Deacon is discovered 'lying in a pool of blood with two large fearful gashes in his head' which, we are told, had clearly been made by 'something heavy and exceedingly sharp' (209).

13. See Arata, *Fictions of Loss*; Danahay.

14. For more on the effect of the character of Holmes upon the public image of the detecting profession, see Worthington.

15. For more on the cultural, social and literary history of London's Soho see, for example, Johnson; Walkowitz; Picard; Nead; Dyos and Wolff.

16. Following the influence of Ronald R. Thomas's work dealing with the links between Victorian detective fiction and physiognomy, it has become something of a commonplace to claim that the criminal is often a

repugnant-looking individual. For Thomas, for instance, in Doyle's *The Sign of Four*, the murderer Tonga is 'naturally hideous' with a 'misshapen head' and 'distorted features', thus telegraphing his criminality (Doyle, *Sign* 141). In a large number of Doyle's later Holmes stories, and other seminal crime stories such as Collins's *The Moonstone*, however, the criminal is a charming and handsome individual, 'hidden' behind an appearance of outward respectability. See Thomas, *Detective Fiction*.

17. Of course, this recalls the apparent fate of the Agra treasure in Doyle's *The Sign of Four*, where Jonathan Small claims to have dumped the jewels into the Thames during a river chase with Holmes and the police. In the novel, though, client Mary Morstan is left with a small amount of the treasure, and she gains Watson as a husband. If Mary had come into possession of the Agra treasure this happy ending would not have been possible, as she would have been too rich to become Watson's wife.

18. As Chandler described the relationship between the detective and the city: 'Down these mean streets a man must go who is not himself mean, who is neither tarnished nor afraid. The detective must be a complete man and a common man and yet an unusual man. He must be ... a man of honour ... He must be the best man in his world and a good enough man for any world ... If there were enough like him, I think the world would be a very safe place to live in.'

6   'A Criminal in Disguise': Class and Empire in Guy Boothby's *A Prince of Swindlers* (1897)

1. The quotation in the chapter heading, 'A Criminal in Disguise', is the title of the first story in the *Prince of Swindlers* collection.

2. This chapter provides the first sustained analysis of the *Prince of Swindlers* collection. One of the stories from the collection, 'The Duchess of Wiltshire's Diamonds', has been reprinted a number of times. See Russell, *Rivals*; Davies, *Shadows*; Greene, *Rivals*; Cox, *Victorian Tales*; Sims, *Gaslight Crime*. *A Prince of Swindlers* gets a one-line mention in Butterss. Simon Carne has an entry in Nevins and Moorcock.

3. Klimo features in Volume 1 episode 5 of Alan Moore's *The League of Extraordinary Gentlemen* comic book series.

4. For more on late Victorian imperial decline, see Shannon; Pearce and Stewart; Brantlinger, *Rule of Darkness*.

5. For more on late Victorian invasion literature, see Otis; Arata, 'Occidental'.

6. Similarly, in what Patrick Brantlinger has termed 'imperial gothic', 'going native' and 'an invasion of civilisation by forces of barbarism' are recurrent tropes (*Rule of Darkness* 230).

7. For more on Doyle's imperial stories, see Wynne; Siddiqi, 'Cesspool'.

8. See Thomas ('Fingerprint'); Siddiqi ('Cesspool'; *Anxieties*); Reitz; Mukherjee. Like Reitz and Mukherjee, I suggest that the colonial setting and the blurring of imperial national and personal boundaries is another way for the writer of detective fiction to interrogate late Victorian master narratives concerning identity, the criminal and the safety of the metropolis.

9. Nikola first appeared in *The Windsor Magazine* in 1895 and was to feature in five novels published between 1895 and 1901. The Nikola books are the only Boothby creations to have been continuously in print since their initial publication over 100 years ago.

10. For more on the role of the Indian viceroy, see Seaman; Kulke and Rothermund.

11. The Black Hole of Calcutta incident: the imprisonment of British soldiers and East India Company employees in a dungeon at Fort William, Calcutta by Indian troops of the Nawab of Bengal.

12. For more on nineteenth-century constructions of Indian criminality, see also Brantlinger, *Rule of Darkness*; Teltscher.

13. For a discussion of cross-cultural dressing and its role in colonial adventure fiction, see Low 84–7.

14. For more on the 'Black Hole of Calcutta' incident, see Teltscher.

15. For more on the odalisque and exotic women, see Singh; Pal-Lapinski.

16. Stephen Arata has also noted this phenomenon. He terms the tainted colonial invaders 'maimed colonials' (*Fictions of Loss* 140). These characters, however, are not the main focus of his discussion. See Arata, 'Strange Events and Extraordinary Combinations: Sherlock Holmes and the Pathology of Everyday Life' (*Fictions of Loss* 133–50).

17. For more on Doyle's views on empire, see Doyle, *Memories*.

18. For more on late Victorian invasion literature, see Otis; Arata, 'Occidental'.

19. Arthur Pearson, who founded *Pearson's Weekly* in 1891, *Pearson's* in 1896 and the *Daily Express* in 1900, proclaimed in the *Express*'s first leader: 'Our policy is patriotic, our policy is the British Empire' (24 April 1900: 1). From its first issue, *Pearson's Magazine* also displays an enthusiastic effort to provide readers with access to the imperial outpost and its inhabitants. The first four volumes alone, published in 1896–97, include factual articles on 'Diamond Digging at De Beers', 'The Native Soldiery of India', 'How the Frontiers of Europe are Kept', 'Rudyard Kipling in India', 'Captain Ronald Campbell's Heroism in the Transvaal', 'Soldiers of the Khedive' and 'A Royal Explorer', which interviews Prince Henri of Orléans about his travels in the French colonies, amongst others. These volumes also include various series of colonial adventure short stories, including Doyle's 'Tales of the High Seas', Cutcliffe Hyne's 'The Adventures of Captain Kettle', Louis Becke's 'Mrs Malleron's Rival', which tells the story of the only white man on Tarawa (Polynesia), and Rudyard Kipling's 'Captains Courageous'.

20. The enduring power of Wells's *War of the Worlds* to play on fears about national security is of course illustrated in the public reaction of panic to Orson Welles's adaptation of the novel which aired on 30 October 1938, amid anxiety about the impending Second World War. The broadcast, which aired on the US Columbia Broadcasting System and transposed the action of the novel to 1930s America, was interrupted by a series of faux-news-bulletins suggesting that a Martian attack was happening in contemporary New Jersey. See 'Radio Listeners in Panic'.

21. 'The Duchess of Wiltshire's Diamonds' has been reprinted a number of times. See Davies, *Shadows*; Greene, *Rivals*; Sims, *Gaslight Crime*.

22. For more on Pear's Soap advertising as an important part of emergent Victorian commodity culture, see McClintock.
23. For more on the ways in which the detective is traditionally read as able to penetrate society see Horsley, *Twentieth* 30–2; Thompson 19–21; Winks 1–10; Cawelti 330–40; Lehman 155–69.
24. For more on nineteenth-century dynamite fiction, see Comerford; Miller, *Framed* 149–222.

Bibliography

Adams, James Eli. *Dandies and Desert Saints: Styles of Victorian Masculinity.* Ithaca, NY: Cornell University Press, 1995.

'Advertising.' *The Argus* 28 Aug. 1888: 12.

'After Grant Allen.' *Pall Mall Gazette* 27 July 1900: 4.

Altick, Richard. *Deadly Encounters: Two Victorian Sensations.* Philadelphia: University of Pennsylvania Press, 1986.

—— *Presence of the Present: Topics of the Day in the Victorian Novel.* Columbus: Ohio State University Press, 1991.

'An Australian Author.' *Otago Daily Times* 12 May 1888: 5.

Arata, Stephen D. *Fictions of Loss in the Victorian Fin de Siècle.* Cambridge University Press, 1996.

—— 'The Occidental Tourist: Dracula and the Anxiety of Reverse Colonization.' *Victorian Studies* 33 (1990): 621–45.

—— 'The Sedulous Ape: Atavism, Professionalism, and Stevenson's *Jekyll and Hyde.*' *Criticism* 37.2 (1995): 233–59.

Arnold, David. 'European Orphans and Vagrants in India in the Nineteenth Century.' *Journal of Imperial and Commonwealth History* 7.2 (Jan. 1979): 104–27.

Ascari, Maurizio. *A Counter-History of Crime Fiction: Supernatural, Gothic, Sensational.* Basingstoke: Palgrave Macmillan, 2007.

Ashley, Mike. *The Age of Storytellers: British Popular Fiction Magazines 1880–1950.* London: British Library Press, 2006.

'Assaults on Women and Children.' *Pall Mall Gazette* 21 Sept. 1885: 10.

'At the Point of the Bayonet.' *Pall Mall Gazette* 14 Nov. 1887: 1.

Auden, W.H. 'The Guilty Vicarage: Notes on the Detective Story, by an Addict.' *Harper's Magazine Online Archive* May 1948. 7 Aug. 2010. http://harpers.org/archive/1948/05/0033206.

'The Author of Madame Midas.' *Illustrated London News* 6 Oct. 1888: 410.

Baker, D W.A. 'The Origins of Robertson's Land Acts.' *Historical Studies* 30 (1958): 166–82.

Bassett, Troy J., and Christina M. Walter. 'Booksellers and Bestsellers: British Book Sales as Documented by *The Bookman*, 1891–1906.' *Book History* 4 (2001): 205–36.

Bennett, Arnold. 'Magazine Sales: What the Public Wants: Love, Beauty, Adventure, Heroism.' *Arnold Bennett: The Evening Standard Years; Books and Persons, 1926–31.* Ed. Andrew Mylett. London: Chatto and Windus, 1974. 82–4.

Berridge, Virginia, and Griffith Edwards. *Opium and the People: Opiate Use in Nineteenth-Century England.* New Haven, CT: Yale University Press, 1987.

Besant, Walter. *The Pen and the Book.* London: Thomas Burleigh, 1899.

Binyon, T.J. *Murder Will Out: The Detective in Fiction.* Oxford University Press, 1989.

Blathwayt, Raymond. 'A Chat with Mr Fergus Hume.' *The Maitland Mercury and Hunter River General Advertiser* 18 Aug. 1888: 5.

—— 'Lions in their Dens: George Newnes at Putney.' *The Idler* Mar. 1893: 161–73.
—— 'A Talk with Dr Conan Doyle.' *The Bookman* May 1892: 50–1.
Bleiler, Everett Franklin [E.F.], ed. *Best Martin Hewitt Detective Stories*. New York: Dover, 1976.
'Books of the Day.' *The Morning Post*. 19 Dec. 1895: 7.
Booth, Charles. *Life and Labour of the People in London*. London: Macmillan, 1891.
—— Maps Descriptive of London Poverty 1898–99. *Charles Booth Online Archive*. 12 Jan. 2011. http://booth.lse.ac.uk/.
Boothby, Guy. *Dr Nikola*. London: Ward, Lock, 1906.
—— Letter to Bram Stoker 12 Nov. 1905. Brotherton Collection MS, 19th C Bram Stoker File. Special Collections. Brotherton Library, University of Leeds, Leeds, UK.
—— *A Prince of Swindlers*. Amsterdam: Fredonia Books, 2002.
—— 'A Prince of Swindlers: The Den of Iniquity.' *Pearson's Magazine*. Jan. 1897: 12–17.
—— 'A Prince of Swindlers: The Duchess of Wiltshire's Diamonds.' *Pearson's Magazine*. Feb. 1897: 167–82.
Braddon, Mary Elizabeth. *Lady Audley's Secret*. Ed. David Skilton. Oxford World's Classics. Oxford University Press, 2008.
Brake, Laurel, and Marysa Demoor. *Dictionary of Nineteenth-Century Journalism in Great Britain and Ireland*. Ghent: Academia Press, 2009.
'Bran-Pie of Current Literature.' *Pall-Mall Gazette* 9 Oct. 1897: 1.
Brantlinger, Patrick. *The Reading Lesson: The Threat of Mass Literacy in Nineteenth Century British Fiction*. Bloomington: Indiana University Press, 1998.
—— *Rule of Darkness: British Literature and Imperialism, 1830–1914*. Ithaca, NY: Cornell University Press, 1990.
'Brevities.' *Launceston Examiner* 25 Aug. 1888: 2.
Briggs, Asa. *Victorian Cities*. Berkeley: University of California Press, 1993.
—— *Victorian People: A Reassessment of Persons and Themes*. University of Chicago Press, 1975.
Broadhurst, Joseph F. *From Vine Street to Jerusalem*. London: Stanley Paul, 1936.
Bullman, Joseph, Neil Hegarty and Brian Hill. *The Secret History of Our Streets: London*. London: Random House, 2012.
Butterss, Philip, ed. *Southwords: Essays on South Australian Writing*. Kent Town, South Australia: Wakefield Press, 1995.
Calder, Robert. 'Arthur Morrison: A Commentary with an Annotated Bibliography of Writings about Him.' *ELT* 28.3 (1985): 276–97.
Carey, John. *The Intellectuals and the Masses: Pride and Prejudice among the Literary Intelligentsia 1880–1939*. London: Faber and Faber, 1992.
Carlyle, Thomas. *On Heroes and Hero Worship and the Heroic in History*. Project Gutenberg. 5 May 2009. www.gutenberg.org/etext/1091.
—— *Past and Present*. Project Gutenberg. 5 May 2009. www.gutenberg.org/etext/13534.
Cawelti, John. *Adventure, Mystery and Romance: Formula Stories as Art and Popular Culture*. University of Chicago Press, 1977.
Chandler, Raymond. 'The Simple Art of Murder.' (1944) *University of Texas American Literature Website*. 25 Sept. 2010. www.en.utexas.edu/amlit/amlitprivate/scans/chandlerart.html.
'Children of the Jago: A Talk with Mr Arthur Morrison.' *Daily News* 12 Dec. 1896: 6.

Churchill, Randolph S., ed. *Churchill Companion. Volume One, Part Two:* *1896–1900*. London: Heinemann, 1967.

Clarke, Clare. 'Horace Dorrington, Criminal-Detective: Investigating the Re-Emergence of the Rogue in Arthur Morrison's *The Dorrington Deed-Box* (1897).' *Clues* 28.2 (2010): 7–18.

Clarke, Marcus. 'A Melbourne Alsatia.' (1869) *A Colonial City: High and Low Life, Selected Journalism of Marcus Clarke*. Ed. L. Hergenhan. St Lucia: Queensland University Press, 1972. 125–32.

Clausen, Christopher. 'Sherlock Holmes, Order and the Late-Victorian Mind.' *Georgia Review* 28.1 (1984): 104–23.

Cohen, William A. *Sex Scandal: The Private Parts of Victorian Fiction*. Durham, NC: Duke University Press, 1996.

Collins, Wilkie. *The Moonstone*. Ed. John Sutherland. Oxford World's Classics. Oxford University Press, 2008.

Comerford, R.V. *The Fenians in Context: Irish Politics and Society, 1848–82*. Dublin: Wolfhound Press, 1985.

'Conan Doyle Tells the True Story of Sherlock Holmes.' *Tit-Bits* 15 Dec. 1900: 287.

'The Condition of the Police Force.' *The Argus* 4 Sept. 1882: 6–7.

'Contemporary Literature.' *Westminster Review* Dec. 1901: 711–13.

Cook, Michael. *Narratives of Enclosure in Detective Fiction: The Locked Room Mystery*. Basingstoke: Palgrave Macmillan, 2011.

Corelli, Marie. *The Sorrows of Satan*. Ed. Peter Keating. Oxford University Press, 1996.

Cox, Michael, ed. *Victorian Detective Stories: An Oxford Anthology*. Oxford University Press, 1993.

—— ed. *Victorian Tales of Mystery and Detection*. Oxford University Press, 1992.

'The Creator of Dr Nikola: An Afternoon with Guy Boothby.' *The Windsor Magazine* Dec. 1896: 129–35.

Curtis, L[ewis] Perry. *Jack the Ripper and the London Press*. New Haven, CT: Yale University Press, 2002.

Danahay, Martin. *Gender at Work in Victorian Culture*. Aldershot: Ashgate, 2005.

Davies, David Stuart. 'Introduction.' *A Study in Scarlet*. Ware: Wordsworth, 2004.

—— ed. *Shadows of Sherlock Holmes*. Ware: Wordsworth, 1998.

—— *Vintage Mystery and Detective Stories*. Ware: Wordsworth, 2006.

Davison, Graeme. *The Rise and Fall of Marvellous Melbourne*. Melbourne University Press, 2004.

'A Day as a Professional Beggar.' *Tit-Bits* 17 Jan. 1891: 5.

'Death of Captain Standish.' *The Argus* 20 Mar. 1883: 6.

'Death of Guy Boothby.' *New York Times* 28 Feb. 1905.

Depasquale, Paul. *Guy Boothby: His Life and Work*. Seacombe Gardens, South Australia: Pioneer Books, 1982.

'A Description of the Offices of *The Strand Magazine*.' *The Strand Magazine* July–Dec. 1892: 594–606.

De Serville, Paul. 'The Double Diary Keeper.' *La Trobe Journal* 80 (2007): 109–23.

—— *Pounds and Pedigrees: The Upper Class in Victoria, 1850–1880*. Oxford University Press, 1991.

'Detective Fiction.' *Saturday Review* 4 Dec. 1886: 749.

Diamond, Michael. *Victorian Sensation*. London: Anthem Press, 2003.

Dickens, Charles. *The Adventures of Oliver Twist*. London: Gadshill, 1897.

—— *Bleak House.* Boston, MA: Ticknor and Fields, 1867.

'A Dinner to Dr Doyle.' *Critic* Aug. 1896: 79.

Dixon, Robert. *Writing the Colonial Adventure: Gender, Race, and Nation in Anglo-Australian Popular Fiction 1875–1914.* Cambridge University Press, 1995.

Dodge, Charlyne, ed. *The Correspondence of Harold Frederic.* Fort Worth: Texas Christian University Press, 1977.

Donovan, Dick [J.E. Preston Muddock]. *Caught at Last! Leaves from the Notebook of a Detective.* London: Chatto, 1889.

—— *Dick Donovan: The Glasgow Detective.* Ed. Bruce Durie. Edinburgh: Mercat Press, 2005.

—— *The Man-Hunter: Stories from the Note-Book of a Detective.* London: Chatto, 1888.

—— *Pages from an Adventurous Life.* London: Laurie, 1907.

Dove, George N. *The Reader and the Detective Story.* Columbus, OH: Bowling Green State University Popular Press, 1997.

Doyle, Arthur Conan. 'The Adventure of the Blue Carbuncle.' *Sherlock Holmes: The Complete Stories with Illustrations from The Strand Magazine.* Ware: Wordsworth, 2006. 541–58.

—— 'The Boscombe Valley Mystery.' *Sherlock Holmes: The Complete Stories with Illustrations from The Strand Magazine.* Ware: Wordsworth, 2006. 484–505.

—— 'The Bruce-Partington Plans.' *Sherlock Holmes: The Complete Stories with Illustrations from The Strand Magazine.* Ware: Wordsworth, 2006. 1146–68.

—— 'A Case of Identity.' *Sherlock Holmes: The Complete Stories with Illustrations from The Strand Magazine.* Ware: Wordsworth, 2006. 469–84.

—— 'Charles Augustus Milverton.' *Sherlock Holmes: The Complete Stories with Illustrations from The Strand Magazine.* Ware: Wordsworth, 2006. 963–76.

—— 'The Copper Beeches.' *Sherlock Holmes: The Complete Stories with Illustrations from The Strand Magazine.* Ware: Wordsworth, 2006. 634–57.

—— 'The Engineer's Thumb.' *Sherlock Holmes: The Complete Stories with Illustrations from The Strand Magazine.* Ware: Wordsworth, 2006. 579–96.

—— 'The Final Problem.' *Sherlock Holmes: The Complete Stories with Illustrations from The Strand Magazine.* Ware: Wordsworth, 2006. 830–49.

—— 'The Five Orange Pips.' *Sherlock Holmes: The Complete Stories with Illustrations from The Strand Magazine.* Ware: Wordsworth, 2006. 505–20.

—— *The Hound of the Baskervilles. Sherlock Holmes: The Complete Stories with Illustrations from The Strand Magazine.* Ware: Wordsworth, 2006. 177–306.

—— 'The Illustrious Client.' *Sherlock Holmes: The Complete Stories with Illustrations from The Strand Magazine.* Ware: Wordsworth, 2006. 1233–54.

—— 'The Man with the Twisted Lip.' *Sherlock Holmes: The Complete Stories with Illustrations from The Strand Magazine.* Ware: Wordsworth, 2006. 521–40.

—— 'The Man with the Twisted Lip.' *The Strand Magazine* July–Dec. 1891: 623–37.

—— *Memories and Adventures: An Autobiography.* London: Wordsworth, 2007.

—— 'The Noble Bachelor.' *Sherlock Holmes: The Complete Stories with Illustrations from The Strand Magazine.* Ware: Wordsworth, 2006. 596–613.

—— 'The Norwood Builder.' *Sherlock Holmes: The Complete Stories with Illustrations from The Strand Magazine.* Ware: Wordsworth, 2006. 866–85.

—— 'The Priory School.' *Sherlock Holmes: The Complete Stories with Illustrations from The Strand Magazine.* Ware: Wordsworth, 2006. 921–46.

—— 'The Red-Headed League.' *Sherlock Holmes: The Complete Stories with Illustrations from The Strand Magazine.* Ware: Wordsworth, 2006. 449–69.

—— 'The Retired Colourman.' *Sherlock Holmes: The Complete Stories with Illustrations from The Strand Magazine.* Ware: Wordsworth, 2006. 1397–1418.

—— 'A Scandal in Bohemia.' *Sherlock Holmes: The Complete Stories with Illustrations from The Strand Magazine.* Ware: Wordsworth, 2006. 429–48.

—— 'The Sherlock Holmes Prize Competition: How I Made My List.' *The Strand Magazine* June 1927: 32.

—— *Sherlock Holmes: The Complete Stories with Illustrations from The Strand Magazine.* Ware: Wordsworth, 2006.

—— *The Sign of Four. Sherlock Holmes: The Complete Stories with Illustrations from The Strand Magazine.* Ware: Wordsworth, 2006. 97–176.

—— *The Sign of Four.* Ed. David Stuart Davies. Kelly Bray, Cornwall: House of Stratus, 2008.

—— 'Silver Blaze.' *Sherlock Holmes: The Complete Stories with Illustrations from The Strand Magazine.* Ware: Wordsworth, 2006. 657–77.

—— 'The Speckled Band.' *Sherlock Holmes: The Complete Stories with Illustrations from The Strand Magazine.* Ware: Wordsworth, 2006. 558–79.

—— *A Study in Scarlet. Sherlock Holmes: The Complete Stories with Illustrations from The Strand Magazine.* Ware: Wordsworth, 2006. 13–96.

—— 'To Mary Doyle, Southsea, March 1, 1888.' Daniel Stashower, Jon L. Lellenberg and Charles Foley. *Arthur Conan Doyle: A Life in Letters.* London: Harper Press, 2007. 249–50.

—— 'Tribute to Sir George Newnes.' *The Times* 9 Sept. 1902: 2.

—— 'The Veiled Lodger.' *The Complete Stories with Illustrations from The Strand Magazine.* Ware: Wordsworth, 2006. 1374–82.

—— 'Wisteria Lodge.' *Sherlock Holmes: The Complete Stories with Illustrations from The Strand Magazine.* Ware: Wordsworth, 2006. 1066–112.

Dryden, Linda. *The Modern Gothic and Literary Doubles: Stevenson, Wilde and Wells.* Basingstoke: Palgrave Macmillan, 2003.

Dryden, Linda, Stephen Arata and Eric Massie. *Stevenson and Conrad: Writers of Transition.* Lubbock: Texas Tech University Press, 2009.

Dryzek, John. 'Including Australia: A Democratic History.' *Australia Reshaped: 200 Years of Institutional Transformation.* Ed. Geoffrey Brennan and Francis G. Castles. Cambridge University Press, 2002. 114–47.

Du Plat, E.A. 'The Thames Police.' *Pearson's Magazine* Jan. 1897: 18–25.

Dyos, H.J., and Michael Wolff, eds. *The Victorian City: Images and Realities,* 2 vols. London: Routledge, 1998.

Dyrenfurth, Nick. '"A Terrible Monster": From "Employers to Capitalists" in the 1885–86 Melbourne Wharf Labourers' Strike.' *Labour History* 94 (2008): 89–111.

Elmsley, John. *The Elements of Murder.* Oxford University Press, 2006.

Emsley, Clive. *Crime and Society in England, 1750–1900.* Upper Saddle River, NJ: Longman, 2005.

Emsley, Clive, and Haia Shpayer-Makov, eds. *Police Detectives in History, 1750–1950.* Aldershot: Ashgate, 2006.

Endelman, Todd M. *The Jews of Britain, 1656 to 2000.* Berkeley: University of California Press, 2002.

'Fashion in Fiction.' *Blackwood's Edinburgh Magazine* Oct. 1899: 531–42.

Fawkner, John P. *Squatting Orders: Orders in Council; Locking Up the Land of the Colony in the Hands of a Small Minority.* Melbourne, 1854.

Feinberg, Joel. *Harmless Wrongdoing: The Moral Limits of the Criminal Law.* Oxford University Press, 1990.

Ferguson, Christine. *Language, Science and Popular Fiction in the Victorian Fin-de-Siècle.* Aldershot: Ashgate, 2006.

'Fiction.' *Academy.* Jan.–June 1899: 458.

'Fiction.' *Speaker* 12 June 1897: 662.

'Fiction.' *Speaker* 16 May 1903: 172.

Flanders, Judith. *The Invention of Murder: How the Victorians Revelled in Death and Detection and Created Modern Crime.* London: HarperCollins, 2011.

'Foreword.' *The Windsor Magazine* Jan. 1895: 1–3.

Foucault, Michel. *Discipline and Punish: The Birth of the Prison.* New York: Vintage, 1979.

'Fracas at the Melbourne Club.' *The Age* 11 Nov. 1876: 3.

Frances, Raelene. *Selling Sex: A Hidden History of Prostitution.* Sydney: University of New South Wales Press, 2007.

Frank, Lawrence. *Victorian Detective Fiction and the Nature of Evidence: The Scientific Investigations of Poe, Dickens, and Doyle.* Basingstoke: Palgrave Macmillan, 2003.

Freeman, R. Austin. 'The Art of the Detective Story' (1924). Reprinted in Howard Haycraft, *The Art of the Mystery Story.* New York: Simon and Schuster, 1946. 11–12.

Friedrichs, Hulda. *The Life of Sir George Newnes.* London: Hodder and Stoughton, 1911.

Frith, Henry. *How to Read Character in Features, Forms, and Faces: A Guide to the General Outlines of Physiognomy.* London: Ward Lock, 1891.

'The Function of Detective Stories.' *Pall Mall Gazette* 22 Sept. 1888: 3.

Gagnier, Regenia. *Subjectivities.* Oxford University Press, 1991.

Garrigan, Kristine Ottesen. *Victorian Scandals: Representations of Gender and Class.* Athens: Ohio University Press, 1992.

Gattrell, Vic, Bruce Lenman and Geoffrey Parker, eds. *Crime and the Law: A Social History of Crime in Western Europe since 1500.* London: Europa, 1980.

Gelder, Ken, and Rachel Weaver, eds. *An Anthology of Colonial Australian Crime Fiction.* Melbourne University Press, 2008.

Gibson, John Michael, and Richard Lancelyn Green, eds. *The Unknown Conan Doyle: Letters to the Press.* London: Secker and Warburg, 1986.

Gillis, Stacy, and Phillipa Gates, eds. *The Devil Himself: Villainy in Detective Fiction and Film.* Westport, CT: Greenwood Press, 2002.

Glover, David. 'Liberalism, Anglo-Jewry and the Diasporic Imagination: Herbert Samuel via Israel Zangwill, 1890–1914.' *The Image of the Jew in European Liberal Culture, 1789–1914.* Ed. Bryan Cheyette and Nadia Valman. London: Vallentine Mitchell, 2004. 186–216.

Gollan, Robin. *Radical and Working Class Politics: A Study of Eastern Australia, 1850–1910.* Melbourne University Press, 1960.

Goodbody, John. 'The *Star*: Its Role in the Rise of Popular Newspapers, 1888–1914.' *Journal of Newspaper and Periodical History* 1.2 (1985): 20–9.

Grant, Charles. 'Observations on the State of Society among Asiatic Subjects of Great Britain, Particularly with Respect to Morals and on the Ways of Improving It.' *Parliamentary Papers* 10 (1812–13).

Gray, William. 'A Source for the Trampling Scene in *Jekyll and Hyde.*' *Notes and Queries* 52.4 (2005): 493–4.

Green, Richard Lancelyn. 'Conan Doyle's Pocket Diary.' *ACD: The Journal of the Arthur Conan Doyle Society* 1.1 (Sept. 1989): 21–9.

—— ed. *The Uncollected Sherlock Holmes.* London: Penguin, 1983.

Greene, Douglas G., ed. *Detection by Gaslight.* New York: Dover, 1997.

Greene, Hugh, ed. *The Rivals of Sherlock Holmes: Early Detective Stories.* London: Bodley Head, 1970.

Greenfield, John. 'Arthur Morrison's Sherlock Clone: Martin Hewitt, Victorian Values, and London Magazine Culture, 1894–1903.' *Victorian Periodicals Review* 35.1 (2002): 18–36.

Greenslade, William. *Degeneration, Culture and the Novel 1880–1940.* Cambridge University Press, 1994.

Grella, George. 'The Hard-Boiled Detective Novel.' *Detective Fiction: A Collection of Critical Essays.* Ed. Robin W. Winks. Englewood Cliffs, NJ: Prentice, 1980. 101–20.

Griffiths, Arthur. *The Rome Express* (1896). New York: Arno Press, 1976.

Grint, Keith. *The Sociology of Work.* Cambridge: Polity, 2005.

'A Guy Boothby Operetta.' *New York Times* 16 July 1897: 4.

Hack, Daniel. *The Material Interests of the Victorian Novel.* Charlottesville: University of Virginia Press, 2005.

Haldane, Robert. *The People's Force: A History of the Victoria Police.* Melbourne University Press, 1986.

Haut, Woody. *Neon Noir: Contemporary American Crime Fiction.* London: Serpent's Tail, 1999.

Haycraft, Howard. *Murder for Pleasure: The Life and Times of the Detective Story.* New York: Carroll and Graf, 1984.

Heath, Deana. *Purifying Empire: Obscenity and the Politics of Moral Regulation in Britain, India and Australia.* Cambridge University Press, 2010.

Heath, Stephen. '*Psychopathia Sexualis*: Stevenson's Strange Case.' *Critical Quarterly* 28.1–2 (1986): 93–108.

Henley, W.E. Letter to Robert Louis Stevenson. 9 July 1885. Stevenson Papers #4841. Special Collections, Beinecke Library, Yale University, New Haven, CT, USA.

—— 'Literature and Democracy.' *National Observer* 11 Apr. 1891: 528.

—— 'Some Novels of 1899.' *North American Review* Feb. 1900: 253–62.

Hennock, E.P. 'Poverty and Social Theory in England: The Experience of the Eighteen-Eighties.' *Social History* (1976): 67–91.

Herbert, Rosemary, ed. *Whodunit?: A Who's Who in Crime and Mystery Writing.* Oxford University Press, 2003.

Hirsch, Gordon. '*Frankenstein*, Detective Fiction and *Jekyll and Hyde.*' *Dr Jekyll and Mr Hyde after One Hundred Years.* Ed. William Veeder and Gordon Hirsch. University of Chicago Press, 1988. 223–46.

Hollyer, Cameron. 'Author to Editor: Arthur Conan Doyle's Correspondence with H. Greenhough Smith.' *ACD: The Journal of the Arthur Conan Doyle Society* 3 (1992): 11.

—— '"My Dear Smith": Some Letters of Arthur Conan Doyle to his *Strand* Editor.' *Baker Street Miscellanea* 44 (1985): 1–24.

'A Home for Her Majesty's Thieves.' *The Argus* 5 Apr. 1856: 4.

Hopkins, Gerard Manley. *Selected Letters*. Oxford University Press, 1990.

Hornung, E.W. *Raffles: The Amateur Cracksman*. Ed. Richard Lancelyn Green. London: Penguin, 2003.

'Horror Upon Horror.' *The Star* 8 Sept. 1888: 2.

Horsley, Lee. 'From Sherlock Holmes to Present.' *A Companion to Crime Fiction*. Ed. Charles Rzepka and Lee Horsley. Chichester: John Wiley, 2010. 28–42.

—— *Twentieth-Century Crime Fiction*. Oxford University Press, 2005.

Houghton, Walter Edwards [W.E.]. *The Victorian Frame of Mind, 1830–1870*. New Haven, CT: Yale University Press, 1975.

How, Harry. 'Illustrated Interviews NO XXIII Mr Harry Furniss.' *The Strand Magazine* July–Dec. 1893: 571–85.

Hubin, Allen J. *Crime Fiction, 1749–1980: A Comprehensive Bibliography*. New York: Garland, 1984.

Hughes, Winifred. *The Maniac in the Cellar: Sensation Novels of the 1860s*. Princeton University Press, 1980.

Hume, Fergus. *The Mystery of a Hansom Cab*. London: Hogarth Press, 1985.

—— Preface. *The Mystery of a Hansom Cab* (revised edition). London: Jarrold, 1896.

Humpherys, Anne. 'Who's Doing It? Fifteen Years of Work on Victorian Detective Fiction.' *Dickens Studies Annual* (1998): 259–74.

Hyde, John. 'An Afternoon with Guy Boothby, the Creator of "Dr Nikola".' *The Windsor Magazine* 5 Dec. 1896–May 1897: 129–33.

'The Hyderabad Diamond.' *The Star* 27 May 1897: 1.

'Imperial Diamond Stolen: Paste Gem Found in Its Place.' *New York Times*. 23 May 1897: 8.

'An Interview with Mr Guy Boothby.' *Academy* 60. Jan. 1901: 116.

'An Interview with Mr Guy Boothby.' *The Advertiser* 1 Mar. 1905.

'Israel Zangwill.' *The Times* 2 Aug. 1926: 11.

'Israel Zangwill: A Sketch.' *San Francisco Call* 25 Aug. 1895: 16.

'It is Much to Be Regretted.' *The Times* 2 Dec. 1845: 4.

Ives, George. *A History of Penal Methods* (1914). Whitefish, MT: Kessinger, 2003.

Jackson, Kate. 'George Newnes and the "Loyal Tit-Bitites": Editorial Identity and Textual Interaction in *Tit-Bits*.' *Nineteenth-Century Media and the Construction of Identities*. Ed. Laurel Brake, Bill Bell and David Finkelstein. Basingstoke: Palgrave, 2003. 11–26.

—— *George Newnes and the New Journalism in Britain 1880–1910: Culture and Profit*. Aldershot: Ashgate, 2001.

Jaffe, Audrey. 'Detecting the Beggar: Arthur Conan Doyle, Henry Mayhew, and "The Man with the Twisted Lip".' *Representations* 31 (1990): 96–117.

James, Louis. *The Victorian Novel*. London: John Wiley, 2008.

Jann, Rosemary. *The Adventures of Sherlock Holmes: Detecting Social Order*. New York: Twayne Press, 1995.

—— 'Sherlock Holmes Codes the Social Body.' *ELH* 57 (1990): 685–708.

Johnson, Steven. *Ghost Map: The Story of London's Most Terrifying Epidemic*. New York: Riverhead Books, 2006.

Jones, Gareth Stedman. *Outcast London: A Study in the Relationship between Classes in Victorian Society*. London: Penguin, 1976.

Jordan, John O., and Robert Patten, eds. *Literature in the Marketplace: Nineteenth-Century British Publishing and Reading Practices*. Cambridge University Press, 2003.

Joyce, Simon. *Capital Offenses: Geographies of Class and Crime in Victorian London.* Charlottesville: University of Virginia, 2003.

Judd, Denis. *Empire: The British Imperial Experience, from 1765 to Present.* London: Weidenfeld and Nicolson, 2001.

Kaemmel, Ernst. 'Literature under the Table: The Detective Novel and its Social Mission.' *The Poetics of Murder.* Ed. Glenn Most and William Stowe. New York: Harcourt Brace Jovanovich, 1983. 55–61.

Kalikoff, Beth. *Murder and Moral Decay in Victorian Popular Literature.* Ann Arbor: University of Michigan Press, 1986.

Kayman, Martin A. *From Bow Street to Baker Street: Mystery, Detection, and Narrative.* New York: St Martin's Press, 1992.

—— 'The Short Story from Poe to Chesterton.' *The Cambridge Companion to Crime Fiction.* Ed. Martin Priestman. Cambridge University Press, 2003. 41–59.

Keating, Peter. 'Biographical Study.' *A Child of the Jago,* by Arthur Morrison. Woodbridge: Boydell Press, 1982. 11–37.

Kelly, Ned. 'The Jerilderie Letter.' Feb. 1879. *State Library of Victoria* 10 Feb. 2013. www2.slv.vic.gov.au/collections/treasures/jerilderieletter/index.html.

Kestner, Joseph A. *The Edwardian Detective 1901–1915.* Aldershot: Ashgate, 2000.

—— Review of *Detection and Its Designs: Narrative and Power in Nineteenth-Century Detective Fiction,* by Peter Thoms. *Victorian Studies* 42.3 (2000): 550–1.

—— *Sherlock's Men: Masculinity, Conan Doyle, and Cultural History.* Aldershot: Ashgate, 1997.

—— *Sherlock's Sisters: The British Female Detective, 1864–1913.* Aldershot: Ashgate, 2003.

Kipling, Rudyard. 'Recessional.' *Recessional and Other Poems.* Whitefish, MT: Kessinger Publishing, 2010.

Kitchin, Frederick Harcourt. *The London 'Times' Under the Management of Moberly Bell.* London: G.P. Putnam's and Sons, 1925.

Knight, Mark. 'Figuring Out the Fascination: Recent Trends in Criticism on Victorian Sensation and Crime Fiction.' *Victorian Literature and Culture* 37 (2009): 323–33.

Knight, Stephen. *Continent of Mystery: A Thematic History of Australian Crime Fiction.* Ann Arbor: University of Michigan Press, 1997.

—— *Crime Fiction 1800–2000: Detection, Death, Diversity.* Basingstoke: Palgrave Macmillan, 2004.

—— 'Crimes Domestic and Crimes Colonial: The Role of Crime Fiction in Developing Postcolonial Consciousness.' *Postcolonial Postmortems: Crime Fiction from a Transcultural Perspective.* Ed. Christine Matzke and Susanne Muhleisen. Amsterdam: Rodopi, 2006. 17–33.

—— 'Enter the Detective: Early Patterns of Crime Fiction.' *The Art of Murder: New Essays on Detective Fiction.* Ed. H.G. Klaus and Stephen Knight. Tübingen: Stauffenburg, 1998. 10–26.

—— *Form and Ideology in Crime Fiction.* London: Macmillan, 1980.

—— *Jack the Ripper: The Final Solution.* London: Harrap, 1976.

—— 'The Vanishing Policeman: Patterns of Control in Australian Crime Fiction.' *Australian Popular Culture.* Ed. Ian Craven. Cambridge University Press, 1994. 109–22.

Koven, Seth. *Slumming: Sexual and Social Politics in Victorian London.* Princeton University Press, 2004.

Kucich, John. *The Power of Lies: Transgression in Victorian Fiction*. Ithaca, NY: Cornell University Press, 1994.

Kulke, Hermann, and Dietmar Rothermund. *A History of India*. New York: Routledge, 2004.

Lang, Andrew. *The Disentanglers*. London: Longman's, Green, and Co., 1902.

—— 'Modern Man: Mr R.L. Stevenson.' *Scots Observer* 20 Jan. 1889: 264–6.

—— 'Stevenson's New Story.' *Saturday Review* 9 Jan. 1886: 55–6.

Legge, J.S. 'Standish, Frederick Charles.' *Australian Dictionary of Biography*. 10 Feb. 2013 http://adb.anu.edu.au/biography/standish-frederick-charles-4632.

Lehman, David. *The Perfect Murder: A Study in Detection*. New York: Free Press, 1989.

Lennon, John J., and Malcolm Foley, *Dark Tourism*. London: Thomson Learning, 2006.

Leps, Marie-Christine. *Apprehending the Criminal: The Production of Deviance in Nineteenth-Century Discourse*. Durham, NC, and London: Duke University Press, 1992.

'A Literary Causerie.' *Speaker* 7 Oct. 1893: 383.

'Literary Notes.' *New York Times* 6 Aug. 1888: 3.

'Literary Recipes.' *Punch* 12 June 1897: 277.

'Literature.' *Glasgow Herald* 5 Nov. 1891: 9.

'The Literature of Vice.' *Bookseller* 28 Feb. 1867: 122.

Lombroso, Cesare. *Criminal Man [L'Uomo Deliquente]*. Ed. Mary Gibson and Nicole Hahn Rafter. Durham, NC: Duke University Press, 2006.

'London Theatrical Talk.' *New York Times* 10 June 1899: 7.

Low, Gail Ching-Liang. *White Skin/Black Masks: Representation and Colonialism*. London: Routledge, 1996.

Luckhurst, Roger. 'Introduction.' *Strange Case of Dr Jekyll and Mr Hyde*. Oxford World's Classics. Oxford University Press, 2006. vii–xxxii.

Ludlow, Christa. 'The Reader Investigates: Images of Crime in the Colonial City.' *Continuum: The Australian Journal of Media & Culture* 7.2 (1994): 43–56.

Lund, Michael. 'Novels, Writers, and Readers in 1850.' *Victorian Periodicals Review* 17 (1984): 15–28.

MacKenzie, John. *Propaganda and Empire: The Manipulation of British Public Opinion 1880–1960*. Manchester University Press, 1984.

'Magazines and Reviews.' *The Leeds Mercury* 6 Dec. 1894: 3.

Maia, Rita Bueno. 'Translation, Censorship and Romanticism in Portugal.' *The Power of the Pen: Translation and Censorship in Nineteenth Century Europe*. Ed. Denise Merkle. Munster: LIT Verlag Munster, 2010. 169–91.

Malmgren, Carl D. *Anatomy of Murder: Mystery, Detective, and Crime Fiction*. Columbus, OH: Bowling Green University Popular Press, 2001.

Mandel, Ernest. *Delightful Murder: A Social History of the Crime Story*. London: Pluto Press, 1984.

Mansel, Henry. 'Sensation Novels.' *Quarterly Review* Apr. 1863: 481–513.

Mayhew, Henry. *London Labour and the London Poor: The Condition and Earnings of Those that Will Work, Cannot Work, and Will Not Work. Vol. 1. London Street-Folk*. London: Charles Griffin and Company, 1865.

McCann, Sean. *Gumshoe America: Hard-Boiled Crime Fiction and the Rise and Fall of New Deal Liberalism*. Durham, NC: Duke University Press, 2000.

McClintock, Anne. 'Soft Soaping Empire: Commodity Racism and Imperial Advertising.' *The Visual Culture Reader*. Ed. Nicholas Mirzoeff. London: Routledge, 2002. 506–19.

McDonald, Peter D. 'The Adventures of the Literary Agent: Conan Doyle, A. P. Watt, Holmes, and *The Strand* in 1891.' *Victorian Periodicals Review* 30.1 (1997): 17–26.

—— *British Literary Culture and Publishing Practice 1880–1914*. Cambridge University Press, 1997.

McLaren, Angus. *A Prescription for Murder: The Victorian Serial Killings of Dr Thomas Neill Cream*. University of Chicago Press, 1995.

—— *Sexual Blackmail: A Modern History*. Cambridge, MA: Harvard University Press, 2002.

McLaughlin, Joseph. *Writing the Urban Jungle: Reading Empire in London from Doyle to Eliot*. Charlottesville: University of Virginia Press, 2000.

Mearns, Andrew. *The Bitter Cry of Outcast London: An Enquiry into the Condition of the Abject Poor*. 1883. *The Fin de Siècle: A Reader in Cultural History c.1880–1900*. Ed. Sally Ledger and Roger Luckhurst. Oxford University Press, 2000. 27–32.

Messent, Peter. *The Crime Fiction Handbook*. Chichester: John Wiley, 2012.

Miles, Peter. 'Introduction' in Arthur Morrison, *A Child of the Jago*. Oxford University Press, 2012. vii–xxvi.

Miller, D.A. *The Novel and the Police*. Berkeley and Los Angeles: University of California Press, 1988.

Miller, Elizabeth Carolyn. *Framed: The New Woman Criminal in British Culture at the Fin de Siècle*. Ann Arbor: University of Michigan Press, 2008.

—— 'Shrewd Women of Business: Madame Rachel, Victorian Consumerism, and L.T. Meade's *The Sorceress of the Strand*.' *Victorian Literature and Culture* 34.1 (2006): 311–22.

—— 'Trouble with She-Dicks: Private Eyes and Public Women in *The Adventures of Loveday Brooke, Lady Detective*.' *Victorian Literature and Culture* 33 (2005): 47–65.

'Monthly Reports of the Wholesale Bookselling Trade.' *The Bookman* Oct. 1900: 4.

Moretti, Franco. *Atlas of the European Novel 1800–1900*. London: Verso, 1998.

—— *Signs Taken For Wonders: On the Sociology of Literary Forms* (1983). London: Verso, 2005.

—— 'The Slaughterhouse of Literature.' *MLQ* 61.1 (2000): 207–27.

Morrison, Arthur. 'The Case of Janissary.' *The Windsor Magazine* Feb. 1897: 370–82.

—— 'The Case of the Mirror of Portugal.' *The Windsor Magazine* Mar. 1897: 458–72.

—— 'The Case of Mr Loftus Deacon.' *The Windsor Magazine* Apr. 1897: 692–707.

—— *A Child of the Jago*. London: MacGibbon and Kee, 1969.

—— 'Cockney Corners: Whitechapel.' *Palace Journal* 14 Apr. 1889.

—— *The Dorrington Deed-Box*. Rockville, MD: James A. Rock, 2002.

—— *Martin Hewitt, Investigator*. Charleston, SC: BiblioBazaar, 2008.

—— 'The Narrative of Mr James Rigby.' *The Windsor Magazine* Jan. 1897: 244–58.

—— 'Old Cater's Money.' *The Windsor Magazine* May 1897: 97–101.

'Mr Guy Boothby.' *The Woman at Home*. Date Unknown. *19th Century British Library Periodicals*. QCAT. McClay Library, Queen's University, Belfast. 16 Oct. 2009. http://find.galegroup.com.ezproxy.qub.ac.uk/bncn.

Muddock, Joyce Emmerson Preston. *Caught at Last!* (1889). Charleston, SC: Bibliobazaar, 2008.

—— *The Man-Hunter: Stories from the Notebook of a Detective* (Dick Donovan Library) (1888). Glenrothes: Gath-Askelon Publishing, 2005.

—— *Pages from an Adventurous Life*. Charleston, SC: Bibliobazaar, 2009.

Mukherjee, Upamanyu Pablo. *Crime and Empire: The Colony in Nineteenth-Century Fictions of Crime*. Oxford University Press, 2003.

Murch, A.E. *The Development of the Detective Novel*. New York: Philosophical Library, 1958.

'Murder in Manchester.' *The Star* [Christchurch, NZ] 25 May 1889: 2.

'Musings on the Question of the Hour – I. By a Saunterer in the Labyrinth.' *Pall Mall Gazette* 10 Aug. 1885: 1–2.

Nabokov, Vladimir, Fredson Bowers and John Updike. *Lectures on Literature*. New York: Mariner Books, 1982.

Nead, Lynda. *Victorian Babylon: People, Streets and Images in Nineteenth-Century London*. New Haven, CT: Yale University Press, 2000.

Nevins, Jess, and Michael Moorcock, eds. *The Encyclopaedia of Fantastic Victoriana*. Austin, TX: MonkeyBrain, 2005.

'New Books of the Month.' *The Bookman* Dec. 1891: 166.

Newens, Stan. *Arthur Morrison*. Loughton: The Alderton Press, 2008.

'New Novels.' *The Graphic* 7 Jan. 1888: 19.

'A Night with the Thames Police.' *The Strand Magazine* Jan.–June 1891: 124–32.

'The Nightmare at the Lyceum.' *Pall Mall Gazette* 7 Aug. 1888: 5.

Noble, James Ashcroft. 'New Novels.' *The Academy* 23 Jan. 1886: 55.

'Obituary: Mr Fergus Hume.' *The Times* 14 July 1932: 17.

'Obituary: Mr Guy Boothby.' *The Advertiser* [Adelaide, South Australia]. 1 Mar. 1905: 5. *Historic Australian Newspapers 1803–1954*. 23 September 2010. http://newspapers.nla.gov.au/ndp/del/page/923420.

O'Connor, T.P. 'The New Journalism.' *New Review* 1 Oct. 1889: 434.

O'Malley, Pat. 'Class Conflict, Land and Social Banditry: Bush-ranging in Nineteenth Century Australia.' *Social Problems* 26 (1979): 271–83.

Otis, Laura. *Membranes: Metaphors of Invasion in Nineteenth-Century Literature, Science, and Politics*. Baltimore: Johns Hopkins University Press, 2000.

'Our Adelaide Letter.' *Inquirer and Commercial News* 2 May 1888: 5.

'Our Booking Office.' [Review of *A Prince of Swindlers*] *Punch* 15 Aug. 1900: 110.

'Our Detective System' *The Star* 18 Sept. 1888: 4.

Ousby, Ian. *Bloodhounds of Heaven: The Detective in English Fiction from Godwin to Doyle*. Cambridge, MA: Harvard University Press, 1976.

—— *The Crime and Mystery Book: A Reader's Companion*. London: Thames and Hudson, 1997.

'The Outcasts of Melbourne.' *The Argus* 20 May 1876: 6.

Paget, James. 'Physiognomy of the Human Form.' *Quarterly Review* 99 (1856): 452–90.

Pal-Lapinski, Piya. *The Exotic Woman in Nineteenth-Century British Fiction and Culture: A Reconsideration*. Hanover: University of New Hampshire Press, 2005.

Panek, LeRoy. *An Introduction to the Detective Story*. Bowling Green State University Popular Press, 1987.

'Past Patterns – Future Directions: Victoria Police and the Problem of Corruption and Serious Misconduct.' Melbourne: Office of Police Integrity, Victoria, 2011.

Pearce, Malcolm, and Geoffrey Stewart. *British Political History, 1867–2001: Democracy and Decline*. London: Routledge, 2002.

Pearl, Sharrona. *About Faces: Physiognomy in Nineteenth-Century Britain*. Cambridge, MA: Harvard University Press, 2011.

Pearson's Magazine. Advertisement. *Pall Mall Gazette* 1 Dec. 1896: 3.

Penzler, Otto, Chris Steinbrunner and Marvin Lachman, eds. *Detectionary*. New York: Overlook Press, 1977.

'The People's Post Box – Our Detective System.' *The Star* 14 Sept. 1888: 4.

Pepper, Andrew. *The Contemporary American Crime Novel: Ethnicity, Gender, Class*. Edinburgh University Press, 2000.

Perkin, Harold. *The Rise of Professional Society: England since 1880*. London: Routledge, 2002.

Pettitt, Clare. *Patent Inventions: Intellectual Property and the Victorian Novel*. Oxford University Press, 2004.

'Physiognomy of the Human Form.' *Quarterly Review* 99 (1856): 453–91.

Picard, Liza. *Victorian London: The Tale of a City, 1840–1870*. New York: St Martin's Press, 2007.

Pick, Daniel. *Faces of Degeneration: A European Disorder, c.1848–c.1918*. Cambridge University Press, 1989.

Pike, Luke Owen. *A History of Crime in England*. London: Smith and Elder, 1876.

Pittard, Christopher. '"Cheap, healthful literature": *The Strand Magazine*, Fictions of Crime, and Purified Reading Communities.' *Victorian Periodicals Review* 40.1 (2007): 1–23.

—— *Purity and Contamination in Late Victorian Detective Fiction*. Farnham: Ashgate, 2011.

—— 'The Real Sensation of 1887: Fergus Hume and *The Mystery of a Hansom Cab*.' *Clues: A Journal of Detection* 26.1 (2008): 37–48.

Poe, Edgar Allan. *The Murders in the Rue Morgue, the Dupin Tales*. Ed. Matthew Pearl. New York: Modern Library, 2006.

'Points About the Murders.' *The Star* 5 Oct 1888: 2.

'Police Alarms.' *The Star* 11 Sept. 1888: 4.

Poovey, Mary. *Uneven Developments*. University of Chicago Press, 1988.

Porter, Dennis. *The Pursuit of Crime: Art and Ideology in Detective Fiction*. New Haven, CT: Yale University Press, 1981.

Porter, Lynette, ed. *Sherlock Holmes for the 21st Century: Essays on New Adaptations*. Jefferson, NC: McFarland, 2012.

'A Possible Clue.' *East London Advertiser* 6 Oct. 1888: 1.

Pound, Reginald. *The Strand Magazine 1891–1950*. London: Heinemann, 1966.

Pridden, Rev. William. *Australia: Its History and Present Condition*. London: J. Burns, 1843.

Priestman, Martin. *The Cambridge Companion to Crime Fiction*. Cambridge University Press, 2003.

—— *Crime Fiction from Poe to the Present*. Plymouth: Northcote House, 1998.

—— *Detective Fiction and Literature: The Figure on the Carpet*. London: Macmillan, 1990.

—— 'Sherlock's Children: The Birth of the Series.' *The Art of Detective Fiction*. Ed. Warren Chernaik et al. New York: St Martin's Press, 2000. 50–9.

'Public Opinion on the "Modern Babylon" Exposures.' *Pall Mall Gazette* 15 July 1885: 6.

Pulling, Christopher. *Mr Punch and the Police*. London: Butterworths, 1964.

Pyrhönen, Heta. 'Criticism and Theory.' *A Companion to Crime Fiction*. Ed. Charles Z. Rzepka and Lee Horsley. Chichester: John Wiley, 2010. 43–57.

Radford, Andrew. 'Victorian Detective Fiction.' *Literature Compass* 5.6 (2008): 1179–96.

'Radio Listeners in Panic, Taking War Drama as Fact.' *New York Times* 31 Oct. 1938.

Reader, W.J. *Professional Men: The Rise of the Professional Classes in Nineteenth-Century England*. London: Weidenfeld and Nicolson, 1966.

'The Real Sherlock Holmes: An Interview with Our Special Commissioner.' *National Observer* 29 Oct. 1892: 606–7.

'Recent Novels.' *The Times* 27 Dec. 1897: 4.

Redmond, Christopher. *In Bed with Sherlock Holmes: Sexual Elements in Arthur Conan Doyle's Stories*. Toronto: Simon and Pierre, 1984.

Reiter, Paula J. 'Doctors, Detectives, and the Professional Ideal: The Trial of Thomas Neill Cream and the Mastery of Sherlock Holmes.' *College Literature* 35.3 (2008): 57–95.

Reitz, Caroline. *Detecting the Nation: Fictions of Detection and the Imperial Venture*. Columbus: Ohio State University Press, 2004.

Review of *Jekyll and Hyde*, by Robert Louis Stevenson. *The Court and Society Review* 83. 4 Feb. 1886: 6.

Review of *Martin Hewitt, Investigator*, by Arthur Morrison. *The Bookman* 7.41. Feb. 1895: 156.

Review of *Martin Hewitt, Investigator*, by Arthur Morrison. *The Times* 22 Feb. 1895: 15.

Review of *A Prince of Swindlers* by Guy Boothby. *Hearth and Home*. 6 Sept. 1900: 676.

Review of *A Prince of Swindlers* by Guy Boothby. *Saturday Review* 90.2. 4 Aug. 1900: 151.

Robbins, Bruce. *Secular Vocations: Intellectuals, Professionalism, Culture*. London: Verso, 1993.

Rochelson, Meri-Jane. 'The Big Bow Mystery: Jewish Identity and the English Detective Novel.' *Victorian Review* 17.2 (1991): 11–20.

—— *A Jew in the Public Arena: The Career of Israel Zangwill*. Detroit: Wayne State University Press, 2008.

Roth, Marty. *Foul and Fair Play: Reading Genre in Classic Detective Fiction*. Athens: University of Georgia Press, 1995.

Rowbotham, Judith, and Kim Stevenson, eds. *Criminal Conversations: Victorian Crimes, Social Panic, and Moral Outrage*. Columbus: Ohio State University Press, 2005.

'Royal Commission on the Police Force of Victoria: Second Progress Report.' *Victorian Parliamentary Papers*, vol. 3, 1881.

Russell, Alan K., ed. *Rivals of Sherlock Holmes: Forty Stories of Crime and Detection from Original Illustrated Magazines*. Secaucus, NJ: Castle Books, 1978.

Ruth, Jennifer. *Novel Professions: Interested Disinterest and the Making of the Professional in the Victorian Novel*. Columbus: Ohio State University Press, 2006.

Rzepka, Charles. *Detective Fiction*. Cambridge: Polity Press, 2005.

Rzepka, Charles, and Lee Horsley, eds. *A Companion to Crime Fiction*. Chichester: Wiley-Blackwell, 2010.

Sadleir, John. *Recollections of a Victorian Police Officer*. London: Penguin facsimile edition, 1973.

Said, Edward. *Culture and Imperialism.* New York: Vintage, 1998.

—— *Orientalism.* New York: Vintage, 1979.

Sala, George Augustus. 'The Land of the Golden Fleece. IX – Melbourne to Adelaide.' *The Argus* 31 Aug. 1885: 7.

Salmon, Richard. *Henry James and the Culture of Publicity.* Cambridge University Press, 1997.

Scheick, William. 'Murder in My Soul: Genre and Ethos in Zangwill's *The Big Bow Mystery* (1897).' *English Literature in Transition, 1880–1920* 40.1 (1997): 22–33.

Schmid, David. 'Imagining Safe Urban Space: The Contribution of Detective Fiction to Radical Geography.' *Antipode* 27.3 (1995): 242–69.

Schooling, J. Holt. 'Nature's Danger-Signals: A Study of the Faces of Murderers.' *Harmsworth Magazine* 1 (1898): 656–60.

Seal, Graham. *The Outlaw Legend: A Cultural Tradition in Britain, America and Australia.* Cambridge University Press, 1996.

Seaman, Lewis Charles Bernard. *Victorian England: Aspects of English and Imperial History, 1837–1901.* London: Routledge, 1990.

Shannon, Richard. *The Crisis of Imperialism.* London: Granada, 1976.

Sharp, William. 'New Novels.' *The Academy* 31 Dec. 1887: 437–8.

'Short Stories.' *Athenaeum* 28 Mar. 1903: 400.

Showalter, Elaine. *Sexual Anarchy.* London: Bloomsbury, 1991.

Shpayer-Makov, Haia. *The Ascent of the Detective: Police Sleuths in Victorian and Edwardian England.* Oxford University Press, 2011.

Siddiqi, Yumna. *Anxieties of Empire and Fictions of Intrigue.* New York: Columbia University Press, 2008.

—— 'The Cesspool of Empire: Sherlock Holmes and the Return of the Repressed.' *Victorian Literature and Culture* 34 (2006): 233–47.

Sims, George R. 'How the Poor Live.' *Into Unknown England, 1866–1913: Selections from Social Explorers.* Ed. Peter J. Keating. Manchester University Press, 1976. 65–91.

Sims, Michael, ed. *The Penguin Book of Gaslight Crime: Con Artists, Burglars, Rogues, and Scoundrels from the Time of Sherlock Holmes.* London: Penguin, 2009.

Sindall, Rob. 'Middle Class Crime in Nineteenth Century England.' *Criminal Justice History* 4 (1983): 23–40.

Singh, Lata. 'Courtesans and the 1857 Revolt: The Role of Azeezun in Kanpur.' *The Great Rebellion of 1857 in India: Exploring Transgressions, Contests and Diversities.* Ed. Biswamoy Pati. London: Routledge, 2010. 95–110.

'Sir George Newnes.' *Otago Daily Times* 11 June 1910: 6.

'Six Novels of the Moment.' *The Bookman* 17 (1903): 256.

Skenazy, Paul. 'Behind the Territory Ahead.' *Los Angeles in Fiction.* Ed. David Fine. Albuquerque: University of New Mexico Press, 1995. 103–37.

Smajic, Srdjan. *Ghost-Seers, Detectives, and Spiritualists: Theories of Vision in Victorian Literature and Science.* Cambridge University Press, 2010.

Smiles, Samuel. *Life and Labour: or, Characteristics of Men of Industry, Culture, and Genius.* 1887. *Internet Archive* 19 May 2009. www.archive.org/details/lifeandlabour00smiluoft.

—— *Self-Help: with Illustrations of Character, Conduct and Perseverance.* 1859. Oxford University Press, 2002.

Smith, Andrew. *Victorian Demons: Medicine, Masculinity and the Gothic at the Fin-de-Siècle.* Manchester University Press, 2004.

Smith, Marie. *Golden Age Detective Stories*. London: Paragon, 1999.
Smith, Richard. 'Bogus Tramp Rakes in £23,000 a Year.' *The Mirror*. 2 Sept. 2010. www. mirror.co.uk/news/weird-world/2010/09/02/beggars-belief-115875-22530671/.
Spivak, Gayatri. 'Can the Subaltern Speak?' *Colonial Discourse and Post-colonial Theory*. Ed. Patrick Williams and Laura Chrisman. New York: Harvester Wheatsheaf, 1996. 66–112.
Spooner, Catherine. 'Crime Fiction and the Gothic.' *A Companion to Crime Fiction*. Ed. Charles Rzepka and Lee Horsley. Chichester: Wiley-Blackwell, 2010. 245–58.
'Squattocracy, Past and Present.' *Illustrated Sydney News*. 15 Sept. 1886: 11.
Stafford, David. *The Silent Game*. Athens: University of Georgia Press, 1991.
Stallybrass, Peter, and Allon White. *The Politics and Poetics of Transgression*. London: Methuen, 1986.
Stashower, Daniel. *Teller of Tales: The Life of Arthur Conan Doyle*. London: Penguin, 1999.
Stashower, Daniel, Jon L. Lellenberg and Charles Foley. *Arthur Conan Doyle: A Life in Letters*. London: Harper Press, 2007.
Stead, W.T. 'Another Murder and More to Follow?' *Pall Mall Gazette* 8 Sept. 1888: 1.
—— *Has Sir Charles Dilke Cleared His Name? An Examination of the Alleged Commission*. London: Review of Reviews, 1891.
—— 'The Maiden Tribute of Modern Babylon – I.' *Pall Mall Gazette* 6 July 1885: 1–6.
—— 'The Maiden Tribute of Modern Babylon – II.' *Pall Mall Gazette* 7 July 1885: 1–6.
—— 'The Maiden Tribute of Modern Babylon – III.' *Pall Mall Gazette* 8 July 1885: 1–5.
—— 'The Maiden Tribute of Modern Babylon – IV.' *Pall Mall Gazette* 10 July 1885: 1–6.
—— 'Notice to Our Readers – A Frank Warning.' *Pall Mall Gazette* 4 July 1885: 1.
—— 'Occasional Notes.' *Pall Mall Gazette* 14 Aug. 1885: 3.
—— 'Occasional Notes.' *Pall Mall Gazette* 10 Sept. 1888: 4.
—— 'We Bid You Be of Hope.' *Pall Mall Gazette* 6 July 1885: 1.
Stevenson, Robert Louis. 'The Body Snatcher and Other Tales.' Lawrence, KS: DigiReads.com Publishing, 2009.
—— *The Letters of Robert Louis Stevenson*. Ed. Sidney Colvin. New York: Scribner, 1911.
—— *Strange Case of Dr Jekyll and Mr Hyde and Other Tales of Terror*. Ed. Robert Mighall. London: Penguin, 1994.
—— *The Wrecker*. Charleston, SC: BiblioBazaar, 2008.
Stoker, Bram. 'Sir Arthur Conan Doyle Tells of His Career and Work, His Sentiments Towards America, and His Approaching Marriage.' *The World* 28 July 1907: 1.
Stowe, William. 'From Semiotics to Hermeneutics: Modes of Detection in Doyle and Chandler.' *The Poetics of Murder*. Ed. Glenn Most and William Stowe. New York: Harcourt, 1983. 366–84.
'Strange Case of Der. Jekyll and Mr Hyde.' *The Times* 25 Jan. 1886: 13.
'The Strange Case of Dr T. and Mr H.' *Punch* 6 Feb. 1886: 64.
Summerscale, Kate. *The Suspicions of Mr Whicher*. London: Bloomsbury, 2008.
Sunlight Soap. Advertisement. *The Strand Magazine* vol. 1. Jan.–June 1891: 5.
Sussex, Lucy. *Women Writers and Detectives in Nineteenth-Century Crime Fiction*. Basingstoke: Palgrave Macmillan, 2010.

Sweet, Matthew. *Inventing the Victorians*. London: Faber and Faber, 2002.
Symonds, John Addington. *The Letters of John Addington Symonds*. Vol. 3. Ed. Herbert M. Schueller and Robert L. Peters. Detroit, MI: Wayne State University Press, 1969.
Symons, Julian. *Bloody Murder: From the Detective Story to the Crime Novel: A History*. London: Penguin, 1972.
Teltscher, Kate. ' "The Fearful Name of the Black Hole": Fashioning an Imperial Myth.' *Writing India, 1757–1990*. Ed. B. Moore-Gilbert. Manchester University Press, 1996. 192–224.
'Theatres: Princess's.' *The Times* 24 Feb. 1888: 8.
Thesing, William B., ed. *British Short Fiction Writers, 1880–1914: The Realist Tradition*. London: Gale Research, 1994.
'Thieves v. Locks and Safes.' *The Strand Magazine* July 1894: 497–506.
Thomas, Ronald R. 'Detection in the Victorian Novel.' *The Cambridge Companion to the Victorian Novel*. Ed. Deirdre David. Cambridge University Press, 2001.
—— *Detective Fiction and the Rise of Forensic Science*. Cambridge University Press, 2004.
—— 'The Fingerprint of the Foreigner: Colonizing the Criminal Body in 1890s Detective Fiction and Criminal Anthropology.' *ELH* 61.3 (Autumn 1994): 655–83.
—— 'Making Darkness Visible: Capturing the Criminal and Observing the Law in Victorian Photography and Detective Fiction.' *Victorian Literature and the Victorian Visual Imagination*. Ed. Carol T. Christ and John O. Jordan. Berkeley: University of California Press, 1995. 134–68.
—— 'Victorian Detective Fiction and Legitimate Literature: Recent Directions in the Criticism.' *Victorian Literature and Culture* 24 (1996): 367–79.
Thompson, Jon. *Fiction, Crime and Empire: Clues to Modernity and Postmodernism*. Urbana and Chicago: University of Illinois Press, 1993.
Thoms, Peter. *Detection and its Designs: Narrative and Power in Nineteenth-Century Detective Fiction*. Athens: Ohio University Press, 1998.
Todorov, Tzvetan. *The Poetics of Prose*. Trans. Richard Howard. Oxford: Blackwell, 1977.
'To the Editor of *The Argus*.' *The Argus* 14 Sept. 1882: 5.
Trodd, Anthea. *Domestic Crime in the Victorian Novel*. Basingstoke: Palgrave Macmillan, 1988.
Twitchell, James B. *Preposterous Violence: Fables of Aggression in Modern Culture*. Oxford University Press, 1989.
Twopeny, R.E.N. *Town Life in Australia*. London: Elliot Stock, 1883.
'Unnamed Melbourne: Memories of Its Beginning.' *The Argus* 25 Dec. 1920: 5.
Veeder, William, and Gordon Hirsch, eds. *Dr Jekyll and Mr Hyde after One Hundred Years*. University of Chicago Press, 1988.
Victoria Parliamentary Debates. Session 1870. Vol. X. Melbourne: John Ferres, 1870.
Vidocq, Eugène François. *Memoirs of Vidocq: Master of Crime*. Charleston, SC: Bibliobazaar, 2009.
'A Visit to an Opium Den.' *Saturday Review* 6 Jan. 1894: 10–12.
Walkowitz, Judith R. *City of Dreadful Delight: Narratives of Sexual Danger in Late-Victorian London*. University of Chicago Press, 1992.
Warden, Gertrude. *The Dancing Leaves*. London: Ward Lock, 1908.
Warwick, Alexandra, and Martin Willis, eds. *Jack the Ripper: Media, Culture, History*. Manchester University Press, 2007.

Weaver, John C. 'Beyond the Fatal Shore: Pastoral Squatting and the Occupation of Australia.' *American Historical Review* 101.4 (1996): 981–1007.

Wells, H.G. 'A Slum Novel: *A Child of the Jago*.' *Saturday Review* 28 Nov. 1896: 573.

Welsh, Alexander. *George Eliot and Blackmail*. Cambridge, MA: Harvard University Press, 1985.

'What We Think.' *The Star* 31 Aug. 1888: 1.

'What We Think.' *The Star* 11 Sept. 1888: 1.

'What We Think.' *The Star* 14 Sept. 1888: 1.

'What We Think.' *The Star* 1 Oct. 1888: 1.

'What We Think.' *The Star* 3 Oct. 1888: 1.

Whitchurch, V.L. 'Donald Penstone's Escape.' *Pearson's Magazine* Jan. 1897: 116–20.

Wiener, Martin. *Reconstructing the Criminal: Culture, Law and Policy in England 1850–1914*. Cambridge University Press, 1990.

Wilde, Oscar. *The Picture of Dorian Gray*. Oxford University Press, 2008.

Williams, Kevin. *Get Me a Murder a Day! A History of Media and Communication in Britain*. London: Bloomsbury, 1997.

Winks, Robin W. *Detective Fiction: A Collection of Critical Essays*. Englewood Cliffs, NJ: Prentice Hall, 1980.

Winslow, Forbes. Letter. *The Times* 12 Sept. 1888: 6.

Wood, H.F. *The Passenger from Scotland Yard*. London: The British Library, 2010.

Wood, J. Carter. *Violence and Crime in Nineteenth-Century England*. London: Routledge, 2004.

Worthington, Heather. *The Rise of the Detective in Early Nineteenth-Century Popular Fiction*. New York: Palgrave Macmillan, 2005.

Wyndham, Horace. *Famous Trials Re-Told: Some Society Causes Célèbres*. London: Hutchinson, 1925.

Wynne, Catherine. *The Colonial Conan Doyle: British Imperialism, Irish Nationalism, and the Gothic*. Santa Barbara, CA: Greenwood Press, 2002.

Wynne, Catherine, and Sabine Vanacker, eds. *Sherlock Holmes and Conan Doyle: Multi-Media Afterlives*. Basingstoke: Palgrave Macmillan, 2013.

'Zangwill.' *Literary Digest* 21 Aug. 1926: 33.

Zangwill, Israel. *The Big Bow Mystery: Three Victorian Detective Novels*. Ed. E.F. Bleiler. Toronto: Dover, 1978. 205–302.

—— 'My First Book.' *The Idler: An Illustrated Monthly Magazine* 3 (1893): 628–41.

—— 'Of Murders and Mysteries.' *Three Victorian Detective Novels*. Ed. E.F. Bleiler. Toronto: Dover, 1978. 201–4.

Films and television

Bad Lieutenant. Dir. Abel Ferrara. Perf. Harvey Keitel. Lions Gate Films, 1992.

Dexter. Perf. Michael C. Hall and Jennifer Carpenter. Showtime, 2006–.

Sherlock. Perf. Benedict Cumberbatch and Martin Freeman. British Broadcasting Corporation, 2010.

Sherlock Holmes. Dir. Guy Ritchie. Perf. Robert Downey Jnr and Jude Law. Warner Brothers, 2009.

True Detective. Dir. Cary Joji Fukunaga. Perf. Matthew McConaughey and Woody Harrelson. HBO, 2014–.

Index

Printed and bound by CPI Group (UK) Ltd, Croydon, CR0 4YY